Born in 19
journalist v
cations thr
been *The Te*
and lives in Dubai with her husband and two
children. *Coming Home* is her first novel.

LOST

ANNABEL KANTARIA

Coming Home

ANNABEL KANTARIA

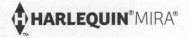

Harlequin MIRA is a registered trademark of Harlequin Enterprises Limited, used under licence.

Published in Great Britain 2015
by Harlequin MIRA, an imprint of Harlequin (UK) Limited,
Eton House, 18-24 Paradise Road,
Richmond, Surrey, TW9 1SR

© 2015 Annabel Kantaria

ISBN 978-1-848-45404-0

60-0315

Harlequin (UK) Limited's policy is to use papers that are natural, renewable and recyclable products and made from wood grown in sustainable forests. The logging and manufacturing processes conform to the legal environmental regulations of the country of origin.

Printed and bound by
CPI Group (UK) Ltd, Croydon, CR0 4YY

ACKNOWLEDGEMENTS

It's taken the support of many to get this book to publication.

My deepest thanks go to my brilliant and patient agent, Luigi Bonomi, who picked my manuscript as a winner and offered his unwavering support at every turn, and to Alison Bonomi for her nurturing support and spot-on editorial advice.

Enormous thanks to the Emirates Airline Festival of Literature (EAFOL) and to Montegrappa for making the Montegrappa Prize for First Fiction a reality. Thanks in particular to Isobel Abulhoul, Yvette Judge and the entire EAFOL team; to Charles Nahhas; and to my talented editor, Sally Williamson, and the marvellous team behind the scenes at Harlequin MIRA.

To the first two readers of the first draft of *Coming Home*, Jane Andrew and Rachel Hamilton, I'd like to say thank you for being so polite.

Heartfelt thanks to the many friends who supported me along the journey, in particular to those who believed in me long before I truly believed in myself: Sarah Baerschmidt, Arabella Pritchett, Claire Buitendag, Vicki Page, Belinda Freeman, Rohini Gill, Julia Ward Osseiran, Sophie Welch and Sibylle Dowding. Special thanks, too, to Ghazwa Dajani and Valerie Myerscough—without your help, I may never have made my deadlines.

And, finally, thanks to my family, who have stood by me every step of the way: to my parents, David and Kay, for making me believe anything was possible; to my children, Maia and Aiman, for their patience when my study door was closed; and to my husband, Sam, for his love, pep talks and fabulous plot ideas, as well as for making me laugh when I most needed to.

For Mum

CHAPTER 1

I hated seeing the grief counsellor, but I couldn't get out of it. My teachers, unsure of how to handle me, had contacted social services and I'd been assigned weekly meetings with Miss Dawson, a sensible-looking lady to whom I was reluctant to speak. I blamed her for that: she should have known better than to tell me to think of her as my favourite auntie; everyone knew I didn't have any aunties.

Every week, Miss Dawson arranged a couple of chairs to one side, near a window that looked out over the playing field. I could see my classmates kicking about in the drizzle. As far as I was concerned, the best bit about the counselling was that I was allowed access to the staff biscuit tin.

I didn't have much to say to Miss Dawson, though. We'd spent the first two sessions locked in silence as I'd eyed the biscuits. Sometimes under the digestives I could see the edge of a custard cream—once, even a Jammie Dodger. But Miss Dawson didn't like me rummaging in the tin, so I had to be sure I picked right the first time. A biscuit lucky dip.

Miss Dawson doodled flowers on the clipboard she kept on her knee.

'Why won't you talk to me?' she sighed after we passed

the first twenty minutes of our third session together marked only by my munching. I looked at her. How stupid was she?

'You can't change what happened, can you?' I hadn't realised I was going to shout, and biscuit crumbs sprayed from my lips. 'You can't stop it from happening! So what's the point of all this?' I jumped up and hurled my biscuit at the wall. The sudden violence, the release, felt good. 'It's just to make the adults feel like they're doing something! But don't you get it? You can't do anything! It's too late!'

I threw myself back into the chair and glowered at her, breathing hard. What was the point? Miss Dawson's hand had stopped mid-doodle. She locked eyes with me but she didn't say anything. As we glared at each other, her eyes narrowed, she chewed on the end of her biro and then she nodded to herself, her lips spreading in a little smile as if she'd had some sort of epiphany.

'OK, Evie,' she said slowly. Her voice had changed. It wasn't all sympathetic now. It was brisk, businesslike. I liked that more. She rummaged in her bag and pulled out a tangle of blue wool stabbed through with two knitting needles. 'I know what we're going to do, Evie. We're not going to talk: we're going to knit.'

'I don't know how to knit.'

'I'm going to teach you.'

She pulled her chair over to mine, arranged the needles in my hand and showed me the repetitive movements I needed to make to produce a line of stitches. It was fiddly and un-natural, and it took all my concentration. For the first time *since June, there was no space in my head for Graham. By the end of the session, I'd knitted five rows; by the following week, a whole strip.*

I was eight when I learned to knit. I haven't stopped since.

CHAPTER 2

I was making béchamel sauce for a lasagne when I found out that my father had died. It was late morning and the kitchen was filled with sunshine. Birdsong and the scent of acacia wafted through the open door; the flowers of the bougainvillea were so bright they looked unreal.

These are the details that stuck in my head as I struggled, in my peaceful surroundings, to take in what my mum was telling me on the phone. England seemed too far away; the news too unbelievable. The béchamel sauce, unfortunately, was at a critical stage.

'He died in his sleep,' Mum was saying. 'Heart failure.' She misread my silence as I continued to stir the sauce, my hand moving automatically as my brain fought to understand. 'Darling,' she said softly, 'he probably didn't even know.'

There was an echo on the long-distance line and I strained to hear her. I flicked off the burner and pulled the pan off the hob, knowing as I did it that the sauce would ruin; knowing also that what I was being told was bigger than that. I sat down at the kitchen table, the phone clamped to my ear, a heaviness in the pit of my stomach. I'd seen Dad in the

summer—he'd been fine then. How could he be dead? So
suddenly? Was this some sort of joke?

'When I realised that he was, you know... dead,' Mum
was saying, cautiously trying out the new word, 'I called the
doctor. I could see there was nothing that could be done; no
need to get the paramedics out. The doctor said he'd been
dead for several hours. He called an ambulance to take him
to the hospital. I followed in the car.'

'There was no need to rush, really,' she added, 'because,
well, you know...' Her words tailed off.

Suddenly I found my voice. 'I don't believe you! Are you
sure? Did they try to resuscitate him? Is there nothing they
can do... no chance... ?'

'Evie. Darling. He's gone.'

I'd dreaded a call like this ever since I'd moved to Dubai
six years ago. There was much I enjoyed about living abroad,
but the fear that something might happen to my parents
lurked permanently at the back of my mind, waking me in
a sweat in the early hours: freak accidents, strokes, cancer,
heart attacks. And now that that 'something' had happened,
I just couldn't take it in.

On the phone, Mum sounded calm, but it was hard to tell
how she was really coping.

'How are you? Are you OK? Where are you?' Now words
poured out of me. My eyes were flicking around the kitchen
and I was thinking ahead, my spare hand raking through
my hair. I needed to know Mum would be all right until I
could get there.

'I'm back home now. They sent me home with a plastic

bag of belongings. Glasses, keys, clothes, wedding ring…'
she said. There was a pause. I could imagine her giving herself a hug in her bobbly cardigan, her spare arm squeezing
around her waist; the silent pep talk she was giving herself.
She rallied. 'I'm fine. Really. But there's a lot to do. The
funeral; the drinks and nibbles? All that stuff. I'm not sure
where his Will is. And I don't even have any sherry.'

'Don't worry,' I said. 'I'm coming. I'll get a flight as soon
as I can. I'll be there tomorrow.'

*

Lasagne forgotten, I went to my bedroom, intending to get
my passport out of the small safe I kept in my wardrobe but,
instead, from my bottom drawer, I pulled out a faded blue
manila folder. Tucked inside it was a pile of tourist leaflets
I'd gathered over the past few months: seaplane rides, retro
desert safaris; deep-sea fishing cruises, amphibious tours
of old Dubai, camel polo lessons; menus from a clutch of
top restaurants.

It was my 'Dad' folder; my plan of things to do when my
father finally made it to Dubai. A year ago it would have been
inconceivable to think that my father would fly to Dubai to
see me: he'd always been 'too busy' when Mum came to
visit. Six years, and not one visit from him—it was something
I tried not to think about. If I did, it made me angry: father
by name, but not by nature. Since I was eight, he'd not only
been physically absent most of the time, but emotionally
unavailable too. But then, last summer, for the first time in
twenty years, he'd started to show an interest in my life.

'So what's it like over there?' he'd asked. He'd brought us each a cup of tea and sat down with me in the garden. 'How hot does it get? What do you do at the weekends?' Then, tellingly, 'What's the museum like?' Dad was an historian. If he was asking about museums, it meant he was thinking about visiting. And, after so many years of feeling like a spare—and not particularly wanted—part in my father's life, the idea had come as a surprise to me—a welcome one at that: I'd lain in bed that night smiling in the dark. With Dad's attention on me for the first time since I was little, I'd felt myself unfurling like a snowdrop in the first rays of spring sunshine. It had been a time of promise, of new beginnings. It had been a chance for us to put things right. Looking at the folder now, I raked my hands through my hair. I should have seized that chance then; insisted that Dad come to Dubai; told him straight out that I'd like him to come.

And now it would never happen.

I picked up one of the leaflets and traced the outline of a camel with my finger. Dad would have enjoyed riding across the sand dunes like Lawrence of Arabia, especially if there was a sundowner at the end of it. He'd have looked great in a *kandora* and *ghutra*, a falcon perched on his arm. Abruptly, I hurled the folder across the room, leaflets spinning from it as it frisbeed over my bed. Jumping up, I kicked out at the leaflets on the floor, sending them skidding across the laminate and under the bed.

'Why?' I shouted at the room. 'Why now?'

*

Getting everything done in time to catch the 8 a.m. flight was a struggle. Booking a last-minute flight with the airline's remote call centre had taken more energy than I'd felt I had to expend; a never-ending round of 'can I put you on hold?' while a sympathetic agent had tried to magic up a seat on the fully booked flight. Tracking down my boss on the golf course was even more difficult.

'How long will you be away?' he barked when his caddy finally handed him his phone at the eleventh hole. 'Will you be back to close the issue?'

'I don't know,' I said. I had no idea how long it took to organise a funeral. 'Emily'll cope perfectly well. I'll leave notes; she knows what to do.'

'Well… she's perfectly capable, I'm sure,' my boss said. 'Make sure you show her what to do.' But then he surprised me. 'Take as long as you need… and, um… all the best.' It didn't come naturally to him to be nice and I could practically hear his toenails curling with the effort, but I didn't care—with my leave approved, I sat down to write my handover notes for Emily.

My phone lay silent on the table next to me. It'd been six weeks but I still hadn't got used to it not buzzing with constant messages from James. I'd been the one to cut him out of my life but I would have given anything to be able to hear his voice again—the voice of the old James, at least. Our lives had been spliced together for so long that my heart hadn't yet caught up with my head. I felt like he should know about Dad, but would he even care? I rubbed my temples, then picked up the phone and dialled.

He picked up on the fourth ring. One more and I'd have hung up.

'Hello James? It's Evie.'

I heard the sounds of a bar in the background: music, laughter.

'Evie.' He was surprised, confused to hear from me. 'What's up?'

'Um. I just wanted to let you know that, um, my dad died last night. I'm flying to England tomorrow. For the funeral.'

James's voice, off the phone, 'Ssh! I'm on the phone, keep it down. Wow, sorry to hear that, Evie.'

'Well, I just thought you might like to know. Y'know.'

'Yes, well, thanks for telling me…' A shout went up in the background. He was in a sports bar; a team had scored.

'OK then, bye.'

'Cheers.'

I shouldn't have called. The 'cheers' grated more than anything. That was what James said to people he didn't care about. I'd always felt a little sorry for them and now I was one of them. I sighed. The truth was that James really didn't care about me; he probably never had. The only person James cared about was himself. I poured myself a large glass of wine and turned my attention to packing.

CHAPTER 3

'*Tell me about Graham,' Miss Dawson said. 'Were you very close? Did you see much of him at school?'*

Rain slid down the windowpanes; the playing field outside looked sodden. I took a biscuit and thought about Miss Dawson's question. Did I see much of Graham at school? Not really. He was two years above me and our social circles didn't overlap much. Sometimes he liked to pretend he didn't even know me. But I remembered one day when I'd been practising handstands up against the wall. The tarmac of the school playground had been gritty with tiny stones—it was the type of grit that, when you fell, dug holes in your knees, making the blood ooze out in mini fountains. After half an hour of non-stop handstands, I'd been looking at the speckles on my palms wondering if I could do any more when I realised the bullies had surrounded me, a circle of hard seven-year-olds.

'Do a cartwheel!' they'd shouted, their arms linked, their faces twisted. They knew I couldn't; they knew I was still trying.

I'd looked at the floor, willing them to find someone else to pick on. *My hands stung but, if I did a perfect handstand, would they go away?*

The ringleader had started up the chant, the sing-song tone of her voice not quite hiding the menace that oozed like oil from her pores: *'Evie can't do a cartwheel!'* The others took up the refrain as they edged towards me, the circle closing in on its prey. *'Evie can't do a cartwheel!'*

The lead bully had stepped forward. *'Watch this,'* she'd said, turning her body over foot to hand to hand to foot, so slowly it looked effortless. *'Let me help you.'* She came closer and I knew, I could tell by the way she approached, that, far from helping me, she was going to shove me onto my knees in the grit, kicking me and rubbing me in it until my socks stained red with blood. It wouldn't have been the first time.

But then a miracle.

'Leave her alone!' a boy had screamed, leaping into the circle and breaking it up. *'Get away from her now or I'll kill you all!'* Graham had stood in a karate stance. *'I'm a black belt! Now shove off!'*

The girls had scattered, and he'd taken me by both arms. *'Are you all right, Evie?'*

I put down my knitting and looked at Miss Dawson. 'I suppose we were close,' I said. 'We didn't see much of each other at school. But, when I needed him, he was always there.'

CHAPTER 4

I laid my lightest clothes—a couple of cotton shirts—
across the top of my suitcase, then sat on the bed, pushing
myself back against the pillows. My wine glass was almost
empty and I upended it now, making a full mouthful of the
final dregs. It was late and my body ached for bed, but my
mind was buzzing. The phone call with Mum replayed in
my head. My dad was dead! Still the news, half a day on
and having been repeated *ad nauseam* on the phone to the
airline, to my boss, was too big to take in; it was like it had
happened to someone else. It was the plot of a book I'd
read, or a movie I'd seen. It was not my life. I knew sleep
wouldn't come.

Instead, I grabbed the house keys and stepped outside. The
night-time air was fragrant with the scent of hot vegetation;
of plants still cooling down from the warmth of the day. I
inhaled frangipani, my favourite scent, with a top note of
jasmine from the bush next door. Breathing deeply, I got a
waft, too, of chlorine from the neighbours' pool.

Slipping quietly through the gate, I waited for a gap in the
beach road traffic. Cars swept past me, a blur of lights and
noise after the silence of my room. Taxis carried tourists to

and from their late-night dinners, bars and entertainments. Eager, sunburned faces peered out at the sights; others went past with their occupants slumped, dozing, in the back. It seemed rude, disrespectful for life to continue when my father was dead.

'My dad's dead,' I said into the night air, to the road, the cars, the tourists and the taxis. 'Have a lovely evening.'

It sounded weaker than I'd imagined. I said it again, louder, to the next car: 'Have a great evening. My dad's dead.'

A taxi beeped, its brakes screeching as the driver slowed, keen for another fare. I saw a gap in the traffic and ran across to the island of the central reservation and stood there, sheltered by the traffic light. Sensing I was a little unhinged, I didn't trust myself to find another gap in the traffic and waited, instead, for the green man.

On the other side, I ducked down a side street between a beauty salon and a dental clinic and picked my way down through the lanes of fishermen's houses to the beach. The sounds of the main road receded and soon all I could hear was the scrunch of my flip-flops on the dusty street, the sound of my own breathing and the thrum of my pulse in my head. 'Dad is dead. Dad is dead. Dad is dead.' I broke into a run to try to make it stop, and, not too soon, there was the beach opening out in front of me: an expanse of moonlit sand, bookended on the left by the Burj Al Arab and contained in front by a low wall. Tonight the hotel had its diamonds on: a twinkling display of lights that shot up and down its spine and belly. I stopped short, realising with a jolt that Dad would now never see this sight; that there

were so many things he'd now never see. I watched through
one full set of the light show then I climbed over the wall
and walked towards the ocean, kicking off my flip-flops
and seeking out the cold under-layer of sand with my toes.

*

The sight of the sea, as always, calmed me. Sitting on
the last edge of warm, dry sand, I stared at the water and
breathed in time with the hypnotic oohs and aahs of the
waves swishing in and out. The tide was receding and
each wave seemed to take the sea farther away from me, a
fringe of seashells marking its highest point. I looked up at
the sky and wondered what happens when you die. Could
Dad see me? Was he up there somewhere now, looking
down on me? Had he known he was dying? Did he think
about me before he died? When his life flashed before his
eyes—did it even really do that?—what did he see? What
was his last thought about me?

   Did he even have a last thought about me?

   You should have come to Dubai, I said silently to the
heavens. *I wanted you to come so badly.* My hands formed
a steeple as if I was praying and my eyes searched for the
constellations Dad had shown me how to find back in the
summer evenings when we were still happy: the Plough, the
Little Bear and Polaris, Orion. Tonight, as usual, all I could
make out above the glow of Dubai's neon skyline was the
Big Dipper and the North Star. I needed Dad there to show
me the more subtle connections between the other stars.
Where are you? I asked the sky.

Would Mum be all right?

She'd sounded all right on the phone but... I shifted as a shiver rippled through me. I hadn't spoken to Miss Dawson for years now but I still remembered the last conversation we'd had about Mum.

'She's like an iceberg,' the counsellor had told me. 'She lets you see only the top layers, the top ten per cent. If that. There's an awful lot that goes on beneath and you'll never see that.' She'd noticed, then, the sadness I couldn't hide. 'It's not just you, pet,' Miss Dawson had added. 'She's like that with everyone. Since the accident, she won't let anyone get close.'

And now what, I wondered. My mother was all I had left, and she was the mistress—the guardian—of The Gap. It was as if she held everyone at a distance; she didn't want to let anyone get close to her again. We wrote each other a daily email but Mum's emails were reports of golf scores, of choir practice and of what she was cooking for supper; they could have been written by anyone. They were information bulletins, memorandums that revealed nothing of the woman underneath. They weren't designed to keep me close. My mum hid emotion. She didn't reach out. She skated the surface of our relationship with prim and proper etiquette but no depth whatsoever. Mind The Gap.

In my replies, I echoed Mum's style. We exchanged huge quantities of useless information in a literary ballet that meant little. I wrote about work achievements and new restaurants, trips to the beach and what my friends were up to. I'd tried in the past to talk about more real things; about how being with James made my blood fizz; how he looked at me like he wanted to devour me. *Is this love?* I'd asked Mum. *Did you feel this way about Dad? How do I know if he's The One?* But the replies came back as dull as the church newsletter. 'Your friend sounds nice, dear. Did I tell you that I'm playing a new course next week?'

By the time I was starting to sense trouble with James, I'd learned that, beyond platitudes, I wouldn't be getting emotional support from my mum: I'd be getting a new lamb recipe and what her choir was singing for the forthcoming summer concert. In our warped relationship, it was I who took care of her.

Miss Dawson had said it was a defence mechanism. 'Your mother's "gap" has become a part of her,' she'd said. 'It helps her define who she is. She doesn't know how to fill it.' Then she'd smiled sadly at me. 'You'll get closeness one day, Evie,' she'd said. 'From a partner; a husband; children.'

I still felt protective of Mum, though. As an adult, I felt it was my job to look after her and the question that bothered me now, sitting on the beach, was of what lay below Mum's gap. Had she really managed to freeze her emotions, or were they still bubbling beneath? I pushed my toes into the cold sand below the surface and wondered if, as far as Mum was concerned, Dad's death would be the earthquake that triggered the tsunami.

CHAPTER 5

Just over twenty-four hours after I first spoke to Mum, at what was quite likely the highest point of the bleak afternoon, my taxi pulled up outside my parents' Victorian semi. They lived in Woodside, a functional commuter town that couldn't decide if it was part of South London or north-west Kent. On a sunny day, there was enough beauty, enough greenery, for you to believe it was Kent; in the drizzle, pavements slick with rain, it looked more like Greater London. It was true, though, that, if you stood at a high point and looked south, all you could see was open countryside.

Wrapped in the pashmina I'd foolishly imagined would keep me warm, I helped the driver haul my bags out of the boot, paid him and crunched across the gravel driveway to the door. Summer's roses, which framed the entrance throughout July and August, were completely gone; the house looked bare without the lushness of their petals. I realised I hadn't been home during winter in six years.

Before I could ring the bell I heard a bolt being drawn back, then another, then, finally, a key turning in a lock: Mum must have been watching out for me. She appeared behind the outer, glass-panelled door. There was the click of another lock, and another, and then the porch door finally opened.

'Hello, dear; that was quick!' she said, looking me up and down and then enveloping me in a hug. Despite the thick sweater she was wearing, she looked small, fragile, and hollow around the eyes. In my arms, she felt tiny. I noticed at once that she had a new haircut, which framed her face. She was wearing a different perfume to usual. It was light, floral, upbeat.

'I got on the first flight I could,' I said, pulling away and blinking in the cold morning light. I felt like I'd been up for twenty-four hours. The shadow of wine drunk on the flight crouched behind my forehead, and my eyes popped with tiredness.

'You've grown your hair,' Mum said, as I lugged my suit-case over the gravel. 'I always thought it suited you shorter.'

I tossed my hair back defensively and followed Mum through the front door and into the living room, breathing in the familiar scent of the house in which I'd grown up. Until I stepped into the living room, the reality of being at home without Dad hadn't hit me; I hadn't given a moment's thought to the physical space his absence would create. But the emptiness of his armchair was tangible. In the doorway, I stopped and stared.

'Glass of champagne?' Mum asked. 'Toast your safe arrival?'

My head snapped round to look at her. It was barely three o'clock.

'Got one open in the fridge,' she said with a shrug. 'Oh, don't look at me like that! It's a good one. I don't want to pour it down the sink.'

'No thanks.' I flopped down in the armchair next to the shelves, my eyes running over the cluttered surfaces, idly clocking what was new; what Mum's latest fad had been — she was an obsessive collector. Every spare inch housed a collection of something: thimbles, decanters, mugs, jugs, stuffed toys, dolls with china faces, books, videos, glassware, figurines. The walls, too, were plastered with paintings. The visual stimulation was overwhelming.

Mum fussed around the room, blowing dust from pieces of glass, holding them up to the shred of daylight and polishing them with a huff of breath and the hem of her skirt.

'Sit down,' I said. 'Talk to me. I want to know what happened. Was it his angina? Are you all right?'

Mum leaned on the back of the sofa and sighed. 'Yes, dear, I'm fine. Fine as can be.'

'So, what happened? With Dad?' Mum had told me on the phone that he'd been a bit breathless lately. I'd thought he was just unfit. 'Had his angina got worse? Or was it just, like… ?' *Bang*, I was going to say but it didn't sound right.

Mum twisted her hands together. 'Oh, you know. He'd gone to see the doctor for his angina a week or so ago because he'd had a bit more pain than usual. I told him to mention the breathless thing, too — it might be linked. I told you about that, didn't I? Anyway, the doctor had said not to worry, but that it was worth doing some further tests. An ECG and some other things. The appointment was supposed to be this week. It was him that I called when I found Dad. He confirmed it was heart failure and issued the death certificate himself.' Mum looked at the floor and, when she spoke, her voice was small. 'He was pottering in the garden earlier that day. We'd had a nice dinner. The doctor said it was just "one of those things". "It happens".'

'I still can't believe it.'

'Neither can I.' Mum gave herself a little shake. 'Still. Onwards and upwards. Life goes on.'

'And I'm here to help.' I wanted her to know she could lean on me.

'Yes, dear.' She turned towards the kitchen. 'I've just made some bread. I'll pop the kettle on and we can have a nice cup of tea and some toast?'

'Sure.'

I looked back at Dad's chair, still trying to take it in, then something caught my eye: under the coffee table lay Dad's cold slippers. Presumably where he'd left them two days ago. Before he died.

As I looked at them, moulded to the shape of Dad's size elevens, it hit me again that he wasn't coming back. Why hadn't I made more of an effort with him? Insisted he come out that autumn? I blinked hard. I'd been protecting my mother since I was eight years old. No matter what I felt inside, I would not cry in front of her.

*

I hadn't known what sort of state Mum would be in. On past performance, she could have been anything from a bit teary to shopping naked in Tesco. So I was relieved to find her acting so normal. She was chomping at the bit, desperate to get things done. I hoped it wasn't just a front; I hoped she wasn't hurtling headlong towards another breakdown. I wanted to ask more about how Dad had died but she didn't give me a chance.

'Toast's ready,' she said, setting the plates on the dining table with two steaming mugs of tea. 'Eat up. We've a lot to do.'

I sighed.

'Apart from the funeral, what else is there?'

Mum pulled out a notebook and ran a pencil down the page as she read a list. 'Well, we'll have to tell people, for a start. So far only a few friends from church know.' We had a very small family—all four of my grandparents were dead; Dad was an only child, and Mum might as well have been one, too: she had an older brother, but I'd never met him and I'd learned years ago never to ask about him—all I knew was that he hadn't come to her wedding. I wondered if things might be different now; perhaps it was my tiredness that made me less guarded than usual.

'Will we let Uncle David know?'

Mum didn't even answer. An imperceptible huff and a miniscule shake of the head, and she was off again, as if I'd never asked.

'Once we've got a date for the funeral, maybe you could help me go through Dad's address book and let people know? Tell them no flowers, too. I don't want people wasting their money on flowers. If they want, they can give the money to charity.'

I nodded, already dreading it.

'And then we have to arrange the funeral. We have an appointment at the funeral place up the road at eleven tomorrow—you don't have to come, but it'd be nice if you did. Then, obviously, the catering for the party. I've no idea how many people will come, but I was thinking at least three hundred for the funeral, maybe a hundred will come back, so we need to think about that. And we need to speak to the crematorium—Dad wanted to be cremated, by the way—and arrange the service there and the committal.'

She looked up to see if I was still listening. I was. But I was also stunned. Dad had only died yesterday morning and already she'd gone through all of this. It was like she was competing to be PA of the year. Either that, or she was clinging onto her list like it was a piece of flotsam in a tsunami.

'I've taken a couple of weeks off from work but, well, if you could help me sort out Dad's papers and make sure that everything's in order in terms of bank accounts, the house, insurance policies, the mortgage, bills etcetera, that'd be very helpful? Dad took care of all of those things and I don't know where to start.'

'Are you still enjoying work? Do you think you'll carry on?' Mum was a part-time administrator at the local hospital.

'Yes. Why wouldn't I? Dr Goodman would be lost without me. You know how he depends on me. I might even go full-time!'

'Really?'

'Yes! Why not?'

I shook my head, lost for words, changed the subject

back. 'What about Dad's computer? Do you want me to close down his email account and stuff?' Mum's fantastic ability at the hospital had never translated to her home life: she was rubbish on the home computer, a fact that even the PC seemed to sense, given it always seemed to shut down on her midway through an email to me, causing her to lose everything.

'Oh, yes please, darling. Maybe you could ping any house-related emails over to my email so I can get the details changed to mine. Good idea.'

Ping?

She looked at her list again. There was more?

'And then, depending on how long you're here for, there'll be the scattering of the ashes. If the crem can get them to us quickly, we could probably fit that in before you go back?'

She looked at me, maybe misinterpreting my silence as reluctance. 'I don't really want to do it on my own,' she said. 'And I couldn't ever be one of those people who keep him in a pot on the mantelpiece. Can you imagine? He'd be home more now than he ever was when he was alive!' She burst out laughing, a raucous sound that jarred.

'I can stay as long as you need me to,' I said, trying not to sound churlish. 'Of course I'll help with the ashes.'

Mum's laughter stopped as abruptly as it started. She opened her mouth to say something then stopped. I waited, but she must have thought the better of it.

'Right,' she said, noticing I'd finished my toast. 'Why don't you unpack and freshen up? We could look at the paperwork later?'

I stared into the middle distance, slightly dazed. Despite, or perhaps because of, the conversation we'd just had, I still had no idea what was going on in Mum's head, and that worried me. Over the years I'd learned how to read her moods; how to avoid her flashpoints; handle her unpredictability; but now I felt I'd lost that skill. I was back to square one, almost as nervous of Mum as I'd been when I was growing up.

Perhaps it was just the lack of sleep, or maybe it was just that peculiar feeling of arriving in a different country without having psychologically left the last one, but suddenly I felt drained. I stood up and turned for the stairs, hauling my suitcase with me.

CHAPTER 6

They say every expat is running away from something. I don't want to believe it about myself but somewhere, in a dark place where I try never to look, I know it's probably true. I was never running away from Graham; I was running away from what had happened after Graham. I heaved my suitcase onto my bed with a grunt worthy of a championship tennis player then went to have a look at Graham's old room. It was now a little-used guest room but, despite the fact that barely anything of his remained in there, I could still feel his essence as if it were ingrained in the walls.

Graham was a typical older brother. I'm not going to lie and say we got on like two members of the Brady Bunch when we were young. There was squabbling, of course there was, and there was hitting, pinching and hair-pulling. Once Graham drove me so mad I pushed him down the stairs and then watched, aghast, as he tumbled down. I thought he'd be dead at the bottom. He cried a lot, but he was fine—still alive, nothing broken—and, boy, was I in trouble.

No one could make me as angry as Graham could—but he was my brother and, when we got on well, he was

my best friend. We'd spend hours inventing games in the
garden; climbing trees, making 'tree houses' and cutting
muddy tracks in the lawn as we raced our bikes up and
down, skidding around the vegetable patch, dodging under
the washing line and trying not to smash into the apple tree.

As was my ritual whenever I came home, I crouched
down and peered under the bed. The box was still there.
Lying flat on my tummy, I stretched my arm out as far
under the bed as I could, trying not to breathe in the dust,
and pedalled my fingers to get a hold on it: our old Mastermind set. Sliding it out along the carpet, I opened the box
and touched my fingertips to the coloured pegs. They were
still in the sequence they'd been in during the last game I'd
played with Dad. Yellow, yellow, red, green.

My mind slipped back to that day. Dad and I usually
played the Mastermind Challenge when Graham was out.
Each time Dad won, I'd be torn between pride and disappointment: disappointed that I'd lost, but proud that Dad
wasn't humouring me—proud as punch that he hadn't
'allowed' me to win simply because I was eight and his
daughter.

On this particular day, Graham had been neither at band
practice nor football training; he'd been outside, playing
Red Arrows on his bike. He'd begged me to join in—Red
Arrows weren't as much fun without a fellow plane to swoop
against in death-defying near-misses—but I'd lost the last
four games to Dad and was desperate to win back at least
one point before the weekend was over.

Yellow, yellow, red, green. I'd chosen carefully, trying to

double bluff, to avoid any obvious patterns. Dad's opening bet had been blue, yellow, green, red—he'd known I'd think 'blue plus yellow equals green' and then I'd have given it a red teacher's tick. Not this time. I'd given him the white peg for the second yellow, and he'd raised his eyebrows and rubbed his chin before slowly placing red, yellow, green, blue.

I'd known what he was thinking there, too: colours of the rainbow. I'd sighed, acting as if he was right, then given him still only the one white peg for the yellow. There was nothing predictable about my colours this time. I'd spent the previous evening in my room, going through all my predictable patterns to come up with something that didn't fit any of them. Who knew how difficult it was to be random?

'Evie! C'mon! I need you!' Graham had shouted through the open patio doors to the dining room where Dad and I were playing. 'Stop being such a boring old fart!'

'Just one more game and I'll come!' I'd shouted back. 'Just let me beat Dad!' I loved playing Red Arrows, too, but it wasn't the same as winning at Mastermind.

'It'll never happen!' Graham had shouted, zooming back down the garden on his bike. 'I'll be playing on my own forever!'

Nine guesses in and Dad had had three white pegs to mark the three colours he'd guessed correctly. But he was having trouble with the fourth—I never put doubles and he knew that. The whole game had hinged on his last guess. Blue, yellow, red, green, he guessed. I'd won!

'Well done, sweetheart!' Dad had said as I'd jumped onto

his lap for a hug. He'd ruffled my hair. 'I'm so proud of you! What a great combination, you completely out-guessed me by choosing that double yellow.' He'd given me a big kiss. 'You know? I think you could be Prime Minister one day with smarts like that. Now, are you going to let me get my own back, or go and play with your brother?'

'I'm going to play with Graham and think about my next combination!' I'd said, putting the set into its box. 'Is it OK if I don't clear this game? I want to remember it forever.'

*

I remembered the day clearly. About a month later, Graham was dead. There was no more Mastermind with Dad after that.

I put the set carefully back into its box and, lying flat on my tummy, pushed it back into its hiding place. Standing up, I brushed the dust off my sleeve and took a deep breath.

'Hello,' I said softly. 'You all right?'

There was no reply, of course.

'Don't worry, I'll look after Mum,' I said. I closed my eyes for a second, then backed quietly out of the room, pulling the door gently to behind me.

*

The only things left in my room from when I'd lived there were the scant clothes I'd left when I moved to Dubai, a couple of old perfumes and some of my childhood books and toys. With my blessing, Mum had redecorated after I'd left, choking the room with flowery wallpaper, adding bright curtains and changing my creaky old single bed for a double with an antique brass frame. If I half shut my eyes, I could still see past the flowers; I could see the contours and colours of the room in which I'd grown up.

Now, I lay on the bed next to my suitcase and tapped a WhatsApp message to Emily to check everything was OK at the office.

Dubai felt dreamlike, a galaxy away. My pillows were comfortable… they smelled like home.

*

Two hours later, as the afternoon started to turn its attention to dying, I went back downstairs, my knitting bag under my arm. I felt much better. I'd had a sleep, unpacked, had a shower and changed into something warm.

I found Mum in the living room having a cup of tea with Richard-from-down-the-road. Although I hadn't seen him for years, I remembered him—he was one of those people who seemed to have been around forever, propping up the local church, leading the Cubs and organising community football matches and bonfires throughout my childhood. He'd taught Sunday school when I was five—and he'd seemed ancient even then. Twenty-three years later, it seems he's only a couple of years older than Mum. A widower, at that.

Dressed in frumpy brown cords and a shabby-looking sweater, the threadbare collar of a beige shirt poking out from the crew neck, and wearing desperately unflattering glasses, he didn't do himself any favours.

'Forgive the clothes,' he said, catching me looking at
him. 'Usually I dress like a pop star but I was trimming the
hedges today.'

I laughed, caught out. I liked his humour.

'Richard just popped round to give us his condolences,'
said Mum. 'He was a huge support to me yesterday morning
when I, um, "found" your father.' She gave a little shudder.
'He came with me to the hospital. It was ever so kind of
him.'

I looked at them both. Mum was smiling at Richard,
her teacup balanced daintily on her knee. She had a bit
of blusher on and she looked pretty. On the mantelpiece,
there was a vase of fresh flowers—thankfully not white
lilies because Mum would have slammed those straight in
the rubbish—and I guessed Richard had brought them. I
wondered how much he knew; if he remembered what had
happened to Graham. It had been talked about enough in
Woodside, even if Richard and his wife hadn't been that
close to Mum and Dad at the time.

I poured myself a cup of tea from the pot and sat down.

'Try the shortbread,' said Mum. 'It's lovely.'

It was only then that I noticed the Petticoat Tails on the
table. Heat flooded my face and I swiped my hand over
my forehead, the sweat wet on my fingers. Petticoat Tails!
Dad's favourite! I blinked hard, the memory of Sunday
afternoon teas before Graham had died, of ham sandwiches,
buttered crumpets and shortbread, hitting me physically in
the gut.

'Have one. You're too thin anyway!' Mum nudged the

plate towards me, and I stared at her. It was all wrong: Mum, Petticoat Tails, Richard.

'Yesterday wasn't the time for condolences,' said Richard, turning his attention from Mum to me. 'So I thought I'd pop by today to see how your mum was bearing up.' He smiled at her and she looked away, almost embarrassed. 'But it seems like she's got everything marvellously under control.'

He nodded to himself. As if to reinforce that his words were definitely true.

I had to agree — on the surface, it did.

CHAPTER 7

'*What do you remember of that that day, Evie? Can you talk about it?*'

I pulled my knitting out and picked up where I'd left off at home that morning. I was knitting my first scarf. There was a bit where I'd dropped a few stitches but I hoped it would be good enough to wear. On the playing fields outside, half of my class was playing football. I could see them through the staffroom window.

'*We were in the garden,*' *I said.* '*Mum and me.*'

Miss Dawson nodded.

'*I remember the sirens.*' *I concentrated on the stitches falling away from my fingers; I tried not to think about the words tumbling out of my mouth. Somehow the 'doing' made the 'saying' easier.*

It had been a beautiful day. The sky had been so blue I'd imagined it reaching all the way up into outer space. We'd heard the sirens while we'd been pulling weeds. I was wearing shorts and a vest and I'd been hot; sweat had been running into my eyes and I was wishing I'd worn a head-band. Mum was throwing big clumps of weeds into a trug; I was copying her, pulling the bits that looked like grass and

*throwing them into my own small trug. I hadn't dared to do
the weeds that looked like flowers in case I got it wrong.*

*'A song came on the radio and we danced,' I told Miss
Dawson. 'It was "Dancing Queen".' Mum had jumped up
and run to the kitchen windowsill, where we'd balanced
the radio. She'd turned up the volume and started dancing,
calling to me to join her.*

*Mum had been strutting up and down the patio, her hands
on her hips, pointing and turning like a pop star. I'd dropped
my trug and tried to copy her moves. Mum had sung along,
pointing at me. I remember thinking how I couldn't imagine
being seventeen.*

*'Mum was going to make lemonade later, and we were
going to take a picnic to the park—maybe even hire a row-
ing boat.'*

*It was then, when I was thinking about ham sandwiches
and lemonade, that we'd heard the sirens. When you hear
them in the distance, you don't think that it's your brother
dying on the road. You just don't think that. 'Sounds like
something's happened on the bypass,' Mum had said.*

*'We heard the sirens,' I told Miss Dawson. 'We didn't
know they were for Graham.'*

'Oh, Evie. No. Of course you couldn't have known.'

*I barely heard Miss Dawson. I was back in the moment,
stitches sliding off my knitting needles as I remembered.
Mum had turned up the radio to drown out the noise. The
song had finished and, out of breath and laughing, we'd
gone back to our trugs. 'Out of breath'. How that haunted
me now.*

I looked at my knitting, my eyes blurring with tears. I'd heard people say that I probably couldn't remember the day—that the shock would have blunted my memory—but it wasn't like that at all. I remembered it too well. It was just hard to find the words.

'We had some biscuits when we went back in.' I stopped. Until I said it, it might not have happened. I took a deep breath. 'After a while, there was a knock at the door. It was the police.'

I remembered how funny I'd thought it was that policemen were calling: we hadn't been burgled. 'Perhaps they heard about the lemonade!' I'd joked to Mum but she'd shoved me into the sitting room and I'd crouched with my ear to the door. I hadn't been able to hear much. I'd heard only bits.

'Very sorry... pedestrian crossing... didn't stop... thrown thirty feet... nothing they could do...'

Then I'd heard Mum. She was stern. 'No, you're wrong! It can't be! Not Graham! You've made a mistake!'

I'd heard her shoes clomp hard across the hall, like she was running, and I'd got away from the door just as she'd shoved through it. 'Evie!' she'd called. 'The police are saying Graham's been run over! Obviously they're wrong because he was with Daddy! I'm going to the hospital to sort it out.'

'Mum went with them,' I said to Miss Dawson. 'She put on her lipstick and went.' I jabbed my needles into the wool. 'The police were right... they were right.' My voice cracked and I took a breath then carried on, my eyes on my knitting. 'Graham had been hit cycling across a pedestrian crossing.

*Dad had seen the whole thing. They put him in hospital, too;
they had to knock him out.' I stared at the window. 'They
should have kept Mum in, too.' I turned to look at Miss
Dawson. 'I wouldn't have minded. But they didn't. Mum
had to come home on her own and look after me.'*

Chapter 8

It turned out that Mum had a pretty good idea where Dad's will might be, after all. As I sat downstairs the next morning, knitting my way through the East-to-West jetlag that had had me up at 4 a.m., I heard her clomping awkwardly down the stairs.

'Uh,' she grunted, kicking open the living room door and depositing four sturdy box files on the dining table. Despite the early hour, she was already dressed, coiffed and scented while I—having been up for half a century—was still in my dressing gown.

'I think the Will might be in here,' she said. 'Your dad kept all his papers in these. It's a blessing that he was such an organised man. Now. Have you had breakfast?'

Before I could reply, she carried on.

'We're due at the funeral place at eleven. We can't sort this out too quickly as there are waiting lists. Poor Lily had to wait two weeks for her brother's funeral.'

And so, after taking a shower, I hunched over the dining table and, feeling as if I might be about to open a Jack-in-the-box, released the catch on the first box. I didn't share Mum's confidence in Dad's organisational skills, but no horrors jumped out; there was no explosion of random papers, just a series of fat folders, each containing what looked like the year's statements from various bank accounts and a couple more folders of credit card statements.

Encouraged, I opened the second box and found another series of neatly labelled folders, these appearing to contain receipts and guarantees for everything that my parents had bought in the last few years, from clothes and electronics to work done on the house and car.

The next two boxes told a similar story. Dad had meticulously filed all of the paperwork essential to keep my parents' lives running smoothly, from utility bills and insurance papers to the tax returns, invoices and payment slips for every little piece of work he'd done.

I smiled a thank you to the sky. It could go either way with historians, I'd found—some of Dad's colleagues had been so disorganised I used to wonder how they managed to dress themselves in the morning, but others, like Dad, got pleasure out of documenting their lives; creating their own historical records, I suppose.

Flicking through the folders, I stuck a Post-it on each thing I thought needed attention—companies that needed to be told of Dad's death; accounts and bills that needed to be transferred into Mum's name; and those that could be closed down. As I put the most recent bank statement back on top of the pile, something caught my eye. A debit of £22,000 made just last week. Strange, I thought, sticking a Post-it on that too. I'd look more closely at it later.

CHAPTER 9

'*How was it when you went back to school?*' asked Miss Dawson. '*It was after the summer holidays, wasn't it?*'

'*Yes.*'

'*So... six weeks? Do you think that was long enough?*'

I sighed. How should I know? I sat back in the armchair and ate my biscuit. School was difficult, but home wasn't much easier. Graham had been the only pupil from our school ever to have died and no one knew what to say to me, his kid sister. On my first day back, everyone had spoken in clichés. 'Don't worry. He wouldn't have known what hit him,' they'd said, way too graphically. 'He's in a happier place now. He's looking down on you from heaven.' My classmates repeated what they heard the adults say. A boy in Graham's class even said, 'Don't worry. He'd have been happy that it was a BMW.'

Dazed, I'd nodded at people as they spun around me, all 'Graham this, Graham that'.

'*When someone dies,*' *I said to Miss Dawson,* '*why is it all about them? They're not there any more. Graham couldn't hear them saying all those things. I could. Why didn't anyone ask how I was? I'm the one who's still alive!*' *I knitted a row furiously.* '*And now no one talks to me about Graham at all. It's like he never existed. But sometimes I just want to talk about him.'*

'That's what these sessions are about, Evie. You know I'm here to try and help.'

I forced myself to smile but my mouth wobbled. I looked down at the knitting on my lap. Miss Dawson hadn't known Graham. How could she talk about him? I wanted to talk about him with someone who remembered the silly pranks he used to play, what his favourite food was, the fact that he was scared of Doctor Who.

'I'd talk to Mum, but...'

On my first day back at school, I'd come home and, out of habit, I'd pushed open Graham's door. The room had still smelled of him, as though his dusky boy-essence had permeated the carpet, the curtains and the duvet that Mum still hadn't stripped from his bed. I'd lain down on his bed and hugged his pillow. For the first time since he'd died, I'd fallen into a deep and natural sleep.

I didn't hear Mum come in but I'll never forget the sound that came out of her mouth when she saw someone asleep in Graham's bed. It was feral, animalistic and seemed to go on forever. Mum had grabbed handfuls of books from Graham's shelf and hurled them at me, screaming 'Get out! Get out! How dare you? How dare you try to fool me? Do you think I'm STUPID? Do you think I don't know my SON IS DEAD?' She'd collapsed on the floor and I'd slunk out, a part of me wishing it was me who'd died.

'I'd talk to Mum,' I told Miss Dawson. 'But it's not always easy.'

CHAPTER 10

10.45 a.m. saw Mum and I walking up the road towards the High Street in a light drizzle. She was smart in a beige raincoat and headscarf ('I don't have anything black,' she'd said. 'Do you think it matters?'), while I was wearing the warmest thing I'd been able to find in the wardrobe—a brown coat of Mum's that had, frankly, seen better days. It wasn't my finest fashion moment.

As we trudged up the street, Mum pointed out all the things that had changed since I'd last been home, and passed on little snippets of gossip. I didn't have the heart to tell her I had no idea who she was talking about. The walk was slightly uphill and into the wind, and I soon became breathless with it, so I let her ramble on—I think she was enjoying having me there to talk to.

'Oh and number forty-two applied for planning permission for an extension, but we lobbied the Council to block it,' she said. 'It would have looked so ugly! You can't mess with these Victorian houses! And this—a conservation area! And look at that ridiculous sports car that Mr Olsen's bought. I mean! How old does he think he is? Twenty-one again? I remember when he was knee-high to a donkey! He's mad to leave that parked outside, anyway—I bet it'll get stolen, just like what happened to that silly Mercedes at number nineteen. Oh look! There's Richard!'

I looked up and, indeed, there was Richard walking towards us, returning from the High Street. Much to my disappointment he wasn't dressed as a pop star, but was wearing a dark green anorak, hood up against the drizzle, and what looked like the same brown cords as yesterday. The jute shopping bag he held seemed heavy. Mum instinctively patted her hair, forgetting perhaps that it was mostly tucked under her headscarf. Her fringe, wet from the drizzle, was plastered against her forehead.

'Off to the High Street?' he asked, once pleasantries were exchanged. Mum took a breath to answer but before she had a chance, a police car screeched past us, its siren deafening. As Richard and I jumped in shock, Mum slapped her hands over her ears and started to shout 'la-la-la-la!' at the top of her voice, like a child pretending not to hear her parents. I knew about Mum's extreme reaction to sirens but I hadn't seen it happen for many years. Mortified, I looked at Richard but he suddenly had Mum in his arms, his hand patting her headscarf, her face on his wet lapel. *It's OK*, he mouthed over her head to me.

Then, as suddenly as they'd started, the sirens stopped, Richard sprang back and Mum's hands dropped back down. She smoothed down her coat and gave herself a little shake.

'Shopping, I wish!' she said. 'We're off to the undertaker's to sort out the funeral.'

'Well, good luck with that,' said Richard, unfazed. He picked up his wet shopping bag. 'Let me know if there's anything I can do to help.'

I looked at Mum, expecting an explanation, but she angled her body purposefully back up the street, leaving me standing with my mouth open. Richard had obviously seen her act like this before, but his dealing with it so smoothly left me feeling uncomfortable, like I'd just witnessed something I shouldn't have.

I hurried to catch up with Mum and, as we rounded the corner, the familiar old High Street hove into view. While much had changed in recent years, many of the landmarks of my childhood were still there. The Indian restaurant where I'd insisted we go for my twelfth birthday because it felt 'so grown up'; the pet shop where I'd bought my only ever pet hamster; and the hidden gem of an Italian restaurant in which I'd had many first dates. People stood huddled as ever at bus stops, puffs of their warm breath mixing with clouds of cigarette smoke. Outside McDonald's, a group of teenagers dipped their hands in and out of brown paper bags—I recalled the warm comforts of a cheeseburger and a bag of hot fries while waiting for the bus in the exact same spot.

We continued on, past charity shops, takeaways and a new crop of pawnshops and cash-converters I hadn't seen the previous summer. On the left, the top end of the double-parked street where Miss Dawson had lived. I remembered the feeling of walking down that street to her house for counselling sessions, which continued even in the school holidays. To this day, Miss Dawson's street still featured in my dreams. I didn't even know if she still lived there.

Mum turned abruptly into the doorway of a dark-fronted shop that sat discreetly next to WHSmith. A bell rang in the hushed interior, and a tall, pale man in a dark suit appeared from a back room. 'You must be Mrs Stevens,' he said softly. 'I'm so sorry for your loss.'

'If you can guide us through whatever we need to do, that would be helpful, thank you,' said Mum.

I wondered if her brusqueness was masking her grief; her upper lip was so stiff you could have stood an army on it. The silence of the undertaker's was oppressive and suddenly I felt clammy and a little light-headed. Two days ago, I'd been living my life in Dubai, that month's magazine about to go to press; a champagne brunch booked for the weekend. How was I now sitting here, in a suburban high street, asking a stranger's advice on what sort of box to put my dead father in? I sat down heavily.

The man showed us a catalogue of coffins. As he joined us at the desk, I caught a waft of his cologne and breathed it in: he smelled of Dad, and suddenly I was playing hide-and-seek in the garden, Graham and I both hunting for our father. As we'd stood next to the raspberry bushes, regrouping after a long and fruitless search, I'd caught a whiff of Dad's signature scent: *Eau Sauvage*.

'He's here!' I'd squealed, digging into the raspberry bush, red juice smearing my fingers. 'I can smell him!'

'I'm thinking closed coffin,' Mum said, moistening the

tip of her finger with her tongue as she flipped through the pages. 'People don't want to *see* him, do they?'

'It's your decision, Mrs Stevens,' said the man.

'That's a nice one, don't you think, Evie?' Mum asked, stopping at a grand-looking box, rectangular, with six handles. 'Dad would have liked that, I think. And maybe with a sky-blue lining? Or yellow like the sunshine? What do you think, darling? I don't suppose it really matters if it's not pure silk—it's going to be burnt to a cinder anyway.'

'Excuse me!' I scraped the chair back and dashed out of the shop.

Around the corner, I leaned heavily against a wall. Dad had gone forever. I breathed in deeply, enjoying the sting of the cold air in my lungs. It gave me something to focus on while I gathered myself.

'Evie? Is that you?' The voice was cautious but familiar. I knew even without looking to whom it belonged.

'Luca.' I ran a hand through my hair, wished the ground would swallow me up. This wasn't how any first meeting with an ex was supposed to be.

'Evie! How are you?'

I nodded and tried for a smile. Words wouldn't come. Luca and I had been one of the only couples to have 'gone steady' at school for the entire two years of the sixth form. I've never since had my life so sorted as when he and I were going out. It's funny how we know it all at sixteen—and then what happens? How does it all fall apart?

Standing within touching distance of him now, I remembered almost viscerally the lunchtimes we'd spent sitting on the bench by the tennis courts at school, his arm draped over my shoulder while we talked about our future. We'd talked about what we'd do when we were married: where we'd live, how many children we'd have and what their names would be. The funny thing was, it wasn't just me leading this fantasy life—Luca had been even keener on it than I was.

Back then he'd worked on Saturday and Sunday lunchtimes in a chichi pub in Chislehurst, where he cleared dishes, washed up and sometimes even waited tables. When I'd turned eighteen, he'd presented me with a tiny solitaire ring he'd saved up his wages to buy and asked me to marry him. I'll never forget the look on his face when I'd said no. He'd thought I was joking at first. 'No. Seriously, Luca. Maybe if we're both still single when we're thirty,' I'd quipped, handing the red velvet box back to him.

It had been the beginning of the end. The relationship had limped on until we left school a few months later, but the magic had gone. We'd gone to different universities and we hadn't stayed in touch.

'It's been—what?—nearly twelve years?' Luca said. 'So what are you up to these days?'

'My dad just died.' The words fell out of me. 'I've just come back to help Mum. For a bit. I live in Dubai.'

Luca touched my arm then pulled his hand back quickly. 'I'm so sorry to hear that. I remember your dad… Look, if there's anything I can do?'

'We're just in the funeral directors now,' I said. 'Choosing the coffin. I just, um, stepped out for a second.'

'I'm so sorry, Evie.'

'It's OK. Not your fault.' I tried to smile.

'Would you let me know about the funeral arrangements? I'd like to pay my respects.' Luca put his hand on his chest and looked down for a second.

'I will.'

'Look, if you need anything at all, Evie. I'm here. Facebook me.'

'Thanks. I will.'

*

Two pairs of eyes turned to me when I stepped back into the undertaker's.

'Would you like to see what we've decided?' Mum asked, looking at me over her spectacles. 'We're going for the oak casket with the blue lining.' She opened the catalogue to a page and pointed. And the funeral's set for a week today. Right, I think we're all done here.'

She pushed her chair back and, together, we stepped out into the drizzle.

CHAPTER 11

The Speckled Hen did a good lunch. Stopping in on our way back to the house, Mum and I ordered salmon fishcakes, salad and thick-cut chips washed down with a warming glass each of Merlot.

'So, shall we get the funeral party thing catered?' I asked, the wine already buzzing in my head. I wasn't expecting a yes.

'Sure,' she said, waving over the waitress. 'Can you ask the manager to come over?'

This was a side of Mum I'd never seen before. When Dad was alive, she'd have stood up all night, on pins if she'd had to, cutting rounds of sandwiches rather than buy them. I was pleased — it was progress. The pub, it turned out, had a home-catering department and the manager was obliging. Within a matter of minutes, it was agreed that uniformed waiters would hand around a selection of sweet and savoury finger foods and hot and cold drinks.

I, however, wasn't making much progress of my own. I'd fully intended to start going through Dad's address book after lunch, letting people know that the funeral had been set for Friday, but the rich food and unaccustomed lunchtime wine took their toll on both me and Mum. Back home, Mum flicked off her shoes, dropped her keys onto the dresser by the front door and collapsed in her favourite chair in the living room while I went to make us each a coffee. But, when I brought it out to her five minutes later, Mum was out for the count, her mouth slightly open, a magazine on her lap. I placed the coffee quietly on the table and looked at my mother. In sleep, her face was softer, free of the worries that plagued her in life.

'Don't worry,' I whispered. 'I'll always be here for you. It's just us now. Just the girls.' I placed a fleecy blanket gently over her lap and went upstairs to lie down. The wind had picked up and I wriggled luxuriously in bed, the duvet half over me as the wind splattered the rain against the windowpanes. We never got afternoons like this in Dubai; I let the rhythmic patter of the rain lull me to sleep.

*

'Aaargh!'

The furious scream that woke me was followed by the crash of the phone being slammed down.

'That woman is so rude!' Mum yelled.

'What's wrong? Mum? What's up?' I leapt off my bed and into the hall where Mum was standing staring at the phone as if it had got up and slapped her on the cheek.

'It's unacceptable! How can people be so rude?' she raged. 'I never even liked the woman!'

'What? What happened?'

'I told her that Graham was dead and she denied it! It's

not as if it's easy telling people, but that woman had the temerity to deny it! She said I was "having a turn"!'

'Oh, Mum, I…' I took a step towards her.

'"Oh, Mum, I" what?' Mum was still staring at the phone, but now she snapped her head to look at me, her eyes flashing.

I reached out for her arm, but she jumped away.

'It's not Graham,' I said gently. 'It's Dad who's died. Robert. Not Graham.'

Mum stared at me, her eyes wide. Then she shook her head. 'I know,' she said. 'Good God, I may be old but I don't have dementia. What kind of idiot do you take me for?'

'I…'

Mum turned for the stairs. 'Cup of tea?'

I shook my head. 'I'm fine.'

CHAPTER 12

I yanked the wool from the tip of my knitting needles, unravelling a row of uneven stitches. 'Please could you help me with my knitting?' I asked Miss Dawson. She'd been waiting for me to say something for several minutes, but the knitting was taking up all my concentration. It hadn't been going right for a few days now and the work I'd produced was full of telltale holes.

'Here.' Miss Dawson took the wool and needles from me, unravelled a couple more rows, cast on and knitted a couple of neat rows for me. 'There you go.' She passed it back.

'Thanks.'

'Are you sleeping all right now?' she asked. 'You said you have sleeping tablets? Are they working?'

'Hmph.'

Nights were bad. I couldn't stop thinking about the accident. Mum had taken me to the doctor and, after that, I got half a tiny purple sleeping pill at bedtime.

The pills tasted bitter and dragged me into sleep but, in my dreams, I met Graham. All night we played, we argued, we messed around. I woke feeling happy. And then I had to remember all over again that he was dead. During the day, I felt like I was walking through melted toffee, my head enclosed in a glass jar.

'I stopped taking them. I don't feel much like myself with them,' I said.

'And are you managing to get to sleep without them?'

'S'pose,' I said.

I'd never tell Miss Dawson, but I'd started talking to Graham instead. Each night, I lay down and told him about my day. I imagined that he could hear me; I imagined his replies. I slept better now—but my dreams were still of Graham.

CHAPTER 13

After Mum had settled downstairs with her tea, I took Dad's address book upstairs. After the scene on the landing, I thought it was better that I make the calls. The address book was faded and worn and, when I lifted it to my nose, I could catch the scent of my father impregnated in the leather. I imagined him sitting in his study, his long fingers thumbing through the pages crammed with carefully written names, numbers and addresses.

I made the calls from my bedroom, not wanting Mum to hear me repeat the same things over and over. 'Yes, died in his sleep… very peaceful… yes, she's fine, thank you… I'm here to help… yes, funeral's on Friday at eleven… no flowers, money to charity…'

It made for a wearing afternoon's work. Dad was one of the first in his peer group to pass away, and many people were so shocked I ended up consoling them rather than the other way around. It was tedious, but I was keen to get it over with; happy that I was able to do it for Mum.

Under 'D' I found the number for Miss Dawson, my old grief counsellor. I chewed my pen and stared out of the window. Would she want to know? She'd seen a lot of me after Graham had died, had almost become a friend. I wondered what she was up to now. I'd have thought she was in her late thirties when she was helping me, so she must be nearly sixty now. I added her number to my phone, clicked 'Call' and waited while it rang.

'Hello?' Her voice sounded muffled, as if she were talking from a previous century.

'Hello. I'm looking for… umm…' I realised I didn't know her Christian name. 'Miss Dawson?'

'Yes, speaking. Who's calling?'

'Miss Dawson! It's Evie. Evie Stevens.'

Not even a pause. 'Evie! How lovely to hear from you. What are you up to now? Still knitting?'

'And some!' I laughed. 'I knit for charity these days. Let's just say there are a lot of sailors in the world wearing warm hats thanks to you.'

She laughed. 'It wasn't as random as you think.'

'What do you mean?'

'I had a theory that you were stopping yourself from talking. I wondered if getting you to focus with all your consciousness on small repetitive tasks might allow thoughts from your subconscious to surface. You were my guinea pig. It was a technique I went on to use on many of my other clients.'

'Wow! I had no idea. I thought you were just trying to fill the time.'

We chatted about Dubai, what I was doing; I told her why I was back. She was touched to be invited to the funeral.

'But how's your mother?' she asked. 'How's she taking it?'

'She's OK, I think. She seems very organised. Together.'

'Well, I'm glad to hear that.' She sighed. 'Look, I probably shouldn't say this, but you know it was her we were worried about most back then.'

'Really?'

'Yes. You were a resilient little thing. A tough cookie. Devastated, obviously, but your grief ran through the natural stages.'

'And Mum's didn't?' I was talking quietly, scared that Mum would come upstairs and overhear.

'Well. It was very—how to say it?—extreme. Wasn't it? It was what we'd call a "complicated grief"—a grief dysfunction, of sorts. Your mother found it exceptionally difficult to accept the loss of Graham. Even when she appeared to start functioning more normally, we were worried she was suppressing it. I tell you this because an event such as this, such as your father passing away, could bring it all back.'

'Hmm.' Just what I was thinking. 'I'm trying to help... you know: be there for her.'

'Evie, you always have been there for her. You can only do your best—and I know your best is very good. But, if you're worried about anything or need to speak to me at any time, please don't hesitate. I'm sure she'll be fine, but keep an eye on her. It's a difficult time.' She gave me her email address.

'Thank you,' I said. 'I hope I don't need it.'

*

As the afternoon wore on, I made good progress through the address book. Luca had been out when I'd called his house, but I left a message and my number. I didn't know, though, what to do about my uncle—Mum's brother—the black sheep of the family. Would he want to know that his brother-in-law had passed away? Did I have the right to tell him if Mum didn't want to contact him?

'How are you getting on?' asked Mum, surprising me, long after I'd had to click on the light.

'Fine,' I said, sighing. I flicked through the remaining pages of the address book. 'Probably only five or six more and I'll be done.'

'We must remember to invite the headmaster,' she said. 'It's probably the "done thing".' She made the little quote marks in the air.

'What headmaster? You mean of the university?'

'Doh, Evie, don't be silly. Of the school!'

I froze. Twice now. 'University,' I said, treading on eggshells. 'Dad worked at the university.'

Mum bent down to pick up a tissue that had missed the bin, placed it in. Then she looked up at me. 'Of course. What did you think I meant! Silly girl. Yes, the chancellor, or whatever, of the university where Robert taught. It's probably only polite to invite him. Will you do that? Anyway. Look. There's one more thing I wonder if you can help me with before you disappear back to Dubai?'

'Sure.' I wasn't paying attention one hundred per cent. I was flicking through the address book, pretending to look at names while Miss Dawson's words circled in my head: *extreme reaction... complicated grief... we were worried she was suppressing it... your father passing away could bring it all back.*

Mum's voice broke into my thoughts. 'I'd like you to help me clear out the attic. All your brother's stuff is up there—' I stared at the address book, unable meet her eye '—and I don't think I can face it. But...'—and I do wonder if she paused here for dramatic effect, or if she was nervous of my reaction—'I'm planning on selling the house. In fact, I've just made an offer on a new one.'

CHAPTER 14

Well, after that bombshell, I begged Mum not to rush into anything, but she seemed adamant that she wanted to sell the house—apparently she and Dad had been planning to do it before he died and had already put in the offer. If I'd learned anything about bereavement from my sessions with Miss Dawson, it was that you shouldn't rush into making any major changes. Such as selling your house.

'The new place is just around the corner,' Mum said, batting away my concerns like lazy bluebottles circling her face. 'Your father liked it a lot and I don't want to lose it. It's a much smaller house—more manageable and cheaper to run, especially now I'll be on my own—but it's in a better location? In the conservation area?' Her intonation rose at the end of each sentence, as if she were asking my approval. 'I'll show you tomorrow, if you like? We can take a walk by. House prices there are just going up and up, and they do say "location, location, location", don't they?'

She stopped talking and I didn't fill the silence.

'Anyway, they haven't accepted my offer yet,' she said eventually. She wasn't looking at me; she was examining the paintwork of the doorframe intently, running a finger over it.

I thought of the £22,000 debit from Dad's account. That must be what it was for. 'So had you and Dad put money aside for the deposit?'

Mum looked at me. 'No...'

'Oh... how about legal fees? Have you had to pay anything yet? For surveys?'

'Why do you ask?' Something in Mum's voice warned me not to go further.

'Oh... no reason.'

There was another silence. To be honest, I was too tired and too shell-shocked by the events of the last forty-eight hours—not to mention by the lack of sleep—to be in a position to talk further about it. Mum and Dad had lived in our house for nearly thirty years; it was the home into which I'd been born. I couldn't understand how or why Mum would want to move so fast. But exhaustion rendered me incapable of expressing even that much.

'Can we talk about it in the morning?' I yawned, looking pointedly towards my bedroom door.

*

I woke the next day with Dad on my mind. I'd dreamed about him in the night, knowing in the dream that something was vaguely wrong, but not understanding what it was. For a few seconds, in that hazy state between sleep and wakefulness, I was unable to place where I was, or why. There was something I needed to do for Dad but where was he? Then, as the morning sun streaked through my curtains, it all came back. I resolved to spend the day clearing out the attic and going through Dad's papers. The missing £22,000 made me feel uneasy and I was determined to get to the bottom of it.

Downstairs, I found a note from Mum saying she'd popped up to the High Street, so I grilled the life back into a couple of croissants I found in the freezer, made myself a coffee and heaved the first of Dad's box files onto the dining table, where I spent the best part of the morning painstakingly matching up each receipt from the 'Receipts' file with each debit from the account, credit card bill or cheque stub.

Kudos to my father, every single one matched—except the most important one; the one that had piqued my curiosity. I could tell the missing £22,000 had been transferred to another bank account—the logical assumption was that it was a savings account—but I couldn't find a record of the recipient bank account in any of the files. I slammed my fist against the table in frustration, figures dancing in front of my eyes. Dad had receipts for new windscreen wipers at £14.99 a pair, for heaven's sake. How could he forget to document where £22,000 went?

Furthermore, I was now in an even worse position than I had been when I started. Instead of finding a solution, going through the papers like a penny-pinching accountant had thrown up a new problem: I'd now found a payment of £1,000 that had gone to the same bank account every single month as far back as Dad's statements went. It, too, was lacking receipts; unexplained. There was a printed screenshot to show that Dad had stopped the payment just before he died, but I couldn't find any further details about it. 'Curiouser and curiouser,' I said, staring at the statements, as if burning the digits onto my retinas might yield an explanation.

If it wasn't for a home deposit, what could it be? A deposit on a new car? A holiday? Garden landscaping? Some sort of investment? A shudder ran through me. James had always been telling me about the dodgy investment scams that people—especially the elderly—fell for: Ponzi schemes, non-existent companies, prime banks and so on. Had Dad been conned into handing over money for something like that? I'd almost rather not know.

Mid-morning, my thoughts were interrupted by Mum bustling back into the house with bags of shopping.

'Morning, darling!' she said. 'It's a gorgeous day! Sorry I took so long! I bumped into Lily and we stopped for a coffee. What have you been up to?' She peered at the table, barely pausing for a reply. 'Ooh, the files. Thank you! Do you think you'll be able to go up to the attic today? I dread to think what's up there—I haven't been up since...' Finally, she tailed off, her attention focused intently on the marmalade jar that still sat on the dining table—the same cut-glass jar I remembered from my childhood. A tiny shake of the head, then, 'Do you have any other plans for today?'

I shook my head.

'You should go out while you're here,' Mum said. 'You haven't seen your friends for so long. Whatever happened to that nice girl who was at junior school with you? You know, the one you shared a room with on the school trip to France?'

'Oh… goodness knows. We were never really friends.'

The phone rang.

'Who's that?' Mum leant over to pick up the clunky handset of her new retro phone. 'Oh hello!' she chirped. I listened as she made plans to meet whoever it was on the phone that evening.

'That was Richard,' she said when she hung up. 'He's got a voucher for a free curry down the road and he's just noticed it runs out today. He's asked me to go out for dinner with him. You don't mind, do you?'

Did I mind? With my father not even buried, I didn't really know what to think. I shook my head, confused. Mum smiled.

'Thanks, darling,' she said. 'He's really quite harmless. And it's only a curry.'

CHAPTER 15

'*And how do you feel?*' *Miss Dawson asked.* '*Are there times when you forget that Graham's no longer here?*'

How did she know? The headmistress must have told her about the day of the school photos. I wished the earth would swallow me up when I thought about that day.

My teacher had been stressed. I could tell by the way she was rubbing her forehead and circling her fingers around her temples as she tried to mark our maths tests. Every now and then, her head would pop up. '*Quiet!*' *she'd say, but it was more of an exasperated sigh than an instruction.*

It had been a rainy morning and the class, like the weather, had been particularly disruptive—aside from the novelty of arriving at school in wellington boots for the first time that autumn, we'd all been excited because it was school-photo day, and that meant a break in routine; something different to working on our never-ending history projects.

At 10 a.m., I'd asked my teacher if I could go for my photo.

'*Sure,*' *she'd said and there'd been a micro-pause as she'd struggled to remember my name. She was new and she always got me mixed up with Emma. Then Adam had howled in pain and her attention had flipped to him and Jason, locked in a battle.*

I'd slipped quietly out of the classroom and headed for the main hall, my plimsolls squeaking with every step on the polished parquet flooring. I loved school-photo day. As we sat in the queue waiting our turn, I loved watching the smiles people put on for their minute in the spotlight; seeing how their faces changed for the camera.

Outside the toilets, I'd hesitated then ducked in at the last minute. Although there wasn't a lot of point in me trying to comb my wild hair—any contact between it and a brush generally earned me the nickname 'Basil Brush'— I'd dampened my fingers and smoothed down the sides as best I could before heading to the hall. Mum would have never forgiven me for having messy hair in the school photo.

The queue wound away from the main stage, the children waiting patiently on the floor in twos and threes. But I was alone. Something wasn't right.

Mrs Hopkins, the headmistress, had bustled towards me, her face creased with concern. 'Evie, dear,' she'd said, putting her hand on my arm. 'Your class photo's not till this afternoon.' I stopped as it dawned on me what I'd done. 'Let me take you back to your classroom,' she'd said, gently taking my hand.

Three months after my brother died, I'd turned up for the sibling photos. A week later, I'd been referred to Miss Dawson.

'*There was only that one time at school,*' I told Miss Dawson. '*And sometimes first thing in the morning when I wake up I forget for a minute and then it all comes back. That's when I miss him the most.*'

CHAPTER 16

Upstairs in my room, I sat at the desk at which I'd revised for my GSCEs and A levels and opened my old address book—somehow, in the rush to pack, I'd remembered to bring it with me. Mum had got me thinking about my old school friends and I wondered who, aside from Luca, was still around. My best friend from school certainly wasn't—she'd met an Australian guy at university, married him and disappeared off to Australia as soon as she'd graduated. I'd been out to visit her once and she'd stopped off in Dubai for a couple of days, too—it was the type of friendship we could just pick up, no matter how many years went by.

My favourite person in the world lived in Warwick. Clem was the reason I'd moved to Dubai in the first place. Since we'd met on the Student Union dance floor doing our Gloria Gaynors to 'I Will Survive' at the Monday night disco, we'd been inseparable throughout university.

'Promise me we won't get sucked into corporate life,' she'd said as we'd studied in her room for our third-year finals, the threat of real life hanging over us like a guillotine. 'Let's travel together, see the world.'

'How?' I'd asked. 'We don't have enough money for the launderette. How are we going to fly around the world?'

'Easy. We get jobs that pay us to travel: we'll be cabin crew or ski chalet girls. We'll get jobs in a bar in Mykonos and party like Tom Cruise in *Cocktail*.'

Huddled in duvets in digs lashed by the relentless rain of the Midlands, she'd dreamed up our plans for a life in the sun; I'd dreamed of a life away from the ruins of my family.

But things hadn't worked out quite as planned. One night, when we'd both been unemployed for several months, we were sitting in a London wine bar making our Happy Hour drinks last as long as we could when Clem had dropped the bombshell.

'So,' she'd said, and I'd known at once it was bad news. Her energy was off-kilter and she'd been preoccupied all night. 'There's something I have to tell you.'

I'd stared at the nicks in the wooden table, wishing I could stop time right there, for I guessed what was coming. I arranged my face, made it smiley, before I looked up at her.

'I've got a job in Dubai,' she'd said. She was trying to break it to me gently but the luminosity of her face gave her away; she'd tried not to smile but I could tell she was fizzing with excitement. 'I'm going to be a PR executive.'

I'd opened my mouth, but words wouldn't form.

'Evie, I have to go. It ticks all the boxes. Sun, sand, a good salary, an accommodation allowance—it's even tax-free.'

I'd bobbed my head like a nodding dog. Of course she had to go. At last the words came out right, but the light had gone out of me. I'd wanted more than anything to be going with her. She'd booked her one-way ticket, and I'd gone reluctantly back to job-hunting in London.

But, despite being unemployed, I hadn't had time to feel lonely. While I'd been away studying, Mum had retreated from everyday life until she'd virtually become a recluse. She lived in a world she perceived to be fraught with danger. Once I was back from university, and with Dad away so much for work, I took the full brunt of this paranoia. I could understand Mum's fear of me crossing the road; I could understand why she didn't want me to own a bike. But everything else?

And now the fear was no longer just for me: it was for herself, too. Mum had let friendships lapse and she rarely went out—when she did, it was a small trip to the closest supermarket to buy groceries. Heaven help if anyone told her about Ocado. She was becoming a hermit and I worried about her. I knew that if I lived nearby it was a small jump till she became totally dependent on me. But we were both too young for that. Instead, I came up with a two-pronged plan of attack.

Part one: I was going to persuade Mum to take a job—it wouldn't only get her out of the house and force her to interact with people, but it would, I hoped, help her get her confidence back. After she was established in a job I hoped she'd enjoy, I'd move on to part two: I was going to follow Clem to Dubai and force Mum to stand on her own two feet. This latter part of the plan I had no problem with—if necessary I'd scrape together enough money for a ticket, fly out on a tourist visa and look for a job while

I was out there. Clem's Facebook updates showed me tantalising slices of life in Dubai and I yearned to be in the sunshine with her.

The former part of the plan, though, was more tricky. Aside from a secretarial job at the university where she'd met Dad, Mum had never really had a career. Working wasn't in her mindset and Dad earned enough that there wasn't really any financial pressure to motivate her.

I'd trawled through the local job ads, looked at cards stuck in newsagent windows and even went to the Job Centre once, but nothing I suggested took Mum's fancy, even the job as assistant in the flower shop, which I'd thought would really appeal to her.

'Oh, good God, no,' she'd said, as if I'd suggested she retrain as an astronaut. 'Have you any idea how cold it gets in that shop in winter? With those stone floors and all that water about? Oh no, darling, that's not for me.'

Eventually, though, I'd secured her an interview at Woodside Hospital, to work as an admin assistant. Mum hadn't been able to come up with an excuse not to go and that, as they say, was that. The job—keeping charge of a busy consultant—had, ultimately, been the making of her and, a couple of months later, I was on the plane to Dubai. Clem and I had proceeded to paint Dubai not just red but scarlet, indigo, magenta and fuschia.

For two single girls living together in a city that never sleeps, the phrase 'burn the candle at both ends' could never have been more appropriate. But then, at a 'fondue and a bottle of white' night, we'd got chatting to Patrick and

James, a couple of well-spoken guys who'd seemed a snip above the usual Dubai blokes.

We'd double-dated them for a while, then flat-swapped — me moving into James's palatial villa, and Patrick moving in with Clem. Finally, a year later and thinking ourselves ever so very clever, we'd all got engaged and thrown a huge party in the lush gardens of The One&Only Royal Mirage Hotel.

But that's where the similarities ended. While Clem and Patrick had got married, moved back to Warwick and had twins, James and I had staggered towards our bitter break-up — infidelity's not a trait I look for in a husband. Clem was now the mistress of a quaint tea shop selling coffee, tea and cake to tourists up to see Warwick Castle while Patrick ran a successful pub. I knew Clem would be busy with the twins, but I sent her an SMS anyway.

That done, I logged onto Facebook on my iPad. After scrolling through the newsfeed, I sucked my cheeks in and typed 'Luca Rossi' into the search box.

He'd mentioned he was on Facebook — that meant it was OK to 'friend' him, didn't it? It had been weird-in-a-nice-way to bump into Luca after so long. Just hearing his voice again had made me feel safe; it was as if he dropped an invisible cloak of protection over my shoulders. Luca was so different to the men I met in Dubai; so very, very different to the razzle-dazzling, lying, cheating James. Luca was what he was; there was no pretence, no show, and I liked that. He knew about Graham. He knew the scars that lay inside my heart. With Luca, I could be myself: no explanations.

'To see what Luca Rossi shares with his friends, send

a Friend Request.' I stared at the tiny picture of Luca that
came up on the screen, my finger hesitating over the mouse.
Would 'friending' him send the wrong signals? I was still
reeling from my break-up with James, the word 'rebound'
pulsing in my mind's eye, and I didn't want Luca to think I
wanted anything more than a connection for old times' sake.

But the pull of seeing someone who knew my past was
too strong and I fired off the request, adding in a message:
'It was great to see you. I'm around for a bit. Let me know if
you fancy a coffee. Cheers, Evie.' Just the thought of being
Facebook friends with Luca made me smile. Although I was
totally off men, he was different… I knew him. I knew his
family, his background, his people. It wasn't like he could
spin a web of lies like James had.

James had dazzled me from the night we'd met—I'd never
in my life come across anyone so handsome, so charming,
so fearless and spontaneous. On our first date—the morning
after we'd met in the wine bar—he'd taken me skydiving
over Palm Jumeirah for goodness' sake. He'd told me he
dabbled in a bit of commodities trading but made most of his
money working as an advisor to a Sheikh. New to Dubai and
green as they come, I'd lapped it all up, naively believing
that James really was 'working on an important project at
the palace' when he was actually sleeping with Shelley or
Susan or Tracey at their airline crew accommodation. Our
engagement had come to an abrupt end when Shelley had
bumped into us having a cosy dinner in the beach restaurant
of the very hotel at which we'd got engaged.

'What are you doing with my fiancé?' she'd asked before

turning her fury on James. I liked to imagine someone had managed to retrieve both our engagement rings from the sea where we'd flung them. Now I shuddered thinking about that night.

I flicked once more through my address book, concluding that, after being away for so long, I had no real friends currently residing in Woodside. But I had one more thing to do. Opening my email, I looked up the address I had stored so recently.

'Dear Miss Dawson,' I typed. 'It was lovely to speak to you today, and thank you for being so kind. As it happens, I am quite worried about Mum. She's not herself (obviously)— she had a really bad reaction to a police car that went past with its sirens on, and now she's told me she's selling the house we've lived in all my life. Dad's not been gone a few days. More seriously, though, she's confused Dad's death with Graham's twice now. Once I could have overlooked, but twice? Is this to be expected? Should I try to get her to see you? Sorry to ask, but you're the only person who knows all the background. With thanks and warm regards, Evie.'

CHAPTER 17

It was a perilous climb up to the attic. Mum positioned the ladder as best she could, adjacent to the door, and held it steady, but I had to haul myself up a good foot between the top of the ladder and the floor of the attic, then transfer myself across sideways. Dignified it was not.

'Right, are you up?' she called, as I dusted myself off and felt around for a light switch. 'If you're OK up there I'll just pop up to the High Street,' she said. 'Do you need anything?'

I said that I didn't. I had mixed feelings about going through the attic and I was glad Mum wasn't going to be hanging around at the bottom of the ladder, waiting to see what I found. I was curious to see what was up there but, like her, I was also slightly nervous of what I might find, of the memories that might resurface.

Easing myself along the ancient floor beams (I vaguely remembered Dad telling me as a child that I must stand only on the beams—was it true? I didn't know), I looked around. The air smelled musty and particles of dust floated languidly in the yellow of the weak electric light.

Every available inch of floor space was choked with boxes. Empty ones, full ones, mysterious ones, labelled ones. Toys, clothes, books, old computers, old stereos, speakers and suitcases. There was more than thirty years' worth of family junk but, as I looked more closely, I realised there was at least some method to the madness: my old toys were grouped together, as were bunches of suitcases, boxes of clothes, hardware, empty boxes and other items. I realised I wasn't going to be able to make a dent in the clearing today—once I'd had a good look around I'd hire a skip and blitz the whole place in a couple of sessions.

In a dusty corner, balanced on the beams near the other toys, I spotted the old wooden doll's house Dad had made for me when I was six. I went over—it was smaller than I remembered but, even under a coat of dust, it was still lovely. Looking at it now, as an adult, I couldn't believe the attention to detail Dad had put into it: different rooms were sectioned off, each with hinged doors and each wallpapered a different colour; there was tiny home-made furniture; a pipe-cleaner family for whom Mum had made wool bodies and tiny clothes; and there were even electric lights.

Feeling like a giant, I slid my hand inside the living room and clicked a tiny switch—long ago, the lights had even worked. Running my fingertips over the neatly painted window frames, I understood for the first time what a labour of love making this house must have been for Dad. I'd played with it countless times as a child, assuming that everyone's fathers hand-crafted wooden doll's houses for them. It was only now—too late—that I realised how special it had been; how much Dad must have loved me. I looked up at the rafters and whispered, 'I loved it. Thank you.'

Reluctantly, I turned back to the attic. By the door was a messy pile of empty boxes—the box that the new retro phone had come in; the new DVD-player's box; the bread-making machine's box. My mother hated to throw anything away—she must have tossed these boxes up into the attic without actually coming up the ladder; she can't have been up for years. As I started to stack the boxes neatly away from the door, I noticed a camp chair and a small table set back behind the door, in a corner where you wouldn't naturally look when climbing into the attic. On the table, there was a lamp, crudely wired into the mains supply, a couple of books and an opened jumbo packet of Minstrels—Dad's favourite sweets.

After stepping carefully past the door, I went over. Surprisingly, the chair, table and books weren't covered in the dust that veiled everything else in the attic. The thinnest book was a school exercise book. My breath caught as I saw Graham's careless writing scrawled on the front: 'NEWS'. I flicked through the book, dipping in and out of Graham's accounts of our weekends, written for Monday morning 'news' at school.

'On Saturday we went to Greenwich Park,' he'd written. 'Me and Evie played hide n seek in the adventur playground. I won. We had Mr Whippy 99s. Evie dropped hers so I shared mine.' He'd drawn a picture of two children holding huge ice creams. He'd put us in identical outfits, but made me smaller and scribbled me some mad brown hair. I sank into the chair and flicked through the book, absorbed in the events so crudely described: our childhood on the page.

Next I pulled the thick book towards me—it was a photo album and, even before I looked, I knew what I'd find inside: Graham. Hundreds of pictures of Graham. His whole life, lovingly tracked out in pictures, with captions written in my father's neat handwriting. I hugged the album tightly to my chest, and squeezed my eyes shut. So this is how Dad coped with Graham's death? He came up to the attic and sat, alone, remembering his dead son? I sat there for some time, imagining how Dad must have felt, the sounds of family life, such as it was, drifting up from the house below as he—as he what? Remembered? Cried? Blamed himself? Talked to Graham?

'Oh, Dad,' I whispered. 'I didn't know. I would have talked to you. Why didn't you talk to me?'

Taking a deep breath, I put the photo album and the News book carefully back into their places and turned to face the attic.

The first brown box I came to was thick with dust. I brushed the label. 'Dresses' it said. Now that was exciting: could they be Mum's? I still remembered the days before the accident when Mum had dressed up every day, following the trends in magazines and trying out different looks. Things had changed when Graham died, and I'd always wondered what had happened to Mum's glamorous wardrobe.

The box was a good weight, tightly packed. I opened it, picked out the top dress and shook it open. It was a powder blue and silver lurex minidress. Holding it to my face, I inhaled, catching—or maybe imagining—a faint whiff of a perfume that triggered memories of Mum and Dad all dressed up and ready to go out: Mum squealing 'Mind my hair!' as she stooped to hug and kiss Graham and me goodnight, her hairdo rigid with lacquer and her shiny white boots reaching well above her knees; Dad, with a twinkle in his eye, taking Mum's hand as they headed out of the door; the crunch of the car tyres on gravel and Lily from next door hustling us up the stairs to bed. Happy memories. Excited to think Mum's dresses had survived all these years, I shoved the box towards the door and moved on.

Dust lay thick on the tops of all the boxes; the cardboard was cold and damp to touch; a fusty smell hung around them all. I slid tatty string over the edges of another box, opened it and gasped in surprise as my old dolls looked up at me, their nylon dresses as bright as the day they were bought.

Since the accident, I'd mastered the art of not dwelling on the first eight years of my life; it was too painful to remember what life had been like with a brother. I'd not given a moment's thought to these dolls since Mum had packed them up, but seeing them brought memories flooding back: the day I threw 'Pattie' at Graham, accidentally smashing the glass lampshade in the living room; the time I threw a dolls' 'pool party' in the bath—a pool party that Graham had gatecrashed with his Action Man; 'Rosie'—a pretty little doll Mum had bought me to keep me occupied on my first ever flight, aged six.

I still remembered that flight; I saw it in snapshots. I'd been wearing a denim skirt that Mum had bought for me— my first denim skirt—and I'd felt so grown up. Graham and I had begged to sit together in the two seats in front of Mum and Dad. Mum had worried what we'd do if there was an emergency, but Dad had pulled rank and Graham and I had spent the flight pretending we were travelling alone as we ordered our apple juice from the cabin crew. I ran a hand through my hair. While I'd gone on to enjoy plenty more flights, Graham had flown just one more time.

Perching on a beam, I put Rosie carefully back and picked out the other dolls in turn, unwrapping them from the crumbling pages of the local paper in which they'd been cocooned. Carefully, I moved their arms and legs, touched their shiny hair and remembered the contours of their plastic faces. Then I rewrapped them all, one by one, closed the box and pushed it to one side. I'd no idea what to do with them.

The next box was packed with old books, teddy bears, games and wooden jigsaws that I remembered bickering over with Graham. As I turned the toys in my hands, half-formed memories chased through my mind like beagles on the hunt. At the bottom was an old radio: Dad's. Wiping the dust from it, I remembered cuddling on his lap while he listened to dreary voices talking about the news. The radio was tarnished now, decades from its prime, but I could still smell Dad on it, the clean scent of his fresh cologne. Sighing, I stood up and pulled my hair into a messy bun: at this rate, it was going to take me days to get through the attic. I'd have to learn be less emotional.

*

An hour or so later, I straightened up, pleased with the size of the 'throw out' pile I'd managed to make of things that obviously had to go. In the far corner of the attic, a glint of metal caught my eye. Stepping closer, I realised it was Dad's old bike. The last time I'd seen it was when the police had brought it back from the accident site. Sitting in the living room, Dad and I had heard the rumble of a truck engine outside.

'Delivery for you,' the driver had said, indicating the two bikes on the back of the truck, one pristine, one a twisted and broken frame. 'You don't have to take them. Some people want them… everyone's different… closure… ' he tailed off.

Mum had come barrelling down the stairs. 'What is it?'

Dad had pointed wordlessly to the truck. The driver shuffled on the doorstep. 'Well?'

Mum was silent.

'Yes, please. Unload them,' said Dad eventually.

We'd watched as the driver had taken down Dad's bike first, propping it up by the side wall, then he'd reverently lifted out the mangled remains of Graham's bike and placed it gently on the gravel.

I'd watched silently as Dad had signed the delivery papers and the truck had driven away. When we were back in the house, I'd cowered against the dresser as Mum had fallen on Dad, pummelling his chest with her fists and screaming, 'How *could* you? It's all your fault!'

Dad had tried to pull her off, tried to hug her. 'Carole, please. You're emotional. Think about it. We'll bury it with him. What else can we do with it? I refuse to let it go for scrap.'

What I hadn't realised was that Dad had kept his own

bike. Somehow, he must have hidden it from Mum; got it up to the attic himself. I brushed dust off the saddle now, and squeezed the brakes. The tyres were flat and the brake pads felt like concrete, but there appeared to be nothing a bit of oil wouldn't cure; ditto with the chain. It was a nice bike; I remember it had been expensive, one of the first things Dad had treated himself to when his first book was published. Not daring to get onto it in the attic, I stood next to it appraisingly as I squeezed the brakes and imagined myself riding it. Dad had been tall but it was still a manageable size. I stared down at my hands on the handlebars Dad would have gripped and thought, *Could I?*

Although the bike was veiled in tragedy, I liked the continuity of me riding it. The bike was a connection to Dad and I really needed that right now. I'd been unable to say goodbye to him and my hopes of us becoming close again had been obliterated overnight. What little I'd ever had of my father was slipping away from me. Like the sky needs the stars, I needed to feel close to him; the ache was almost physical. But what would Mum say? The accident had been twenty years ago and the bike was nondescript, black; maybe she'd even forgotten what it had looked like. If I got it down without her seeing, could I pass it off as a friend's? I wheeled it carefully towards the attic door then turned back. What next?

CHAPTER 18

'So how are things with your dad?' Miss Dawson asked. Today she'd brought sweets and I sucked on a sticky Drumstick, softening it up before I bit into it, while I thought about what to say. Graham wasn't the only person I'd lost in the summer.

'He doesn't play Mastermind with me any more,' I said.

'Oh? Is that something you used to do a lot?'

'Yep. He stopped reading with me as well.' I thought about the books we used to read together at bedtime. The way he did the silly voices.

'Have you tried to speak to him? Properly?' Miss Dawson's voice was gentle.

'He's never home. He's away on lecture tours. It's "very important" for his "career".' I mimicked the way Dad said it.

The truth was, Mum and I hardly saw Dad these days. He worked long hours and started going away on lecture tours a lot of the time.

'Why won't he speak to me?' I said, a sob catching in my throat. 'I'm still here. It's like he thinks I'm dead, too.'

'He must be at home sometimes?'

'He locks himself in his study.'

'Working?'

'Huh.' Usually he was writing papers and books and whatever else historians did, but sometimes—and I knew this because I'd peeped around the door—Dad just sat with his head in his hands. 'He's really busy with work,' I said. 'He's really famous. He's in the papers, magazines and everything. Once he was on the radio. And the telly.'

'Wonderful. You must be proud of him. What does he do?'

I knew she knew. 'He's a historian. He writes papers. And books, and he's made TV shows and everything. He's just finished a series of books for children. He's been on TV.'

People talked about how my dad managed to make history 'come alive' for children. Mum's friends stopped mentioning Graham when they came to the house; they stopped asking how we were. All they wanted to do was meet Dad; you could see it in the way they looked past me and Mum. Everyone talked about the way Dad could 'connect' with his students. I didn't know what that meant, but it sounded nice. I wished he could 'connect' with me.

'I just want him to notice me again,' I said. 'I want it to be how it was before.'

'Oh, Evie. It will get better. Everyone deals with tragedies differently. Your dad lost his son. It'll take time.'

'But I'm still here,' I said. 'Can't he see that? I'm still here.'

CHAPTER 19

It wasn't easy getting the bike down from the attic but, somehow, I managed. I was keen to do it before Mum got back and, somehow, after a struggle that broke two of my nails, gouged out a small section of wallpaper and left a smear of oil on the paint of the attic door, both the bike and I were on the landing. I bumped it down the stairs and into the kitchen, where I examined it more thoroughly, remembering the do-it-yourself tutorials Dad had given Graham and me in this very room; the reluctant (on my part) Sunday afternoons spent learning how to oil our chains, flip off the tyres and change the inner tubes. The bike needed a bit of a service, a good re-grease and a couple of new tyres, but, aside from that, it was in good shape. I lay newspaper over the kitchen floor, dug out the toolkit and the oilcan from under the stairs and, cranking up the radio, got to work.

I didn't hear Mum come in, not until she snapped off the radio, causing me to jerk up from where I was slowly dripping oil into the chain. I was starting to wonder if I'd actually have to take the bike for a professional service; the chain was more dilapidated than I'd originally thought, and the brake blocks definitely needed changing.

Mum was breathing heavily, her basket of shopping dropped at her feet, Richard hovering behind her. 'What are you doing?' Her voice was quiet, but a red spot high on each cheek belied her calmness.

'Oh hi!' I said, realising at once that I'd underestimated her. Woefully underestimated her. Of course she would remember Dad's bike. I looked at the floor, my cheeks burning in shame. I could have handled it so much better. How could I have been so stupid to think she wouldn't recognise the bike?

'WHAT. IS. THAT?'

'Umm…'

'Is it your father's?'

I nodded feeling like an eight-year-old. I could feel my lip curling like I was going to cry. *I made a mistake!* I wanted to say. *Go away and I'll put it back and we'll pretend it never happened!* 'It was in the attic,' I said.

'And what are you doing to it?' Mum's words were clipped.

'I was just taking a look at it…'

'Why?'

'Oh, no reason. Just… I wondered what you wanted to do with it.'

'Well, mark my words, young lady. You will not be riding that bike. You hear me?'

'What?'

'I said, you are not riding that bike.'

'But…'

'But nothing. Now you've got it down, you may as well

put it outside for the bin men. But mark my words, if I catch you…' Mum let out a stifled scream and steamed out of the room, fury stuck to her like a swarm of bees.

'It was twenty years ago!' I shouted after her, suddenly furious myself. 'When are you going to face up to it? He's *dead*! They are *both dead*!' I dropped the oilcan and collapsed onto my knees on the kitchen floor.

Richard looked sadly at me and shook his head. 'To be fair, Evie, that was a bit much.'

'To be fair, Richard,' I snapped, 'it's none of your business.'

I waited for him to leave the room, then stood up, rubbing out the ache in the small of my back. I wheeled the bike out into the garden and around the side of the house, where I propped it up by the bins. I'd decide what to do with it later.

CHAPTER 20

'*E*vie, what happened?' Miss Dawson asked. 'The school called. I came as quickly as I could. What happened?'

I liked that Miss Dawson didn't ask if I was all right. Even my teacher had spotted that I wasn't all right. When I hadn't been able to stop crying in class, she'd led me to the nurse's room and asked her to phone my mum.

'No! Not Mum!' I'd curled in a ball on the narrow bed and wished I could stay there forever.

'Who then?' Nurse had asked. 'Is your dad around?'

I'd shaken my head.

Nurse had tut-tutted. 'Who then? Miss Dawson?' and I'd agreed with a nod.

Now Miss Dawson was here, I knew I had to talk to her. I pulled myself up so I was sitting on the bed.

'It's Dingbat,' I said.

Miss Dawson waited.

'Hamster,' I hiccupped. 'He's dead.' I scrubbed at my eyes with the balled-up tissue I'd been holding all morning, my breath still jagged.

'Oh, Evie. I'm sorry to hear that.' Miss Dawson rubbed a hand over her face.

But it wasn't that Dingbat was dead. Well, it was, but it wasn't like Miss Dawson thought. Dingbat had been Graham's hamster. He'd got him when he'd turned ten— for his last birthday. He'd begged and pleaded, claiming he'd look after the hamster one hundred per cent himself. Mum hadn't thought Graham would manage, but Dad had persuaded her to give him the benefit of the doubt and Graham had hand-picked Dingbat from a heap of ginger- and-white fluff at the pet shop. And, to Mum's surprise, he'd looked after Dingbat really well, feeding him, changing his water, peeling grapes for him and even cleaning out his cage. He'd really loved him. After the accident, I'd taken over caring for Dingbat. It made me feel like I was with Graham.

'He was Graham's,' I said.

'It's very sad when pets die,' Miss Dawson said carefully. 'And it must be very hard for you with… Dingbat? … because he was a link to Graham?'

'Mmm.' I didn't know what to say. I was supposed to be able to tell Miss Dawson anything, but I didn't know if I could tell her what had happened yesterday after school. Whenever I thought about it, I started to shake.

I'd gone into the kitchen to ask for a biscuit. Mum had been standing at Dingbat's cage. The cage door was open and Mum had been holding Dingbat, letting him run from one hand to the other as she stared out of the window at the garden. At the exact moment that I opened my mouth to ask for the biscuit, Mum had spun around with a scream and hurled Dingbat at the kitchen wall. I could still hear the crunch of his little body slamming into the wall, the thud of him landing on the tiled floor.

'Mummy!' I'd screamed and she'd noticed me for the first time. She'd stared at me, then she'd pushed a strand of hair out of her eyes and come towards me with her arms held out and a smile splitting her face in two. On the floor behind her, Dingbat twitched and then was still, blood oozing from his mouth and ears.

'Evie, darling. What's wrong? Come here. Let me give you a cuddle.' She'd wound her arms around me, stroking my hair, and I'd sagged against my mother, clinging to her, breathing in the scent of her clothes, her perfume. It was the first time she'd hugged me since Graham had died.

'I love you, Evie,' she'd said, kissing my hair and running her hands through it. 'Don't ever leave me. Promise you won't leave me.'

It was awful, but the attention was nice and I hated myself for liking it; hated myself for choosing Mum's hugs instead of running to Dingbat.

'It's Mum,' I told Miss Dawson.

'OK,' she said. 'She probably misses Dingbat as much as you do. I expect he reminded her of Graham, too.'

I twisted the tissue in my hand, my eyes raw. Mum had killed a living creature. Would Miss Dawson have to tell the police? Would Mum have to go to jail? What was worse: Mum like this, or Mum in jail? I took a deep breath and made my decision: 'It's just that… I don't think she'll let me get a new hamster,' I said. Well…at least that bit was true.

CHAPTER 21

Slightly squiffy from having discovered Mum's stash of good gin, I decided to spend the evening catching up on back episodes of *Casualty*. Right near the start of one episode, a man had a dramatic heart attack in a shopping centre. He clutched his chest as he dropped to the floor, groaning.

'Hollywood heart attack!' I shouted at the television, realising as I did so that I sounded just like Dad. It's exactly what he would have said. 'Most heart attacks don't look like that,' he'd say. And now he'd know, I thought, wondering what he'd felt—if anything—when his heart had failed him in his sleep. Had he woken up? Had there been a moment when he'd panicked? Known he was dying? Or had he simply slept through it, as Mum clearly wanted to believe? I had my doubts. Suddenly, grief ambushed me and I pressed 'mute' on the television, picked up my phone and flicked through my contacts to the entry for 'Dad'. I stared at the word for a few seconds then, before I even had time to think about it, I pressed 'dial' and put the phone to my ear.

'Hello. You're through to Doctor Robert Stevens. I can't

take your call right now. Please leave a message after the tone.'

'Dad,' I whispered. I clicked off the call, but kept the phone at my ear.

'Hello, Dad. It's me,' I said into the handset. 'I just wanted to… say hello. See how you are. I hope… it wasn't painful… I hope you're in a good place now.' Suddenly, I felt silly. 'OK, bye.' I put my phone out of reach on the coffee table and clicked the TV's sound back on.

Outside, there was the scrunch of gravel, a pause while goodnights were said, and then the scrape of Mum's key in the door. I turned off the television as she stuck her head around the door.

'How was your evening?'

'Oh very nice, thank you,' Mum said, flopping into an armchair and easing her feet out of her shoes and then her pop socks. 'We had some poppadums, chicken tikka and tiny samosas to start, then I had chicken *korma* and Richard had lamb *biryiani*. We shared the *naan* and a bottle of red wine. I couldn't manage dessert so we just had coffee.'

'Sounds lovely, but I meant how was the evening? With Richard?'

'Oh.' Mum looked at her watch. 'We've only been gone two hours. No time at all!' She was wearing her 'going out' perfume and a stylish skirt and top; they could have been Ghost. So much for 'just a curry'.

'So, did he make a move on you?' I asked.

'Of course not!' I was glad she seemed affronted.

'So?' I asked again, raising an eyebrow. 'How was it?'

Mum tutted. 'It's not like that. He just had a voucher and knew I was on my own. He thought I might like cheering up. For goodness' sake, Evie. Dad's not been gone three days.'

'Do you miss him?'

Mum flopped onto the sofa. 'Of course. I was married to him for thirty-three years. Do you?'

I sighed. My head was starting to spin with the gin; I could feel blood throbbing at my temples. 'Oh, I don't know. It's weird. You know what he was like. After... ?' I couldn't say it. 'He was distant. He wasn't interested in me. But he was better last summer, wasn't he? Did you notice how he asked questions about Dubai? It was like he wanted to come. And I wanted him to see what I've achieved. I wanted him to be proud.'

It was the most I'd ever said to her about Dad. What I didn't tell her was about the other, unexpected conversation I'd had with Dad out in the garden last summer.

'I still blame myself,' he'd said, *apropos* of nothing, but I'd known at once what he meant.

'Well, you shouldn't. It wasn't your fault,' I'd said. 'The car jumped the lights. No one could have stopped that, not even Mum. It was a quirk of fate that it was you with Graham, not her.'

Dad had looked so grateful then that I'd had to look away.

'You really don't blame me?' he'd asked.

'Of course not. I never did.'

He'd reached out and touched my hand. It was the most contact we'd had in over two decades.

Now, in the living room, Mum didn't say anything. I

rubbed my temples, trying to smooth away the giddiness from the alcohol. 'Well, too late now, isn't it?' I said.

Mum flattened her lips into a line. 'Your father loved you very much, Evie. He just didn't know how show it. He was ever so proud of you going off to Dubai on your own.' She shifted in her chair and pulled at her skirt, smoothing it down over her thighs.

I raised my eyebrows. Apart from last summer, I'd not seen any evidence of Dad being proud of me.

'He never stopped blaming himself, you know,' she said.

'But it wasn't his fault, was it?'

'No, of course not. It was a terrible tragedy. But Graham was under his care. He couldn't forgive himself.'

'I never blamed him.' I needed her to see that, to understand it.

Mum was quiet.

'Last summer we spoke about it,' I said. 'I told him I didn't blame him.'

Mum stood up, yawned and stretched her arms out behind her.

'Well, he never stopped blaming himself. That much I know. Goodnight.'

The white elephant in the room practically headbutted me: Dad had never stopped blaming himself because Mum had never stopped blaming him.

'Goodnight,' I said.

*

I may have intended to sleep that night, but the gin had

other plans for me. As soon as I lay down, the matter of the mysterious debits slithered snake-like into my mind and flicked its forked tongue at my consciousness, keeping me awake. I'd bet my last Rolo that Mum knew neither about the lump sum nor the regular debits and, if the money wasn't for the house, what was it for? I tossed about in my bed, turning this way and that, then flipping the pillow and finally lying on my back staring at the ceiling. What on earth would my parents have spent £22,000 on? They were hardly known for their extravagant purchases.

Lying in the dark, I ran through possibilities. Could Dad have been putting money aside for a surprise for Mum? A new car, maybe — but it would have to be a really nice one. An exotic holiday? A Caribbean cruise? Maybe it was more practical: an advance payment to a retirement home? Or had he really fallen victim to a financial scam?

Giving up any pretence of sleep, I grabbed my knitting bag and sat up in bed. Knit one, purl one, knit one, purl one… the ribbed base of the hat I was knitting took shape in the light of the bedside lamp as my mind whirled. What could it be?

As my needles clicked, I tried to convince myself Dad must have spent the money on something so obvious I'd completely overlooked it. I finished off the hat's ribbing and packed my needles away, resolving to go through the receipts with a toothcomb as soon as I could. I plumped the pillows one more time and settled into my favourite sleeping position, but still I couldn't sleep.

After fumbling for the torch I kept on the bedside table,

I padded into the bathroom and opened the medicine cupboard. I was hoping Mum might have an old box of herbal sleeping tablets somewhere in there, but what I actually saw, as the torch lit up the contents, was a shock: the entire right-hand side of the cabinet was given over to sleep remedies ranging in strength from Night Rescue Remedy to boxes of prescription tablets. I checked the dates on the prescription labels — all were under six months old. I'd had no idea. Had things really got that bad?

*

When I finally got to sleep, I dreamed about moving house. Mum and I watched the movers put the last boxes into the lorry, slam the door shut and drive off with a cheery wave. The driver was Dad. Mum and I followed in the car, but we weren't able to catch up. The faster we drove, the further from us the lorry drew, as we span along dark, wet roads, trying to find shortcuts and straining always for a glimpse of the van that contained my father and the memories of my childhood.

I woke in a tangle of sheets.

CHAPTER 22

'*Are things improving with your mum now?*' *Miss Dawson asked. We were sitting in her living room—each of us in a big armchair. It was the school holidays but my sessions didn't stop for holidays. Dad was waiting in the dining room. Miss Dawson had bought me a KitKat.*

I bit my lip. 'Not really,' I said.

'What makes you say that, Evie?'

The truth was, Mum wasn't coping at all. I hadn't told anyone about what had really happened with Dingbat: all I said was, 'He got out; he died.' Then, last week Mum had gone to the supermarket in her pyjamas. They were red-and-white checked and Mum had matched them with red high heels and a pillar-box red lipstick. She'd stood in the hall, finalising her shopping list with her basket over her arm and I'd thought she was doing it for a joke; trying to be funny; trying to cheer me up. My heart had filled with love and I'd laughed.

'What's so funny?' she'd snapped.

I should have spotted the warning tone in her voice, but I was still laughing. I'd thought the joke was still going.

'You're going to the shops in your pyjamas!' I'd giggled.

Already I was imagining telling my friends about it. My mum was the funny one!

'They are NOT my pyjamas!'

I froze.

'This is my suit! I am wearing a SUIT!' she'd shouted. She'd jabbed at her lips, kicked a foot out at me. 'See? I am wearing lipstick! I am wearing RED SHOES! Don't you know what a SUIT looks like?'

She'd kicked hard at the stair I was sitting on and left, slamming the front door so hard behind her that the hall had seemed to reverberate for minutes.

I was upstairs when she'd come back with the shopping. I heard her put it away in the kitchen then go into her bedroom. When I went down for lunch she was wearing a dress and her lipstick had gone.

'What would you like for lunch?' she'd asked, smiling at me as if nothing was wrong.

'She sometimes wears her pyjamas to the High Street,' I told Miss Dawson.

CHAPTER 23

Even through my eyelids, I could tell that it was sunny when I woke the next morning, remnants of the anxiety of my dream still coursing through my veins. Lying motionless, not daring to move after the skinful of gin I'd drunk the night before, I felt gently around inside my head for signs of the hangover I knew I deserved, and was both relieved and grateful to discover that I'd been spared.

The sound of music drifted up from downstairs. An uplifting piano concerto on the radio—Mozart, maybe. I lay in bed, letting the waves of sound wash over me. The music stopped abruptly and restarted a few bars back and I realised that it wasn't the radio at all: Mum was actually playing the piano downstairs. It had been so long since I'd last heard her play that I'd almost forgotten that she did. The piano in the corner of the dining room had long been buried under a collection of dusty knick-knacks, photographs and old sheet music.

Dust particles pirouetted in the sunshine as I entered the dining room. Mum's fingers danced over the keys as she strained forward to read the music. I stood and listened for a minute; I hadn't seen her looking so alive in years; her body moved with the music and the word 'graceful' came to mind. When Mum realised I was standing there, she broke off, flexing her wrists and bending back her fingers.

'Wow,' I said, shaking my head. 'Impressed! I didn't know you could still play.'

Mum smiled. 'Still got it!' she said. 'I should do it more often.'

I remembered childhood evenings, sing-songs around the piano. 'Dad loved it when you played.'

'I know...' said Mum. 'Anyway. Sleep well?'

'Yes. You?'

'Oh...you know.' She shrugged and turned back to her music while I fixed myself some breakfast. Mum absently played a few scales and their arpeggios, smiling to herself as she got each one right.

'G major. Oh. I have an appointment to see the new house again this afternoon,' she said, her fingers fluttering over the keys. 'A major. Would you like to come? Or have you got something else planned? B major.'

'Have you heard back from the estate agent yet?' I asked.

'Not yet, but he said he might hear today. C-sharp major. I can't believe I still remember all these!'

'So there's still time to back out?'

'Why would I want to back out? It's the perfect house for me, and just around the corner.' She played the arpeggios as chords. The sound of the last chord fell away and I didn't fill the silence.

'It's what your father wanted, too.'

I sighed. 'Sure. If you want me to, I'll come.'

'Thank you. If you like it, there's no reason why I shouldn't go ahead and buy it. There's no chain and Dad had worked out the finances…'

'Oh really? Had he put the money aside?'

Mum shot me a look over her glasses, her fingers still holding the chord for D-sharp major. Evie Stealthy Stevens, I was not. 'As I said last time you asked: no. But the point is that this house is smaller, so we—' she rolled her eyes upwards laughing a little at her mistake '—*I* would be able to free up a bit more capital. I think it's really exciting. I can't wait to move. F-sharp major. That was always my favourite.'

I decided to spend the morning in the attic.

*

Three and a half hours later, I straightened up as far as I could under the eaves of the attic and rubbed the small of my back with a grubby hand, surveying my work. I'd managed to get rid of all the empty boxes and all the old suitcases that were broken or falling apart with age. Mum now had a respectable collection of usable cases and in-flight trolley-bags in different sizes, every single one of which could be seen in public.

I'd also managed to get through a few boxes of junk but, as I got further into the boxes, I was finding it increasingly hard to know what to do with the stuff. I rolled one of Graham's shiny little Matchbox cars to and fro across my grimy palm, remembering the intricate cities we'd built with cardboard roads and shoebox car parks. Clem's voice echoed in my head: 'Who can afford to store memories?' she'd said when she left Dubai, selling what she could and giving the rest to me. 'Clear the old; make space for the new.'

Sighing, I put the car back in the box with all its playmates. For now, I'd shove all the things I wasn't sure about into a corner. Maybe the new house would have at least a small attic.

The phone rang in the hall below.

'Darling!' Mum's voice floated up from the bottom of the ladder. 'It's *Luca*! *Luca Rossi*!' His name was stage-whispered to indicate the significance of being phoned by an ex-almost-fiancé. I heard the drama, the matchmaker in her voice: *Ooh… Evie could do worse than Luca. He's handsome, nice family, would be a good bet…* 'Can you come down? Or shall I ask him to call back?'

'Coming!' I shouted, slithering down the ladder and landing heavily as I missed the bottom step. 'Don't get ideas,' I whispered to Mum as I took the phone from her. 'It's not like that… Hello?'

'Hi, Evie.' I turned my back on Mum, seventeen again, Luca's voice transporting me to the long evenings I'd spent curling the phone wire around my finger as the two of us had run up his parents' phone bill chatting about nothing. 'I saw your message on Facebook,' Luca said. 'I was going to ask you for a coffee but, well, I suppose we've missed the boat now it's nearly midday. But are you free for lunch? Could I tempt you with a bit of… oooh… Pizza Express?'

Aside from the curry place, a Chinese and a clutch of fast-food joints, there wasn't a lot of choice in Woodside—and I was hungry. Because it hadn't been there ten years ago, we had no 'date' memories from Pizza Express, no history to hang over us.

'Sure,' I said. We agreed to meet in half an hour.

CHAPTER 24

While I'd hurried up Mum's road towards the High Street, my steps slowed as I approached Pizza Express. Shyness gnawed at my confidence and I felt inelegant, inarticulate, flumpy with awkwardness. What would I say to Luca? Was I kidding myself to think we could ever be more than Facebook friends? The whole 'Luca and Evie' thing was water under a bridge so distant I'd forgotten what it looked like but, if we were to forge some sort of adult friendship—which, given my lack of other friends, would be nice—I needed to let Luca know how sorry I was for rejecting him so coldly; it was something I still felt guilty about. He was probably too much of a gentleman to bring it up, but I couldn't let it stay unsaid. I suppose what I was looking for was his forgiveness. This lunch would be a good place to start, but the thought of how he'd take my apology made me nervous.

I had to pass the restaurant's window before I got to the door and I could see Luca already there at a table, his back to the glass, and busy with his phone. His profile was familiar yet firmer, filled out, more mature. It was peculiar to see the older Luca; as a teenager I'd tried to imagine what he might look like as a man—and here he was. Better.

The restaurant, only a few tables taken, smelled of fried garlic. The warmth of the central heating hit me as I entered and, in the open kitchen, the chef sang a few bars of music, his voice bass, vibrato. I paused, tossed my hair back, took a deep breath and marched up to Luca's table. A glass of white wine and a jug of water stood alongside the menu.

'Hey, stranger,' I said, brusquer than I'd intended. 'Morning. Or is it afternoon?'

'Evie,' said Luca, standing up to greet me. He was wearing blue jeans and a sweater, a brown leather jacket slung over the back of his chair. He looked amazing, but I couldn't tell if he'd made an effort because I had no reference point on which to base it. I didn't know how Luca dressed these days. Personally, I'd put a lot of effort into trying to look effortless.

A slight touch of cheek to cheek; the ghost of an air-kiss; the scent of cologne on warm, clean skin.

'Same hair,' Luca said, as he sat back down. 'Very Kate Middleton.'

I laughed and patted my hair, realising that it did look almost exactly the same as it had when we'd been at school. '*Now* it's the same hair,' I said. 'But in the last ten years it's gone full circle. Short, bobbed, highlights, lowlights, long—blonde, even.' I remembered how Luca had always said he liked the combination of dark hair and blue eyes.

'Suits you like this.'

'Thanks.' There was a short silence. 'You look, um, the

same, too,' I said. It wasn't strictly true: he did and he didn't, but the silence was awkward and I needed to fill it.

'Thanks,' said Luca. 'I think.' He gave a short little laugh. 'I didn't know what you'd want so I didn't order a drink for you. I hope you don't mind.' Luca nodded toward his wine glass. 'And, just for the record, this isn't the first time I've had pizza and wine for breakfast—and neither will it be the last.'

'Wine would be great,' I said. 'Just what I need. I'm sure the sun's over the yardarm in Dubai.'

'Really?' he asked, looking at his watch. It must only be, what, four-thirty there?'

'We have low yardarms in Dubai.' I looked at Luca from under my lashes and we both laughed. He ordered a bottle of wine and another glass.

'So how's your mum?' he asked.

'Oh, you know. It's early days...' I paused and then remembered I could actually talk to Luca about her. He would understand. 'I don't know what to expect. She seems all right sometimes, and then she does something really unexpected. I don't know what's normal.'

I took a slug of wine and exhaled deeply as it hit my bloodstream. My muscles softened and I leaned back in my chair, realising that my shoulders had been hunched all morning.

'The dad of one of my colleagues died,' said Luca. 'I remember him saying his mum was all over the place for a while, you know, losing things, being scatty and distracted. Once he found her glasses in the microwave. Stuff like that?'

I frowned. 'Not really.'

'Does she cry?'

'I haven't seen her cry.'

'It'll come. It takes time for them to process this stuff. It's not been long, has it? A week?'

'Less than. It was Friday night.'

'Well. Give her time. It'll take her at least six months to get used to the idea, probably longer.'

But Graham's accident complicates everything, I thought. This is not a normal situation. 'So far she seems to be taking it well,' I said. 'She seems quite together. Organised, like, she's got everything under control. She even went out for dinner last night. With a man.'

Luca raised an eyebrow. I mirrored it and nodded, half a laugh escaping with my breath.

'I thought so, too. It's odd, isn't it? He's only been gone five days.'

'When you put it like that, yes. But would she have done that anyway? If your dad was still alive? He was away a lot, wasn't he? She must have friends?'

'Oh I guess. I don't know. But shouldn't there be like a mourning period, or something?'

Luca took a sip of wine. I could see he didn't know what to say. But he didn't have to say anything; I could see that it wasn't just me who thought it was a bit odd.

'She's also put in an offer on a house.'

Luca's eyes widened. 'Wow. That's big. And sudden? She's lived there all your life, right?'

'Yeah. Thirty years. But she says the house is too big, and

that she and Dad were planning the move. Apparently, she put in the offer the day before he died. But surely she can retract it now? It's not binding, is it? Until it's been accepted and everything? The last thing she needs now is to move house. Isn't moving house right up there, along with death of a spouse, as one of life's most stressful events?' I paused. 'Or am I being unreasonable?'

'I don't know what to say,' said Luca. 'If they were planning to move before your dad... you know... then maybe it's not as sudden as it seems? Maybe it'll give her something to focus on. Like, a sense of purpose?'

'Yeah... maybe.'

We sipped our drinks.

'So how long are you here for?' he asked eventually.

'I'm here for the funeral, which is on Friday. And Mum's asked me to help her clear out the attic ready for a potential move. After that, I haven't really thought. My boss said to take as long as I needed, but I can't be here forever, really. I don't think he meant "stick around for three months".' I wished I had a sibling to help me keep an eye on Mum and simultaneously squashed the thought. 'Anyway, how are you?'

Luca exhaled slowly; took a sip of wine. 'I'm fine,' he said. 'All good.' He stared out of the window, shaking his head. 'Your poor mum. How is she?'

'She's OK. She's coping well.' My eyes slid away from Luca's and I twisted the wine bottle around to face me, making a show of reading the label.

'Anyway.' I topped up Luca's glass. 'Tell me. What have

you been doing for the past ten years? Did you ever set up that art gallery you used to dream about?'

'Well, I'm a freelance photographer, by way of a law degree, but my dream is still to set up a gallery with a coffee shop, and maybe a bookshop, too. Woodside needs some beauty. It needs a photography gallery, no?' His eyes were brimful of passion.

'And I've every faith you're the man to bring beauty to Woodside.' I smiled back at him. 'But, seriously, good on you.'

'Anyway,' said Luca, changing the subject, 'what have you been doing since you jilted me at the altar?'

I snorted, wine tickling my nose. 'That's not fair! It was hardly the altar!'

'Altar. Engagement. Same thing. Pff.' Luca was laughing at me.

'Look, about that,' I said. Luca raised an eyebrow. 'I'm really sorry.'

'Sorry for what? For turning me down?'

'Well, that… and the way I did it.'

'I should bloody hope so.' Again, he was laughing and I squirmed in my seat, not entirely sure if he was teasing or serious. Luca reached for my hand, put his over it.

'Look, Evie, just so you know…' He paused. 'I'm really glad you turned me down.'

'Really?'

'Really. Can you imagine being married at nineteen?' He shuddered. 'You did me a favour.'

'I still feel so guilty.'

'Well, stop that right now.' He squeezed my hand. I squeezed back, grateful. 'Don't worry. I took the ring back. Got a refund. Argos is great about returns.' He said it deadpan and a laugh exploded out of me. I pulled my hand away, the tension of the moment dissipated.

'But, seriously, do you ever wonder how it would have turned out? Do you think we'd still be together now?'

'Who knows. I'd like to hope so. But we were very young and we had university still to get through. The odds were stacked against us. I don't know what I was thinking proposing like that. Honestly, Evie? I suspect you saved us both a lot of heartache.'

'Oh, don't you worry on that account: seems like I managed to get myself plenty of heartache without any help from you whatsoever.'

'Really? I half expected you to be married by now.'

'I was, almost. Well, I got as close to being married as you can get when you're engaged to a pathological liar who already has a fiancée.' Now I had someone to talk to about James, I suddenly didn't want to waste my energy dragging through it all. Sitting with Luca, it no longer seemed important. 'A story for another day,' I said.

Luca read me well. 'So,' he said after a moment, 'what took you to Dubai? Not the pathological liar, I hope?'

I laughed. 'No. I had the joy of meeting him there. Oh, you know how it was with me. Like I always had ants in my pants?'

'Yep. You always had your nose in a travel brochure. I remember how you used to stare at those pictures of blue sky and beaches and yearn to be anywhere but the UK. I wished we'd had the money to travel to some of those places.'

'Ha. I loved my brochures, didn't I? Well, after I finished uni, I wasn't ready to do the nine-to-five thing in London. I just couldn't do it. My best friend from uni got a job in Dubai and I followed her over.' I hesitated, then plunged on. 'I did it for Mum as much as for me. Dad was away much of the time and she was too dependent on me. I wanted to force her to stand on her own two feet.' I looked at Luca and saw that he got it. 'I wanted to make a clean break, as well. There were too many memories here. Too much sadness in Mum and Dad's house... you know what I mean?' He nodded. 'Anyway.' I shrugged. 'I had nothing to lose, no ties. You know how it is.'

'Now or never. Before the kids, the car and the mortgage.'

I returned Luca's smile. 'Exactly.'

'And now?' he asked. 'Still got ants in your pants, or ready to come back?'

'Well, goodness,' I said, surprised by the way the question got me. A couple of weeks ago I wouldn't have even considered moving back to the UK but now, sitting in Pizza Express with Luca, I started to wonder. 'Never say never.'

While I wasn't surprised to see that Mum's house-to-be was located in what I called her 'magic triangle' — an area of about one square mile centred on the existing house, outside of which she didn't think it was possible to breathe oxygen — what I was surprised to see was Richard hanging around on the pavement outside it.

'What's he doing here?' I hissed.

'Oh! I invited him! He loves property; very interested in property. Thought he might like the chance to look around.'

I rolled my eyes at the sky. 'Marvellous.'

'Hello!' said Richard as we approached. He gave Mum a little air-kiss and nodded to me. 'Exciting times, eh? See you've gone for a new-build, too. Far easier to maintain than those draughty old Victorian heaps.'

'Oh, tell me about it!' laughed Mum. 'No more cleaning those leaded windows! I can't wait.'

'It's not yours yet,' I muttered, but Mum and Richard were already halfway up the garden path. Despite Mum's protestations that there was nothing between the two of them, it certainly didn't look like that. I watched for a minute as they walked together to the front door, every inch the married couple.

Tucked away from the main street, the house was a two-bedroom bungalow in a conservation area and it was detached, which I knew would have scored points with Mum; she hated being able to hear anything through the shared wall of our house. I wondered how Dad had stomached the idea of living in a new-build. As a historian, he'd always been quite scathing about 'shoebox' houses. Still, the outside of the house was covered in climbing ivy and other plants and the front garden was lush with foliage. It looked friendly.

Sheltering from the wind in a small porch, grey clouds scudding across the sky, we knocked on the door, and were invited in by the owner, a middle-aged man wearing the England football strip.

'Mrs Stevens!' he said. 'Come to have another look at your new home? Did that sorry excuse for an estate agent tell you I accepted your offer?'

'Oh,' Mum said, her mouth pursed. 'No, he didn't. I'll give him a call this afternoon.' She exchanged a glance with Richard.

'Right you are, love,' said the man. 'It's chain-free, so I'm ready to move just as soon as. Now, I'm in the middle of something. Do you mind taking a look around by yourselves?' We shook our heads and he disappeared back into the house.

I looked around. We were standing in a tidy little entrance hall with pillar-box red walls and carpeted in a green so bright I jokingly slid my sunglasses back over my eyes once the owner had disappeared

'I'm trying to look past the décor,' I whispered, pretending to peer through my sunglasses.

'What's wrong with the décor?' she asked. 'I quite like it.'

The house was U-shaped, built as if its arms were hugging a little garden that could be seen from almost every room. There was a sense of light and space, which I liked at once. Richard and I followed Mum around and she presented each room to us with a flourish, clearly enjoying seeing the property again now she knew her offer had been accepted. I could see from the way her eyes narrowed that she was trying to picture her things in each room. The study was very small. I couldn't imagine how Dad would have managed to work in it.

'I'll need to get some new furniture,' said Mum. 'Most of mine is too big. But wait till you see the bedroom. The bedroom's gorgeous.'

She led us through the long, narrow living room nodding apologies to the owner, who was watching television, opened a set of French doors and stepped outside onto a patio that faced the small, neat garden.

'It's not very big,' said Mum. Already I could see her saying the same thing to her first guests as she showed them outside.

'But isn't that the point?' I asked. 'Wasn't the old one too big for you to manage? Especially now you're on your own.'

'Not that your father—God rest his soul—was ever that

much of a help in the garden,' she said. 'He was always bloody away.'

The master bedroom was a beautiful space. With French doors to the garden as well as a glass wall through to an *en suite* with windows facing the end of the plot, it was bright and airy. Richard nodded to himself. 'Very nice,' he said.

'Ta-da!' said Mum, doing a twirl as if she owned the house already. 'I love this room. There's room to swing a cat—and I won't need to do a thing to it.'

I frowned. 'Did Dad see it?'

'Yep.'

What, I wondered, had he made of the pink carpet, flowery wallpaper and chipboard fitted wardrobe?

*

'So. He accepted the offer despite what the estate agent said,' said Mum, as we walked home after we'd said goodbye to Richard. The wind whipped our hair around our faces. Mum did a silent cheer, clearly pleased with herself. 'What did you think? Do you like it? Can you see yourself visiting your old ma there?'

'I liked it,' I said. 'Yeah. Nice choice. But you really will have to get rid of a lot of furniture before you move.'

'I know. I'll have to get a smaller dining table and maybe just the one sofa instead of the two three-seaters. But you're getting through the stuff in the attic, aren't you? I don't want to be taking all that stuff with me.'

I nodded.

'I don't think that house even has an attic. Nowhere to

keep my secrets!' Her laugh took flight on the wind. We walked in silence for a bit. Then: 'Have you found...' she hesitated a fraction '... your brother's things yet?'

Nothing of Graham's had been thrown out. Absolutely everything he'd owned had been bundled in black plastic bags and shoved into cardboard boxes, presumably by Dad.

I hadn't known what to do with them. I hadn't wanted to bring up the subject of Graham's things so they were in that corner pile, waiting for either inspiration or instruction.

Before I could reply, Mum continued, 'I think we should give them to charity. I bet some of his toys and books are in really nice condition. Would you mind if we did that? Just take anything you want for yourself first, and we'll donate the rest.'

'Sure,' I said. Wow, I thought. Maybe we're getting there.

*

I cooked *saag aloo*, butter chicken and *dhal* for dinner that night. I made an effort, serving the dishes with rice and *naan,* and throwing a few poppadums under the grill as an accompaniment. I'd learned the recipes from an Indian friend in Dubai and, although very simple, they never failed to impress. The table between Mum and me was a sea of exotic chutneys I'd sourced from the grocery up the road.

'Nice,' said Mum, nodding, after her first spoonful. 'Very nice, Evie. Thank you.'

I smiled and we chinked our wine glasses. 'Cheers.'

'How are you getting on with Dad's papers?' she asked.

'Mmm-nn,' I said, off guard.

'Is there a problem?'

'Uh, no. No, not at all.' I sipped my wine, tried to sound nonchalant: 'Did Dad have any more files, by the way? Anything else you need me to go through?'

Mum laughed. 'Not as far as I know. Is something missing? Or have you found something exciting? Had he been siphoning money into a Swiss bank account?' She gave a little shiver. 'Imagine the jewels I could buy!'

I laughed with Mum to take the heat out of the moment. Something about the conversation was off-kilter and I didn't think it was just from my side. Maybe Mum was more tipsy than I'd thought.

She stood up and started to clear the dishes. 'Anyway, unfortunately—or fortunately—your father was very particular. All of the bank papers are in that file. He didn't have anything else kept anywhere else. I'm absolutely sure of that.'

I took another sip of wine, pressing the cold glass against my lips and inhaling the scent of the wine.

'By the way,' Mum said, 'what are you planning to do with all those dresses from the attic? The boxes are cluttering up the hall.'

'I need you to go through them before I throw any out. Do you feel like doing it now?'

'*Are you able to talk about what happened? That night with your mother?' Miss Dawson's voice was gentle. My knitting needles and a fresh ball of wool lay on my lap. My scarf and the following blanket had been such a success I was excited to start work on my first sweater.*

'*Please can you help me cast on?'*

Miss Dawson fiddled with my needles, did the first couple of stitches for me.

'*There you go.' She sat back and waited. I knitted a full row while I thought about where to start.*

'*She was in the bath,' I said eventually.*

Miss Dawson nodded. Unlike most adults, she didn't interrupt when I was talking. I looked at my knitting and remembered that night. I'd been so proud when Dad's TV show had been shortlisted for an award. He and Mum were going to London for the awards ceremony and I told everyone that they were going to 'the British Oscars'. Even the bullies fell quiet. For once, I wasn't 'poor little Evie' whose brother had died.

The day before the event, Mum had called me to her bedroom and asked me to help her choose what she was going to wear. She'd swished a long black dress from a smart dust cover. 'I bought it specially,' she said, the ghost of a smile dusting her lips. 'I just knew your father would be shortlisted.'

She'd put on the dress and I'd helped her choose a faux *fur stole and strappy silver heels to go with it. She looked like a movie star. 'I'm not done yet,' she said, fiddling with her hair as she folded it into a French pleat. Then she'd powdered her face, added some mascara, rouge and her new red lipstick. 'There. Do I pass?' she asked and I ran to her and hugged her hips, careful not to ruck up the dress.*

'You look like a princess,' I said.

'One day, darling, this dress will be yours, and you'll look like a princess, too.' Mum kissed my hair.

On the day of the awards, I rushed through my spellings so I could watch TV before bed. Mum was having a bath. I'd called her through the bathroom door, but there was no reply. Not even the sound of water swishing. I banged on the door, shouted again.

'What is it, Evie?' Dad had called from the bedroom. 'What do you want?'

'Can I watch telly? I've done my spellings.'

'What did your mother say?' Dad came to the bedroom door, fixing a cufflink as he spoke.

'She's not answering.'

There was a pause then Dad crossed the landing and knocked loudly on the bathroom door. He shouted, but Mum didn't reply. He banged on the door so hard I thought Lily would hear next door.

'Carole! Please answer me! Carole! Are you all right?'

We looked at each other, panic sliding into Dad's eyes. He told me to stand back. He rammed his shoulder at the door like they do in movies. It must have hurt but nothing happened. Then he stepped back and kicked with his heel to the side of where the lock was. He kicked again and again and then suddenly the door splintered and burst open.

I rushed towards the door but Dad got there first. He screamed at me not to come in. I'd never heard him scream before. I stopped, but it was too late. I'd already seen Mum's blue-white feet floating, the water swirling red around them.

'Evie, call an ambulance. Call an ambulance!' Dad was shouting. 'Quickly! Run! Dial 999 and tell them she's bleeding. Badly! Quickly, Evie, please!'

I knew what to do because we'd practised it, but I was frozen to the spot. It was like my legs wouldn't work. I still feel guilty that I hadn't been able to move; I still wake in the night, my heart hammering and my limbs glued to the bed because, in my dreams, I don't get the ambulance to come in time.

I stopped knitting and looked at Miss Dawson. 'I saw her feet and I called the ambulance,' I said, my voice a whisper. 'I ran downstairs and called the ambulance.'

Miss Dawson nodded. 'That's excellent Evie. Very good. You know you saved your mother's life?'

CHAPTER 27

After we'd done the dishes, I pulled Mum's dresses out one by one from the boxes and held them up against myself as she watched from an armchair with her coffee and her glasses.

'I feel like Sharon Osbourne on *The X Factor*.' Mum let a little laugh slip out, so I played up to her, mincing about on the carpet with the dresses held up against me and pulling silly poses.

'Ta da! Look at this gorgeous little number,' I said of a white leather minidress with patent leather details. 'Just add a pair of over-the-knee boots and it's perfect for a ladies' lunch at the golf club…'

'Oh crumbs!' said Mum. 'Did I ever really wear that? What was I thinking? I bet it barely covered my bottom!' She made an 'X' for 'no' with her forearms and the charity-shop pile grew.

'And for her next outfit, Evie will be modelling a—' I looked at the label '—maxi dress by Kenzo.' Seeing that the buttercup-yellow concoction was roomy enough to fit over my clothes, I left the room and pulled it on over my head, reappearing with a catwalk mince. The fabric swirled around my ankles as I twirled in front of Mum.

'Oh, that was from the seventies,' she said. 'I used to love that dress. It was so comfy. I saved up forever to buy that.'

'Cut the memories. Keep or throw?'

Mum rubbed her temples. 'Ohh… throw.'

I pulled the dress over my head, slung it on the reject pile and reached back into the box. My hands felt the satin silk of an evening gown; I'd pulled it almost all the way out before I realised what it was. I tried to stuff it back but Mum had seen.

'Oh, what's that one?' she asked.

'This?' I pulled out a different dress. A safer one.

'No, the black one. What was that?'

'Oh… not sure.' I rummaged in the box, trying to bury the evening gown. Mum came over.

'This one, I meant.' She grabbed the silk evening gown and pulled it out of the box, the fabric slipping through her hands as she took in the exquisite workmanship; the delicate beading; the lines of the elegant bias cut. It was an expensive dress.

'I remember this,' she said. 'I bought it for the awards ceremony. You remember when your father won that award?'

My eyes glued to the dress, I gave a small nod. Words wouldn't come.

'I looked so beautiful in it.'

Tears pricked my eyes. 'Mum, please.'

She looked at the dress appraisingly. It was as if she didn't even remember the night she'd tried to slash her wrists. 'It looks big for a twelve,' she said. 'I wonder if I can still get into it.'

CHAPTER 28

At first glance, my old junior school looked the same as I remembered. As I cycled towards the gates, my hair streaming out behind me in the cold wind, my head swam with memories: cars, parents and children crowding this same narrow street at pick-up time; the Friday afternoons when I was given a few coins to spend in the sweet shop; walking home with friends' mums for play dates, good as gold and slightly nervous; the last day of school when we all came out, our shirts inked with messages from our friends. There was a time when this tiny part of Woodside had been the centre of my universe.

The high metal gates where Mum used to wait for Graham and me each afternoon now sported huge padlocks and a notice outside explained that, for safety's sake, they were locked during school hours. Still out of breath from the sudden burst of exercise, I peered through the wire fence at the classrooms where I'd learned to read and write; at the gritty playground where I'd cut my knees too many times to count. It was paved with that multicoloured rubber stuff now, and I hoped it was impossible to rub people's knees in it till they bled.

There was a phone number for the school office on the sign outside the gates. I toyed with calling it and asking to have a look around, but then thought the better of it. I'd not been there for seventeen years—the likelihood of any of the teachers either being there or remembering me was slight. The thought of trying to explain myself was too exhausting. They'd probably think I was a paedophile.

I looked at my watch, swung my leg over the saddle and set off on my old route home from school. I reckoned I had about half an hour. I hadn't been able to put Dad's bike out with the rubbish. Instead, I'd convinced myself that it would make no difference to Mum if I got it fixed and gave it away to someone who could use it. What she didn't know couldn't hurt her, right? While she was out, I'd managed to pump up the tyres enough to get to the bike shop, where I'd had the moving parts properly re-greased and new sets of brakes and tyres fitted. Now the bike was roadworthy I was going to take it to the charity shop; even so, I really wanted to be back home, with it all done and dusted, before Mum got back.

I passed a parade of shops: the sweet shop where Graham and I used to buy bubble gum, sherbet pips and aniseed balls with our weekly sweet allowance was now a Tesco Metro; the shops next to that converted into contemporary flats.

My head full of memories, I pedalled on up the hill to the park. On the left of the tennis courts (now with a lick of new paint and bookable online) was what used to be the tarmacked play area with its swings, roundabout and mas-

sive, daredevil slide—now replaced with far safer, more
child-friendly apparatus and kid-friendly wood-chip flooring—and, on the right, the little copse where we'd spent
whole days playing cowboys and Indians, creating dig-outs
behind the bushes and blowing whistles made from reeds
of wild grass.

After leaning the bike up against a tree, I walked into the
woods, breathing in the cold air, sucking up the earthy scent
of the vegetation and remembering the intense excitement
of being chased by the other team; how my heart had
pounded as I stalked one of theirs back to their hide-out.
Twigs cracked under my shoes and my stomach leapt with
remembered excitement. But the copse looked small now;
the bushes not big enough to hide whole villages of mud-
smeared cowboys. My phone rang. It was Mum.

'Where are you?'

'In the park. I just popped by school for a quick look. I'll
be back soon.'

'How did you get there? Did you take the bike? It's gone,
and it's not rubbish day.'

My stomach constricted.

'No. I walked. I, umm, took the bike to the charity shop
first.' Again, I felt six years old.

'Really, Evie? What use is that bike to anyone in that
state? They wouldn't want it. Don't lie to me.' Her voice
was rising. 'Don't lie to me, Evie Stevens. What did you
do with the bike?'

'OK. I took it to the bike shop and had new tyres put on
it. All right? The rubbish men would never take it. It's too

big. I'm just giving it a quick test run before I take it to the charity shop. I thought it may as well be of use to someone.'

Mum was suddenly screaming. Not even screaming like a normal person, but like someone demented. I could picture her face contorted with rage, spit on her lips as she screamed down the phone.

'How *dare* you? How *dare* you take that bike—*that bike*—after I told you to *throw it out?* Have you any idea how that makes me *feel*? Get back here at once! *Get back here now!*'

'But, Mum… !'

There was a clatter, like she'd hurled the handset back onto the phone, and the line went dead.

'Shit. Shit, shit, shit.' I rammed the phone back in my pocket, stomped through the copse and slumped onto the first bench I reached, not caring that it was damp. Now what? I could see Mum's point of view but… Oh God, what had I been thinking? Again, I could have handled it better.

'Shit,' I said to the pavement. 'Seriously? Shit.'

I covered my face with my hands. What was I doing sitting here in suburban London, hiding from my mum like a child? So much for brave Evie forging a new life in Dubai. Rain started to fall, a few spots at first, then steadily harder and at last I cried—for Dad, for Graham and, ultimately, for me. Sitting there on the bench, it all came out, all the pent-up emotion, the sadness about Dad, the worry about Mum, the old feelings of loss for Graham and even the break-up with James. I was full of self-pity. Is this what my life had come to? Sobbing on a bench in the rain?

I don't know how long I sat there, but eventually the rain petered out and so did my tears. I heaved myself up, retrieved the bike and dried the saddle as best I could with the sleeve of my jumper. I wheeled it slowly out of the park, sucking in lungfuls of the cold air as I walked. At the other end of the park, I saw a florist's; outside on the pavement were buckets of colourful flowers, £4 a bunch. I stopped and looked. They had white lilies. On a whim, I went in and asked for a few stems tied with a blue ribbon. Wedging the bundle of flowers carefully under one arm, I cycled lopsided up to The Crossing.

Trying not to focus on the road, on that particular spot of tarmac where my brother had breathed his last breath, I laid the lilies gently on the low wall next to the pavement, blew a kiss to the moody sky, then turned for the charity shop, followed by the slow walk home, the spectre of the inevitable row with Mum chafing at my subconscious like my wet socks chafed against my heels.

*

At Mum's gate my steps slowed; I hesitated before crunching across the gravel, the sound of my footsteps announcing my arrival. Was Mum watching me from inside? Pausing in the porch where she hopefully couldn't see me, I took a few deep, calming breaths to gather myself and rolled my shoulders backwards and forwards to release the steel cables of tension I could feel running up to my neck. I couldn't challenge Mum. I was in the wrong. I knew that; I was just going to have to suck up her anger. Pick my battles.

I put the key in the lock, my body on the defensive. I fully expected Mum to be waiting in the hall ready to launch her fury at me. It wouldn't surprise me if she was waiting on the stairs. I could see now that I shouldn't have taken Dad's bike. How could I have been so stupid?

Inside, the house was silent. I stood still, listening for a clue as to where Mum was, but I could hear nothing— no television, no radio, no clattering about in the kitchen. Had she gone out again? I went through to the kitchen and then I saw her. She was in the garden with Richard, both of them closely examining the lawn. Slipping on Mum's spare gardening shoes, I walked slowly towards them, dread crawling through my intestines.

'Oh hello, darling,' she said. 'Glad you're back. Nice bike ride?'

'Hello,' said Richard. He didn't look alarmed; didn't seem to have any idea of the storm about to be unleashed.

'Mmm,' I said to Mum. Was she setting me up before laying into me? I examined her face. No signs of anger; in fact, it looked like she may have applied a little extra powder and blusher. I looked from her to Richard and back, confused, nervous. I remembered his words to me when I'd first got the bike in the kitchen. Were they in this together? Was it some sort of good-cop, bad-cop double act?

'Jolly good,' said Mum. 'Good you got the bike fixed. I'm sure someone will be thrilled to have it. Richard was just looking at the moss for me. It's starting to choke the lawn and I was going to try to get a grip on it for the new people. I bought some moss-killer from the garden centre but it hasn't worked.'

'I was telling your mum that the garden's probably too shady,' said Richard, straightening up. 'Moss likes cool, shady spots. Trimming back those oaks might give the grass a bit more light. We also need to make the lawn a bit more resilient. It's a constant battle with acidic soil in Woodside.'

I looked hard at Richard. Had he seen Mum's outburst? Had he been the one to calm her down?

'Have you been here long?' I asked.

He looked at his watch, frowning as he looked at the dial and then up at the sky as if it could remind him what time he'd come.

'Hmm. A few minutes,' he said finally, his face giving no clues as to what state Mum had been in when he'd arrived. He turned to her. 'Raking might help at this stage. I could give it a go, if you like? It would have to be quite vigorous, though. Or, if you really want to make an effort for the new people, maybe we could find somewhere to rent a mechanical scarifier?'

What on earth was a scarifier? I raised my eyebrows.

'I'll leave you to it,' I said. I turned back to the house, my back a wall of tension. I felt as if I was walking across a minefield: with every step I took, I expected Mum to hurl something after me.

CHAPTER 29

'*How is it now your mum's in the, um, hospital?*' *Miss Dawson asked, as I knitted. We were back in the staffroom, the school holidays over. 'Do you feel it's doing her good?*'

I sighed. I had to visit Mum in what my classmates called the 'loony bin' after school on Fridays. I dreaded it all week. Mum, dressed all day in a nightie and a gown, couldn't care less if I was there or not, but the social worker had said it was good for her to see me to remind her of what she had waiting at home. I felt like bait, slung out on a fishing rod in the hope that the shark might bite; I felt like an experiment: social services' attempt to winch Mum back to normality.

'I just want to know why she did it,' I said, my eyes on my knitting. 'No one's said why she did it.'

Miss Dawson nodded and waited for me to carry on.

'Doesn't she love us? I know Graham's dead, but I'm not. I'm still here. What about me and Dad?'

I reached for the tissues and blew my nose heavily.

Miss Dawson smiled. 'Good, Evie,' she said. 'Very good.'

'I mean Dad never asks her. I just want him to say, "Why did you do it? Don't you love us? Did you want to leave us?" but all he ever talks about is how bright the flowerbeds

are or what she wants for lunch or if she needs anything from home.'

I slumped back in my chair. It was even worse at school. Dad had told my teacher that the other kids were teasing me, so she'd tried to help. I mean, what was he thinking? Everyone knows teachers can't help.

'Now, class, let's all say a happy "Good luck!" to Evie today because she has something very important to do after school!' she'd say in her bright, sparkly voice. 'Evie's going to visit her mummy! Isn't it lovely that Evie's going to see her mummy this afternoon? Let's all give her a nice, "good luck" clap!' What she didn't see was the boys making 'crazy cuckoo' signs at me behind her back; some even stuck their tongues behind their lower lips and leered at me. I wanted the ground to swallow me up.

'I just want my family back,' I said.

CHAPTER 30

The next morning there'd been no mention of the bike at breakfast—but then I hadn't expected there to be: brushing things under the carpet was very much the Stevens' way. After she'd washed her dishes, Mum had disappeared off upstairs. I heaved Dad's file of bank statements onto the table. How much money would you need to have to be able to consider a lump sum of £22,000 an insignificant amount? I wondered. Mum and Dad were well off thanks to ongoing royalties from Dad's various books, which had been on all the non-fiction bestseller lists for the past ten years, as well as from a series of successful documentaries he'd produced for the BBC. Still, I'd never have described them as rich enough to justify spending £22,000 without even noting what it was for. I was convinced the answer must lie somewhere in Dad's files: he'd been too careful to let that kind of money go missing.

Now I took every folder out of the bank statements file, hoping to find some clue that I'd overlooked—an extra statement, a letter from the bank—something to explain the transfers. I found nothing.

'Come on, Evie. Don't give up.' I hauled the next box file onto the table with a sigh.

I went through the next two files, looking between every sheet of paper in every folder for something—anything— that I might have missed the first time. Finally, I did the same with the 'Receipts' file, taking out each folder one by one. The bottom of the file was lined with a piece of old newspaper, yellow with age. I took that out, too, intending to read it front and back to see if there was a reason it had been saved but, as I lifted it up, I found what I'd been looking for: tucked beneath the newspaper was a manila folder, its faded yellow cover almost winking at me.

'Yesss,' I breathed, picking it up and opening it carefully. Inside, just an old photo of Graham as a toddler and a fax so old the ink had faded, the handwriting appearing and disappearing like a will-o'-the-wisp. Still, I could just make out the date on the top sheet: eighteen years ago. I struggled to read the body of text: it appeared to be some sort of agreement for the sum of £500 to be paid monthly to someone called Zoe Peters. The sum was to be reviewed annually. Pulling out Dad's most recent bank statement, I compared the bank account details—bingo—it was the same. So this Zoe Peters had received a monthly amount from Dad for donkey's years, as well as the lump sum just the other week. But who was she? I tapped my pen on my front teeth as I puzzled over it. Some sort of colleague? Were they royalty payments? But why wouldn't they go direct from the publisher?

I looked at my watch then slipped the fax and the photo

back into the folder and placed it beneath the newspaper. I couldn't do any more on it now—Mum would be down any minute and I knew she'd be fussing: the funeral was at eleven.

Chapter 31

I don't think anything can prepare you for the sight of a box that contains the remains of one of your parents. I don't know why this thought didn't hit me before I reached the worn stone steps of the church, but, suddenly, after Mum went in with the Reverend, I found myself standing outside the door, unable to follow her through it.

'I'll just be a sec,' I called, leaning on the wall for support, my legs suddenly weak. I took a few deep breaths to calm myself. It had only just hit me that I was going to have to walk down the aisle in front of everyone, towards the coffin I knew would be waiting at the altar. I could feel panic looming, my body trying to breathe faster and shallower. I fought it, counting each breath in and each breath out.

Thank heavens Mum had insisted on a closed casket.

I couldn't believe I hadn't thought to prepare myself for this: I'd made the arrangements for the funeral without giving any thought to what I was about to go through. I'd even been joking with Mum when we'd paraded our black outfits around her bedroom, as if we were getting ready for a night out, not my father's funeral. And now I realised that

I hadn't been inside this church since the day of Graham's funeral. I felt a hand on my arm.

'Are you all right?' I turned to see a lady, perhaps in her early forties with a friendly smile. She was wearing black with a powder-blue scarf. It suited her pale skin and dark hair.

'I was just wishing I smoked,' I said. 'It seems like a good moment for a fag.'

'Oh. Sorry. I don't have any. I don't smoke; I just needed some air.'

'Me neither. It was just thinking it. Is it busy in there?'

'Almost full.' If she realised that I was 'the daughter', she didn't show it.

'Oh,' I said. I looked at the church door, but neither of us moved. I felt like I might be sick. I imagined haring down the steps and away. Away from the church, from Mum, from all the mourners, the funeral and Woodside. Running so far that no one could find me. I felt beaten; tired of life. Did I really have to do this?

'Going in makes it more real, doesn't it?' said the woman. 'But I suppose we should. My son will be wondering where I am.' She held out her arm with a kind smile. Obediently, I tucked my hand under it and let her lead me through the door. With Mum inside, I had no better option.

The church, both elegant and large, was packed with well-wishers. I was amazed. I hadn't realised how many people Dad had known. In addition to friends and ex-colleagues, there must have been legions of ex-students, too, and, as the door banged behind us, everyone turned to look; an ocean of black; a sea of faces, young and old; faces pinched with grief, some already crying, some looking sympathetically at me and some craning to see my grief. I saw the back of Mum's head, right at the front. I couldn't make eye contact with anyone.

'Stay strong,' said the woman, letting go of my arm and sliding into a pew near the back. I fixed my eyes on the coffin, not catching anyone's eye, and walked slowly down the aisle to Mum, the woman's words echoing in my head.

*

If the funeral was difficult, the cremation was worse. The chapel was small and claustrophobic. We followed Dad's coffin inside and took our places on rows of chairs, as he was placed in front of 'the curtains'. It was then that the finality really hit me. The funeral in the church had been all very well, with its singing and its emotional eulogies, but there was something utterly final about a cremation— there really was no second chance. After tomorrow, there'd be nothing left of Dad. I realised I hadn't seen the body.

I shifted in my seat, my insides icy and my eyes tearing up. All my instincts told me to jump onto the coffin, to lie on top of it and stop him from going through the curtains. Shifting to cross my legs, I hid my face behind the Order of Service and tried to compose myself. I couldn't sit still. I fanned myself with the flimsy paper.

The service was short, but the minister's voice droned on. I pinched myself to try to make myself focus, but it was like

I was watching a film of someone else's life. Mum took my hand and squeezed it.

'Nearly done,' she whispered.

A tear slid down my cheek.

CHAPTER 32

The funeral, everyone said, had been a good one. I'd no idea what that meant, but now everyone and his wife were back at our house singing Dad's praises and enjoying the refreshments. People clutching sherry glasses filled the two reception rooms, spilling through the kitchen onto the patio. For once the sun had deigned to shine; it was chilly but fresh, a light breeze ruffling blue rinses and bringing a flush to powdered cheeks.

I stood quietly in the corner, sipping at a glass of Tio Pepe and people-watching. The majority of guests hadn't been at the crematorium and, now that the sadness of the funeral was done, the noise level increased and the occasional peal of laughter rose above the din. I was looking for the woman I'd seen outside the church. I'd felt a connection with her and I wanted to talk more with her—to find out how she knew my dad.

As I watched the crowd, I was accosted by a bulky lady with a lavender-tinged rinse. It was one of Mum and Dad's oldest friends, a woman whose imposing presence at Christmas parties, barbecues and lunches had punctuated my childhood. Today she was wearing a black skirt suit with black pop socks, and the veiny flesh of her knees was bulging out over tops that weren't quite hidden under the hemline of her voluminous A-line skirt.

'My condolences, dear,' she said, pulling me to her scented bosom. 'So terribly sad. And Robert so young.' She took a sip of her sherry, leaving a coral-pink imprint of her lips on the crystal. 'Mind you, a blessing to go so quickly. No need for Dignitas after all!' She chuckled.

'Dignitas?' I looked at her fleshy, painted lips, which opened and shut like a goldfish when she spoke.

'Oh, you know Robert and Dignitas? He was always going on about it. "You won't catch me waiting around to die," he said, gosh, what, at Christmas? He and your mum fair entertained all of us with their talk of how they'd get on a plane over to Switzerland should they ever have to. Far better to go quickly and quietly, he said, and, I have to say, dear, I couldn't agree more.'

'Me too,' I said flatly. 'Heart failure. Fabulous way to go! Now, if you'll excuse me…' Dignitas? I pushed through the crowds, nudging elbows and banging hips, in search of Mum.

'Evie!' exclaimed a deep voice. 'Not so fast!' I turned to see Richard, holding court in a black suit that was slightly too big for him. He waved his glass at me and I went over reluctantly, my eyes still searching the room for Mum. He stepped away from the women to whom he'd been chatting.

'She's doing well, isn't she?' he said.

'Do you really think she's OK?'

'Yes. I mean: look at all this.' He nodded at the room full

of chattering guests. 'Marvellous job she's done. Marvellous. Hardly falling apart, is she?'

'Well, um…'

'She's strong as an ox your mother.'

'If you'll excuse me…' I motioned with my eyes towards Mum, whom I'd spotted heading into the kitchen.

'Of course,' he said and I made a beeline for the door, smiling and thanking my way across the room on autopilot. Had Mum and Dad been serious about going to Dignitas? How could I not know this stuff?

I closed the kitchen door behind me. Mum was bent down, rummaging in the fridge. She looked up at me.

'Going well, isn't it? I'm just looking for some olives. I'm sure I had some Kalamatas. They'd go ever so nicely with this sherry.'

'Yes, I guess it's going well,' I said. 'Aside from the fact the guests are discussing my late father's apparent plan to top himself. I mean, personally, I don't think it's in particularly good taste to be discussing a person's potential suicide at his funeral. Do you?'

'Oh…' Mum straightened up and closed the fridge, holding on to the kitchen counter for support. 'The Dignitas thing?'

I nodded. We were on opposite sides of the kitchen, boxers in the ring.

'Who brought that up?'

'That's not the point!' I snorted. 'I'm far more interested in why I didn't I know when half the town appears to!'

Mum looked at my face. I stared back, challenging her.

'Well? How come you didn't tell me?'

Mum opened her mouth to say something, but the door burst open and a uniformed waitress pushed her way in, bottom-first, an empty plate in each hand.

'Oh, sorry!'

I smiled and we waited, suspended in the pause, while the waitress replenished her load and left. The sounds of the party faded as the door closed behind her.

'Well?'

'Oh. Oh, darling. This is hardly the time and the place.'

'Well, if that's so, how come half of Woodside is currently discussing Dad's decision to end his life at Dignitas in our living room? It wasn't a nice way for me to find out.'

'Sweetheart, please. I'm sorry you found out like this. But it wasn't an issue. If it had been, I would have told you.' Mum turned back to the fridge; she was speaking not to me, but to the butter. 'Can we talk about it later? It's kind of irrelevant now, anyhow.'

My head throbbed. I shut my eyes and pressed my fingers onto my temples.

She stood up, the Kalamatas in her hand. 'Now. If you don't mind, I need to get back to our guests.'

Turning my back on the door, I stood at the sink and stared out at the garden. What had become of my life? I was supposed to be sunning myself in Dubai not standing at my father's funeral worried that my mother was going mad.

Despite Richard's protestations that Mum was doing all right, I was desperately worried about her. Miss Dawson had replied to my email, mentioning the possibility—

unconfirmed without her having seen Mum, of course—
that Mum was suffering from some sort of long-term grief
dysfunction. She'd said it was quite possible that Mum had
suppressed her grief after Graham died and that Dad's death
had triggered all those unresolved issues. 'Ultimately, Evie,
she blamed your father,' Miss Dawson had written. 'While
he was present in her life, she was unable to move on. Now
he's gone, she's able—for the first time—to grieve properly
for Graham. There's a lot hidden under the surface. It's
bound to come out somehow.'

It sounded credible, but was it possible, too, I wondered,
that Mum was simply knocked sideways by the loss of her
partner of thirty-odd years? People acted strangely when
they were bereaved, didn't they? Sold houses and hooked up
with inappropriate people? That didn't have to mean she was
mentally ill. I thought about Richard. Although he appeared
to be a pillar of support to Mum, he was too protective, too
familiar. Mum had denied there was anything going on, but
I wasn't convinced. Were they a couple? So soon?

*

When everyone had gone and the pub staff had cleared
up the mess, Mum and I sat down in the living room. The
air was laced with perfume mixed with the acrid tang of
the cigars some of the men had smoked in the garden; it
reminded me, strangely, of Christmas. After taking my
socks and shoes off, I rested my feet on the coffee table and
circled my ankles. My Dubai pedicure looked obscenely
bright in the flatness of the northern European light.

'That went well, didn't it? I think everyone had a nice time,' Mum said brightly.

'So what was all that about Dignitas?'

She picked up a magazine and stared at it. 'Evie. It was nothing. It never came to anything. Had it done so, we would have talked to you about it. Of course we would. But Robert died suddenly. He had an underlying heart condition and his heart failed. The Dignitas talk was nothing more than bravado after a few too many mulled wines at the church Christmas party.'

'So it really was that quick? Just, like, one day he was fine, the next…' My voice trailed off.

Mum put down the magazine again. 'Robert had suspected something was wrong with his heart and he'd been to the doctor, I don't know… Ten days before he died? As I said, when I "found" him, I called the doctor and he confirmed it was heart failure. There wasn't even a need for an autopsy.'

I shook my head. 'That fast.'

'It's the best way, Evie.'

'You too!' I snorted.

'It could have been worse, darling. Cancer, for example. That can take months. It's a horrible way to go.' Mum looked at me. 'To be honest, we were lucky. Robert had had a problem with his prostate…'

'What? Cancer?'

'Well. We didn't know if he had cancer. He'd been going to the loo a lot at night so he had some blood tests done. They'd found enough whatever it is in his blood to recommend he go for a biopsy. He'd just done that. We were waiting for the results when he died. All I'm saying is, heart's a much better way to go.'

'How can you say that? Even if it was cancer, it could have been early stages. It's treatable, isn't it? If you catch it early enough?'

'Well, it's all academic at this stage anyway. But, honestly, both your father and I knew he would have made a terrible patient.' Mum shook her head. 'Trust me. It turned out for the best.'

I chewed my lip, looked at the floor then at the window, anywhere but at my mother. 'I know. It's just… I'd have liked to say goodbye.'

'Oh, darling. I'm sorry you didn't get to do that. But no one could have predicted what happened. The heart thing was like a shotgun. Not even the doctor spotted it.'

We sat in silence for some time.

'Anyway,' Mum said, eventually, 'I think the funeral went well. People seemed glad to have come and the food was nice.'

'The pub did a good job,' I said. 'I'm glad we got them in. I hadn't realised Dad knew so many people. There must have been, what, two hundred people back here? Five hundred at the church?'

'Well, he met a lot of people through his work. And there were probably some there who didn't even know him, but who enjoyed his books and felt moved to come.'

'Oh, I meant to ask you,' I said. 'Do you know who that elegant woman with the pale blue scarf was? Dark hair?

Forty-ish? I talked to her at the church, but I didn't see her at the house? She seemed really nice.'

Mum didn't reply and, when I looked up from my pedicure, I saw that she was halfway to the kitchen. 'I'm gasping for a cup of tea,' she said, over her shoulder. 'Do you want one?'

'Did you hear me?' I called. 'Did you know who that woman was in the blue scarf?'

'No idea who you're talking about, dear. No idea. Was that yes to tea?'

*

'Since you're the creative one,' Mum said when she returned with the tea, 'have you any ideas where we could scatter the ashes? They should be ready by Monday if not tomorrow.'

I had no idea where you could scatter human ashes. Were you allowed to just throw them into the atmosphere? Anywhere? I'd managed to connect my iPad to the Wi-Fi Mum had denied that she had, so I grabbed it now and did a quick search.

'"The law on scattering ashes in the UK is fairly relaxed",' I read out to Mum. '"You can even scatter or bury ashes in your garden if you wish. There is nothing explicit in the legislation to restrict people in disposing of cremated ashes."'

I looked up from the iPad. 'He loved the sea. Maybe we could go to the coast and throw them out to sea? What do you think?'

'That's what I thought,' said Mum. 'Remember how he used to drag us down to the seaside when you were little? Sandy sandwiches, weak orange squash and a windbreak? Maybe we could have a little ceremony on the beach, just you and me? When shall we do it?'

'As soon as we get them?'

Mum nodded. 'It'd be weird to sleep in the house with Dad on the mantelpiece.'

I couldn't have agreed more. There were enough ghosts in this house already.

CHAPTER 33

'*Your mum's back at home now, isn't she?*' Miss Dawson asked. '*Is it nice to have her back?*' It was the first real day of spring and I could see my classmates playing leapfrog and kiss-chase on the field outside. The trees were full of cherry blossom; some of the girls had put sprigs in their hair. Optimism bubbled all around me; I was an island of misery.

'*It's not like it was before.*' I started to knit, my lips twitching as I tried to work out how to say what I wanted to say.

It had started well. On the day Dad brought Mum home, I'd sat, a bag of nerves, on the stairs waiting for the scrunch of the gravel, the turn of the key in the lock. Lily, who'd been looking after me while Dad went to the Unit, hovered in the living room. I'd watched the silhouettes of my parents behind the bobbled glass panel of the front door; held my breath as the door slowly opened—then Mum had held out her arms to me.

'*Evie!*' she'd said. '*Come 'ere!*' and I'd cannoned into her, squeezing my arms around her waist as she knelt on the floor and inhaling the scent of her, while she'd hugged me so tight it was as if she wanted to eat me. I'd thought, then, that it was over. That we'd survived.

But Dad had told me it would be difficult for a while when Mum got back. He'd taken me out for an ice cream and asked me to be patient with her; to try and make life easy for her by taking care of my own things and helping out around the house. It was because of that that I'd decided to do the cleaning.

After school the next day, I'd changed into jogging bottoms and a sweatshirt then I'd done the dusting. After that, I'd vacuumed the living room and dining room, sucking up every last crumb that had been dropped. It wasn't easy because the Hoover was heavy. I'd struggled, but it was satisfying to see the stripes of clean carpet appear under me. I'd had a quick rest, then I'd cleaned the bathrooms, wiping over the sinks, the bath and the loo seats with a sponge and a squirt of Jif.

Happy with my handiwork, I'd moved to the kitchen, where I'd squirted more Jif all over the surfaces before wiping it off with a cloth. Then I'd filled a bucket with hot water and bleach and mopped the floor, taking with it the splits and splats. I couldn't bear for Mum to notice the squalor in which Dad and I had been living while she was away.

It was when I was wiping over dirty marks around the light switches that Mum had appeared from her afternoon nap.

'What are you doing?' Her voice was sharp, but I was deaf to the danger. Maybe she was confused to see her daughter *doing the cleaning. I stood tall by my handiwork, a proud smile on my face, the cloth in my hand.*

'Just doing a bit of cleaning?' I said.

The silence could have stung a bee.

'To help?' I added. 'I'm old enough now.'

Mum walked over to the light switch, examined it closely, then screamed like a wild animal having its guts torn out. She ripped the cloth from my hands then collapsed on the floor, smelling the cloth, rubbing it against her face.

'How dare you?' she screamed. 'How dare you take him out of my life like this? Do you think you can wipe him out of this house just like that?'

Jumping up, she picked me up by my arms and shook me violently. Dad—having heard the commotion from the office—came crashing down the stairs and grabbed me from her. He shoved me, hard, out of the kitchen. 'Leave her, Carole. She didn't mean it. She didn't know. Leave it.'

I listened through the door as Dad calmed her down, like a horse-whisperer handling a wild stallion. It was only then that I realised what I'd done: I'd wiped Graham's greasy fingerprints off the light switch. The last physical reminder Mum had had of her son was gone.

'I don't know how to make her happy again,' I told Miss Dawson.

CHAPTER 34

The front of Richard's house was neat and well kept. I marched up the driveway to the front door and rapped smartly on it. I heard Richard's voice behind the door.

'Coming!' The door opened and Richard was there in his customary brown cords. 'Oh hello, Evie. What can I do for you?'

We stood in the doorway. I glanced over my shoulder, paranoid that Mum, still across the road in our house, would spot me talking to Richard.

'Would you like to come in?' he asked, opening the door wider.

'Just for a second,' I said. 'Won't take long.'

'Come through. I'm afraid it's not much, but, hey, what do I need? A man alone?' He laughed a little, rubbed his hands together.

Richard was apologising for the humbleness of his home, I understood that, but I saw nothing that deemed apology necessary. I was focused one hundred per cent on what I wanted to say to him. I suddenly felt less brave now: it seemed outrageous that I should march into this widower's home and ask him about his personal life.

I took a deep breath and fixed my eyes on the wallpaper behind him. 'I just wanted to ask…' I began. 'About you and Mum.'

'Yes?'

'Is there… is there anything I should know?'

'This is a conversation you should have with your mother.'

'I tried. But she said nothing. As if she would tell me. So I thought I'd ask you.'

Richard sighed. 'Would you like to sit down, Evie?' He pointed to an armchair.

'I don't need to sit down. I just want to know. Is there anything going on between you and my mother?'

Richard paced the room. 'Carole is a friend,' he said gently. 'Your mother has many friends, through golf, through the church, and I am one of them. One of many friends.' He stopped and turned, faced me. 'But I happen to live very close by and, well, when Robert was away so much, I…' He started again. 'Since my wife died…' He sighed. 'Look. Carole and I aren't spring chickens, and we look out for each other, Evie. Do you know what I mean by that?'

My insides sagged. What had I expected him to say: 'I've had the hots for your mother for years. The day your father died was the happiest day of my life'?

I nodded. 'Sure. Of course. That's all it is?'

'I care about your mother, Evie.'

I felt monstrous for insinuating anything different. I turned to leave.

'I know your mum very well, Evie,' said Richard. 'I look

after her. That's something I think you should be pleased about, given you live overseas.'

If I hadn't been in such a rush to leave, I might have thought more about what he meant by that. As it was, I bundled myself out of the door, apologising for having disturbed him and it wasn't until much later that I realised he hadn't really answered my question at all.

*

Later that evening I went up to the room that my parents called 'the office'. It was small and chilly, with just a single radiator to warm it and a small window overlooking the garden. With its walls lined with shelves of dusty history books, the room looked like a relic itself.

I switched on my parents' computer, and waited while it groaned into life. To be honest, I was grateful for the rest: Mum and I had spent the bulk of the day blitzing the attic; me heaving boxes, bags and packages down to Mum, who'd sat on the landing deciding what to keep, sell or throw. I'd passed down the black bags of Graham's things without comment and watched as she'd put them gently in the 'charity shop' pile.

I knew Dad's email password because I'd set the account up for him in the first place, making a note of it on a slip of paper that was still—how many years later?—tucked under the keyboard. As I went through his emails, giving each a cursory glance before deleting or forwarding to Mum, the hairs on the back of my neck prickled, as if I was expecting Dad to walk in at any moment. I've never hacked into anyone's email and I couldn't shift the feeling that I was spying on my father.

'Found anything interesting?' Mum asked, making me jump as she walked up behind me. I flicked the screen onto Facebook, feeling strangely protective of Dad.

'No, it all seems in order,' I said. 'I've forwarded anything important to you, with instructions on what to do with it. I've deleted everything else. I'll close up the account when I'm done.'

'Thank you, darling. Thank you so much for doing that.' Mum ruffled my hair. 'I do appreciate you being here.' She stood silently behind me for a second waiting, maybe, for me to continue. I waited, too. 'The crem called, by the way,' she said. 'They're allowing us to pick up the ashes tomorrow instead of Monday. Maybe we could drive down to Brighton straight away and get it over with.'

'Sure. But that's very quick, isn't it?'

'It is. I asked the woman if they'd still be hot.'

'Mum!'

'Sorry, but... well, y'know!' She chuckled. 'Right, if you don't need me for anything, I'm going to have a nice, oily bath and get to bed. Big day tomorrow. Goodnight.'

Mum backed out of the room looking pleased. Hearing her shut and lock the bathroom door behind her and turn on the bath taps, I flicked back onto Dad's emails. After reading and deleting twenty more, I finally reached the bottom of his inbox — the last email was one he'd sent to himself when he'd first opened the account. It contained all his passwords. That was something I'd suggested he did when he first got into email and had worried he'd forget them all, and I was ridiculously pleased to see that he'd done it. I opened it up, smiling to myself. Who knows, maybe there'd even be a clue as to who Zoe Peters was and why he'd sent her the mystery twenty-two grand.

But there was no magical information in the email. Just log-in details for various online accounts and memberships and details of another email account of Dad's: '*robsteve@yahoo.com*' it said.

Oh God, not another one. My eyes hurt and I couldn't face working my way through another account tonight. I emailed Dad's final email to myself, then—with a huge sense of finality—followed the onscreen instructions on how to delete the email account. I'd look at the second one after we got back tomorrow.

CHAPTER 35

'*So, Evie. I saw your dad has a new series running on the BBC. Is he still travelling a lot?*'

I wasn't knitting today. I'd been working on some doll's clothes quite late the night before and my fingers needed a break. I took a biscuit and chewed it as I mulled over what to say. Dad seemed to be away every weekend these days, travelling around the country giving lectures, presentations and library readings, making documentaries or whatever. When I asked Mum why it always had to be over the weekends, she just pursed her lips and said, 'It's your father's choice, darling.'

'Mmm. But Mum and I do fun things,' I told Miss Dawson. 'She really makes an effort.'

We had a routine. Every Saturday morning we'd walk up to the High Street together. Mum would pick up the paper and a few groceries in the supermarket. At the greengrocer's, I was allowed to ask for a kilo of peaches, a half of cherries or a couple of punnets of strawberries, which I put in my basket, then, business done, we'd look at the display in the jewellery shop window, seeing if they had anything new, and pointing out which pieces we liked the most.

Some weeks, if Mum was in a good mood, we'd wander all the way up the High Street—never anywhere near the crossing, mind—browsing books, clothes, antiques, shoes and toiletries. Mum would hold my hand tightly as we went to cross the road—it was a bit embarrassing given I was ten and perfectly able to cross the road on my own, but I never said anything.

We rarely bought anything, but we always ended up in the baker's shop which, heavy with the scent of bread, had a couple of tables squeezed in the corner. Mum always let me choose a treat from the trays in the window while she sat with a coffee and we talked about what we were going to do for the rest of the day.

'How is your mum?' Miss Dawson asked.

I thought about a Saturday, not long ago, when we were sitting in the bakery. I'd got a pink iced bun and Mum had been absently flicking through the paper with her coffee. We were thinking about going to Greenwich Park for the afternoon.

'We could take a picnic?' Mum had suggested. 'Sit on the grass at the top of the hill? Then walk down to the river, wander down through the market and look at the boats? The Book Boat should be there?'

I smiled. Mum knew how much I loved the Book Boat. It was like a deal we did: I had to be patient while she browsed the jewellery and handicraft stalls of the market, then I got a book of my choice at the Book Boat.

But before I'd been able to answer, Mum had suddenly leapt out of her seat, knocking her coffee flying, her chair bashing into the legs of an old lady standing in the queue. She shot out of the shop and ran down the High Street towards Woolworths, her coat flying behind her like Superwoman.

   'I'm so sorry,' I apologised to the old lady, checking she was all right. The baker brought over a wad of tissues to clean the split coffee. I didn't know if anyone in the shop knew who Mum was or why she'd just done that, but I did. I knew she thought she'd just seen Graham. I knew it because, in the gait of a boy who walked past the window, I thought I saw him, too.

   'Yeah. She's good,' I said. 'But she still has moments when she forgets… we both do.'

CHAPTER 36

I didn't envy the lady at the crem her job: handing over mortal remains to grieving relatives couldn't be easy. Still, she didn't seem to mind it: she welcomed me into the reception area with brisk sympathy and asked me to take a seat while she disappeared out back. Mum waited in the car.

I looked around: the room was bland and impersonal, just another waiting area with a few black *faux* leather armchairs, a low coffee table smothered in magazines and leaflets, a noticeboard pinned with ads for various support groups and a framed print of some daffodils on one wall. I wandered around, picking up leaflets and reading notices—doing anything I could do, really, not to have to think about what was about to happen; what I was about to hold in my hands.

Suddenly, the woman was back. She placed a jar gently on the counter and I caught my breath: I don't know what I'd expected the ashes to be in—some sort of urn I supposed—but they were in a container that looked more like one of those old-fashioned sweet-shop jars. I glanced at the door: no way did I want Mum to see this.

'Would you like a bag?' the lady asked, but I'd found Dad's old school scarf in the attic and, thanking my lucky stars I'd thought to bring it, I pulled it out of my handbag and wrapped it over and around the jar.

The lady cleared her throat. 'Forgive me for saying but, if you haven't yet decided what to do with the ashes, we have some suggestions.' She handed me what looked like a catalogue.

'Some people have them incorporated into pieces of jewellery?' Her voice was gently hesitant. I held my breath. 'So their loved one is always with them... Or we do some lovely wee necklaces? Paperweights are popular, too. It's ever such a nice way to keep a loved one with you.'

I took a step towards the door. 'Um, I don't think so.'

'If you want to keep the ashes in the house, there are various receptacles that look, you know, less urn-like.' She flipped through the pages of another catalogue stopping on the image of a Viking longboat. 'If the deceased liked the sea?'

'Thank you, but no. We're fine. Thank you.'

Tucking the wrapped jar under my arm, I moved towards the door and opened it carefully. The last thing I needed was to drop the thing: I was surprised how heavy it was. I'd kind of been expecting Dad to be weightless now he no longer existed, but the ashes must have been a good couple of kilos.

Without actually discussing it, Mum and I had skirted around the issue of where in the car Dad was to travel and concluded that the front was too creepy and the boot too much like cargo. So, back at the car, I opened the door and placed the container carefully in the footwell of the rear seat. I hoped Dad didn't mind.

'Here you go. All done.'

Mum didn't turn around to look. 'Are you sure it's him?' she asked.

*

I suppose there's no established etiquette for driving the remains of your father down to the coast wrapped in his old school scarf; well, if there was, I'd never heard of it. I'd imagined—if I'd thought about it at all—that we might drive in a respectful silence, but we didn't: we sang. Mum started it, turning up the volume on the radio and singing along to Madonna's 'Holiday'.

I snuck a sideways look at her; the song seemed wildly inappropriate yet a smile licked at the corner of her lips. She seemed unusually carefree. I sucked my teeth: who was I to ruin her fun?

As the song drew to a close, Mum turned the dial back down. 'I suppose once we've done this, I should think about getting back to work. "Life goes on", and all that.'

'Sure.' I had no objection to her going back to work. Her job at the hospital was such a positive influence on her it could only be a good thing. Moping around the house wasn't going to do her any good.

'I wonder how they're doing without me.' She laughed and shook her head. 'Dr Goodman is so busy he doesn't know if he's coming or going. I almost feel irresponsible taking time off. I doubt any of the patient letters have been sent out.'

'Seriously? Isn't anyone standing in for you?'

'They got a temp, I think. As if she'd know how to handle Dr Goodman! He never even reads the letters; just likes them in a pile on his desk at the end of the day so he can whip through with his pen.' She paused, smiled to herself. 'Yes, I think I'll go back later this week. You don't mind, do you?'

''Course not. Unless you need me to help with the house, I'll probably head back to Dubai soon, too.'

'Well, if you have time to stay and help, yes? But it's fine if you don't.'

We drove along companionably for a while, both of us humming along to the radio.

'Maybe we could have a wander through The Lanes,' I suggested as we drew close to Brighton. 'I'd like to buy us each a ring as a sort of memorial for Dad? Gold bands? We could get the dates engraved on the insides? What do you think?'

'You mean a bit like a wedding ring?' she asked. I looked at her left hand on the wheel: her wedding ring was gone. She sighed. 'If you want to waste your money, dear.' She tut-tutted in that way that only mothers can.

*

If you were asked to provide a definition of 'bleak', Brighton Beach on this winter's day would provide more than ample inspiration: looking out to sea, it was hard to tell where the grey water ended and the grey sky began.

Closer to shore, a strong wind whipped up whitecaps that sent spray flying up onto the few figures huddled along the length of the pier.

Crunching over the shingle to the edge of the water, Mum and I sang a quiet and not very confident rendition of Dad's favourite hymn—'To be a pilgrim'. To check the wind direction, I turned a slow circle on the beach, noting which way my hair blew, then I took the top off the jar and gave it, still wrapped in the scarf, to Mum.

'It's OK, the wind's not coming back at us. If you sort of point that way, they should go towards the pier.'

'Goodness,' said Mum, holding the jar out in front of her like you might someone else's screaming baby. Gingerly at first, and then with more force, she started to shake the ashes into the murky water. There was a small splash as a lump fell in. Mum gasped and I clapped my hand over my mouth. Neither of us said anything.

I took a look around the beach; it was deserted, and I was glad no one was close enough to see. Although I was pretty certain we were allowed to scatter the ashes in the sea, I hoped no one would realise what we were doing; I was scared someone would try to stop us halfway through. I could imagine the horror of only managing to get half the ashes in the sea and having to carry the other half home. Or the even greater horror of the ashes landing on a toddler out for a paddle in her pink wellington boots.

'Would you like to do a bit?' Mum asked. I shook my head. Mum turned back to the sea and emptied the rest of the jar with a two-handed underarm hurl. We watched

for as long as it took for the last flecks of ash to disappear
from sight, then, feeling strangely released, yet deflated, we
picked our way back off the beach.

'What now?' I asked.

Mum didn't respond. 'Mum? What do you fancy doing
now?'

Still no response. She was staring down the beach, her
hand on her chest.

'Mum!'

I followed her line of sight and saw what she was watching: a man, walking further down the beach. There was
something about the colour and cut of his coat; his height;
his careful, slightly stiff gait.

'Oh, Mum,' I said.

'I… I just thought… oh, how could it be? Silly me! We
just threw him in the sea!' She gave herself a little shake.
'Come on, let's get some fish and chips.'

'Perfect.'

We sat by the window of the chip shop, snug in the fug
of frying, and ordered a glass of wine each.

'Cheers,' said Mum.

'To Dad.'

We clinked glasses and watched the seagulls circling
over the sea as we waited for our food. Afterwards, we
wandered into The Lanes, where, in a quaint little jewellery
shop, I chose us each a thin gold band decorated with three
tiny diamonds. Mum protested, told me not to waste my
money.

'I don't expect you to wear it every day, but I think it's

nice to have a memento,' I said, as I handed over my credit card.

Mum sighed. 'Thank you, darling, it's lovely.' As the transaction went through, I admired my ring on the fourth finger of my right hand, turning it this way and that so the diamonds caught the light. Mum put her ring, inside its velvet box, carefully into her handbag, her lips a thin line. 'I shall treasure it,' she said.

CHAPTER 37

'*So...*' *Miss Dawson said once we'd settled into our seats. Now I was in senior school, we used a private interview room, not the staffroom. Somehow, the small room with just the two of us in it felt more intense and I shifted a little on my chair; wished I'd brought my knitting. 'How are things?'*

I hadn't seen Miss Dawson since before the summer. Our meetings were now just once a term.

'It's good. School's good,' I said.

'You've settled in well? Made some new friends?'

'Yes. A few of my old class moved up with me, so it's fine. Really.'

'You sound unsure?'

I sighed. 'School's fine. I'm enjoying it. It's just...'

Miss Dawson waited. Was I being pathetic? I wondered. I knew why it was that Mum insisted on picking me up from school even though I was eleven years old; I knew why she wouldn't let me walk or cycle home with my friends. But it was so embarrassing after school when everyone would walk out in a big gang, heading off towards shops, and I'd see Mum standing there at the gate waiting for me.

Now that I was in a new school, the majority of my year didn't know my history; they didn't know why it was that Mum picked me up and they didn't stop to think there might be a reason. The taunts were cruel.

'Evie needs her mummy to take her home. Off you go now, Evie,' they'd tease. 'Don't forget to hold Mummy's hand, now, out in the big, wide world!' I'd taken to hanging around in the loos after school, waiting for everyone to leave before I headed out.

'It's just Mum,' I said to Miss Dawson. 'I don't know what to do about Mum. She won't let me walk home from school without her.'

'I see. Have you tried talking to her?'

I closed my eyes and nodded. Of course I'd tried talking to her. When I'd suggested I walk home from school alone, Mum had fallen silent. She'd sunk into a chair at the kitchen table, her head in her hands.

'Mum?' I'd asked. 'I'll make sure I cross the roads safely.' I knew not to mention the word 'crossing'. 'I'll always walk with someone. I'll be OK. I will!'

Mum said nothing, just rocked with her head in her hands.

'It'll be OK, just let me try? Once... Mum?' I'd put my hand on her arm, trying to pull her hands off her eyes, but she'd shrugged my hand off.

Then she'd snapped her head up. 'So this is it, is it, Evie?' she'd barked, and I'd flinched away, instantly on alert for one of her outbursts. 'This is how I lose you, too? Is it not enough for me to lose my son? I have to lose my daughter too? You of all people, Evie! I thought you would know why this is so important. How life can turn in a second!' Her voice caught and I realised she was crying. 'It doesn't have to be you who makes a mistake!' she sobbed. 'It doesn't have to be your fault, just you in the wrong place at the wrong time and that's it! Gone!'

We'd stared at each other. I'd been too scared of her reaction to push it further. These days, I treated Mum with kid gloves. 'OK,' I'd said, backing away. 'It's OK, Mum. It's fine. I'll see you at the gate.'

'It's because she loves you,' Miss Dawson said. 'You know that, don't you?'

I sighed. 'Yeah. I get it. She's scared she's going to lose me, too. But she's making my life a misery. You don't do that to people you love!'

'Would you like me to try to talk to her?' Miss Dawson asked. 'I mean, I could try?'

I sighed. 'I don't think there's much point. She's never going to let me go. Not unless I move to Timbuktu.'

CHAPTER 38

We drank a little brandy at home that night before retiring upstairs for the evening—Mum to her bath, and me to check and delete Dad's second email account. Having scattered the ashes, everything seemed so very final. Now it really was just Mum and me. I couldn't bear to imagine how she would feel once I left. Just her alone, in this big, old house, filled with ghosts and memories. The sooner she moved, the better.

As I sat at the desk in the office waiting for the computer to boot up, my phone pinged. It was Emily on WhatsApp.

Imagining Emily messaging me from a crowded carriage on Dubai Metro as she commuted home after work, I breathed in and tried to feel the warmth of the sun, to remember the scent of the frangipani, feel the texture of the sand under my feet. I'd be lying if I said I didn't miss Dubai, but I was keen to stay just a little longer to help Mum move house. The fact that I needed to protect my mother had been tattooed on my soul since Graham's death; I didn't want her to go through such a momentous thing alone, especially when she was so vulnerable. The estate agent had said the sale would go through quickly and I really hoped I could stay in Woodside for a few more weeks, even if it meant taking unpaid leave. Besides, a little voice in my head said, it would give me an opportunity to see Luca again.

As soon as I replied and put my phone down, it pinged again. This time it was Luca. *'Hey, Evie. I just wondered how you got on today. Was it ok?'*

I smiled at my phone and typed my reply at once.

'Yeah. Got through it ok, thx. At least it's done and Mum can move on. How are you?'

'All good here, thanks.'

'Great.'

'Do you fancy meeting up in the next day or two? If you're still around?'

'Yeah, that'd be great.'

'Cool. I'll call you.'

At last I turned my attention to the computer. I opened up my email and retrieved Dad's username and password. 'Zeepee93'. I said it out loud as I typed it in—it was unlike Dad to choose rhyming passwords. His were usually a functional, code-based mix of random letters and numbers. But before I had time to think about it further, the inbox opened and I saw that there were only four emails: all from Zoe Peters. ZeePee.

So who was this mysterious Zoe? I racked my brains. Was she a colleague? A cousin? I couldn't think of any Zoes ever being mentioned at home. Why did she warrant a separate email account?

I opened the top email, dated the week before Dad had

died. It was short, but to the point: *'Why £22,000? Call me when you can.'*

'Oh marvellous!' I huffed. Even 'Zoe' didn't know what the money was for.

Dad didn't seem to have replied to the email, so I opened the next one. It was dated the Friday a week before Dad died: *'Are you coming tonight?'*

Why would he meet her on a Friday night? Hunched over the computer, rubbing my temples with my left hand, I opened the second-from-bottom email. Its title was 'Photo-sharing: Tom' and it was dated over a year ago. I read it three times, squinting at the screen as I tried to make sense of it. My brain was unwilling to accept what my eyes were telling it; I must have misunderstood, left out a crucial word.

'Rob, I just wanted to let you know I've finally managed to set up an account on a photo-sharing website so I can post whatever pictures your son deigns to share from uni. I added a few baby ones, too, just to remind you. Wasn't he cute? Don't laugh at my clothes—it was *nearly 20 years ago! Here's the link. Z x'*

Maybe 'Zoe' had made a typo. I read it another time. 'Your son'? Surely not. Graham was dead. Wasn't he? For a minute I questioned myself, but I went to his funeral! Graham wasn't at university. And why would this Zoe woman have pictures of him anyway? I stared at the email, massaging my temples as my brain tried to compute something a deeper part of me didn't want to understand. What was she saying? Was Graham still alive?

My head swam—and then the mist cleared and then, slowly, like a monster emerging from a swamp in a D-rate horror movie, the truth dawned. 'Your son,' she'd written. The email was about photos of someone called Tom. Zoe wasn't talking about Graham at all. There was another child. Another son of Dad's who was alive, well and at university. The payments? Maintenance.

I got to the toilet just in time, and vomited until there was nothing left in my stomach. After wiping my mouth, I flushed, put down the seat and slumped back against the cistern, my hands over my face, trying to block out the sight of the words I'd just read.

'Are you all right?' Mum called from the bathroom. She must have heard me retching. On autopilot, I dashed into the study, logged off the email and closed down the computer. I couldn't risk her stumbling on it. Did she know?

CHAPTER 39

On my bed, I hugged my knees to my chest as I ran through the email in my head.

'No!' I said every time I got to 'your son', my head shaking from side to side as if the movement could wipe out the words. 'No. No. No!' Dad wouldn't have a secret like that. It went against everything I knew about him. He was an upstanding person; people respected him. What he had was a strong moral compass, not a secret son. I knew we weren't perfect, but things like this didn't happen to families like ours. They just didn't.

I couldn't even begin to think about the circumstances that had led up to the birth of this 'Tom'. True, you come to learn, as an adult, that your parents have a life that you don't see, but Dad just wasn't the sort to cheat on Mum.

I stared unseeingly at the curtains. All I'd come home to do was help Mum bury my father—I hadn't come home expecting to have the story of my life rewritten. Since I'd been back, I'd stumbled on so many secrets that I no longer knew what was real and what was illusion. Had my parents hidden anything else from me? Curled up in the foetal position, I barely dared to move for fear of what else might come crashing down. Was there anything else?

And then, as I lay there, it hit me almost physically that, if Dad had a son—*if* Dad had another son—what I had, after twenty years, was a brother. A half-brother. I moaned into the pillow. A child who's lost both her parents is called an orphan. The world acknowledges her pain and bows to it. But there's no word in English for a child who's lost her only sibling. Like an amputee who still feels tickles and itches in a lost limb, I'd felt the absence of Graham, physically, every day for the past twenty years. And the thought that there'd been someone out there—someone who could never be Graham but who, purely by dint of his genetic make-up, might have been able to dip even just a toe into the brother-shaped gap that had yawned in my life for two decades—was almost too painful to bear. I hugged myself, staring unseeingly at the curtains. My mind ran in circles. Was it true? How could it be true? How could Dad not have told me?

*

Sleep, unsurprisingly, eluded me. I didn't even try. Galaxies away from the unconsciousness I craved, I sat up with my knitting, thoughts exploding like fireworks. What circumstances could have led to Dad having another son? Without any facts, all I could do was speculate. As my needles clicked, I came up with my own scenario. Given Tom was, according to the email, nearly twenty, he must have been born a year or so after Graham died. Maybe

Dad, eaten up with guilt and sadness, had turned to this Zoe for support. But who was she? Someone Dad had worked with? A television producer? An editor? I thought back. Twenty years ago, Dad had had a book out, but he'd worked mainly at the university. His media career hadn't yet taken off. Maybe 'Zoe' was a fellow lecturer. A student. The thought made a shudder run through me: Dad, about forty at the time, and a teenager? Please, God, no.

But, somehow, he must have ended up having a one-night stand, and Tom was the product. Being a decent man, Dad had offered to take financial responsibility for his son— hence the debits—while not being able to leave the wife and daughter that he loved. Happens all the time—right?

Even coming up with that scenario failed to bring me peace of mind. What was Tom like? Was he like Graham? Like me? Or something completely different? Would I like him? What if I didn't? I couldn't bear the thought of having a brother who was alive but not liking him. But, again, I couldn't imagine having a brother who wasn't Graham. And then my blood ran cold as another thought struck me: had I ever met him? Tossing my knitting aside, I picked up the spare pillow and hugged it to me as I remembered a film I'd seen in which a dad with children from two different mums arranged for them to play together unknowingly in the park. Oh my goodness, had Dad ever done that? I racked my brains for any encounters with a boy called Tom: nothing. Then: why *hadn't* Dad done that?

And what about Mum? This was hard enough for me, but did she know? I couldn't imagine that she would have kept something this big from me, so I could only deduce that she didn't know. Which then begged another question: not *should* I tell her, but *could* I tell her? There was no doubt that she should know, but was she strong enough to hear that my father had betrayed her? That he'd had another son? A replacement? Complicated grief disorder, Miss Dawson had said—a long-term dysfunction. How could I possibly tell her this? It would send her over the edge.

My thoughts went back to Zoe—the mysterious Zoe—and I remembered the faxed agreement downstairs. With them had been a photo of a small boy. I'd thought it was Graham, but what if it wasn't? Why would there be a photo of my dead brother in with her fax? I jumped out of bed and ran down the stairs, the carpet quietening the sound of my feet. In the dining room, I ripped open the box file and dug under the newspaper for the yellow manila folder and the photo. Putting everything back in place, I sped back up to my room, where I got into bed and looked properly at the picture.

Slightly out of focus, it wasn't great. Like any toddler, he'd been in motion when the lens had clicked; he wasn't looking directly at the camera and it was difficult to see his eyes. I moved my head around the picture, as if I could somehow see around the angles that prevented me from looking him in the eye. Still, to all intents and purposes, it could have been Graham. He had the same, curly dark hair and was of a similar build. But the outfit was not one I'd seen in photos of Graham at that age. I squeezed my hand over my mouth, inhaling deeply through my nose. Breathe, Evie, breathe. Was I really looking at my half-brother?

Desperately needing to talk to someone, I dialled Luca's number, my fingers clammy on the touchscreen.

'Please pick up, Luca,' I whispered. 'Please. I need you.'

'You have reached the voicemail of…' said the automated voice, 'Luca Rossi,' said Luca's voice. I hung up, opened WhatsApp and bashed out a message for Luca.

'Hello. How are you? Really, really need your advice. Please can we meet tomorrow? It's urgent. E.' Then I tried to go to sleep.

*

It didn't work, of course. My curiosity was a woodpecker jabbing at my brain. Once more I sat up in bed and groped for the light switch. When my eyes had accustomed to the light, I opened my iPad and read the final email in the ZeePee account. Dad had emailed himself a document containing all Zoe and Tom's personal information, from phone numbers and addresses to the bank account number that I knew so well. Now there was just one thing left for me to do: open the photo-sharing site and see once and for all what my half-brother looked like.

I didn't know if I could do it.

I snapped the cover over the iPad and lay back on my pillows, my heart thumping so loudly I thought the house would shake.

'Come on, Evie,' I told myself, trying to think logically. 'Do you want this or not?' Once I'd seen the pictures, there'd be no going back: Zoe and her son would become more real and would take up residence in my head (as if they hadn't anyway). Did I want that? I was burning with curiosity, but it would kill me *not* to see them. Sweating on the pillow, I realised that I'd definitely look at some point—it was just a matter of how soon.

So, with shaking hands, I opened the iPad cover, clicked the link and entered the password. I closed my eyes while the page loaded and, when I opened them, there he was, laughing in the sunshine in what looked like a pub garden: my half-brother, Tom Peters. Woodside—the whole of England—could have been obliterated by a meteor at that moment and still it wouldn't have torn me away from the picture in front of my eyes. With a hand pressed to my chest, I stared.

CHAPTER 40

I woke the next morning to the sound of Mum's clock radio roaring into life. I was still slumped up against the pillows, the iPad still open on my lap. My eyes felt puffy; a crumpled tissue was still in my hand.

I felt sick at the thought of what I had to tell Mum. I was rehearsing sentences in my head—'Could you pass the butter, please, and, by the way, Mum, did you know Dad had another son?'—when I heard her bustling across the hall. I managed to slide the iPad under my pillow and lie down properly just in time.

'Morning, darling!' she said, knocking and entering in the same fluid movement. 'How are we today?'

'Uh. Not that great. I feel all congested, like I'm coming down with something.'

'Maybe it's all the stress, dear. It's not been an easy time,' said Mum. 'Anyway, you need to get up. We're going out. I'm treating us both to a spa day!'

'What? Today? Have you booked?'

'Yes, today! I wanted to surprise you. Also because tomorrow—I hope you don't mind—I've been asked to play in the Ladies' Morning Challenge at the golf club. You don't think it's too unseemly, do you—' she didn't pause long enough for me to gather my thoughts, let alone reply, rattling on '—but the girls really need me. Anyway, so I thought we'd do something nice together today. I've arranged for us to go to Hinton Hall—it's only half an hour on the motorway and we're booked in for a full day's pampering.' She walked over to the window and pulled open a curtain.

'It's a lovely thought,' I said. 'But I really don't feel well. Maybe we could do it another day?'

'Oh, come on, Evie. We'll have a nice massage, then a facial and a "spa cuisine" lunch. After that, we're free to use the facilities, so bring a book. I think there's a nice indoor pool to lounge around, and some exercise classes and stuff. I'd quite like to try yoga. In the afternoon, we've got manicures and pedicures followed by afternoon tea.'

'Mum. It sounds lovely. But I'm really not up for it today.'

She rolled her eyes at me. 'It's a spa! It'll make you feel better! All you've got to do is loll about in a dressing gown being pampered. You don't have to come to yoga if you don't want.'

'Can you take anyone else? One of your golf friends? I'm sure they'd love it.'

Mum's voice dropped its cheery tone. 'I really need this, Evie. And I'd like you to come with me. Please humour me.'

I sighed.

'Good. Thank you.' Mum looked at her watch. 'But you really need to get up now. We need to leave by nine-thirty.' She bustled out of the room.

But I wasn't ready to leave my new half-brother. I needed

to see his face again, and this time I needed to look more
objectively. I needed to find a trace of Dad in him; I needed
to know that he wasn't a fake, an imposter. What if that Zoe
woman had tricked Dad? Had he ever had any proof that the
baby was his? Had he asked for a paternity test?

My mind flooded with doubts as I took the iPad into the
bathroom, locked the door and sat on the toilet. I opened
up the photo-sharing site with shaking fingers. And there he
was again. There was no doubt that he was Dad's son: my
new half-brother looked uncannily like my dead brother.

Once I got beyond the shock of seeing what Graham
might have looked like grown-up, I couldn't stop looking
at Tom, devouring every detail of his face. I held the iPad
close to my face and stared into Tom's eyes; I pulled it
away and looked at him from the corner of my eye, as if
I'd just caught sight of him. Would I have recognised him
in the street? What had he got from Dad? Did he look at
all like me?

Tom's hair was entirely from our side: he had the same
shock of curly nut-brown hair that Graham and I had shared,
and he had Dad's light-hazel eyes while I'd got Mum's blue
ones. His teeth were white and even, his cheeks rosy over
a tan; there was something familiar about the shape of his
mouth, but I couldn't place it. The physical resemblance to
the Stevens side of the family was strong—I was sure I'd
have done a double take had I seen him out and about. I
traced my finger round the outline of his face, touched it to
his cheek. My brother.

But the picture of Tom didn't tell me anything more about

him, about this person who was suddenly my family. He looked nice, but I wanted to know what he was really like; whether he was kind or arrogant, friendly, sporty or bookish. I wanted to know how he filled his days. Did he know about me? Did he wonder who his dad was?

In the photo, Tom was in a pub garden, wearing a polo shirt and jeans and half-standing up from a picnic table, a pint glass in his hand. There was a handful of pretty blonde women behind him, and two more guys. I clicked onto the next picture. It was a 'selfie' of him and an attractive, middle-aged woman, their laughing, windswept faces squashed together as they struggled to get in the shot. I recognised her at once: the woman outside the church. Zoe. Tom's mother.

I yanked my towel off the rack, bunched it up and slammed my fist into it as hard as I could, again and again. At the funeral, that woman — that adulterer, my father's mistress — had known exactly who I was.

I felt sick to remember that I'd liked her. And then I remembered what she'd said before she went into the church: 'My son will be wondering where I am.' I spun around and retched into the toilet.

CHAPTER 41

When Mum said she'd booked a spa, I'd imagined one of those community fitness-centre jobs—a blobby manicure and a no-frills massage in an afterthought of a treatment room shoved behind the squash courts—but Mum had really pushed the boat out: Hinton Hall was a huge Jacobean country-house hotel, which stood magnificently in its own sprawling grounds in the Kent countryside, and its spa was no afterthought. Franchised by Six Senses, it was the real deal—walking through the double doors into the rarified air of the spa made me feel like we'd walked into a little piece of Thailand. As we stood at the reception desk, my shoulders dropped and I took a deep breath, inhaling the scent of the aromatherapy oils that infused the air.

Although I sometimes went for the odd massage in Dubai, this wasn't a natural scene for Mum. She'd always avoided spas, re-gifting any vouchers people bought her for Christmas and claiming she didn't have time for all that 'touchy-feely' stuff, so I was surprised how enthusiastic she was. She'd been as giddy as a goat all the way down in the car—an infectious mood that hadn't allowed me to dwell on my thoughts. It continued now, as we were shown to the changing room and asked to slip into the thick bathrobes and unflattering mesh spa pants.

'Thank you for coming with me,' Mum said, as we opened our lockers. She sighed. 'What would I do without you, Evie? You're the best daughter I could ever have asked for. I hope you know that.' She smiled tenderly at me.

I took a deep breath. 'Mum, while we're being all serious, there's something I…'

But her head was once more inside the locker.

'What on earth are these?' she asked, pulling out the spa pants.

'They go on your head,' I said, deadpan. The moment was over. 'Keeps the oil off your hair? And these?' I held up the slippers. 'These go on your hands. They're spa mittens.'

Without missing a beat, Mum obediently put the pants on her head and the slippers on her hands, which she then flapped about like a seal, and we both collapsed in fits of giggles that neither of us could stop. Each time one of us straightened up, our giggles erupted again. We doubled over in our gowns, snorts of laughter bursting out of us like geysers.

The door swung open and the spa manager, clearly fed up with waiting for us, came in, a disapproving look on her face. Mum whipped the pants off her head and, mouth twitching, I fought to look serious. Mum's hair was still mussed up from the pants and I felt another round of giggles starting in my belly. I stared at the floor and turned my laugh into an explosive cough, while Mum dutifully followed

the manager out into the relaxation area, where she took us
through our massage choices.

If only there was one that could soothe the mind as
well as the body, I thought: while the giggles had relieved
a lot of tension, the problem of how to tell Mum about
Tom resurfaced during my treatment and my thoughts slid
around like eels, tangling themselves up until I felt queasy.
Could I tell her during the afternoon tea, when she was
all relaxed? Or should I wait till we were back home and
she didn't have to get in a car and drive? Or would it be
better to tell her while she was distracted with driving?
My mind swam.

I didn't see Mum again until after our facials when
we met up in the relaxation room. Sipping from a cup
of ginger tea, Mum was glowing—the facial seemed to
have plumped up her face, making her look younger and
fresher.

'Don't get settled,' she said, as I plopped down in a wick-
er chair opposite her. 'It's nearly time for the yoga class.
Will you come?'

'Sure.' I did a bit of yoga in Dubai. Maybe that would
calm my thoughts.

As it happened, we were the only two who turned up and
the teacher suggested that she take us through a series of
gentle stretches and twists to get us warmed up before we
started on some easy 'chest-opening' *asanas*.

I was belly to the floor, hands at chest level, doing my
best impression of a cobra when I heard a strange noise:
a stifled sob. Mum was really struggling to hold the pose.

She slumped back down onto her front, her head flopping into her hands.

The sobbing noise continued.

'Sorry,' Mum whispered and I thought she was apologising for not doing the pose right, then I realised that she was crying.

'Oh, Mum,' I said, releasing my own baby cobra and sitting up to pat her back. I passed her a tissue from my pocket and she blew her nose, struggling to compose herself. I didn't think I'd seen her cry for twenty years.

'Sorry,' she kept saying. 'I don't know what happened. Sorry. I don't know why I'm crying. I feel fine, it was just… it just came over me. Sorry.'

'Maybe we should call it a day?' I said. I helped her into the changing room then went back to the studio to apologise to the teacher.

'Chest-opening *asanas* often have that effect on people,' she said, as she wiped down the mats. 'They open up the heart area, which can trigger a release of bottled-up emotion. Is your mum under any kind of emotional strain?'

I gave a little laugh. 'You could say that. Her husband— my father—died, just over a week ago. They'd been married for over thirty years.'

I felt awkward talking about it with a stranger.

'I see,' she said. 'I'm sorry to hear that.' She paused long enough to be decent, then continued. 'But that would be it then. It's perfectly normal for the emotions to come out like that—you can't keep them bottled up. It does more harm than good. But your mum's reaction was quite extreme.

Are you able to keep an eye on her? I think she's probably feeling a lot more than she's letting you see. Maybe she's trying to be strong for you?'

Given I'd been planning to drop an emotional atom bomb on her later that day, I didn't really want to hear that and, slightly taken aback at getting Psychology 101 from a yoga teacher when all I'd expected was some sun salutations, I edged towards the door, muttering a thank you as I left.

I found Mum in the relaxation room and poured us each a glass of water from a jug packed with lemon, lime, cucumber and mint leaves.

'Are you all right?' I asked.

'Sorry, darling,' she said, much more composed. 'I do miss him. I know he wasn't perfect, and he could be an awkward old goat sometimes, but we'd been married for thirty-three years. It's odd not to have him there. Just you and me now, darling.'

I gave her a sad little smile.

'You must miss James, too?' she asked.

I stiffened. I didn't want to talk about James. He'd taken me for a complete fool. But that didn't mean there weren't times when I missed his physical presence in my life.

'It's hardly the same,' I said. 'We'd only been together three years.'

'Hmm,' said Mum. 'Now, how are we placed for some lunch? What's spa cuisine anyway? I hope it's not blended with massage oil.'

*

While we'd been spa-ing, I'd left my phone on silent in the locker and it had clearly been active. There was a string of concerned messages from Luca followed by a suggestion that we meet at my local at eight. After the emotion and physical release of the day, I'd rather have had an early night, but I was more desperate to talk to him about the Tom situation. My own thoughts were going in ever-decreasing circles—I really needed some outside perspective to help me decide what to do.

'Thanks so much,' I typed. *'See you then.'*

CHAPTER 42

'*It's lovely to see you again, Evie,*' said Miss Dawson. '*It's been a while.*'

I only saw Miss Dawson on an ad hoc basis, now: maintenance, not crisis management.

Two coffees sat on the table. I smiled to myself, remembering the days when I'd been so excited about the staffroom and the biscuit tin. Now I was in the sixth form, Miss Dawson picked up decaf coffees for us on her way in.

'*So how are you?*' she asked.

'*Look—no knitting,*' I said, showing her my empty hands. '*Ta-da!*'

'*Well, that's a good sign.*' She stirred her coffee. '*So, what's been going on? How's that boyfriend of yours? Luca?*'

'*Ah.*' I looked out of the window. Trust Miss Dawson to hit the nail on the head. There were so many positive and happy things I could talk about but, today, Luca was not one of them. I pressed my lips together. '*He asked me to marry him.*'

'*Well, well, Evie!*' Miss Dawson sat back in her chair.

'That's big news. And what did you say? You love him, don't you?'

I exhaled hard while I nodded, tears suddenly clouding my vision. I talked to the table. Miss Dawson shifted forward as she tried to catch my reply.

'I said no.'

'OK.' She pushed a box of tissues towards me. 'Let's look at this. You've been together how long? Nearly two years?' I nodded. 'And you love him?' I nodded again. 'And he obviously feels the same or he wouldn't have asked...' She cocked her head at me. 'So what's the problem?'

I shook my head, unable to speak.

'Do you think you're too young?'

'Mmm-hmm. A bit.'

'OK. I see that. You are only eighteen. But, you know, some people meet their life partner at an early age. It can work out. Even if you go to different universities. People do make it work.'

I sniffed. 'It's not that.'

Miss Dawson waited.

'I should have brought my knitting after all,' I said.

I got up and walked to the window. Outside, the clouds had gathered. A storm was brewing. The smaller trees bent under the force of the wind; leaves flurried through the playground. I turned and perched on the radiator, its warmth flooding through my clothes. 'I love him too much.'

'That's not a good thing? I don't think you can ever love a person too much.'

'I'm scared. What if I lose him?'

'Lose him, as in he'll leave you? Or lose him, as in… ?'

'Lose him like Graham,' I said, my voice small. 'I lost Graham. I nearly lost Mum. I've practically lost Dad. I lose everyone I love. If I marry Luca, what if I lose him, too?'

CHAPTER 43

The pub at the end of the road was never going to win awards, neither for its design nor for the menu. A converted run of four terraced houses now painted cream and self-styled as a commuter-belt gastro-pub, it had a tiny patch of muddy grass out the front, nestled against the main road. Three wooden picnic tables floated on the grass like rafts in a radioactive sea.

Just before 8 p.m., I stood outside it and, with fingers stiff from the cold, jabbed a number into my phone. I'd marched up the road from Mum's full of righteous bravado and now my breath came out in puffs that floated up into the orange sodium glow of the High Street. But, before the line connected, I disconnected it and shoved my phone back in my pocket. Then I dithered on the pavement: should I or shouldn't I call Zoe? What was the worst that could happen? That she'd be nice and I'd get drawn into a conversation with her? I shook my head at the thought, then I turned and walked slowly back towards the pub's doors. But then... I spun on my heel and walked back down the pavement.

Trying to look as if I knew where I was going—as if I had a purpose in mind—I walked down towards the estate agent's and stood staring unseeingly at the pictures of houses for sale and rent. I needed to do it. Already I knew I'd have no inner peace if I didn't make this call. Turning my back to the estate agent's window, I dialled again.

Ring-ring… ring-ring.

'Hello? Zoe speaking.'

'Hello. This is Evie. Evie Stevens?'

'Oh… Evie… hello.'

'I just wanted to tell you that I know. I know all about you and Tom.'

'Oh. Oh my goodness. Evie…'

'Are you positive my dad was his father?'

'Yes. Yes, of course.'

'There's no doubt?'

'No. No doubt. It wasn't that kind of…'

'That's all. I just wanted you to know that I know. Bye.'

'Evie, wait! I—'

Click.

CHAPTER 44

Call made, I pushed my way through the double doors, trying to look like I walked into suburban pseudo-gastro-pubs every day of my life. Despite the interior being full of 'atmospheric' nooks and crannies, I spotted Luca at once, but paused, suddenly shy. After being in Dubai, where five minutes constitutes a long relationship, the shared sense of history I had with Luca was incredibly comforting. I bit my lips as I walked slowly towards the table, embarrassed by the rush of warmth and gratitude that swamped me. My life in Dubai suddenly seemed very far away.

'Hey.' I tapped Luca on the shoulder.

'Evie.' He jumped up, gave me a peck on the cheek and pulled out a chair for me and indicated the bottle of wine on the table. 'Are you all right with Chablis?'

'Of course.' I smiled at him and he poured me a glass.

I took a sip, rolling the wine appreciatively around my mouth.

'That's good. Thank you.'

'So...' Luca looked at me expectantly. 'I was worried about you today. What's up? Is your mum all right?'

Clutching my glass, I took another sip, stalling for time.

Once I admitted what I'd found out, it would become real. Once Luca knew, I wouldn't be able to hide away, pretending the whole thing hadn't happened. A large part of me wished I'd just jumped on a plane and flown back to my other, relatively uncomplicated life, leaving no one any the wiser. I shook my head.

'I don't even know where to begin. It's so complicated.'

'The beginning's a good place.'

I took a deep breath and blew it out through my nose. 'OK. You remember what happened to my brother?'

Luca nodded. He was the only person I'd really talked to about the accident and he'd known the depth of my grief. Even ten years afterwards, I'd cried in his arms.

'And you remember what happened with my mum after that? You know what she did before she was sectioned?'

He nodded again. I stared at my wine glass, noticed I was tapping my fingernails on the table and gripped my hand into a tight fist to stop myself from doing it. I chewed the inside of my lip and thought about how to say the next bit.

'Well. I've just found out what my dad did around that time. He…' I squeezed my eyes shut, opened them, took a breath and tried again. 'He had another son. I have a half brother!' The unfamiliar word came out with a sob.

Luca shook his head slowly. 'No. I can't believe it. How? How did that happen?' He paused. 'Do you know?'

I shook my head, my lips a thin line. 'No idea. But the guy – Tom - is nineteen, so I'm guessing that Dad met the mum while he worked at the university. The Zoe woman looks about forty now so she must have been about twenty then—maybe she was a student of Dad's, or maybe they met somewhere completely different—who knows—' I threw my hands in the air '—and had a one-night stand? Anyway, the upshot is, she got pregnant and didn't get rid of it. So I have a half-brother. At university.'

There was a short silence as Luca processed what I'd just said. I looked up at the ceiling; I couldn't make eye contact with him: the merest whiff of sympathy would break me. He seemed to know that.

'How did you find out?' he asked. 'Did he contact you? Or did the mother? Or did your mum tell you? Does she even know?'

'None of the above. Just call me Sherlock.' I paused. 'This is going to sound really weird,' I said, 'but I've actually met this "Zoe". She was at Dad's funeral. Get this: with Tom.' I took in Luca's shocked expression. 'I know!' I shook my head. 'The mum was really nice to me at the funeral, but I didn't know who she was then.'

Luca was still shaking his head.

'I called her just now,' I said. 'Told her I knew.'

'Sorry, what? Evie, you called this woman? You're crazy!'

'Well, what would you have done?' The words shot out of my mouth like bullets. Was I coming across as unhinged? I didn't know any more what was real. My world had tilted; everything was suddenly skewed, off balance.

Luca took my hand and squeezed it. 'I'm not judging you. I'm just taking it in. Sorry.'

I twisted my wine glass. 'The worst thing is, I don't think Mum knows. I found out when I was closing Dad's email account. I found a secret email account with correspondence between him and this woman, Zoe, and I pieced it all together. It must have happened soon after the accident. I just don't know how to tell Mum. We went to a spa today and I was going to tell her, but she cried during yoga. The teacher told me she's really fragile and I just don't know what to do. She has to know — right? I have to tell her?'

Luca's forehead wrinkled.

'You do have to tell her, Evie. It's just a matter of when. Personally, I'd tell her as soon as possible. But how is she? If she's "fragile", you don't want to risk…' He tailed off. He looked down at his wine glass, as if the answers lay there. Then he sighed, and looked up again. 'Look, if I were your mum, I'd want you to tell me as soon as you found out. I'd be hurt if you kept it from me.'

'But how can I tell her now? It's too soon.'

'Look at it this way: How did you feel when you found out your dad had kept it from you for so long?'

'I'm not planning on keeping it from her for twenty years!'

'Sure. But what if it drives a wedge between you and your mum? What if she blames you for keeping it from her? You need to be open with each other. She's all you've got left now. Family secrets always end in tears. You can do it, you can tell her, but you have to play it really carefully.'

I drew patterns with my nail on the condensation on the side of my glass.

Luca spoke again. 'And you don't want to meet this Tom person? If it were me, I'd have to. I couldn't know there was someone who shares my genes out there without making an effort to meet them. I just couldn't.'

We sat with our thoughts.

'Telling your mum might be painful,' said Luca softly, 'but it'd be for the best. It might even be good for her. You could make sure she got the right support this time. As there's a history?'

'He looks just like Graham. I've seen pictures.'

'You think it might be too much for her?'

'Oh God. I don't know. Buggery shitty fuck fuck. Why is life so complicated? I just don't know!' I banged the table in frustration, making our glasses jump.

There was another silence.

'So do you think you'll get in touch with your… um… brother?' Luca asked.

'I don't know. I haven't even thought about it. What if he's awful? What if he looks like Graham but is nothing like Graham?'

'Evie. The chances of him being just like Graham are pretty non-existent,' Luca's voice was gentle. 'Please don't expect that of him. He's not Graham. He's never going to be Graham.'

'I know.'

We sat in silence with our wine. Luca picked up the empty wine bottle. 'Another one?'

I shook my head. 'Maybe just a glass. My round.'

When I came back from the bar, Luca was busy on his phone. 'Have you looked for this guy online?' he asked. 'I've got a signal. What's his full name again?'

'Tom Peters.' I looked around the pub, pretending not to be interested.

Luca tapped his screen. 'Right. Got him. Loads of entries. Facebook, Twitter. He appears to be at Warwick University. God bless social media. Here. Have a look?' He held out his phone.

I shook my head. 'Thanks, but no. Not like this. I want to do it properly at home when I've got time to take it all in. Not half drunk in a pub.'

'Fair enough.'

*

'So I have to tell her?' I asked Luca as we stood outside the pub.

Luca shoved his hands in his pockets and shuffled his feet against the cold. 'Yes. But pick your time.'

'OK. Thanks for coming tonight. I really appreciate it.'

'No problem. It was a pleasure.'

Our eyes locked, then Luca stepped forward and pulled me into a hug that was half polite, half something more. He went to kiss my cheek but got my hair. My lips connected with his ear. I remembered with a jolt of embarrassment how much he liked having his ears kissed.

'OK, bye then.'

'Bye.'

I walked slowly away from Luca, then glanced quickly over my shoulder. He was walking purposefully down the High Street, his phone clamped to his ear. I felt a surge of jealousy for the recipient of the call and, reflexively, got my own phone out. Without stopping to think if what I was doing was right or wrong, I opened the email I'd forwarded to myself from Dad's account, double-clicked the mobile phone number for Tom and waited while it rang one, two, three times, then, 'Hello? Tom speaking?' Crisp and efficient; a smile in the inflection, the timbre of his voice achingly similar to Dad's.

I stabbed 'disconnect'.

CHAPTER 45

I was glad to see the living room light off when I got home. I crept upstairs and poked my head around Mum's bedroom door when I saw that her bedside light was still on. She was sitting up in bed, looking intently at a photo album. From it, Graham's ten-year-old face smiled up at her.

'Oh hello, darling. How was your evening?' Mum closed the album quickly. I pretended I hadn't seen.

'Good, thanks. G'night!' I started to back out of the room. My head was full of Tom.

'The funeral was beautiful, wasn't it?' said Mum.

I paused in the doorway. 'Yes. It was lovely.'

'All those white lilies. So beautiful.'

White lilies? There had been no flowers. We'd made sure of that by asking people to donate to charity instead. Unless… ? Oh God.

'They were lovely,' I said, non-committal, looking for my escape. But Mum patted the bed. 'Come and sit with me for a bit, Evie. I'm just remembering. There's no harm in remembering, is there?'

I smiled the trace of a smile, and sat on the bed, carefully out of touching distance. I couldn't look at Mum, just at the bedspread. I studied the patchwork and wondered who'd made it—it hadn't been Mum: that much I knew. I picked a repeating pattern of tiny daisies and stared at it. Mum was on a roll.

'The coffin was so small, Evie, just him and his elephant inside—Ellie, wasn't it? I put Ellie on his chest—no parent should have to see such a small coffin. I think the white made it even worse.' I realised I was holding my breath. 'Maybe we should have gone for oak, after all. But it was your father's choice. He asked for the white. And he was right: the white lilies looked so special, didn't they? Arranged on top?'

I traced the patchwork with my finger, forced myself to breathe. I didn't know what to say.

'And the readings—his teacher, what was her name? Mrs Wilson? Mrs Wilcox? She did such a special reading, didn't she? She really captured his spirit. He was such a character. But I cried when that little boy from his class read out what he'd written himself. "Graham was the best friend I could ever have wished for and I can't wait to see him in Heaven"—that's what he said, wasn't it? I cried then. It was so sweet. I wonder how he is now.'

'Mum, stop.'

'And then how we sang his favourite hymn, "All things bright and beautiful". It was lovely. I'll never forget that… I did my reading after that. Do you remember how the vicar had to support me so I didn't fall?'

Mum's eyes were unfocused, she was lost in her thoughts, rambling. 'I'll never forget the sound of that first clot of earth hitting the coffin. I'm glad I threw it, but I'll never forget the sound.' Suddenly, her eyes snapped back to me, took in the expression on my face. 'I'm just remembering, darling. I'm not sad. I'm just remembering my boy. There's no one else left to remember him now, darling. Just you and me.'

There was no harm in remembering. I got that. But Mum was not remembering. Mum hadn't gone to Graham's funeral. She'd locked herself in the bathroom, screaming that he wasn't dead and she wasn't going to pretend he was. No one could get her out, not even me. In the end, I'd gone alone with Dad.

''Course not, Mum. Goodnight,' I said.

*

Back in my room, I sat on the edge of my bed, my knees hugged to my chest, and stared at nothing. Was this part of the 'grief dysfunction' Miss Dawson had mentioned? Was Mum regressing? Twice she'd confused Dad's death with Graham's and now she remembered a funeral she hadn't even been to. I didn't care what Richard had said about her being OK: it terrified me. I'd seen Mum go through a psychosis, depression and a suicide attempt once in my life and I didn't want to see it again. She may be getting through her day-to-day life with a wave and a breezy smile, but she didn't fool me. Something was amiss far below the surface and I was terrified of what might happen. I couldn't let her deteriorate like she had after Graham's death.

I flung myself back on the bed and stared at the ceiling. I thought we'd got through this; I thought we were safe now.

Mum had got her job, got her life together. She'd got her golf, the church, her friends, even her cosy little friendship with Richard. I couldn't let her lose all that. Taking a deep breath I pulled myself up and marched back into her bedroom. Her light was off.

'I know you're not asleep and there's something I need to say. You don't have to answer, but please listen to what I have to say.' I paused. Mum was so still I knew she was listening. 'Graham's funeral,' I said. 'You weren't remembering it. You weren't there. You've pieced things together from what other people told you, but they're not memories. It's important that you know that. I'm not going to let you get confused. Don't go down that route now, Mum. You've got through all that and you're fine. You're on the right track. Don't bring it all back up again. Please.'

Silence.

'Mum. Do you hear me? *You weren't there!*'

I crumpled against the bedroom wall, the fight having suddenly left me, and waited for a response, something, anything at all to show that Mum had heard me. When nothing came, I turned to leave. Only as I reached the door did her voice come, tiny, from the bed.

'I know,' she said. 'I do know that.'

CHAPTER 46

Mum's golf club wasn't at all what I'd expected. I'd never played golf, but I'd always imagined clubhouses to be quite plush places with oak-panelled walls and over-stuffed sofas, the scent of a million old cigars ground into thick carpets. But Mum's club, with its sticky Formica table tops, self-service cafeteria and lingering smell of last night's chips, bore more resemblance to a motorway service station than any sort of members' club. It was, Mum told me apologetically, only a temporary base while the real clubhouse was given a much-needed refurbishment.

Mum was happy, though. She'd worried that it might look unseemly to play golf so soon after her bereavement, but she'd told me that she'd had a chat to her friends, who'd assured her that no one would think the worse of her if she came and, furthermore, had insisted that she'd regret it if she didn't take part in the annual Ladies' Morning Challenge — it was the highlight of the recreational golfing calendar.

'Would you mind dropping me off?' she'd asked coyly. 'I'd like to have a drink or two at the Ladies' Lunch.'

I didn't mind at all. The scene with her in the bedroom last night had left me shaken. Even though Mum had said that she knew she wasn't at Graham's funeral, part of me felt she'd said that just to appease me; that she'd lied to shut me up. Maybe she thought I was the mad one. I had no idea what was going on in her head. Anyway, the fact was, I was more than happy to drop her off: although I'd had to concentrate hard on making normal conversation with her in the car, it meant I'd be alone till after lunch — and I had plans of my own.

All Mum's 'golf girls' were there. It was a mark of how well they knew Mum that they didn't make a fuss of her over Dad's death, welcoming her instead with a mix of bawdiness and laughter that made me smile. She was in good hands. Feeling more than a little deceptive, I waved them off to the first hole then headed home to make a start on my own little projects: first, Uncle David; second, Tom.

*

I found Mum's address book tucked in the desk drawer where it had lived for as long as I remembered. Some of the pages were so well thumbed the paper was thinning. I don't know how long it had been since she last had any contact with Uncle David, but the book was old enough to give me some hope that his address might be there.

Although Mum had indicated that she didn't want me to contact her brother, I'd decided to do it anyway. Over and above everything else, it was only polite to let Uncle David know that his brother-in-law had passed away but, besides that, I was twenty-eight years old, for goodness' sake, not a child who did whatever her mother thought best. Mum's acting weird had given me the strange feeling that I was the adult in the relationship, like I was the one protecting her, and not the other way around.

Anyway, I reasoned, maybe enough time had passed for whatever it was that had caused Uncle David and Mum to become estranged to have faded into insignificance; maybe they were both too proud to make the first move. But he was Mum's closest living relative and the pair of us were hardly in the position to pick and choose our relatives: we were currently a family of two and a secret half, and I'd welcome the addition of an uncle, however elusive. Desperate times call for desperate measures.

I found Uncle David's details under 'E' for Evans—Mum's maiden name. But then there was a problem: no email address. Of course, back when Mum wrote it down, there was no email. There was a phone number and a postal address in Oxford. I wasn't going to phone, so it would have to be a physical letter. Sighing, I searched my parents' heavy wooden desk for the pad of watermarked Basildon Bond I knew would be there somewhere, chose a pen and started writing.

Half an hour later, when I was happy with my handiwork, I sealed the envelope, dug out a stamp from the tin my parents kept in the desk, and walked down the road to the postbox. I stared at the envelope for the last time, crossed my fingers and pushed it through the slot.

*

Next on my agenda was Tom. I was desperate to find out

more about him. It fascinated me that there was this person out there who shared so many of my genes. With Luca's warning still ringing in my ears, I needed to find out as much as I could. I knew Tom wouldn't be Graham—of course he wouldn't be Graham—but, before I could decide whether or not I wanted to meet him, whether it was safe to tell Mum about him or anything, I needed to know what sort of person he was. Settling myself with a coffee at the dining table, I opened up Google on the iPad and typed 'Tom Peters' into the search box, flinching as the screen suddenly filled with images and links to mentions of my half-brother.

Two hours later, I had a more complete idea of the entity that was Tom Peters. In a nutshell: he was a second-year law student at Warwick University; he had a girlfriend called Sophie (blonde, beautiful, also studying law); 267 Facebook friends—about 150 of whom appeared to want to replace Sophie as far as I could tell by the flirty comments and selfies of themselves in various states of undress that they posted in his timeline. On Twitter, he had 1,094 followers. '@TeePee94', ran his bio. 'Amateur sportsman, comedian and lawyer-in-waiting. Live and let live.' He was sports-mad, played in the university cricket and rugby teams, and wasn't averse to delivering a bit of stand-up comedy, usually to good reviews. I loved that he seemed to be an all-round good-egg sort of a bloke. Staring into space, I wondered what Graham would have been like had he been able to grow up. Definitely a good egg, too.

Still, these facts weren't enough. I needed to know as

much about Tom as was humanly possible without meeting him. I clicked on the link to a review of one of his stand-up gigs in Coventry and smiled as I read it. I loved that my half-brother was funny. Had he got the 'performance' gene from Dad? I wondered. One of the reasons Dad had become so successful was his ability to engage an audience and deliver quite dull facts in an amusing way. Flicking onto YouTube, I searched for videos of Tom performing, but nothing came up.

How would we meet for the first time? I wondered. Did Tom even know about me? My friend Clem lived in Warwick. Maybe we'd be sitting in the tea rooms that she ran, enjoying a cream tea and cackling like witches, when in he'd walk, unmistakably my brother. He'd do a double take as he passed by my table.

'Excuse me, but do we know each other?' he'd ask.

'I do believe you may be my long-lost brother,' I'd reply, super-cool. I shook my head at my corny imagination. I'd been watching too many Hollywood movies. It'd probably be far more mundane than that. *If* I decided to meet him.

I scrolled through Tom's Twitter feed and saw with a jolt, as newer tweets loaded, that he wasn't currently in Warwick. He was actually staying down in Maidstone for a couple of weeks, working at a café while he revised for exams. Maidstone was about half an hour away by car. I typed 'Harry's Café' into the search box and clicked 'images'—there it was, the place my brother most likely was right now. I looked at the café's door and imagined him walking through it each day. The thought of it blew my mind.

*

I didn't hear the phone ring at first, so intense was my concentration on the iPad screen. I'd toyed with the idea of following Tom on Twitter but had decided it was too risky. Instead, I was scrolling through his Tweets, sucking up every last piece of knowledge I could about him, trying to get to know as much about him as possible before I decided whether or not I wanted to announce myself as his secret half-sister.

'Hi, darling, it's just me,' said Mum. It was hard to hear her over the background noise. She was in the bar or restaurant. I looked at my watch—it was already three o'clock.

'How was the match? Did you win?' I asked.

'We won! No thanks to me, though: the third hole took me nine shots! Nine! I usually do that in about four, but thank heavens Margot got a birdie!'

'Wow, congratulations! Nice one! So have you been celebrating?'

'Can't you hear, dear? It's like a hen night in here! The prize was a magnum of champagne and we've drunk the lot!' I could hear the unaccustomed giggle in her voice now she mentioned it. Mum rarely drank more than the odd whisky or glass of wine. 'Are you able you come and pick Richard and me up in about twenty minutes? It'll take us that long to sort out the bill.'

I raised an eyebrow. Richard? At the Ladies' Morning?
'Sure. Glad you had a good time.'

'What have you been up to?'

'Oh nothing much, you know, pottering about at home.
A bit of work.' Lying to my mother. 'I'll see you in a bit.
Bye.'

CHAPTER 47

I didn't consciously decide to go and see Zoe: I woke in the wee hours, absolutely sure of the fact that I had to. I've no memory what I was dreaming about, no idea why the thought came to mind, no clue why it woke me, but it did. My eyes snapped open and I lay rigid in bed, my muscles still paralysed with sleep, arms by my sides, and I knew with every fibre of my being that I had to see her again.

And, as soon as I knew it, I wondered why I hadn't thought of it before. I'd thought that the phone call — hearing her voice knowing that Dad had fathered a child with her — would have been enough. I'd wanted her to know that I knew; that she no longer had one up on me, a secret over me. But it hadn't been enough. The curiosity demons inside me weren't sated; now I knew who she was, they wanted to see this woman properly; to look at her, to talk to her, to try to see what Dad had seen in her. I hadn't taken in a lot when I'd seen her outside the church. Did she get dimples when she smiled? What did her laugh sound like? What exactly was it about her that had snared my father all those years ago? Had she loved Dad? Had she seriously expected him to leave Mum?

But how could I see her? Zoe was, after all, the 'other' woman—the woman with whom Dad had betrayed Mum. It was seedier than anything I'd ever imagined would happen in our family, and to make any sort of contact with her made me feel like I, too, was betraying Mum.

I re-plumped the pillow and sighed. To plan a meeting seemed too deceitful. I would drive down to her house. I would park outside and I would look at the house in which my half-brother had grown up. And then I would knock at the door and take my chances. If it was meant to be, she'd be in. Happy with my decision, I fell into the deep sleep of the decided.

CHAPTER 48

Luca drove a small, black hatchback. I waited like a teenager, curtains twitching, for him to arrive then, as soon as he drew up outside, I opened the door, shouted bye to Mum, and crunched across the gravel. When I'd messaged Luca at breakfast with the news that I'd decided to go down to Zoe's house, he'd called me back immediately, insisting on driving me down to Maidstone himself. 'However it goes—and you have to prepare for the fact that it might not go well, Evie—it's going to be emotional,' he'd said. 'Better you've got someone with you. And I'm free.'

Now, he jumped out of his car and came around to greet me, holding me by the elbows as he kissed me firmly on both cheeks.

'How are you? Are you sure you want to do this?'

I nodded. I wanted to see where Tom had grown up, I wanted to see Zoe, and, after my night-time realisation, I wanted it now. I knew I could have called her first, agreed a suitable time, but I also didn't mind catching her unawares, seeing what her spontaneous reaction would be. I have to admit, it wasn't the best thought out of plans and I was glad Luca would be with me.

Luca pulled me into a little hug. 'Good girl. I'll be there. Don't be nervous.'

He opened the passenger door for me with a flourish and stood back to let me climb in and I felt a little *frisson*, the flutter of the tiniest butterfly. Getting into a car with Luca brought back almost visceral memories of when we'd been dating. He'd barely had his licence back then but he'd sometimes managed to borrow his dad's Audi to take me out on special occasions. An image from my seventeenth birthday popped into my head: Luca, in a suit, picking me up for my birthday dinner in Bromley. I remembered that he'd held the door for me then exactly the same way as he was doing now.

The car smelled subtly of his cologne—the same citrus blend as the other night. He was wearing jeans, a sweater and a battered leather jacket. His tough-looking brown leather shoes were muddy. My tummy fizzed.

'I've come straight from shooting over the river,' Luca said. His eyes slid towards me for a nanosecond and I knew what he was thinking: I, too, remembered the lazy, sensual afternoons we'd spent by the river when we were dating. Just us on a picnic blanket in the sunshine, kissing. I didn't meet his gaze, but I felt my cheeks heat up and I turned away.

'I got some great shots,' Luca said, his eyes back on the road, his voice steady. 'The light at dawn is just incredible as the orange spills over the horizon and reflects off the water. The swans were out, too, which was an unexpected bonus. I love it when they're there. They're so majestic.'

I smiled weakly. My mind was not on swans.

'Thanks for doing this, Luca,' I said, trying to bring my mind back to the present and the task that lay ahead.

'Any time, Evie. Do you mind if we just drop my equipment off at my flat first? I'd rather not drive around with it all in the back unless I have to. I've got the tripod today. It'll only take a couple of minutes extra?'

'Sure,' I said.

Luca lived in a one-bedroom apartment near the station. The building hadn't been there when I last lived in Woodside and its modern shape stuck out from the redbrick terraces that surrounded it. The awkwardness returned as Luca parked the car.

'You coming in?' he asked.

I bent down in the car and fiddled in my handbag to give myself time to think. I didn't need to go in but curiosity got the better of me. I picked up my bag and stepped out of the car.

Carefully avoiding any body contact with Luca, I followed him into the lobby. I was relieved he ignored the lift and headed straight for the stairs. 'Take the lift if you want—fifth floor. I always do the stairs—saves me going to the gym!' I followed him up the stairs, though nowhere near as fast, my nostrils flaring with the effort. The stale smell of old food hung heavy in the air of the stairwell. I carved my way through it, trying not to breathe too deeply.

Luca's front door opened straight into a small hallway. Ahead and to the right, I could see the door to what must be his bedroom. I pressed a hand to my chest.

'Unfit!' I wheezed.

Luca laughed and led me left into a bright and airy open-plan room. At one end was a small kitchen area with glossy white units and a small dining table, which had nothing but a notepad and a pen on it; at the other, a reasonable-sized living room. It was surprisingly clean and I wondered if there was a girlfriend around to help, or if he kept it that way himself. My eyes flicked around, found no evidence of a resident female.

The floor was oak parquet and two sets of French windows not only let in masses of light but looked out over a huge terrace. The décor was a tasteful blend of style and comfort, with more than a nod to Ikea. Luca's sofa was a modern, minimalist piece in black leather and chrome — not my taste, but very masculine — and white walls formed the perfect backdrop for a gallery of what I presumed was his photographic work.

While Luca went off to store his tripod in his bedroom, I looked at his photographs. He definitely had a talent for capturing the moment — all the pictures were in black and white; some were of his friends, some of landscapes, but the uniting theme was the play of dark and shadow on un-expected angles.

'Do you like them?' Luca was back.

'Gorgeous photographs. I was just looking… you really have a gift.'

'Thanks.'

'Nice flat, too.' I smiled at him. He used to say my smile was my best feature and now I gave him my brightest, mega-watt beam.

'I bought at the right time.' Luca smiled back, then looked away, modest. 'It's already worth more than I paid. I'm hoping to sell it on for something bigger one day. Do you want to see outside?'

He didn't need to ask twice. I felt the heat of his body as he leaned past me to unlock the terrace doors. Together, we stepped out onto a huge terrace.

'Wow,' I breathed, spinning around with my arms held out. 'It's massive! You can see for miles.' There was almost a 180-degree view of the surrounding area. 'It's so... liberating!'

'I know. I love it up here.' Luca walked over to the edge and looked into the distance. He talked into the sky. 'I feel like I can get away from the world. I sit here on summer evenings with a glass of wine and read. Sometimes there's still enough light at nine-thirty.'

'It's gorgeous.'

'It is, isn't it? Best bit of the flat. That and the fact I can be at the station in two minutes. Right... come on.' He jangled his keys. 'Enough property viewing. Let's hit that crazy motorway.

*

Zoe lived in the outskirts of Maidstone. After a couple of false starts, we finally turned into her road. Luca slowed down so I could scan the house fronts for number sixty-eight.

And, there it was: an unassuming semi at the end of a quiet residential street. Cars were parked bumper to bumper down one side of the road—none of the houses had garages or driveways. Zoe's house was painted white in contrast to the neighbour's beige brickwork. Its gutters stood out in black, its roof was tidy and well maintained. Three windows faced the street—two upstairs and one larger one downstairs—and a path down the side of the house led to the front door. The tiny patch of front garden was paved over but neat, a wooden bench parked under the window—a spot from which to catch the sun maybe. It looked like there might be a larger garden at the rear and I thought I could just make out the top of a conservatory. I wondered if Tom had grown up here. If this had been the landscape of my brother's childhood. I felt sorry that he hadn't known his father; sad that my own upbringing had probably been richer, in so many ways.

'So,' said Luca. 'How does it feel?'

Weird. Weird was how it felt, to be sitting in a car looking at the house in which my dad's ex-mistress had lived with my half-brother for, presumably, the past twenty years— although I was just guessing that bit. Maybe Zoe and Tom had started out somewhere smaller, an apartment. Had Dad bought the house for her?

Luca interrupted my thoughts with a discreet cough. 'Are you sure you want to see her? We can just go now you've seen the house. No pressure.'

I did want to see Zoe—so badly—and, yet, I didn't. I didn't know what I'd say to her. I had so many questions, I didn't know where to start. Maybe I needed to plan a strategy before announcing myself to her. But, sitting here faced with her house, I had to try.

'Do you mind waiting?'

'No problem. If it's going well, and you think you'll be ages, just drop me a quick text and I'll wait in town. Otherwise, I'll be here.'

I opened the car door, got out and walked slowly up the front path to the door, concentrating on putting one foot in front of the other. I stood for a second, then picked up the heavy brass knocker and let it drop back onto the door. The rap sounded like a gunshot; a handful of birds exploded into the air from nearby trees, wings flapping. I tried to hang on to the fact that I'd met Zoe before — I'd met her and I'd liked her.

No response. I knocked again, louder this time. More confident.

No reply. Seriously, she was out? Logic left me; the fact that I'd come unannounced left me. All I could think was that I'd come all this way after twenty years and she was out. Bitterly disappointed, I walked back down the path to Luca's car, all the while straining for the sound of the door being opened behind me. Perhaps she'd been in the loo?

'No reply,' I said. 'She's out.'

Luca tried to rally, but he looked as defeated as I felt.

'At least you tried. We'll come back another time. Maybe on a weekend? I don't mind.'

I fastened my seat belt, looking back at the house. Did I imagine a shadow in the upstairs window?

'Thanks so much for bringing me here, Luca,' I said. 'I really appreciate it. Maybe we can get a coffee or something so it's not a completely wasted trip?' Then I remembered that he had work; new photos he presumably needed to download and process. I didn't want to be a nuisance. 'I mean, if you've got time?'

'Sure,' he said and a plan, as yet unformed, pushed its way into my head; a maggot of a thought popping through the apple's skin. A way that maybe, just maybe, I could get to see my half-brother in the flesh.

'There's a café in town called Harry's,' I said. 'Maybe we could go there?'

'Sure,' he said.

CHAPTER 49

Harry's Café was easy to find. Clearly the *café du jour* with Maidstone's coffee-drinking set, it had a prominent position on the High Street and looked, in the flesh, just as it had on the website: white shutters, white window frames, a neat awning, 'Harry's' painted in black italics. Luca paused, his hand on the door, and turned back to look at me.

'Come on! I thought you said you wanted to try this place?'

I'd stopped further back on the pavement, my courage on strike. Luca cocked his head and looked closely at me. His eyes narrowed, then he nodded.

'Is there something you're not telling me, Miss Stevens?'

I bit my lip and looked at the pavement. Luca came over, bent down so his head was below mine, and looked up into my face. 'I know you, Evie Stevens. I used to know you better than you knew yourself. And I know there's something going on. What is it?'

He looked so funny upside down I had to laugh. I pushed him away.

'Look, it might be that someone I know works here.'

'Someone like who?'

I stared at Luca, one eyebrow raised, willing him to guess.

'Oh God.' Luca slapped his forehead. 'Oh, don't tell me, Evie. Someone who could maybe, for example, be your half-brother?'

'Got it in one.' I turned on my heel and started walking away. 'Anyway, it's all academic. I can't do it. Let's go to Prêt.'

Luca ran after me, grabbed my arm and spun me around. I looked anywhere but at him.

'Look at me, Evie.' He gave me a little shake. 'We've come all this way. You didn't see the mum. You have the perfect chance to see Tom. He won't even know who you are.'

'Nope.'

'OK, let's try this. Imagine going home without having seen him. Come on.' He pulled me in the direction of the car park. 'Come on, we're going. "Bye Maidstone. Bye Tom. Was nice not-quite seeing you." How does that feel?'

'Oh, Luca.'

'How does it feel, Evie?' His voice softened and he brushed a wisp of hair off my face, tucked it behind my ear. 'We can just nip in and get a takeout if you like. You don't have to sit there and gaze at him for half a day. Two minutes max. He might not even be there. What do you say?'

My nod was almost imperceptible. 'Just a takeout.'

'OK, great. I'm gasping for a coffee. Come on.' Luca turned back towards the door. I hurried to catch up with him.

'Hold my hand,' I whispered.

*

Luca pushed the door, a bell jangled overhead, and then we were inside the warm fug of the café. The scent of coffee and toasted panini made my mouth water. Luca squeezed my hand and I hesitated behind him, feeling suddenly sick.

Despite the fact that there were two other young men working, I saw Tom at once. Standing behind the counter, he was taller and broader than I'd imagined from the photos — at least six feet tall — and, although he had curly brown hair, he looked far less like Graham in real life than he'd done in the pictures. Would I really have recognised him in the street? I flicked a look around the café: two young guys were waiting tables. One was blond and the other Asian. Yes, assuming Tom was working today, this had to be him.

He was flirting with an old lady he was serving, laughing and joking with her as he pressed the coffee into the espresso maker and steamed the milk.

'Is that him?' Luca whispered. I nodded. He squeezed my hand and I leaned into him, as if his strength could transfer to me through his jacket sleeve. Together, hands clasped, we walked over to the counter, over to Tom. We waited our turn.

Finally, the lady tore herself away and Luca and I faced Tom directly.

'Morning,' said Tom. He looked from Luca to me and back. I stared. He looked more like Graham when he smiled. It was like seeing a ghost. 'What can I get you?'

'Two Americanos to take away,' Luca said. I barely heard: I was focusing on Tom's name badge. Despite everything, it didn't say 'Tom', it said 'Sebastian'. It couldn't be. I was so sure this man was my brother. I looked around the shop again, strained to see into the kitchens as the door flipped open. While Tom's back was turned, I nudged Luca and jabbed my finger at my chest.

'Badge!' I hissed.

Tom turned back and placed the two coffees on the counter between us. 'Milk, sugar, blah-di-blahs all over there.' He pointed to another counter. 'Four ninety.' His voice brought an image of Dad to my mind.

'Let me get this,' said Luca to me, not that I'd moved to get my purse. He rummaged in his pocket and pulled out a handful of pound coins.

'Sebastian,' he said thoughtfully, running the word through his lips. 'Got a kid brother called that. So, are you a Bastian or a Seb?'

Tom twisted his badge up so he could see it. 'Oh God, no. He's done it again, the idiot. No. This is my mate's badge. He likes to swap them. Thinks it's hilarious to confuse the old ladies. No, no. I'm Tom.'

'Oh well.' Luca shrugged. 'Neither a Bastian nor a Seb. Nice to meet you, anyways, Tom.' Luca picked up the coffees. 'Come on, Evie. Places to see, things to do.'

At the door, I turned and looked back. Tom was still looking at us. He raised a hand in a static wave.

*

I floated out of the café, light and free, like I had a thousand helium balloons tied to my shoulders. I'd done it. I'd seen my half-brother and the world hadn't stopped turning.

Luca and I sat with our coffees in the park. It was cold but sunny and we perched side by side on a wall like a pair of oversized crows. I couldn't stop smiling. I also couldn't stop gabbling. It was all I could do to sit still. My entire body jiggled with energy.

'He seems so nice! He was so much taller than I thought! I can see Dad in him. Did you see my dad in him? Do you think Graham would have looked like that when he was older? Do you think he knows about me?' It was a monologue: replies not required. When I finally ground to a halt, I looked over at Luca. He was drinking his coffee, a study of patience. I leaned into him and kissed his cold cheek.

'Sorry,' I said. 'I'm just excited. Thanks so much for doing that. And for the "Sebastian" thing.'

'You're welcome.' Luca turned to look at me. 'But you knew, didn't you? You knew it was him? He has your smile.'

'Oh I don't know. I thought I knew, but then I wasn't sure. The name thing really threw me. But looking back, it was obvious it was him.'

'Er… yes! So. Glad you did it?'

'Glad you made me do it, you mean?'

'Glad I made you do it?'

'Yes. Thank you. I really appreciate it.' I shivered and he put his arm around me, giving my back a brisk rub.

'You're welcome, Evie. Now can you sleep well tonight?'

'I hope so.'

'Forgotten about Zoe?'

The funny thing was I had. Now I'd seen Tom with my

own eyes, meeting her seemed less important. I was on fire
with the idea of having a secret half-brother. It was like
having a bit of Graham back, as well as a bit of Dad.

'Yep.' I swirled my coffee in the cup. I'd still only had one
sip. 'I still can't believe he made me this. My brother—who
I didn't know existed till two days ago—made me a coffee.'
I shook my head. 'God! It's so bizarre.'

'He makes a mean coffee,' said Luca.

'I want to see him again,' I said. The words fell out of
my mouth before I really thought about them. But as soon
as they were out I knew it was what I wanted.

'What?'

'I want to go back.' Having got over my fear of seeing
Tom, having walked into the café without the world falling
apart, I was like a child who discovers a new skill: I wanted
to do it over and over again. I could see myself sitting there
with the papers, watching Tom surreptitiously.

'Well,' said Luca slowly. 'Now's probably not a great
time. I'd give it a while. So it doesn't look odd. Or are you
going to admit who you are?'

'No. I can't do that. Not while he's at work. That wouldn't
be fair.'

We were quiet for a minute, alone with our thoughts. I
could hear the roar of distant traffic, but the air in the park
itself was still. We were the only people there.

'So, how's your mum?' Luca asked.

'Oh, I dunno. Up and down and round about. I suppose
it's par for the course.'

Luca nodded. 'It'll take time. Did you ever get in touch

with that uncle, by the way? You know, the mad one in the tower?' He was referring to conversations we used to have at school when we tried to guess what Uncle David must have done to make Mum so angry.

I laughed. 'He's not mad. Well, maybe he is. I've still no idea why he and Mum don't speak, but yes. Yes, I wrote to him. A proper letter! I thought it was only fair to tell him about Dad. He lives in Oxford, by the way. Not in a tower.' I laughed.

'Interesting. I wonder if he'll get back to you. It'd be cool to find out what they fought about. I bet it's something really mundane. Like she got more pocket money than him. Or he beheaded her Barbie doll or something.'

'It happened as adults, you muppet.' I shoved my elbow into Luca's side. 'Kids living in the same house can't be estranged from each other.'

'You should have lived in my house,' said Luca. He stood up and held out his arm for me. 'Shall we? I'm freezing my brass monkeys off here.'

We strolled slowly back into town, stopping only to look in the windows of estate agents.

'Wow,' I breathed, 'look at that one!'

'Bagsie this one,' Luca said, pointing out an even more extravagant mansion in the Kent countryside. 'Seriously, can you imagine living in a place like that? Swimming pool, gym, tennis courts, basement cinema, media room, stables, riding arena… all it needs is a private airstrip.'

'Perfect for you and your girlfriend,' I said.

'Oh yes, the lovely Miss Non-Existent,' said Luca. 'Evie,

meet my invisible girlfriend.' He bowed at the empty pavement. 'I love her to bits.'

'Because she never says anything?' I asked, deadpan. 'So that's how a girl gets to keep you.'

Luca went to poke me in the ribs, but I scampered away. 'I think you'll find it was you who dumped me. Actually. If we're telling the truth here.'

'Terribly sorry about that,' I said, offering my arm to him. 'You should have tried harder.' I gave him a cheeky wink and he dodged after me and grabbed my arm, linking his through it.

'Come on,' he said. 'Let's walk.'

'So tell me, Mister Rossi,' I said, after we'd strolled a little down the street, stopping here and there to peer into more shop windows. 'Did I leave you so damaged you've never dated anyone since?'

Luca patted my arm patronisingly. 'In your dreams, short stuff.'

'No... seriously?'

He sighed. 'There was someone...'

'Just the one?' I teased.

'Actually, yes. Just the one.'

'Really?'

'Yes, really. Is that so strange? I met her at university. We were together for nine years.'

'I'm sorry. What happened?' They must have split up within the last year or so.

'Oh... y'know. We grew apart.' Luca fell silent. I looked at him, waiting for more. His mouth moved as he searched for the right words. 'I guess she fell in love with someone who was going to be a lawyer. But what she actually got, after all that time, wasn't a high-rolling legal hotshot but a penniless photographer.'

'Seriously?' I didn't want to say how shallow she sounded.

'That's probably the essence in a nutshell. Though it took an awful lot of fighting to work that out.'

'I'm sorry.'

'Don't be.'

'And there's been no one since?'

'Let's just say nothing I'm proud of. If you know what I mean.' Luca grimaced. I nodded. We walked on. Coffee segued into lunch.

CHAPTER 50

I was thinking about Luca as I unlocked the front door
later that afternoon. I'd enjoyed spending time with him;
he'd always been good company and I felt that he understood me better than most of my Dubai friends. I loved
that he took the mickey out of me and didn't stand for any
nonsense. I loved that he knew me so well.

What was interesting me most, though, as I pushed open
the door, was the lingering kiss I'd given him in the car
just now. It had taken him completely by surprise, though
perhaps not by as much as it had me. As we'd pulled up in
the driveway and I'd remembered my cold, lonely arrival
from Dubai the other week, I'd suddenly felt overwhelmed
with gratitude to Luca for taking me to Maidstone, for
being with me when I saw Tom for the first time and for
being my friend when I so badly needed one. Before I'd
even had time to think about it, I'd leaned across and
touched my mouth to his. There'd been a fraction of a
second when his eyes had caught mine in surprise, and
a delicious pause while it had seemed the most natural
thing in the world to be sitting in a car kissing Luca Rossi,
but then I'd broken the moment, scrambling from the car

before he'd had a chance to say anything. I put my fingers to my lips now as I unlocked the door, remembering the familiar taste of him.

Perhaps if I hadn't been thinking about that, I'd have noticed the pile of stuffed bin bags stacked just inside the front door. Instead, I fell over them, landing awkwardly on my knees. The floor near the door was almost entirely taken up with bin bags, their tops neatly tied into rabbit ears. Rubbing my knees, I realised Mum must have tackled her wardrobe—she'd been saying forever that she wanted to throw out some of her older and more dated clothes. I hadn't realised how much she had that she didn't wear.

'Yoo-hoo! Is that you, darling? I'm upstairs!' came Mum's voice.

'Yes! Just me!' Who else had a key? I threw my coat over the bannister and padded up the stairs into Mum's room, expecting to see her trying on some ludicrous golfing outfit, but I stopped dead when I saw the chaos within. The carpet was an ocean of bin bags. Drawers were open, the wardrobe doors were open, piles of trousers, jumpers, shirts and ties were laid out on the bed. Stuffed suit carriers dangled from the picture rail. But none of it was Mum's: every single item was Dad's. Mum was throwing away his things. I stopped short in the doorway, my hand over my mouth. Mum straightened up.

'Goodness!' she said. 'Your father had a lot of stuff he never used! Who knew he had so many jumpers? He only ever wore the same ratty one! Remember?' She held up Dad's familiar old grey jumper for me to see—the one with

the leather patches on the elbows—then shoved it into the
nearest bin bag. 'Won't be sad to see the last of that!'

Maybe she saw, then, the look on my face because she
continued, her voice artificially bright, trilling, 'I decided
to go through all his stuff, darling. It's not as if Graham's
around to take it, is it? And there's no point in me moving
it all to the new house. There's so little storage space there
anyway, and what would I do with all this? Far better the
charity shops make use of it.'

'But, Mum,' I started. But Mum what? I didn't know
what to say. She was right. She had no use for this stuff,
but I didn't like the way she was throwing it all out without
consulting me. Did she need to consult me? Probably not.
But I'd have liked to have been involved, liked to have
looked through Dad's things with her, chosen a keepsake
or two. It could have been something we'd done together,
mother and daughter, remembering as we went through
Dad's things for the last time. I reached into one of the open
bin bags, pulling out a small box: cufflinks. The silver ones
I'd bought for Father's Day when I was sixteen. I'd saved
my Saturday job wages to get those. A sob caught in my
throat. 'Mum! How could you? You know I bought these!
What else have you thrown out?'

'Put them back, Evie. We're not going to keep them.
Everything's going. I've decided that's how I want it. Now
put them back!'

I should have recognised the brittleness in her voice, but
I was too upset to notice. I pulled Dad's wallet out of the
bag. 'You're throwing this away? How could you?' He'd

had the wallet as long as I could remember. It was tatty, but it was the essence of Dad, part of his identity. I touched the leather, imagined it in Dad's hands.

'I'm warning you, Evie.'

I put the wallet on the bed and reached back into the bag. Wham! Mum's hand connected with my cheek in a slap that echoed around the room. Then silence. The world seemed to stop as we stared at each other—me in shock; her in unconcealed fury. Mum hadn't hit me since I was a child. I raised my hand to my cheek, already feeling the blood rushing to the skin's surface, my cheek starting to throb.

'I warned you, Evie,' she said. 'I told you not to.' There was no apology in her voice, no sign of regret at what she'd done. She walked over to the window, wrestled the catch open and slid up the sash as far as it would go. Purposefully, she walked back to the bag I'd been looking at, tied the top, heaved it to the window, balanced it on the ledge, then shoved it out onto the gravel below. I ran to the window.

'Mum, no!'

But she was on a mission. I struggled to close the window, but she shoved me aside.

'Get out of my way!' She lifted her hand as if to strike me again and I dodged backwards. Moving faster now, she started grabbing things and lobbing them out of the window. 'Happy, Evie? I mean it! Just watch me! It's all going! All of it! I'm keeping nothing! Everything's going! And don't you *dare* try to stop me!'

I watched, unable to move, as my father's possessions were jettisoned out of the window. His tuxedo—the one he'd put on for the awards ceremony he'd never made it to—his work shoes, his slippers, his glasses, photos in frames, a dusty box of birthday cards from me—Mum was merciless.

'Mum, please! They're mine! Let me keep them!' I ran over and tried to grab the box of cards from her. 'Let go!' I shouted. 'They're mine! You've no right!'

'No! Get out!' Mum shouted. 'It's none of your business!'

We wrestled with the box until the ancient cardboard split and cards rained all over the carpet, my childish handwriting visible. Mum scooped them up and Frisbeed them out of the window by the handful.

'Mum! You don't know what you're doing! These are my memories too! You're upset! Stop it!'

'Don't try to stop me, Evie! I'm warning you!'

Our eyes locked and I saw it was no use: she was insane. Stifling a sob, I scraped up the few cards I could and left the room clutching them to my chest.

'You've no idea!' she screamed after me, her voice rising even higher. 'No idea!'

*

When I finally ventured downstairs, long after the last light had faded from the sky, I found Mum asleep on the sofa, an empty glass next to her on the side table. I didn't need to smell it to know she'd had a whisky; it was her usual evening tipple. Her mouth was slightly open and she was snoring quiet little snores. Grabbing bin bags from under the stairs, I crept past the living room door and out to the driveway, where I started gathering up Dad's things from the places where they'd landed: on the rose bushes, in the flowerbeds, on the gravel, in the hedge.

I picked up every last thing I could find, packing it all into bin bags, which I dragged around the side of the house, out of sight from passers-by. When I finally went back inside, Mum was no longer on the sofa. I smelled onions frying—she was in the kitchen. I didn't want to talk to her; I had nothing to say and I felt the onus was on her to apologise, to make the first move. I turned on the television, got out my knitting and waited, paying absolutely no attention to the screen. My fingers moved fast in the rhythm I found so calming. As the needles clicked and new rows appeared, my mind was going in circles: how would Mum and I move forward from this? It was a hurdle almost too big to negotiate.

'Dinner!' called Mum. My fingers stopped moving, but I kept holding the knitting. I sat completely still. I hadn't anticipated this: I'd thought Mum would come over to me, full of remorse. Maybe bring us a couple of drinks, apologise. My cheek still smarted.

'Did you hear me, darling? Dinner!' I heard Mum put the plates on the table, pull out her chair, uncork the wine, pour it into two glasses.

I sighed. I didn't have the luxury of a big family; of others behind whom I could hide. I put down the knitting and went to the downstairs bathroom, where I splashed cold water on my face and washed my hands. Then I took a deep breath and headed for the dining room. If she wasn't going to face this head on, I was.

'Care to explain what that was all about?' My voice was clipped, controlled.

Mum looked me in the eye. 'I was clearing out, Evie. It's what you do when people die.' Her tone was that of a primary school teacher explaining something to a class of five-year-olds. 'It helps you move on.' She picked up her glass. 'Cheers.'

We ate in silence.

*

I was woken in the night by my phone buzzing underneath my pillow. I'd set the alarm for 2 a.m. but, really, I needn't have bothered because I'd lain awake since midnight. Silently, and by the light of my phone screen, I got dressed and padded downstairs.

Letting myself quietly out of the kitchen door, I went round the side of the house and retrieved the bin bags from where I'd left them. I held my breath as I turned the key in the conservatory door, the click sounding way too loud for the time of night. I waited a moment, listening intently for sounds from upstairs, then quickly pulled the bags inside. The conservatory was at the back of the house — crucially, it was completely out of sight of Mum's room. I'd be able to sit in it with the light on and go through everything bag by bag. It wasn't my ideal scenario, but I didn't see what other choice I had.

*

It was nearly 4 a.m. when I retied the last bag. I hadn't

taken much stuff—certainly none of Dad's clothes—but
I was happy with what I'd managed to salvage. I now
had Dad's old-fashioned SLR camera with its boxes of
additional lenses; his silver business card holder with a
few of his old business cards; just for memory's sake, his
wallet; his watch; the box of birthday cards I'd sent him;
the cufflinks I'd bought him and a couple of pairs of his
favourite ones. I'd also retrieved all of the family photos
from the broken frames.

As I sorted through the bags, it had occurred to me that,
if I met Tom and things went well with him, he might also
want something of his father's so I put aside Dad's watch,
a good pair of cufflinks and a couple of photos for him, too.
It seemed like a long shot, Tom probably wouldn't want
anything, given he'd never known Dad, but it seemed only
right that I offer.

When I was completely done, I carried the bags back
into the front hall, and stacked them neatly there, ready to
take to the charity shop. I didn't want to leave them outside
because the foxes had a habit of ripping open bin bags: the
last thing I wanted was Dad's things strewn all over the
garden a second time.

Finally, I locked up then I took the stuff I'd saved upstairs
with me. I put it carefully into my suitcase, locked the case
and hid the key.

*

In what little of the night was left, I dreamed about Graham.
We were out on our bikes. Even in the dream, I knew how

it ended: dread lurched in my stomach as we cycled up to the crossing. It was a dangerous spot as cars came flying off the roundabout on the dual carriageway, so we pressed the button for the pedestrian crossing and waited not just until the traffic light was red, but until the pedestrian man was green, just like Dad had taught us.

Then we kicked off from the kerb and, even in the dream, I knew that something bad was about to happen. The speeding BMW came from nowhere, shooting around the corner so fast that no one had a chance to react. As I watched, Graham was tossed in the air, thrown thirty metres down the road, his body landing back on the tarmac with the dull crunching thud of flesh and breaking bones.

Tonight the dream was different to usual: when I rushed over, it wasn't Graham lying on the tarmac. It was Tom. I woke pinned to the bed, my limbs useless and glazed in sweat, the image of another broken brother imprinted on my mind.

'Tom,' I whispered into the darkness.

CHAPTER 51

I was tired when I woke later that morning. Tired, and nervous of what the day would bring. Ideally, I wanted an apology from a contrite and sane mother, though I didn't fancy my chances—apologies for emotional outbursts were not the Stevens family's style. We Stevenses were like ostriches: heads in sand as far as they would go. Sighing deeply, I rolled over and stared at the curtains, wishing I could climb out of my window and run away without having to see Mum. In fact, I wished I could keep on running, all the way to the airport.

But, much as I might dream about running back to my little life in Dubai, there were three things that were keeping me in Woodside: Mum's behaviour—conversely, the more unhinged she acted, the more I felt I couldn't just leave her; Luca—I smiled to myself as I thought about Luca; and Tom. I needed to see my new brother again. Not to talk to—just to see. Harry's Café was like a beacon to me. I had to go back.

With another sigh, I dragged myself up and wrapped myself in my dressing gown before treading carefully down the stairs, listening all the while for signs of my mother. Although the scent of coffee hung in the air, the house felt

empty. I padded through the living room. There was no
Mum, but a note lay on the kitchen counter.

'Thanks for clearing up outside. I've got to hit some balls
at the club. Back after lunch. Mum xx'. She'd even drawn
a smiley face.

'Aaargh!' I shouted at the note. I scrumpled it up and
hurled it across the kitchen.

*

Later that morning I pushed open the door of Harry's Café
and stopped in my tracks: far from being the quiet haven in
which I'd imagined myself reading the paper, the café had
been ambushed by a mother-and-toddler group. They'd
taken over almost every table I could see. Pushchairs
blocked every available space; Lilliputian children ran
around between tables; the noise level was unbelievable. I
hesitated. Coming back to Harry's had seemed like a good
idea two hours ago when I'd stepped out of the shower, my
head full of steam, but I wasn't so sure now. I felt a touch
on my arm.

'Looking for a table?' It was a waiter—the blond guy,
Sebastian I guessed, with a tray of dirty cups balanced in
one hand.

'I guess,' I said, shrugging at the chaos.

'Here, follow me.'

With a glance back at the door, I took a deep breath and
followed him through the maze of high chairs, buggies, toys
and toddlers to a small table by the window. I could see his
badge now. He was indeed the real Sebastian.

'I'll just clear it for you. Gimme a sec.' Sebastian loaded the cups from the table onto his tray, disappeared off to the kitchen, then reappeared with a cloth. I stood awkwardly next to the table while he gave it a quick wipe.

'There you go. I'll send someone over to take your order.'

'Cheers.' I looked around quickly. I couldn't see Tom in all the disarray. I pulled out my iPad and the newspaper, arranged them on the table, put my bag on the other chair, rearranged the iPad and the newspaper, picked up the iPad, remembered it wasn't connected, put it down and picked up the menu. It could have been the weather report. Nothing registered. A shadow fell over me.

'What can I get you?' I knew without looking that it was Tom. Hiding behind my hair, I pointed to the menu. 'An Americano, please. And a palmier. If you've got them?'

Only then did I look up, a stiff smile pasted on my lips. I'd gurned to myself a block away from Harry's this morning, trying to loosen my facial muscles from the nerves that had threatened to paralyse them. Tom was standing over me, pen scribbling over the order pad.

'Oh hello!' he said. 'Welcome back!'

'Thanks,' I mumbled. There was a pause.

'Eating in today?' he said.

'Yep. I have some work to do.'

'Great.' Another pause. 'Well. I'll bring you over a Wi-Fi token. You get an hour.' He lowered his voice. 'Ask me if you need more.'

'Thanks.' He walked away. Even his walk was like Dad's. I pulled my eyes off him.

*

Even without looking, I knew precisely where Tom was all morning. You could have spun me around blindfolded and I'd still have been able to point him out. When he moved behind me, the hairs on the back of my neck stood on end. But my not looking didn't last long. My eyes slid back and followed him around.

He did his job gracefully, moving fluidly around the café taking orders, getting bills, taking money and returning change. He clearly enjoyed chatting with the customers, and the mums loved him. I cringed to see the way they exchanged glances with each other and acted coy, twirling their hair around their fingers, and beaming at him, all teeth, lashes and lips. 'Get your claws out of my brother!' I wanted to shout to them. 'Pick on someone your own age!' It was strange to feel protective.

After an hour, I closed the iPad, the Wi-Fi token expired. The café had quietened considerably. The coffee-morning mums had gathered their belongings and left as one, as if they'd been sucked through the door by an enormous vacuum cleaner. I watched Tom buzzing about, gathering crockery and cutlery, reuniting chairs with tables, mopping spills and restacking high chairs in the corner. There was something about the way he moved that reminded me not only of Dad, but of Graham. I half shut my eyes and looked obliquely at him: it was like seeing Graham's ghost grown up. Tom caught me looking and smiled.

Wi-Fi? he mouthed across the tables.

I nodded. He disappeared behind the counter then came

over, acting as if he were on some sort of stealth mission. He looked around, eyes wide, and leapt theatrically between the tables. Sebastian, behind the till, rolled his eyes, clearly used to such behaviour. Eventually Tom made it to my table and tucked the slip of paper under the salt cellar.

'Don't tell everyone!' he whispered *sotto voce.* 'I could be forced to work *in the kitchen*!'

'OK!' I whispered back. Tom looked around again with wild eyes and made his way back across the café. I smiled to myself, feeling old in the face of his teenage jinks.

At midday, I looked up again, the newspaper finished and the iPad battery threatening imminent death. The café was starting to fill up with customers once more, but Tom saw at once, and walked towards me, normally this time.

'Can I get you anything else? Some lunch?'

'No… no, I'm good, thanks. Just the bill.'

'Sure.' He nodded at the iPad. My Twitter page was open. 'You on Twitter?'

'Yeah. It's kind of handy. I live abroad. It's a good way to stay in touch with friends and family. Not that I have much family. Small family. No siblings.' Stop blabbering, Evie. I rubbed my hands together vigorously then steepled them in front of my mouth to hide my nervousness as much as to shut myself up.

'Where do you live?' Tom asked, writing out my bill and placing it on the table.

'Dubai.'

'Wow. I have family there.'

I froze. 'Really?'

'Yeah. Never been, though.'

'Why not?'

'Oh…' His eyes hooked into mine and I couldn't look away. Time stretched, went saggy in the middle, like chewing gum pulled between shoe and pavement. 'Long story,' he said eventually. 'It's complicated.'

Silence. Breathe, Evie. Breathe. 'You should go,' I said faintly. I fumbled in my purse, put money on the table. 'It's a nice place. For holidays.'

'I'd love to go,' said Tom.

'You should. Just avoid the summer. It's hot.'

'When's a good time?'

'April. October.'

'OK. Cool. I'll start saving.' He picked up the money.

'Bye then,' he said.

'Bye.'

*

Dazed, I stepped out of the warmth of the café and into the cold air, wrapping my scarf about me as I went. What had just happened between Tom and me? Although we'd only made small talk, I felt like a completely different conversation had transpired without words; a whole different layer of communication had taken place. I slumped against the wall of the neighbouring shop.

But then, a commotion to the side; the clatter of the café door opening, banging back on its frame, the jangle of the bell and a loud shout: 'Evie! Wait!'

I snapped to attention, turned towards the shout. Tom, in

his barista's apron, stood in the doorway of Harry's Café, his arm raised and his mouth still open. He stared at me and I stood on the pavement and stared back at him. The world — the buses, the people, the cars, the shops — it all fell away. It was just my half-brother and me on the pavement staring at each other. Did he feel the pull? Did he know? Looking into his eyes it was impossible that we were not related. I was Alice falling down the rabbit hole. Was Tom falling, too?

He took a step towards me, letting go of the door, which swung shut behind him.

'Yes?' I said, my voice a croak.

The moment broken, he passed a hand through his hair then took a step towards me. 'Sorry,' he said. 'It is Evie, isn't it?'

I nodded.

He opened his mouth, then closed it again. Started to say something and stopped.

'What is it?' I said.

'I… I just…' He shook his head, running his hand through his hair again. 'I'm sorry. I made a mistake. I thought I gave you the wrong change. But no. You're all right.' He turned back towards the café.

'You know, don't you?' I said, not knowing where my voice came from; how I found the courage to say perhaps the bravest four words I'd ever said.

Tom turned slowly back to me, his eyes burning into my soul. 'Yes,' he said. 'I do. I hoped you'd get in touch.'

CHAPTER 52

I realised that Tom was holding out his hand to me. I took it in my own, hyper-aware of the dry warmth of it and we shook hands like business associates.

'Nice to meet you,' said my half-brother.

'Nice to meet you, too,' I said, feeling absurd. We let our hands drop and there was a silence.

'I'm sorry,' I said finally. 'This is a bit surreal. I hadn't expected this at all. I don't know what to say.' Tears suddenly sprung into my eyes and I brushed at them, embarrassed. 'Oh God. That's all I need.'

'You've only just found out?' he asked.

I nodded, swiping my hand across my face.

'Ahhh.' He exhaled slowly through his mouth, like he'd been for a run. 'Did you come here just to see me?'

I nodded again. 'I saw you worked here. On Twitter.'

'Ahh,' he said again. 'That makes sense.' A pause. 'Sorry about your dad.'

'Yours too. Technically!'

'Yes.' He looked up and down the pavement. 'Does anyone know you're here? Your mum?'

I shook my head.

'OK,' he said. Then he looked anxiously back at the café. 'Look. I'm really sorry to do this to you right now, but it's the start of the lunch rush and we're short-staffed today. The boss is a complete dragon. I really need to get back in there.'

I must have looked crestfallen for Tom reached out and squeezed my arm. 'Don't get me wrong,' he said, searching for my eyes. 'I'm so glad you came. But rather than us having a half-baked conversation on the pavement, let's do this properly. Why don't we take some time to think about it and then get back in touch when the dust's settled a bit and we've got time to talk properly? Does that sound like a sensible plan?'

Wordless, I nodded. Tom felt in his pocket for his order pad, scribbled on it and handed me the slip of paper.

'Here's my email address, and my mobile. Get in touch when you're ready.'

'OK.'

'Promise?'

I nodded.

'OK then. Bye.'

'Bye.'

*

The bus home went via Timbuktu. I say that to give an indication of how long the journey seemed to take but, in reality, it could actually have gone via Mars given the amount of attention I paid to my whereabouts. I collapsed into the first available seat and rested my head on the window while I replayed the meeting in my head. Tom had known. He'd known. God, it must have been awful for him growing up. Zoe must have told him who his father was to reassure him that he'd been a good person, rather than some random drunk round the back of the student union. I imagined her buying Dad's books for Tom, taping some of his TV appearances, and showing them to her son.

'That's your father,' she might have said. She'd have been proud. 'He's a very clever man.'

Maybe Tom had Googled Dad and found out about me that way. It was no secret that the famous Dr Robert Stevens had a wife and daughter.

I shut my eyes and let the vibrations of the bus's diesel engine soothe my brain. While my own childhood had been far from perfect, at least I'd had two parents while Tom had grown up an illegitimate child with a presumably impoverished twenty-something mother. I'd seen their house. Our lives had been so different.

On my lap, my bag buzzed. I pulled out my phone and saw a notification from Twitter: 'Tom Peters followed you. @TeePee94.'

I clicked 'Follow', then, before my sensible self could prevent it, quickly typed a Direct Message: 'Hello again' and pressed send. As first words between siblings went, they weren't outstanding, but this wasn't a time for poetry. I stared out of the bus window and waited for a return ping, relaxed as soon as it came, then held off looking at the message, savouring the moment. Not only did I have a half-brother, I was holding a phone on which there was a message from my half-brother. I was in touch with my brother. Finally, I took a deep breath and opened the message.

'Hello. Nice to meet you today,' was Tom's reply.

'Likewise.'

I waited. There was no response, so I typed in 'What time do you finish?', then deleted it. I thought for a bit, muttering sentences out loud to myself. I wanted to say something light-hearted and engaging, but nothing sprang to mind. Sighing, I wrote, 'Did you know it was me yesterday?' and clicked send.

'Sort of,' came the reply. 'Wasn't sure until your bf said your name. Then I realised; Evie's not common. When you came back today… #happy'

'How long have you known?' I ignored the bit about Luca being my 'bf'—boyfriend, I guessed he meant—in the general scheme of things, it wasn't important.

'A few years. It's complicated.'

'I've only just found out about you!!! I had no idea!!'

'You said. Judging by the !!! it was a shock. I'm not that bad :p'

'Understatement. There's so much I want to ask you.'

'I'm back to uni day after tomorrow. Exams. But we'll get together soon. Talk. Long overdue.'

'OK.'

*

The afternoon had broken by the time I slid the key into the front door. The house alarm started beeping: Mum was out. I made a cup of tea and collapsed on the sofa, shoving one of Mum's property magazines out of the way. Picking up my phone, I checked in case Tom had sent any more messages—nothing. Unable to settle, I got up, went to the bookshelf, pulled a book down, read the blurb, flicked the pages, put it to my nose, inhaled the scent of the ink, and placed the book back. I ran my finger along the shelf, drawing a line in the thin layer of dust. I looked in the mirror over the fireplace, flipped my hair about, thought about getting a haircut, put it in a ponytail, then took it out again. How was I supposed to relax after a morning like that?

Throwing myself back on the sofa, I dialled Luca's number.

'Tom knew about me,' I said, as soon as he picked up.

'What?' said Luca. 'How do you know? What's happened?'

'I went back.'

'To Harry's Café? On your own?'

'Yep. I had a coffee, did some work there, had a chat to Tom…'

'And then what? How did you find out that he knew?'

'I asked him!' I twiddled my finger in the phone cord, enjoying reliving the moment. 'It was kind of obvious that he knew. He heard you say my name yesterday and put two and two together.'

'Wow, Evie. I'm impressed,' said Luca. I pictured him sitting on his black leather sofa, stroking his chin. 'Very impressed. So what happens now? How did you leave it?'

I started to explain about our Twitter conversation and

our plan to meet up later when there was a crash and a laugh from outside, then the sound of Mum's key in the lock.

'Gotta go!' I cut the call and slid my phone back into my bag. The living room door burst open and Mum practically fell into the room, her hair whipped from the wind, her eyes bright and her cheeks rosy. Richard, right behind her, did a double take when he saw me.

'Oh hello, dear,' Mum said. 'Bumped into Richard at the club. We did a quick nine holes.'

'Hello again,' Richard said smoothly. 'Your mum was ever so kind to let me tag along. I'm still learning. Bit of a hacker, really.'

'You do yourself down,' said Mum. She held an envelope. 'Oh, post for you, by the way. From Oxford.' She examined her brother's writing. 'Who do you know there?'

'No idea,' I said. 'But, if you'll both excuse me?' I took the envelope and headed up to my room, closing the door carefully behind me. I slit open the envelope with my finger and pulled out the folded page. My uncle's writing looked like a drunken spider had danced the tango across the page and I squinted to read it.

'Dear Evie, It was kind of you to let me know that your father had passed away. My thoughts are with you at what must be very a difficult time. I saw Robert's obituary in the papers and wondered if I should get in touch with you now it's just you and your mother. Although I agonised over it, I decided, in the end, not to, as I would never wish to cause any trouble between you and your mother. Would I be right in assuming that she's unaware that you wrote to me?

'Evie, I hope that you are all right. You mention briefly that your mother had some sort of a mental breakdown after your brother's accident and that you're concerned about her. Although I doubt I'd be of much use at all, sometimes it helps to talk these things over with someone who's not caught up in the epicentre, so to speak. As your uncle, I'd be very happy to do that if you felt it might be useful. Perhaps I could be of some help. I've included my telephone number and I leave it with you. The last thing I want is to cause trouble between you and your mother.

'With fond regards, David.'

*

I read the letter again. Was there a hidden message in there? *'Evie, I hope that you are all right.'* Was he trying to tell me something? He'd practically asked me to call him. Was there something he wanted to tell me?

CHAPTER 53

'*So, Evie. Are you all set for university?*' It was our last ever session and Miss Dawson had brought us each a muffin to celebrate.

'*Hope so!*'

She took out a book of matches, placed a small candle on my muffin and lit it. '*Make a wish!*' she said. I shut my eyes and blew.

'*It's an exciting time,*' she said, as we sat down with our muffins. '*You'll have a blast.*'

'*Yeah.*' I looked at my plate. '*But it makes me sad to think that Graham never got to go to university. I often wonder what he'd have been like as a teenager. You know—sporty, a swot, serious, the class clown?*' Miss Dawson smiled and I laughed. '*Probably the latter. The thing is, Graham is always held up as this perfect kid. He was, like, the golden boy when he died. But who knows if that would have lasted? He might have gone totally off the rails. He was idolised aged ten. He can't make mistakes. His future is always golden.*'

'*Goodness, Evie. But yes. That's something you can never know.*'

'*And what about me and Graham? When he died, we*'

were really close. I always imagine we would have stayed close. But, having seen the way my friends fought with their siblings as they got older, it probably wouldn't have lasted.' I bit my lip. *'He'd be twenty now; possibly at university— maybe have a girlfriend. Or maybe he'd have got a job and moved out. Maybe we'd have grown apart, never been close again. I hate that I'll never know.'*

Miss Dawson moved to say something, but I held up my hand. *'I often wonder how things would have turned out for all our family if he hadn't died. I mean, it's easy to pin all our troubles on what happened—Mum's suicide attempt, being put in the hospital, Dad becoming distant—but what if it wasn't just that? Who's to say none of that would have happened anyway?'*

'We'll never know.'

'No, I guess we never will.'

Chapter 54

I was desperate to email Tom. But finding time without Mum asking what I was doing was tricky. Whenever I opened up the iPad, she was there, looming over me, offering cups of tea or asking coquettishly about how things were going with Luca. Suddenly, I missed my home; the peace and solitude I had living in my own little space. But my salvation came in the form of rubbish television. I'd had no idea Mum liked it so much. In the past, my parents had spent their evenings either watching 'edifying' programmes or reading—either that, or Dad had slunk off to work in his study.

But Mum was now revealing a side of herself that I'd never known. Each week when the TV listings arrived with the Sunday paper, she spent a good hour going through the booklet marking the programmes she wanted to watch and I realised that this was my chance. After we'd washed and dried the dishes, when Mum settled down in front of the telly, I was able to settle myself at the dining table with a glass of red wine and my iPad. Tonight, I was going to email Tom. My fingers were tacky on the screen as I sweated over what to write. In the end, after several false starts when I

260   ANNABEL KANTARIA

was trying to be more than I really was, I just went for the questions: How did you know it was me? How did you find out? What did you think when I walked into the café? Do you want to stay in touch?

Tom replied the next evening, his answers more guarded than I'd imagined from what I'd seen of him—one-liners. He'd found out about me at sixteen; he'd seen pictures of me on the internet; he wasn't sure when I walked into Harry's, but then Luca had called me 'Evie' and he'd suddenly thought 'OMG, maybe that was her'. He'd Googled me again that night and, when I'd walked in again the next day, he'd been sure. He'd love to stay in touch; he'd love to meet me again, but was already back in Warwick. 'Exams... bet you don't remember what they are!'

I replied and we fell into a routine. As I got to know Tom, it became increasingly important to me to share as much of my father with him as I could, as if to make up for the childhood that he'd never had. I was the only person on earth who could tell him what it had been like to be a child of Robert Stevens. My need to chronicle our history for Tom became a fire in my belly. I needed desperately to let my new brother in on everything that he'd missed. I suppose the upshot was that I felt guilty that I'd grown up with my father while Tom had not. Guilty that Dad had chosen to stay with us, not him. I spent the long evenings in Woodside writing down my memories for Tom.

I tried to put myself in his shoes and think what I'd want to know if I were him. I imagined he'd want to know what type of a father ours had been, so I told him little stories and anecdotes to illustrate. I was tempted to make Dad out to be perfect, but I tried to keep it realistic. I told Tom about the Mastermind championships, about the bike rides and the family trips abroad that always had a historical bent; how there was never just a simple beach holiday—there always had to be ruins and history lessons disguised as fun.

I wanted Tom to know, too, what it was like growing up with a famous father, a man who was revered by both his peers and the media, so I talked about how absent Dad had become after Graham's accident; how badly affected he was; how he retreated from family life and spent every weekend on lecture tours. 'That was probably why he became so successful,' I wrote, suddenly realising that, for my dad, some tiny good could have come out of Graham's death after all. 'He was devoted to his career; he spent so much time touring and making his name that, by the time I was ten, I didn't see much of him either!'

To be honest, though, it was me who did most of the writing—Tom mentioned that he had exams coming up, so I didn't really expect replies. But I hoped my emails provided him with some light relief between exams; I hoped that he enjoyed hearing from me, enjoyed finding out about me and his father. He sent me the odd message on Twitter, but I knew he had better things to do in the evenings than write long emails back to his sister. I understood that.

*

It was Tom, however, who made the next move in our game of sibling chess; it was Tom who picked up a castle and progressed the game two squares while I was still shuffling my pawns. I'd just sent him an email when a reply dropped into my inbox with a ping.

'Hey, Evie,' it read. 'Thanks for the emails. I really appreciate what you're trying to do and I'm sorry I haven't had time to reply. But my exams will be over next week so I wondered if you're ready to meet up for a proper chat now? We really need to talk; there's stuff I want to tell you, too. Much better face to face than on email. Can you come up here or shall I come back down?'

As soon as I read it, I knew a trip to Warwick to meet Tom was exactly what I needed. Not only was the time now right since I'd got to know him a bit, but I needed to get away from home and away from Mum. She hadn't mentioned the bin-bags saga since leaving her 'thanks' note that morning and I needed to clear my head in a different setting. I was running in ever-decreasing circles here in Woodside, panicking about what to tell Mum, worrying about Tom, worrying about Mum's mental health, worrying about her getting over the loss of my father and wondering, too, whether I should meet Uncle David or if that was a whole different can of worms. What I needed was some space, some clarity and an independent viewpoint. A trip up to see Clem—and Tom—was the perfect solution. Excited, nervous and full of trepidation, I dialled her number.

'Clem! How are you?' I smiled into the phone when she picked it up—she always had that effect on me.

'Evie? Is that really you?' she asked. 'It's so great to hear from you! You got my reply, right? I'm so sorry to hear about your dad. Are you all right?' A micro-pause and then, 'How's your mum?'

'We're fine, thanks. Mum's... Mum seems OK. But, oh God, Clem, so much else has happened.'

'What do you mean? Is everything all right?'

'It's a long story. How long have you got?' I asked, listening for squawks from her twins in the background—there were none.

'Ages,' she said. 'The beasts're at nursery and the shop's covered. So tell me.'

And so I sunk to the floor and explained as much as I could on the phone, wrapping the cord around my finger as I talked. Clem was unflappable. I loved that about her. You could tell her you'd murdered someone and hidden the body in her car and she wouldn't panic; she always knew what to do. The news of my father's death she'd taken well, but the story of my new half-brother took her by surprise.

'Bloody hell, Evie. I wasn't expecting that. Your dad was definitely a charmer, but he always looked so strait-laced! But, listen, this is too big for the phone. Can you come up? We need to talk about this in person. Come up and spend some time with me. Please?'

'Well, actually, that was why I was calling. Tom's asked me to meet him in Warwick and I wondered... ?'

'You don't ever need to ask, Evie.'

We agreed I'd come up the next day.

CHAPTER 55

I've always liked train journeys. I don't see them as dead time; for me, they're time to think, to daydream, sometimes to read. Today, though, on the train to Coventry, I was too keyed up for any of that. I tried to relax: I bought myself a cup of tea and settled back in my seat with my knitting, my iPad and my book to hand, but I couldn't focus on anything. I knitted a few stitches but my heart wasn't in it, the iPad wouldn't connect to the in-train Wi-Fi, and I certainly couldn't focus on my book. Tapping my fingers on the table, I stared out at the passing countryside.

My entire body was fizzing with so much nervous energy I could have lit up London. I was dying to see Clem again, but I was even more desperate to see Tom, properly this time. He hadn't said much to me in the scant emails he'd sent, so I had loads of questions for him: How did he feel about me? Did he want to stay in touch? He'd lived his entire life as an only child—maybe there wasn't room in his life for a sister, even part-time.

We'd agreed to meet the following day at Clem's tea rooms. I was trying not to overplay it in my head, trying not to get too keen, to expect too much, but I couldn't help but let thoughts about how it might go run through my head as I looked out of the window, watching the landscape slowly change from urban London to the Home Counties, then the washed-out fields of the countryside dotted with sheep so static they could have been painted onto the muddy grass.

After what seemed like a lifetime, the train pulled into Coventry Station and there, jumping up and down with excitement, was Clem, her curly brown hair whipping around her face in the wind. The last time I'd seen her was when James and I had dropped her and Patrick at the doors to Dubai International Airport and I'd watched her walk away with an ache in my throat.

'Darling, buck up,' James had said, pulling away from the kerb, as I'd craned my neck backwards for a last glimpse of my best friend. 'She's only moving to England, not Outer bloody Mongolia. You'll see her every summer and no doubt we won't be able to beat her and Pat off with sticks when it comes to visiting us.'

And although in theory he was right, it hadn't happened in reality and now, for the first time in a couple of years, here she was.

'Hello, gorgeous!' said Clem, flinging her arms around me as I dropped my bag to hug her. 'Welcome to Coventry.' She said it with a perfect, but ironic, Midlands accent. 'How was the journey?'

'Oh, you know—on time.' I was too excited for small talk. 'I can't believe I'm here! Look at you! You look amazing!'

And it was true. I'd worried about how Clem—the biggest
sun-worshipper I knew—would reacclimatise to life in the
UK. She'd once joked that, in Dubai, all she owned was
work clothes and twenty-eight bikinis. Given she spent
every single weekend at the beach or by the pool, it was
probably true. But looking at her now, she glowed with
health and happiness.

'You look so healthy!'

'It's all the fresh air. Pushing the twins around in the
buggy all the time! I walk everywhere here.' She held me
at arm's distance and looked me up and down. 'So sorry
to hear about your dad, but, wow, it's so good to see you!'

She led me through the car park to a silver estate car,
the back of which was stuffed with baby paraphernalia:
two baby car seats inhabited the back seats and a double
stroller filled most of the boot. Clem flicked her eyes at it all.
'Kids. Take over your life. No more sexy cars for me—just
the Mummy-wagon. Is there space for your bag?' I could
see, though, that having the twins had been the making of
Clem. She was a natural mum, one of those women with
unending patience and unlimited kindness to give. She was
in her element. Was I jealous? A bit—of the direction she
had in her life; the purpose.

'Where are the twins today?'

'They go to nursery. Now they're running about and into
everything, I couldn't run the shop with them at home. They
love it, anyway. Once a week, the whole nursery decamps to
the woods for "forest school", where they look for insects,
chase squirrels and do bark tracings, even in the rain—it's

probably far better for them than sticking around with me yelling at them not to bug the customers. You might not see them, though—they're terribly excited to be going for a sleepover at Mum's tonight.'

We pulled out of the station car park onto the Coventry ring road.

'So,' said Clem. 'Have you ever seen Warwick University?'

My heart quickened and I looked at her sideways. Did she mean what I thought she meant? Had she read my mind? She gave me a cheeky smile, her brows raised in innocence, but she had that mischievous look on her face that I remembered from the crazier of our nights in the past.

'It's a lovely campus university.' Her tone was light, innocent. 'You can drive right through it. It's on our way, just a small detour.'

'And you're telling me this because… ?'

'Just thought you might like to do a little sightseeing on the way to Warwick?'

'Sightseeing?'

'Yes? You know, drive through the university, take a look around—see the students, get a feel for the place. You don't need to get out, we'll just drive through?'

I smiled. Clem didn't need me to reply.

*

The chances of us seeing Tom randomly walking to class must have been next to nothing. But my eyes were swivelling right and left as Clem drove us slowly through the heart of the university campus. Forget forest school,

I couldn't believe I was looking at the natural habitat of my half-brother. This is where he lived; where he worked and played. This was the air he breathed. Maybe we'd see him.

We didn't see him.

CHAPTER 56

After the concrete of Coventry, Warwick High Street looked picture-postcard pretty, its mix of Georgian, Tudor and Victorian architecture so quintessentially English I couldn't believe it really existed. Clem's tea rooms took up the first two floors of a Georgian townhouse in the middle of the High Street. Behind a large picture window at street level, she'd packed wooden tables and chairs in tightly to accommodate the rush of tourists that flooded the shop each time a tour bus disgorged its occupants— already her cream teas, with their generous pots of luscious clotted cream and home-made strawberry, raspberry and blackcurrant jam, were gaining a reputation. As we walked through, I looked around for Tom. I knew it was silly— what would a student be doing in a place like that?—but I couldn't stop myself.

Clem took me upstairs to what she called the drawing room—it was a more intimate, quieter space frequented by locals looking for a calm spot. One wall was covered in bookshelves, the books there for the taking.

'It's a sort of exchange,' said Clem. 'People take what they want and drop off when they're done.'

I slumped into an armchair by the open fire and Clem asked the waitress to bring us each a cup of English Breakfast tea and a slice of her Victoria sponge.

'Oh, Clem,' I said. 'How do you always manage to get it so right?'

She raised her eyebrows at me, questioning.

'Your life, I mean. Your life choices. First Dubai—the perfect choice at the time. Then Patrick, marriage, the twins—this?' I flicked my hand at her tea rooms. Clem had the life I knew my parents had wished for me. They'd have loved me to be married with kids at thirty, happily settled in Britain. My life went wrong, though, when I thought I'd be the one who could tame James. Even then I'd known that there wasn't a single ex-girlfriend that meant a thing to James. How I'd thought I'd come out the other side of an encounter with him smiling, I don't know.

Clem, on the other hand, had chosen well with Patrick, James's wingman. What Pat lacked in sculptural good looks, he made up for in personality, loyalty and staying power. I was proud of Clem for getting it right that night at the wine bar, when I got it so spectacularly wrong.

'Right, I'm desperate to talk about your new "brother"—' Clem said the word carefully, trying the feel of it in her mouth—for so long it had been a word people were scared to say around me,'—but, before we get to that, can we talk about James?'

Clem knew we'd split up, but I hadn't gone into details on Facebook—just changed my status to 'Single' and mentioned I was loving living in my own little place—

and I doubt James had bragged to Patrick about what had happened. To be honest, I hadn't really spoken to many people about the break-up—I'd withdrawn a bit from the social scene, become more private.

The waitress arrived with the teas.

'It's OK if you don't want to talk about it,' Clem said when she'd left. 'But I need to know that you're all right. What happened? How come you moved out? Are you OK?' She leaned over and put her hand on my arm. 'Sorry for the questions.'

'No, it's all right,' I said. 'I'm OK now. In one sense, coming to England has really helped.' I looked at the cake. 'That looks divine. Shall I be mum?' I poured us each a cup of tea.

'So what happened?' Clem asked when I was settled back in the chair.

'Oh God, you couldn't make it up.'

'Try me.'

'Do you remember how charming James was? Remember that night we got together—me and James and you and Pat—and he made me feel like the luckiest woman alive?' I bit into the cake.

'Yes. He got that song played for you, didn't he?' Clem, her mouth full of cake, sang a bar of Prince's 'The Most Beautiful Girl in the World'. It sounded cheesy now, but I'd thought it was romantic. At the time.

'Well, that wasn't the real James.' I wondered how to phrase it, the fact that her husband's best friend was, in my opinion, not just a pathological liar but a narcissist and a sociopath, too. 'He's quite… difficult.' I said. 'I suppose the signs were there all along. I just didn't want to see them.'

Clem was shaking her head. 'I never saw any signs, Evie. He always seemed totally devoted to you. Like the world's most perfect fiancé. Goodness, you two were going to have the most perfect kids.'

'He was clever, Clem. When he was with me, he was amazing. I thought the sun shone out of his you-know-what. But he wasn't with me all the time. And that's where the problem lay.'

'What do you mean?'

'Remember he worked as an advisor to the Sheikh?'

Clem nodded. 'Yes. Yes, I do. He was always being called to the palace at weird hours.'

'Exactly. Except he wasn't an advisor to the Sheikh. That wasn't the Sheikh calling him at weird hours. It was his other fiancée.'

'WHAT?' Clem's outrage was gratifying. 'Evie! How can you sit here so composed and tell me this? You were going to marry the man; have children with him. He was the poster boy for perfect.' She shook her head in disbelief. 'You must be in pieces!'

I gave a bitter little laugh. 'You know what? I was devastated. I thought my world had ended. I'd imagined growing old with him. I'd really thought he was the one.'

Clem reached for my hand. 'It wasn't just you. We all thought he was the one. Even Patrick had no idea. He fooled us all.'

I squashed the cake crumbs on my plate with my fork and

dabbed them into my mouth. 'But this is Evie Stevie you're talking about. You know what, Clem? I've been through worse. A lot worse. One night, I realised that I was the only one in charge of how I reacted to this. I could either sit at home and cry or I could get on with my life. I thought back over everything that I'd learned about grief when Graham died because, in a strange way, it felt similar. I made myself busy. I took up running; I started meditating, did some yoga. I got my knitting out — in a cold ocean somewhere, a whole ship of sailors have got new woolly hats thanks to James.' Clem laughed. 'I have bigger fish to fry than James bloody Carruthers.'

'Well said!' said Clem. 'I don't know how you do it, Evie. You're amazing. It's been how long now?'

'A couple of months.'

'If it was me, I'd be a mess. You seem so together.'

'I was a mess, trust me. But, you know, I don't care any more.' As I said it, I realised it was true. In Dubai, James had consumed my thoughts night and day but, since Dad had died and I'd come to England, things had changed. James no longer dominated my feelings. And then there was the matter of the little shiver I felt when I thought of Luca. I was surprised how much I was enjoying his company.

'And what about James?' Clem asked. 'Did he marry the other one… What was her name?'

'Shelley.'

'Shelley?' Clem shook her head slowly. 'Did he marry her in the end? Is he still in Dubai? Do you ever see him?'

'Yeah, he's still in Dubai. I doubt he got married. We were

having dinner at the One&Only when Shelley confronted him. She and I both lobbed our engagement rings into the sea.'

'That's hilarious. The One&Only?'

'Yep.'

'Nice symmetry, Miss Stevens.'

'Thanks.'

'I wish I could have been there for you.' Clem smiled at me. 'But you seem to have managed so well on your own. I'm so proud of you.'

I smiled back. It hadn't been an easy journey, but I was getting there. 'The main thing is that James is firmly off my radar. The only people I care about now are Mum, you, me and Tom Peters.' *And Luca*, I added silently.

'Ah yes,' said Clem. 'Tom Peters. I can't wait to hear all about Tom Peters.'

CHAPTER 57

Clem and I picked up the thread again once we were back at her house. Pat had kindly offered to go out for the evening, leaving us alone to order in a pizza and crack open the wine.

Clem and I settled down with our takeaway while I told her everything from the moment I got the call about Dad to how I found out about Tom. Even though Clem knew what was coming, it didn't stop her from gasping as I got to the bit about finding the email from Zoe that told me about Tom.

'Oh my God! When she said "your son", you thought she was talking about Graham?' she asked, aghast.

'I didn't know what to think. As far as I knew, I only had one brother and he was dead. The first thing I thought was that maybe he wasn't dead at all. I mean, what would you think? I started to think his dying had all been some sort of sham and he was alive and at university. But I'd been to his funeral. I just couldn't understand it.'

'I bet you couldn't. It's not the kind of thing that happens every day. You poor thing. I can just imagine you there, all on your own in your mum's study, wondering what in God's name was going on.'

Her sympathy was too much. Suddenly overwhelmed, I felt the humiliating prick of tears.

'Sorry,' I said, looking up and trying to blot the wetness with my fingertips, trying to save my mascara. 'It's just... Oh God.'

Clem leapt over to the sofa and put an arm around me, patting my back. 'It's OK. Let it out. Let it all out. You've had so many shocks. It's all right. Let it out. You've experienced more emotion in about a week than most people get in a lifetime. It's OK.'

'Oh no. I think it's a tissue situation,' I said, wiping my face with the back of my hand. There was snot everywhere and mascara down my cheeks. 'Have you got any?'

Clem dashed out to the kitchen and brought back a box. 'Here.'

Rubbing at my eyes till they were scratchy, I tried to compose myself but, every time I thought I'd pulled it back, the tears started again.

'I'm sorry,' I said. 'It's all been too much. Oh, Clem. I'm a rubbish friend. I come here, drink your wine and cry all over your sofa.'

'I wouldn't have it any other way.'

Slowly, I struggled to regain control. Finally, I raised a wobbly smile and realised that I was ravenous. 'Is there any pizza left?'

'That's my girl,' said Clem. She loaded up my plate and refilled our wine glasses.

'Cheers!' Emotions out, I felt better than I had all week.

'So let me get this straight,' said Clem. 'You've already

met Tom once, right? But you didn't get much of a chance
to talk.' I nodded. 'And now he's asked you to come up here
and meet him properly?'

'Yep. I've got loads of questions for him, and there's stuff
he wants to tell me, too.'

'Like what?'

'No idea. Probably how he found out. I dunno. Stuff like
that.'

'It's unbelievable,' said Clem. 'I can't believe you've had
a brother for nearly two decades and not known about him.
It's like a Hollywood movie. What's he like? Do you think
you're going to get on?'

'He seems nice. I'm sort of excited,' I said. 'But it's
tempered by all the other stuff—Dad, for example. I'm so
angry with Dad. Can you understand that? And it's so difficult
being angry with someone who's dead. I wish I could have
it out with him but I can't. It kills me to think that he knew
how much I missed Graham, he knew I had another brother,
and he *hid* it from me. I know it was difficult for him, but I
just wish there was a way I could have grown up knowing I
had a brother, even if I didn't meet him. I can't bear to think
of all those years I felt so alone, with Dad off working and
Mum going loopy. I know Tom wouldn't have been able to
do anything—he was a baby for half of it!—but just knowing
I had a brother. It would have made a difference.'

Clem sighed. 'I know.'

'And then I've been worrying about how to tell Mum.
You remember what happened after Graham? I told you
about that, right?'

'I do. But she needs to know. I think you have to tell her at some point—it's just a matter of when. How is she?'

'She's all over the place, that's how she is. One minute she seems fine, then she's going loopy, throwing Dad's stuff out of the window, screaming at me, getting Dad confused with Graham. She's selling the house. She even hit me, Clem.'

'What?'

'Miss Dawson, the grief counsellor I saw when Graham died, thinks she might have some grief disorder thing. A psychotic thing. I'm walking on pins around her, watching, waiting, trying not to upset her. Nothing's turning out to be as simple as I thought it would be.'

Clem swilled her wine around the glass.

'When I came over, I thought I'd just be helping Mum with Dad's things, helping her arrange the funeral and all that. But now Mum has these, I don't know, "episodes". She totally loses it, then she's fine the next minute. I feel like I don't know her at all. We had a whole conversation about Graham's funeral—she remembered all the details, right down to hymns and readings, but she didn't even go to Graham's funeral. And when I confronted her about it she said she knew she hadn't gone. I mean, talk about a head-fuck.'

'Oh God, that's awful.'

'Anyway, the point is, after all this, how can I tell her that Dad had a secret son? Conceived when Graham died? And that all the time she was grieving for Graham, he was sending money for his other son?'

'Well, are you absolutely sure you've got your facts right? Are you sure your dad really is Tom's father?'

'Yes, I asked the Zoe woman outright…'

'You *spoke* to her? Oh my God! You're crazy, Evie. You are unbelievable!'

'I called her to ask if she was sure Dad was the father. Once a journalist, always a journalist, right? Got to get my facts right. But aside from that, he looks just like Graham. Short of getting a DNA test, I can't be any surer.'

'Hmm,' said Clem thoughtfully. 'Well, Tom and his mum obviously know about you, so why don't you see what he has to tell you tomorrow. Then, depending on how that goes, I think you should try to talk to the mum. She's the only person who can tell you what happened with your dad. When you know all the facts, let the dust settle, think about the best way to do it. When do you have to go back to Dubai?'

'I can take as long as I need—unpaid, of course.' I rolled my eyes. 'And while I don't want to take the mickey, I need to be here right now to keep an eye on Mum, even if it means losing my job.'

'You'll never lose your job. Your boss loves you.'

'Ha.' It was true. All my boss knew about running magazines was that I made money for him. What's more, after I'd told Emily I'd like a bit more unpaid leave, she'd managed to persuade him to divert a little chunk of what he was saving on my salary into a freelance budget to help her through— clearly there were benefits to being the boss's niece.

'I'd like to be here to help Mum move house,' I told

Clem. 'It's chain-free, so maybe she'll get the keys in a couple of weeks.'

'OK great. Then you've got plenty of time to decide what to do.'

'Mmm.' While I was curious and excited to meet Tom again, things were different when it came to Zoe. With her, I felt conflicting loyalties. She wasn't a direct relative of mine; she was a person with whom Dad had betrayed Mum—Mum didn't need me to betray her, too.

*

'Can you imagine what it'd be like to lose a child? You're a parent, Clem. Can you?' It was late, we were tidying up the kitchen before bed, and it was a question I'd never have dared ask her sober.

Wiping the kitchen counter, she shuddered. 'Where did that come from, Evie?'

'I'm just trying to imagine what Mum went through.' Clem stopped wiping and looked at me. 'When Graham died, it was all about me. About me losing my brother. I never stopped to think what it would have been like for Mum and Dad, losing their son.'

'You were so young.'

'Yeah. I was. I was eight. Too young to think about what it was like for them. I was wrapped up in my own shock and grief. I guess, if I imagined anything, I thought it would have been the same for them as it was for me. But it wouldn't have been, would it?'

Clem shook her head.

'I can't even imagine it,' she said. 'Just thinking about it… it makes my blood run cold. I can't put that thought in my head.' Her eyes slid to a family photo on the wall, to the twins' messy artwork, which threatened to consume the fridge door. 'It makes me want to call Mum now and check the twins are OK. Your children are like a part of you, Evie. I can't explain it. It's like they're a part of you walking around the world and you feel for them as you would for yourself.'

For the first time since Graham died, I tried to put myself in my parents' shoes. I tried to imagine what Mum must have felt to have lost her only son — the perfect, blue-eyed boy. I tried to imagine the anger she must have felt towards Dad for being there and not preventing it. And I thought about Dad, not just devastated by the loss of his son, but regretting, constantly, the moment that he let Graham step into the road, replaying the accident, wishing he could change things.

I imagined what it must have been like for Dad afterwards, watching helplessly as Mum broke open, the life literally spilling out of her, and feeling that it was his fault. Coping with the blame she threw at him; dealing with her suicide attempt and incarceration while trying to keep things normal for me. I ached to think of the two of them trapped in their separate worlds of grief. Is that what had driven him into Zoe's arms?

'Do you think losing Graham could have changed Mum forever? Do you think she might never have got over it?'

'Totally.'

'I never realised. At the time, I never realised.'

CHAPTER 58

My room was at the top of Clem's house, up the main staircase, then an immediate right and up another narrow stairway that led to a small gap under the eaves, presumably once an attic. Clem had made it homely, though, painting it in soft shades of grey and white. Underfoot was a luxurious dove-grey carpet which softened sounds in the room, giving it a cosy feel. The wrought-iron bed took up most of the space; a matching chandelier hung directly above. I looked at my watch now, squinting at its face in what little light came in through the Velux windows. It was 4 a.m. I sighed and flipped onto my back. In the moonlight, the chandelier cast a shadow halfway down the wall. With its 'legs' facing up, it looked not unlike a dead spider.

My insomnia was only to be expected, really. I always got it at the times when I probably most needed my sleep: at stressful times; on the nights before important meetings; when I had a lot on my mind. The best part of a bottle of wine hitting my liver hadn't helped, either. Having fallen straight into a drunken sleep just after midnight, I'd woken now, my mouth dry and my mind racing.

I remembered fragments of dreams. Anxious dreams about Tom; about him coming into Clem's tea room but not seeing me; me chasing him down Warwick High Street shouting his name. Mum chasing me, asking who I was calling, and me stuck, torn, between the two of them. A dream, too, about me screaming at Dad. I couldn't recall what it was about, but the feeling of anger remained with me, the upset.

And now I was wide awake. With another sigh, I got out of bed and pulled on the dressing gown Clem had left hanging on the back of the door. Opening one of the windows, I stuck my head out and felt the cold, clean air rush in. It carried the scent of cows, manure, countryside, and a freshness that I really missed in Dubai. The air there, except in the dead of what you might call winter, was always heavy with heat and often peppered with dust particles that clogged my sinuses.

Clem's house was just outside Warwick and looked out over open fields. During the day, I'd been able to see for miles from my window but now, with the sky still inky black and the sodium glow of Coventry presumably in the far distance on the other side of the house, I leaned as far out as I could and started to count the stars.

Please, I mouthed to them. *Please let it go well with Tom today.* Butterflies danced in my belly as I thought of the meeting that lay ahead. Looking east over the distant hills, I searched the sky for signs of dawn. There were no pinks, no oranges, no glorious colours of the sunrise—it was too early for that. Straining my eyes, though, I could just make out what looked like a gentle softening of the unforgiving blackness in the far distance—a hint of something that lay just out of sight: the start of a new day. The day I was to get to know my brother.

CHAPTER 59

The next day dawned grey; the clear sky of the night hadn't lasted and clouds loomed ominously overhead, casting their shadows over the landscape and threatening rain, as Clem and I drove the short journey into Warwick. It was hardly the auspicious weather I might have hoped for. I shivered. Clem turned up the car heater. My stomach twisted itself into knots. I hadn't been able to eat breakfast.

'You said Tom had "stuff" to tell you,' Clem said to break the silence. 'Do you think it's anything specific?'

'No idea. Stuff about his life? What it was like growing up?' I shrugged. 'Or maybe nothing like that at all. Maybe he wants a summer job in Dubai!' My nerves about the meeting translated into silliness. 'Maybe he's discovered that we don't have the same dad after all; the whole thing's been a massive mistake.' A part of me was even hopeful that this was the case. Clem joined in the game.

'No, not that. He's so glad to have a sister he wants you to move to Warwick and has bought you a house — with your dad's money!'

'Maybe he wants me to get to know his mum. Maybe he's bringing her.'

'He forgot to tell you you've got a secret half-sister, too.'

'Oh don't! I couldn't take any more secret siblings!'

*

At five to ten, Clem gave me a hug and left me alone in the drawing room, pulling the door closed behind her. She had offered Tom and me the use of the upper level of her tea rooms for our meeting—the secret sitting room. She was going to close it off so we could talk in privacy. It was thoughtful of her, but I wondered if we might have been more at ease in a crowded room; if the distraction of having other people around might have made things feel more natural. Although Tom and I had already spoken once in person, it felt completely different to have an arranged meeting with him.

I sat down, legs crossed, and looked around, my bottom foot tapping a rhythm on the polished floorboards. After a minute, I got up and dragged another chintzy armchair over to where I was sitting, trying not to dislodge the rugs. That done, I sat down in the chair that gave the best view of the door and flicked through the paper. Nothing went in. Rain slid down the leaded windowpanes; noise from the street below was muffled; the air inside stuffy with central heating.

I went to the bookshelf. With my head turned sideways, I browsed the spines. There was a good selection of bestsellers, most of which I'd read, and a surprising amount of historical romances. I say 'surprising', but maybe it's only to be expected that the middle-aged clientele of a tea shop in a historical town would like historical romance.

These were the thoughts running through my head when Tom arrived, catching me by surprise despite the fact I was waiting for him. I heard the door open, I turned, and there he was, looking completely incongruous and larger than life in this low-ceilinged, flowery room. He stepped in, bringing with him a slice of sound—the buzz of conversation, the chink of china, a stab of laughter—from the shop below, and the scent of the fresh air and rain. Then he pushed the door gently to, shutting out the rest of the world with a click.

'Hello again,' he said.

'Hello.'

We looked at each other. I smiled, still nervous. 'Thanks for coming here. Did you find it OK?'

'Yes, great directions, thanks. A friend dropped me off.' He looked around. 'Great place. How did you find it?'

'It belongs to the friend I'm staying with. Apparently, residents usually hide up here, away from the tourist crowds. She's locked them all out today, though.' My laugh was brittle.

'That's kind of her.' Finally, Tom stepped further into the room. He unbuttoned his coat and looked around for somewhere to hang it, deciding with a shrug to sling it over one of the other armchairs instead. We stood facing each other.

'So,' he said. 'Here we are.'

'Yes. I hope you didn't think I was stalking you. In Harry's.'

'No. You'd only just found out. I'd have done the same.'

'So why didn't you? Track me down, I mean?'

'Long story,' he said. 'I've had a few years to get used to the idea. But, look, I just want to say that however you want to play this, it's fine by me. I've had an "absent" sister for three years so I'm kind of used to it.' He shrugged. 'I'm cool with it. Whatever you want to do… if it's too weird and you want to just…' His voice tailed off.

'Oh God, no, I… I mean… thank you.'

We smiled at each other then looked away, suddenly shy.

'Look, I'm dying for a coffee,' Tom said. 'Shall we try to get some? How do we order? Is there some sort of dumb-waiter hidden behind the bookshelf? Do we shout down the shaft?'

'Clem—my friend—said she'd send up a waitress.'

No sooner had I said it than there was a knock and the door opened—a young waitress with a peaches-and-cream complexion appeared and took our orders. When she left, I perched on the edge of an armchair. Tom paced around the room. When he got to the window, he spun around to face me, rubbing his hands together.

'So,' he said. 'I can't believe we're finally sitting here together. Where do we start? I mean, shit. What do we do in this situation? Tell me something interesting about yourself.'

'Umm, let me see.' I bit my lip and thought. 'I knit hats for sailors.' Tom looked suitably surprised.

'Wow. I didn't see that coming. Fantastic. So you knit them, and then what? Sell them at sailors' conventions?'

'No, it's a bit more organised than that. I do it through a charity. But, come on, play fair: now it's your turn. You tell me something about you.'

'I used to have a stutter.'

'Really? I saw on Twitter you do stand-up comedy!'

'Well, yes,' he said. 'That's actually why I started doing it: to try to beat my stutter.'

'Brave. Did it work?'

'W-w-well, w-w-what do you th-th-think?' We laughed; the tension dissolved. A pause, then Tom leaned forward in his chair. 'So you really didn't know about me until just recently?' he asked.

'Seriously. I had no idea. It was quite a shock. But a good one. And you've known for three years?'

'Yes. I was sixteen when I found out.'

'And you didn't want to try to find me?'

'There was no finding to be done. I knew your name and that your family lived in Woodside. But I wasn't allowed to contact you. Mum was adamant about that. She didn't want to upset your mum. Believe it or not, she's not the type to go around having children with other women's husbands. I think she just wanted to pretend that everything was above board.'

'So, if my dad hadn't died, I still wouldn't know?'

Tom shrugged.

'Weren't you curious? About me?'

'Oh God. I was everything. Curious, furious, happy, confused, excited, terrified. I was all over the place, like you must be now. Only you're probably far more in control of your emotions than I was at sixteen. I didn't know what to think. It was a rocky time. But, ultimately, when everything had calmed down again, you can't miss what you never had.'

'So you didn't try to look for me?'

'I wasn't allowed to. I Googled you once. Saw that you worked in Dubai. But I'd grown up as an only child.' He paused. 'I suppose I guessed it would all come out one day. And—well, here we are.'

'Indeed. Here we are.' There was a silence and I struggled to know what to say. There was so much. 'You sound like him.'

'Mum says that.'

'You sound like Dad but look like my brother… Graham?'

The waitress returned with our order and we sat with our thoughts as she set out the coffees, the pastries.

'I know it's a huge thing for you suddenly to get another brother. How do you feel now?' Tom asked when she'd gone again. 'To see me looking so like your brother, and sounding like Dad? Is it odd?'

Why, I wondered, had Tom referred to my dad, a man who'd fathered him after a one-night stand, as 'Dad'? Maybe he was trying to make me feel at ease. I smiled. 'God. It's beyond weird—but, depending how we get on… ' I gave him a quick smile. 'It's nice, too. It's kind of nice to have a brother again.' My eyes slid to the floor, shy.

Tom doffed an imaginary cap and bowed low from his chair. 'I'll try to do my best in the noble position of brother.'

'Thank you.' We laughed. There was another silence. I became aware of the clock ticking on the mantelpiece. I didn't dare look at it; didn't want to be reminded of the passing of time. 'I couldn't believe it when I saw that you were going to be working at Harry's Café. The badge thing threw me, though,' I said.

'Oh yeah. That was funny. Your friend was asking me about my name deliberately, wasn't he?'

'Yep.'

'He doesn't have a kid brother called Sebastian, does he?'

'Nope.'

'That's really sweet, what he did for you.'

'It is, isn't it?'

Tom nodded, eyebrows raised. 'He seemed like a nice guy. So how did you find out about me in the end? How did you break Fort Knox?'

'Well, let's just say Dad wasn't as careful as he might have thought. He hadn't buried you without a trace.' I realised as I said it how inappropriate it sounded, but Tom looked expectantly at me. His fingers drummed on the armrest. I carried on. 'I found an email your mum had sent to Dad with a link to a photo-sharing website. There were pictures of you and she referred to you as "our son".'

'Ahh.' There was a silence. 'Anyway, Evie, thanks for your emails.'

'Oh, you're welcome. I wanted you to know what a great dad he was. Even if you never got to know him.'

Tom's energy seemed to shift. 'Thanks,' he said, his mind not on the subject. He looked away, his face tense once more. Then he looked back up at me. 'Look, Evie, there's something you should know. I don't know how to say this. But I have to. Please don't take it the wrong way.'

'What?' My nerves of earlier flooded back. 'What's up?'

Tom sighed. 'Your emails? It's very sweet the way you want me to learn about Dad.' There was that word again. Why 'Dad'? 'But the thing is. Oh God, Evie. If you're going to be able to have any relationship with me, and with Mum, you have to know this.' It was obvious he didn't want to say what he had to say; that it was taking him a lot of effort to find the right words.

I felt sick. This wasn't about a summer job in Dubai.

Tom was struggling. He tried again, a different tack. 'When you say that our dad was a good dad, I agree— sometimes he was. He tried to be and, most of the time, he was. But he didn't always succeed. He had his flaws.'

I stared at Tom, the hairs on the back of my neck prickling. I could tell something bad was coming—maybe even on some level I knew what it was that was coming—but I didn't want to hear it.

'How do you know? How do you know he wasn't always a good dad? Just because he wasn't always there doesn't make him a bad dad.' I shook my head. 'He had a lot to deal with after Graham… and he worked. Really hard! He was successful.'

'Evie, I know because he was my dad, too.' Tom looked at me, as if to check I understood what he was saying.

I laughed, the ten-year gap suddenly making me feel old, wise, like an aunt not a sibling. 'Oh please! Only biologically. Not even in name!'

Tom looked sadly at me. 'No, Evie. Not only biologically. Those weekends he spent on "lecture tours"? He didn't go on lecture tours. Well, not that many. He lived with Mum and me. In our house. In Maidstone.'

'Seriously, Tom, I like you, but you need to get a grip. I know it must be hard for you, knowing that Dad chose to stay with Mum and me, not you. It can't have been easy growing up without a father, but really.' I stared at him. He looked so normal, but was obviously delusional.

Tom shook his head. 'Evie, think about it. Think about all the weekends he disappeared after work on a Friday and came back only on Sunday night. He wasn't touring the country, Evie, he was at home with Mum and me.'

'No.' I was shaking my head. 'If that was true, he'd have left something for you in his Will. And he didn't. I've seen it. You and your mum aren't even mentioned.'

'We don't need to be in the Will. He set up a Trust for us.'

I stood up. 'Sorry, Tom. I'm not buying it.' I picked up my bag, my coat, and prepared to leave—if he had nothing sensible to say, we were done. I was so disappointed, bitterly disappointed. I'd spent hours wondering what my relationship with Tom might be like, but never in a million years would I have guessed it would all turn sour. What was he trying to do? Claim something from Dad's estate?

Tom stood up, too, tried to get between me and the door. 'He played Mastermind with me, too.' His voice was gentle. 'Four reds? His default position?'

Well, that was true. But I may have mentioned that in an email. Still, I paused and Tom grabbed the opportunity. 'Your trip to Corfu? Did you ever wonder how he knew the area so well? Knew where to stay, where to eat? He'd already been with Mum. I was only little, but Mum has the photos.'

I slumped back into the armchair and Tom paced the room, nibbling at his thumb.

'My favourite bedtime story? *Paddington*—same as yours, right? Dad put on that funny voice when he read it to me, too. He read it to me every night he was with us, till I was too old. And even then some, too.'

He paused. Still I couldn't say anything. My head was shaking in disbelief. Could Tom be making all this up? Could he be? What kind of a person would make this up? What sort of a stalker was he?

'If you'd talked properly with Mum the day you phoned her, she'd have told you the same. She actually wanted to be the one to tell you. It wasn't supposed to be me who told you.' He laughed bitterly.

I struggled to comprehend what Tom was saying. I had to admit it could be true. But how would we not have noticed? It was obvious: with his work, Dad had had the perfect cover. We never expected him to be home at the weekends. He could have had ten wives, thirty children and a house in Spain and we wouldn't have known. I couldn't believe—didn't want to believe—that Dad would have lied to us for twenty years. If he was living a lie, we all were. How would he have kept that up for so long? I was finding it hard to understand the enormity of what Tom was saying he'd done.

'But I don't get it. Why would he do that? Why would he lie to us? Why wouldn't he just choose one way or the other? There's no shame in divorce these days.' I stood up again, ready to leave.

'Funnily enough, I grew up believing that Dad was away all week for work. I guess he had his reasons. Maybe he loved us all in his own weird way.'

I said nothing. Tom carried on: 'I also couldn't believe he'd been living with another family. My first question was why the bloody hell he couldn't just choose one family and stick with them. We talked about it a lot. I was really angry with him, Evie. You have to understand that. I thought he was weak. I was furious; I raged at him, I despised him. I wouldn't acknowledge him in the house; I even tried to run away. But Dad argued that he couldn't leave your mum because she was too fragile.' Tom was speaking fast, trying to get everything in. 'He loved you and he was scared that if he left, your mum wouldn't let him see you any more. Or that she'd do something stupid and you'd lose her as well as your brother. He said she'd tried in the past...' He stopped himself, then carried on. 'You were always his priority, Evie. Dad cared a lot about your mum as the mother of his children but honestly? He didn't stay with her for love.'

'That's ridiculous! How can you say that?' But even as I said it, I realised it could have been true. Mum had been far from stable in the years after the accident. Maybe she would have tried to kill herself again. Maybe she would have made Dad cut off all contact; I didn't know. It was all too much. I didn't want to hear any more.

'I'm sorry. I should never have come. This was a really bad

idea. At least we tried. What were we thinking, imagining this could work?' I picked up my bag and rushed to the door, ripping it open and almost falling through it.

'Evie! Wait!' Tom shouted.

I ran down the narrow staircase and straight through the tea room. I tore open the front door, sending the bell jangling, and tore out onto the street. I could hear Tom's footsteps clattering behind me. Looking both ways, I chose right and dodged down an alley that ran behind the tea rooms, my feet slipping on the wet cobblestones. In the delivery bay that lay behind, I doubled up against the wall behind the bins while I got my breath back. The stench of rotten food filled the air.

'Evie! Evie!' Tom had followed me down the alley. I held my breath, hoping he'd go away, but suddenly there he was, standing in front of me, hands on hips, breathing hard. A fine drizzle misted us both.

'Go away!'

'He loved you very much.'

'I don't want to hear it!'

But Tom persisted. 'He said he'd already lost one child and he couldn't bear the thought of losing you, too.' His voice was earnest. 'He wanted to do the right thing by all of us, I think.'

'So he split his time between us? How very convenient for him! Two women! Two families! My poor mum!' I looked up at Tom, disgusted.

'I know it's no excuse, but she doesn't know. He was always very careful.'

'Duplicitous? Devious?' I spat. 'Anyway, he wasn't *that* careful—I managed to find out after about, ooh, three days? Without even looking? He's lucky Mum wasn't great with computers!'

'He used different names. He was Rob Peters when he was with us. I wanted to come round to your house and meet you and your mum when I found out. But they begged me not to say anything.' Tom's words were staccato like gunfire; they rained down on me like bullets. 'Mum hated the idea that he was someone else's husband. She didn't want to cause a scandal; she tried to accept that he'd only ever be a weekend husband to her.'

'Why did she accept it at all? If she felt that bad about stealing someone's husband, why didn't she let him go?'

'She wanted me to grow up knowing Dad. But mainly I think because she really loved him. She was crazy about him till the day he died—probably still is. He was the love of her life. She was completely in love with him—and him with her.'

I shook my head. 'You're wrong! Of course he loved Mum. He stayed with her. He didn't leave her. That tells you everything!' Even as I said it, I wondered, Had he really loved her all this time? Or stayed with us out of duty? Convenience?

Tom looked at his feet, nudged at a piece of loose stone with the tip of his shoe. 'There's just one more thing, Evie. I can't get this far and not tell you everything.'

'Oh please. What more could there be? How could this be any worse than it already is?'

'Mum's pregnant. We're going to get a baby brother or sister. Mum found out just before Dad died…'

I shoved past Tom and stormed down the alley.

He shouted after me. 'He didn't know! She hadn't had a chance to tell him!'

As if that made it any bloody better.

CHAPTER 60

I slumped in the car, unaware of my surroundings, as Clem drove me to the station. She'd been hovering near the door, waiting for me after I'd crashed past her earlier and now she drove in silence, patting my hand when we stopped at the traffic lights.

All I could hear was Tom's voice in my head: 'Mum's pregnant, Mum's pregnant, Mum's pregnant'. I squeezed my fingers against my temples, trying to stop the loop from playing. The fact that this woman was pregnant scared me: a baby was immediate, it was real, and it was the future. What would it do to Mum? I scrunched my head into my hands and moaned.

Things had started off so well with Tom. That morning of hope in Harry's Café now seemed a lifetime away. I'd imagined we were going to forge a glorious relationship and now everything lay in tatters—not just my relationship with my new brother, but my memories of my father, too. Dad may have been distant, but I'd never have guessed he'd do something like this. I'd built it up in my mind that Tom's birth was just a one-night stand, a lapse at a critical time, but Dad had lied to Mum and me for twenty years. In a matter of minutes, Tom had redrawn the landscape of my child-hood. My life, since Graham had died, had been a sham; my family's existence based on lies. I hadn't known my father at all. The man I'd called Dad had been nothing more than a pencil sketch—and Tom had just rubbed him out.

I shrunk back in the car seat as I remembered Tom talking about how Dad had been with him. Dad had stopped reading bedtime stories to me when Graham had died, yet he'd read *Paddington* to Tom until he was 'too old' for it. He'd also played Mastermind with Tom. I felt like such a fool for writing those emails to him. What was going to happen now? Was my fledgling relationship with Tom over already?

*

Back in Woodside, I took the bus to the edge of the fields that flanked the town's little river. From the road, a narrow footpath led through a thicket of tall trees to the fields and the water beyond. The path was smaller and narrower than I remembered from my childhood and neither did it look as safe and inviting as it had twenty years ago. Checking my mobile phone was on in my pocket, I set off towards the river.

Mum and Dad used to bring us here on sunny Saturday afternoons. Dad would lug the heavy picnic basket and Mum would carry the groundsheet and blanket while Graham and I skipped along, constantly stopping to adjust the fishing nets and gaudy plastic buckets we were carrying in the hope of catching tiny minnows, tadpoles and other minute river-dwelling life. It was a long walk from home and my legs would often be aching before we even got to the open fields that spilled down to the water's edge. Although a river in name, it was essentially a small, fast-flowing stream, which, at the part where we used to play, could almost entirely be traversed in children's wellies.

Dad had loved nothing more than being by water and I long suspected the Saturday afternoon outings with sandwiches, biscuits and orange squash—and a flask of tea for the grown-ups—enjoyed on the grey groundsheet with the car blanket over the top, were more about him watching the water and daydreaming than any thought of fun for us.

Still, we loved it, loved the challenge of catching something and even the long trudge home at dusk, the thought of hot, buttered crumpets reeling us back in to the warmth and light. These outings were as much a part of the furniture of my childhood as school and Brownies.

Today, the trees looked unfriendly, their bare, winter shapes stark against the cold, grey sky. When the footpath ended, I followed a well-walked trail through wild grass down to the part of the river where it widened and shallowed—the prime fishing spot for small children and, I think, just downstream from the place where Luca had photographed the swans at dawn.

I stood where the water licked the gravel at the shallowest part of the riverbed, and I took ten deep breaths in, expelling them slowly in an attempt to rid myself of the stress and tension of the disastrous meeting with Tom.

'I know, by the way,' I said to the water that scurried over the shingle. 'I know about your other family; your double life.' Between each sentence, I paused before carrying on. 'I bet you never imagined we'd find out? Mum and me... Why didn't you tell us?' I stared at the river, willing myself to see some connection to Dad in the movement of the water. 'Were you really trying to protect us, or were you too much of a coward? You couldn't face it, could you?' I kicked angrily at the gravel scattering it into the water. The sky was unforgiving. 'What a mess. What. A. Mess. Now what am I supposed to do?' I kicked out again, enjoying the violence of the movement. 'You should have told Mum. Why should I do your dirty work? Why should I clear up your bloody mess? Thanks a lot!'

The water continued to run, as it always had, under the bridge, its fast current already starting to push back the gravel I'd disturbed with my kicks. A raindrop hit my cheek. Another. I took one last look at the water, then turned to start the long walk home.

*

Mum was in the garden with Richard when I finally got back. By the looks of it, he'd managed to get hold of a scarifier: he was attacking the moss with gusto while Mum hovered about, raking leaves. They barely noticed me arrive. The walk had helped to dissipate some of my anger and I slunk quietly up to my room and lay on the bed, my mind playing over events from the past, replaying them now in the light of my new knowledge. It was horrible to think that every day of my life, from when I was nine till his death, Dad had duped Mum and me. Had done it deliberately.

Try as I might, though, I couldn't find any clues; Dad had never acted odd in any way. I hadn't suspected a thing when he'd gone off on his 'lecture tours'; I wondered if Mum had. Had we really both been so blind? Or had Dad been that good at covering his tracks?

The phone interrupted my thoughts. Luca's name was flashing on the screen.

'How was your meeting with Tom?' he asked. 'I've been thinking about you.'

'Don't ask.'

'That bad?'

'Worse.' A bark of a laugh.

'How about you tell me everything over dinner?'

'Oh, Luca. I really don't feel like dinner. You know, dressing up, conversation blah, blah. I just feel like crying. On my bed. On my own.'

'Therapy,' said Luca. 'Think of it as therapy. Don't do your hair. Come as you are. Honestly, you'll feel better after talking to Dr Luca. My treat.'

I laughed again. He always knew how to make me feel better.

'Please?' he said. 'I've missed you.'

*

We met at the Indian restaurant in the High Street—the same one that I'd begged my parents to take me to for my twelfth birthday. As I walked in, it smelled exactly the same as I remembered it smelling all those years ago: a welcoming blend of spices, chutneys and poppadums. I inhaled deeply, my eyes closed, feeling again the excitement of that first 'grown-up' birthday dinner.

Luca was at a window table. When he saw me, he jumped up and enveloped me a big hug. I closed my eyes, my face pressed against his chest, listening to the steady thump of his heartbeat. I let go reluctantly only when he started to unwind himself from me.

'So what happened? Exactly how bad are we talking?' he asked after the waiter had settled us at the table. The whole sorry tale came tumbling out.

'It's a shocker about your dad: agreed. But I don't think you've ruined your relationship with Tom,' said Luca when I'd finished. 'He's a bloke. He seemed pretty easy-going. He'll understand.'

'Funny. He said the same about you. Said he thought you looked like a nice bloke.'

'Well, there we are. If he likes me, he's a good guy. Don't worry about it, Evie. Let the dust settle. So much has happened in—how long? A week? Ten days? Don't be too hard on yourself.' He reached for my hand and squeezed it across the table. 'I think you're doing really well.'

I smiled weakly.

'You know what I think you should do now? Forget the whole thing for a bit. Have a glass of wine. Have some fun.' He looked closely at me then carried on. 'So, tell me… I'm changing the subject here… but which of our dates—back in the day—was your favourite?' He tapped his fingers on his chin, hamming it up. 'Let me see. Was it that time—that *one* time, mind—that you beat me at tenpin bowling?'

*

As we stepped out of the restaurant much later that evening, Luca slung his arm gently around my shoulders like he used to do ten years earlier. My body remembered; unconsciously, it moulded itself into the contours of his and our steps synched as we walked towards Mum's house. I slid my hand up under the bottom of his jacket and slipped it into the back pocket of his jeans.

'Is this how I used to do it?' I asked.

'Perfect,' he said, giving me a squeeze.

We walked towards the row of bus stops outside the old cinema.

'Come,' said Luca, guiding me towards the last one. Gently, with his hands on my shoulders, he positioned me against the glass of the bus stop shelter. He looked me up and down and stepped closer; so close I could feel the warmth of his breath on my face.

'It's this one, isn't it?' he breathed. I nodded, my whole body tingling. Luca moved even closer. 'Twelve years ago and I still think about it.'

'Really?'

He nodded and moved closer. 'Yes. Every time I walk past.'

Holding my face in his hands, he placed his lips softly

on mine. 'Was that how it was?' he asked, referring to
our first ever kiss. 'Or was it more like this?' His mouth
touched mine again, and he pushed me up against the bus
shelter and kissed me with a passion I hadn't thought about
for a decade.

*

I couldn't sleep that night. Kissing Luca had been a
revelation. I'd thought that James had left me too damaged,
too cynical to get involved with anyone for a long time.

   But the possibility of a relationship with Luca showed me
options that I hadn't previously wanted to admit existed; it
pushed me to question how my future might pan out. Until
tonight, I'd seen myself alone in Dubai, striving to achieve
in my career; living a comfortable life, but a life away from
family and true friends. I'd never questioned that; although
a boyfriend would be nice, Dubai was what I thought I
wanted more. Luca, tonight, had swayed the way I saw the
world. It was as if the blinkers had fallen away. The future
opened up in front of me, a smorgasbord of possibilities,
of different directions... despite everything else that was
going on in my life, I felt a flicker of optimism.

   I tossed and turned in bed, admitting to myself the
possibility that one day I could move back home; I could
live in London, close enough to keep an eye on Mum. If
I moved back, much of the subliminal worry about Mum
that I carried with me in Dubai would disappear. Maybe
Luca and I would even try to make a go of it, get married,
have children of our own. James had dangled all those

things in front of me then snatched them away, but now I realised that it wasn't him I missed as such, it was what he represented, what Clem had: the next stage of life. I dared to imagine a future that included my new brother. My head swam with possibilities.

CHAPTER 61

Pushing open the living room door the next morning, I found Mum stranded in a sea of boxes. Bubble wrap, brown tape and crumpled pieces of brown paper were strewn all around her. She looked not unlike an over-grown child on Christmas Day.

She didn't notice me at first, so intent was she on what she was doing. I stood and watched her — this woman who was my mother; this woman whose life had been built on the lies of her husband; this woman who was soon to find out that her late husband had had another son and now had a baby on the way — and I felt a huge surge of love for her. I shifted and then she looked up and jumped, surprised to see me. She brushed a strand of hair from her eye with dusty fingers.

'Oh! There you are! I was wondering when you'd surface.'

It was 7.30 a.m., hardly late, but it looked like Mum had been up for hours, maybe even all night.

'I'm clearing out the china!' she said, unnecessarily. Her eyes were shiny and bright, her face slightly flushed. 'Why don't you get a coffee and join me? It'll be fun!'

I could tell Mum was on a high — manic, perhaps. Still, I

did as she said and we passed a happy couple of hours going through the mountains of crockery and glassware she'd accumulated over the years. She was very considerate this time, asking me about each item before deciding to throw it out. It was exactly how I'd hoped we'd have gone through Dad's things. I knew it was her way of apologising about the other night.

'Would you like this, Evie?' she'd ask, producing a coffee pot, a tea set or a pair of salad servers. 'It was my great-grandmother's… ? But it's quite vile, isn't it!'

I enjoyed the closeness with her, the rare normality. When she was like this, Mum was brilliant—giggly and fun. But by 9.30 a.m., we began to tire. Mum sat back in an armchair, let out a deep breath and admired our handiwork. The pile for the charity shop was five times the size of the 'keep' pile.

'You got back late last night,' she said.

'I had dinner with Luca.'

'Dinner?' she asked. 'With Luca? Just the two of you?'

I flushed, remembering the way we'd made out like teenagers in the bus shelter.

'He's a good catch, you know, Evie,' Mum said. 'You could do worse.'

'Oh, Mum, really. We live in different countries. '

Mum snorted. 'So you think you're going to meet a husband in Dubai? Like that James? Seriously, Evie? He was a no-hoper from the start.'

'Hmph.'

Mum settled back in her chair. 'Marriage isn't about

skydiving and champagne for breakfast, darling. It's about companionship, trust, respect, not Flash Harries.' I didn't say anything. 'James wasn't the right man for you.' Mum's tone was soft. She didn't mean to hurt me. 'All I'm saying is don't ignore what you've got right in front of your nose, just because it's familiar... the love of a good man is a valuable thing.'

I couldn't help myself: 'Is that what you had with Dad?'

Mum sighed. 'Oh, Evie. Meeting your father was like being hit by a train. He knocked me off my feet. He was so charming, so totally convinced that he and I were meant to be together and he was relentless in his pursuit of me. He made it clear he wouldn't give up until I married him.' She paused, rubbing the finger where her wedding ring used to sit, then said quietly, 'It was very flattering. But maybe I should have taken things slower.'

I looked at the floor. This was my moment. I may never have such a good opportunity again. I took a deep breath and looked up at her. 'What do you mean?'

Now Mum was quiet. She stared out of the window, a pensive look on her face. I counted slowly to fifteen trying to control my breathing, then Mum's eyes snapped back to me. 'Oh... oh nothing, darling.'

I was tired. Tired of the lies, tired of hiding what I knew and tired, almost, of life itself. I did a little cough to clear my throat and then I said it: the sentence that was to start unravelling what was left of our family. Had I known where it would lead, I might have shut up, packed my bags and gone straight to the airport.

'There's something I need to tell you… about Dad.' I pressed my lips together.

Mum shifted back in her chair, but said nothing. I looked around the living room, looked anywhere but at her. I took in the familiarity of the room: the trinkets and glassware jostling for space on the shelves, the walls covered in paintings, the familiar old sofa with its floral covers, the cream carpet that showed a little too much of the wear and tear it'd been subjected to over the years, and I felt wretched. Mum looked expectantly at me and nodded, as if to make me spit it out.

'It's not easy to tell you this, Mum, especially given what happened… you know…with Graham…' I paused, but still she didn't say anything. I took a deep breath and jumped.

'Do you remember when I went to Coventry' Mum nodded. 'Clem wasn't the only person I saw. I met someone else. I went there to meet him.'

Mum's brow furrowed. 'Who did you meet?'

'A guy called Tom. A student.' Mum got up and went to the window. I couldn't see her face—leaning against the windowsill, she was looking at the floor, examining the carpet as if the secret to life was inscribed in its pile. My eyes followed her gaze. The carpet was paler, bushier, behind the television, where no one ever trod. A layer of fine dust lay like icing sugar on the top of the skirting board in the corner. It was to this layer of dust, to that patch of pristine carpet, that I talked.

'When I was going through Dad's papers I found that he had a second email account. It was how he communicated with someone called Zoe.' I paused to see if Mum was going to say anything. She stayed quiet. 'He was having an affair. Had been having it for years.' It sounded so tawdry. I would never have imagined the words 'affair' and 'Dad' in the same sentence. I ploughed on. 'And they had a child. A boy. He's nineteen now. Dad stayed with them every weekend. When we thought he was away for work?' I paused. 'That's who I was seeing in Warwick. Tom. I'm so sorry. It wasn't about you. It was about me: he's my half-brother and I needed to meet him.'

Mum didn't say anything. She was also staring at the carpet. I could just about make out the faded stain where I'd spilled the Mother's Day cup of tea I'd made her when I was six—the dark spot of tea in a patch of lighter carpet where Mum had scrubbed. I wondered if she was remembering the same thing. I couldn't bear the silence. 'He's at university there.'

I buried my face in my hands. I didn't want to see Mum's reaction. I wanted to shut everything out; shut it all out. I heard her get up. She sat down next to me, peeled my hands off my face and held them in hers.

'Darling,' she said. 'I know. I've known for years.'

CHAPTER 62

Mum put her arms around me awkwardly as we sat next to each other on the sofa, and stroked my hair. I clung onto her. She felt so small and thin.

'How could you put up with it?' I sobbed, my tears making Mum's jumper wet. 'Why didn't you do anything? I can't believe you knew all this time!'

'Ssh,' she said. 'Shh, Evie. It's OK. Shh.' She rocked backwards and forwards with me.

Eventually, I pulled away and sat up. Mum took out her hanky, looked at it and handed it to me. 'It's clean, I think,' she said. She brushed her own eyes with a finger. 'Now I'm going to make us a nice cup of tea.' She picked her way through the piles of boxes and china and I heard her clattering about in the kitchen.

I went in after her, propping myself up on the counter. 'Why didn't you tell me? About Tom, I mean? Why didn't you confront Dad? How could you live knowing he was cheating on you every weekend? Oh, Mum. I don't know how you did it.' As she bustled about making the tea, it hit me that maybe she blamed herself for him straying. Was she ashamed?

'Darling, let me just finish making this and we'll sit down and I'll answer all your questions. Now go. Go and wait. I'll be through in a sec. You want normal or Earl Grey?'

I flopped back onto the sofa, flummoxed once more by the secrets my parents had kept from me; by the lies that had couched my childhood; the pretence of normality that had been constructed around me. The feeling was unsettling, like trying to walk against the direction of motion on a fast-moving train. Out of everything, I kept coming back to one thing: both Mum and Dad knew how much I'd missed Graham—they knew about that hole in my heart—so why hadn't either of them told me I had a half-brother?

Mum came back in, a pot of tea and two cups and saucers rattling on a tray.

'Why didn't you tell me?' My voice was whiney. I sounded like a child. Mum held up a hand to stop me, but I had too many questions.

'How did you find out?' I asked. Mum poured the milk and strained the tea leaves like it was any other normal day at home; like we were the normal family we appeared to be, not the tangled mess of death, infidelity and lies that we actually were. '*When* did you find out?'

'Evie, your dad may have been a clever man,' she said finally, 'but he wasn't as clever as he thought he was and, although I have my weaknesses, darling, I'm nobody's fool.'

'But how did you find out?'

'Well, funnily enough, you told me.'

'I told you? How could I tell you? I didn't know myself till the other week!'

'You told me by accident. A year or two, I suppose, after Graham died. You didn't know what you were saying.'

'But how?' I couldn't understand what Mum was telling me. How could I have told her something I didn't know myself?

Mum sighed. 'One afternoon I'd gone shopping,' she said. 'Or out somewhere. I forget where. Probably the High Street. We didn't have the big supermarket in those days; I had to get everything from the High Street. Anyway, I'd nipped out and you were home from school. You were full of excitement, practically flying with it. I hadn't seen you look so happy for a long time. "Are you going upstairs?" you kept asking until I realised that you wanted me to go up; that there was something waiting for me. I imagined it was some artwork or a little gift you'd made for me in crafts at school—do you remember how you used to like making me those little brooches?

'Anyway, so I went upstairs and there, on the bed, you'd laid out my best dress—a black cocktail dress—high heels, your favourite of my necklaces and the cream, patent leather handbag you thought looked like the Queen's. You were practically jumping up and down with excitement so I asked you what was going on. You were never the best at keeping secrets and you couldn't keep this one in: "You're going out for dinner! I'm not supposed to tell you but I heard Daddy on the phone. He booked a table for two at The Blue Orchid! He's going to meet you there straight from work. And I want you to look nice!"'

I remembered the afternoon, remembered The Blue

Orchid—at the time, it'd not only been the only Thai restaurant for miles, but the most romantic restaurant around. I think it's a takeaway now.

'I'd no idea about this dinner plan,' Mum continued. 'Your father hadn't mentioned it to me—he'd actually told me he'd be away lecturing—and I imagined you'd got the story wrong; that your father was taking a work colleague there. Still, I was a little suspicious—if it was work, why not go somewhere closer to the university?' Mum looked at me, her face clouded with the memory. 'You must have noticed, Evie, as you got older, that your father wasn't always the easiest man to be with? I saw the same thing in James, by the way. They were peas in a pod.'

She shook her head then picked up the thread again. 'Your father had been acting odd for some time and I'd been wondering if something was up. He'd bought some new clothes and got a spring in his step. Yet, when he was home, it was like a light had gone off. His attention was no longer on me. It was quite obvious; like being left out in the cold. I don't think he could deal with my… my… well. You know what happened after "the accident"?' She was referring to her suicide attempt. 'Your dad was a man who liked to be adored; he liked to be the centre of attention. And, when I was sick, that wasn't the case. It was the beginning of the end, Evie, but I tried to keep it together for you: I was scared.

'Anyway, that night, I decided to play along. I got dressed; we made a game of it. You helped me put on the necklace, spray my perfume and choose a lipstick to put in the bag.'

I nodded, the memory coming back to me. Mum had let me put some lipstick on, too. 'Then I called a cab and went to the restaurant. Lily was only too happy to babysit.

'I sat in a café across the street and I watched until your father arrived. And I saw them, Evie. I saw your father with his arm around that woman and I knew the moment I saw them. It was something in the way he moved with her, a lightness; an intimacy. I knew at once that this was no fling; that he thought he loved her.'

'But what did you do? Why didn't you go in and confront them? I would have.'

Mum's eyes misted. 'I know you would—you always were impulsive. And maybe I should have confronted him then, Evie. Maybe I should have had it out with him then and there and let him run away with her. It's easy to say now. Maybe that would have been the better thing to do. If I knew now how it would all turn out, how that decision was going to affect so many people, maybe I would have let him go. But back then all I could think was that I didn't want to make a scene. I wanted to go home and think about what to do, not barge in and risk ruining my life—and yours. You'd already lost your brother—all I could think was that if Robert chose that woman—' she curled her lip around the word, as if the feel of it repulsed her '—our family would have been ripped apart. I couldn't bear for you to lose anyone else. Your father may not always have been the best, but he was your dad and you loved him.'

I pressed my hands to my chest. 'Oh, Mum… So what did you do?'

'Well, I did all that I could: I paid my bill, I got up and called a cab home. You were in bed so you didn't see me come in without your father. In the morning, you assumed he'd already left. I told you that, far from being the romantic date you'd imagined, the dinner hadn't gone very well — that Dad had got a bit upset about Graham — and that it'd be better not to mention it. You obliged. Always were a good girl.'

I remembered that. I remembered that morning. Graham was the one topic that could be relied upon never to be brought up in our house. His death was the subject we swept collectively under the family carpet. How sneaky Mum had been to cash in on that.

'And you never said anything? To Dad? Or Zoe?'

'No.'

'But then? As I got older? Why didn't you confront Dad then? You had a job, you were independent. You could easily have left.'

Mum sighed, and refilled her teacup. 'Evie. Things are never as clear-cut as they seem. For a while I thought he'd stopped seeing her; that whatever little thing they'd had had burnt itself out. Although I should have known better. I'd done my research, found out her name. I spied on them every now and then, too — once I followed your father down to Maidstone on a Friday night and I saw her open the door, the child at her feet shouting "Daddy!"'

'Oh my God!'

'Yes, that was a shock. Actually, "shock" is an understatement. When I first found out, I'd no idea there was a baby.'

I was shaking my head, over and over. I tried to remember what Mum had been like a couple of years after the accident. I'd thought she was getting better. 'Did you talk to anyone about it? Does "she" know that you know?'

'No, she doesn't. And I couldn't tell anyone else. We were busy during the day, you and me; I had to keep going for you; try to keep your life normal. Do you remember the little outings we used to go on? Greenwich Park? Swimming? People were sympathetic because of what happened with Graham. If I looked a bit morose, they assumed I was grieving—which I was, but for far more than they ever knew. The doctor was more than happy to keep me in sedatives. I got through.'

I thought of the bathroom cabinet still full of sleep remedies.

'And then, as time went by, I realised it suited me to stay married to your father. I didn't want to let her "win"; neither did I want to be a single mother, a forty-something divorcée with a child. It's not how I saw my life panning out. And I liked being married—I didn't want to have to find someone else and start again. Who wants a middle-aged woman with a child? And then your father became successful—I can't lie, Evie, I enjoyed his success. I enjoyed the money, the prestige, the social standing. I enjoyed being Mrs Robert Stevens.'

'So you turned a blind eye? It was that easy?'

'I've told you. It wasn't easy to block it out, but I got used to it.

'Is that what the sleeping pills are for?'

She laughed. 'In the end, it became like a game for me. A challenge. He could easily have gone to her but, despite her youth, whatever it was that she had, I kept him here. Ultimately, he loved me enough to stay.'

'Did Dad know that you knew?'

'No. I was always one step ahead of him. I had him under my thumb.' She laughed again. 'Men aren't that complicated.' A pause. 'I just wish he'd been a bit more careful.'

'In what way? In making sure you didn't find out?'

'No. In leaving a trail of destruction—the children. Child, I mean.'

I caught my breath. 'You know?'

Mum sighed heavily, looked out of the window. 'Know what?'

'You said children. You know? That Zoe… ?'

Mum turned around and, in the instant that she did, I saw something I'd never before seen in her face: hatred. 'Yes. I know. She's expecting.' She spat the word out.

'How?'

'Oh, Evie.' Mum shook her head sadly. 'I work at a hospital. The biggest one in the south-east.'

'What do you mean? You saw her there? She can't even be showing.'

Mum shook her head, her lips a thin line. She looked hard at me, as if she were assessing me; she opened her mouth to say something then closed it again with a tiny shake of her head.

'What's the point of working in a hospital, Evie, if you can't use it to your advantage now and again?' She rolled her eyes at me as if I were stupid. 'Medical records. Long ago I pulled up her records. Wouldn't you if you could? And I checked them every now and then, just to see what was going on with her. That's how I found out about the baby. Thanks to NHS cuts, we have the only maternity unit in the area.' Mum counted on her fingers. 'She must be, what, fourteen weeks now.'

I shook my head in disbelief. But Mum was so calm.

'How can you stand it? Doesn't it kill you to know?'

Mum lifted her chin. 'You don't need to worry about me, darling. I'm stronger than you give me credit for.' She laughed to herself, a small chuckle, and shook her head again. 'Oh, Evie. You've no idea.'

I wasn't convinced of that. Given the 'episodes' I'd witnessed her having, I thought Dad's death had knocked her far harder than she thought. Another thought crossed my mind. 'Did you know Zoe and Tom came to Dad's funeral? Was it you who invited them?'

'I didn't see either of them at the funeral. Well, I was hardly looking—there were so many people there. I'm glad they didn't come back to the house afterwards. Some decency, I suppose. But I suspect it was you who invited them. Her name's in your father's address book. He'd put it in way back before anything happened and he kept it updated, I suppose not to look suspicious. When you went through it, you probably called her.'

I racked my brains; I wanted so badly to remember that call, but the more I thought about it, the more I think I imagined it.

'I sometimes wondered if it was all my fault.'

'What do you mean?'

Mum shrugged. 'Well. It's too late now.' She stood up, collected the teacups, put them back on the tray with a little laugh. 'Anyway, I'm glad you know. I can stop pretending. Perhaps you'll understand now why I'm not really knocked sideways about your father's death.' She picked up the tray. 'Do you fancy helping me go through the books now?'

Confession hour, it would seem, was over.

CHAPTER 63

Lying upstairs on my bed, a pillow hugged to my chest, I could hear the muffled sound of the radio coming up through the floor. I don't know what Mum was listening to and I couldn't catch any specific words but a man's voice was reverberating up through the floorboards, the sound as irritating to me as that of a bluebottle stuck in the net curtains. Bzz. Bzz-bzz. Bzzzzz. Bzz.

I was rerunning in my head the conversation we'd had. As far as Mum was concerned, the topic of Zoe and Tom was closed—she'd taken the tea things back to the kitchen, washed them up and gone back to sorting out the books. I think she genuinely felt the issue was resolved. She'd been relieved that the lies were over; that she could stop pretending—the word made me wince—to be sad about Dad's death. She'd said she hadn't been 'knocked sideways' but I didn't think that was true. Maybe she didn't see it, but she'd been acting odd the whole time I'd been in England.

For my own part, I was struggling. To some extent I was relieved, but the rest of me felt as if I'd been disembowelled, my insides scraped out. Admittedly, the weight I'd carried around with me since finding out about Tom had gone—the

problem of how to tell Mum and how she'd take it simply
ceased to exist. But what did all this tell me about Mum?
How could my mother have kept this to herself for so long?
I knew what James's infidelity had done to me: when I'd
found out, I'd wanted to kill him slowly and painfully with
my bare hands. I'd even fantasised about how best to do it.
How had Mum lived with the knowledge of Dad's infidelity,
constantly and continually? She'd have been reminded of it
every weekend when he packed his bags and disappeared off
'on lecture tours'. How had she lived with that knowledge
and not exploded? Was her strange behaviour since I'd been
here a symptom of that?

'Maybe,' I said to the room. 'Maybe...'

Miss Dawson had suggested that Mum had been unable
to move on from Graham's death while Dad was alive; that
she had suppressed her grief about it; and that Dad's death
had finally enabled her to 'bury' Graham. That made a lot of
sense to me and it largely fitted what I'd seen: Mum's reaction to the sirens, for example. Her 'memory' of Graham's
funeral; the screaming fit over Dad's bike. It was only since
Dad had died that she'd started to have these 'episodes'. But
was that all that was going on?

How did the night of the black bags fit into it? Certainly,
Mum had blamed Dad for Graham's death, but was there
something more going on? After being so emotionally
controlled for two decades, had Dad's death also given
Mum some sort of emotional release? Had her fury that
night been directed at him, rather than at me? I sighed
and propped myself up on my bed, pulling over my bag

of knitting. Something was out of kilter and I couldn't put my finger on it.

I was startled from my thoughts by the sound of my phone ringing. I saw it was Tom and scrambled to pick it up.

'Hey, Evie.' His voice was questioning, as if he wasn't sure whether or not I'd hang up on him.

'Hey. How are you?'

'I'm great. I was just calling to see... um, how you were? After the other day?'

'Bruised,' I said. 'But getting better.' I smiled into the phone, surprised at how happy I was to hear from him. The fact that Mum had known all along about Dad's double life changed everything. I didn't need to worry about her finding out any more; she even knew Zoe was pregnant.

'Look, Evie, I don't want to leave things like that. I know it was a shock for you. But I just want to say that when you're ready, I'd love the chance to talk to you properly.'

'You know what? I'd like that, too.'

'Great! I can come down to London over the weekend, if you like? Meet you in the West End?'

'No need.' I was more than happy to go back up to Warwick. I could do with some time out from Woodside.

I hung up with a massive smile on my face then I stomped down the stairs, rehearsing my words in my head as I went. Mum was tidying up the boxes of china. I stood behind the sofa, its flowery bulk squatted between us.

'Just to let you know,' I said, 'I'm going to see Tom tomorrow.'

She didn't look up.

'I'm sorry,' I said, 'but it's not all about you. I lost my brother. I can't believe you knew about Tom and didn't tell me I had a half-brother.'

'It wasn't my news to tell—'

I held up a hand to stop her. 'And now I know about Tom, I'm not going to miss the chance to get to know him. I'm telling you because I don't think we should have any more secrets, especially now it's just us.' I waited, but Mum didn't say anything. I wanted a reaction. 'You can't stop me,' I said. 'It's bad enough you hid it from me all these years. The least you can do is let me get to know him now.'

Finally, she looked at me, her mouth pursed into the little flat line I remembered from times I'd misbehaved as a child.

'I'm not stopping you, Evie,' she said, and turned back to the china.

CHAPTER 64

The Dirty Duck was Warwick University's campus pub. I wondered how it'd got its name. Still, the pub itself was much smarter than I remembered the bars being in my own university days and it was already, at midday, packed with students. I found a table and ordered a pint of my own—I barely ever drank beer but, given I was already about ten years older than most of the clientele, I put it down to camouflage. The last thing I wanted was to draw attention to myself.

The customers seemed a friendly crowd, jovial, joshing and more carefree than the stressed professionals I tended to hang out with, too young as they were for mortgages, job stress and babies. I kept my eyes on my phone, pretending to be tapping away at some important task while all my senses, my peripheral vision, and the nerves in the back of my neck took in what was going on around me. The steady buzz of conversation was punctuated by an occasional shout or burst of laughter. I was aware of the scrape of cutlery on plate, the clunk of glass on table. Even though I started every time the door opened I still, somehow, missed the moment that Tom walked in.

Suddenly, my brother was beside my table. After years of squeezing the word 'brother' out of my vocabulary, it felt odd to think it. I wondered what Graham would have thought had he been able to see me now. It occurred to me that Tom would have been Graham's half-brother, too. Three of us. Soon to be four. That was weird.

'Hi.' Tom shrugged off his coat, threw it over the chair across from me.

I jumped up, knocking the table and slopping beer over the side of my glass despite the fact I'd already drunk a good quarter of the pint.

'Hi!' A pause. 'So what can I get you? My round—to make up for last time?'

'You can stop apologising about that right now,' said Tom. 'But I'll have a pint, cheers.' He looked around, waved hello to a few people, sat down.

'Are you… OK now?' Tom asked, as I deposited his glass in front of him at the table and slid back into my seat.

'Yeah. Look, I'm sorry about what happened. It was a massive shock. I'd had no idea.'

'Understandable. It's hardly a normal situation, is it?'

'You can say that again.' There was a silence as we both sipped our drinks.

'I just wish he'd come clean. It may have been horrible for a while, but it would have made things so much better in the end,' Tom said. 'No more secrets.'

'I know. How did you feel about him when you first found out? I'm going round in circles. I can't help thinking he was a coward in the way he handled all this.'

'I went through the same thing. I blamed him, too,' said Tom. 'I guess, ultimately, it was his mess and he should have manned up and sorted it out. I can just imagine how much better it would have been for us: no more creeping around. You know we were banned from ever going to Woodside? In case we bumped into you? And Mum didn't ever want anyone to question my "legitimacy", so she pretended to be married? She's spent her whole adult life pretending to be married.'

'I haven't thought about that side of it. It never occurred to me that you were illegitimate.'

Tom laughed, rueful. 'Yup. I'm the "bastard" of the family. It obviously bothered Mum because she wore—still wears—a ring on her wedding finger. I never questioned it when I was growing up. I suppose she just put it on so no one would ask questions, and referred obliquely to Dad as her "husband". She told everyone he worked away from home.'

'Were you ever jealous? Of me?' My finger traced patterns in the condensation on my glass. I'd have been jealous had the situation been reversed.

'Well, I didn't know about you for ages. And when I found out, I suppose yes, for a bit. But when I calmed down I started thinking about what Dad had given Mum and me. It's not like he was an absent Dad. Mum kept telling me that he didn't have to spend time with us; he came because he wanted to. And, honestly, he was great when he was with us.'

'How do you mean "great"?'

'Well, you must remember? He must have been the same with you? The Mastermind Challenge? Lego? The bedtime

stories? He never missed a night. I loved having him read
to me; it was my favourite part of the day, the way he did
those funny voices. I used to love his Paddington voice.
Do you remember how he used to say "Please look after
this bear. Thank you."?' Tom laughed. 'I can't do it as well
as him. He used to help me with my homework as well.
That was brilliant, as I used to have projects to do over
the weekend—if it was history, wow, he was amazing at
coming up with ideas for history projects. He was good at
science, too. He loved building junk models and all that
crap we had to do. He must have done the same with you?
Maybe that's why he was so good—he'd already gone
through it all with you.'

Tom laughed, but I shook my head. I couldn't say
anything. I hadn't had homework before Graham died, then
Dad had changed, withdrawn. He'd never, not once, asked
me about my homework, let alone helped me with it. He'd
stopped reading to me when I was eight; stopped playing
Mastermind with me; never played Lego with me. It was like
Tom had had everything that I should have had; everything
Dad should have given me but, somehow felt he couldn't.
It was my turn to be jealous. I'd never have imagined he'd
have been such an attentive dad to his illegitimate child.

'He taught me to ride my bike, too,' said Tom. He looked
carefully at me; his voice was softer.

'No. No, he wouldn't have done that.' I sat stock still, my
voice barely audible. 'After… after…' I thought of Dad's
bike, banished to the attic.

'He didn't want to. But Mum made him. She said he

mustn't let Graham's accident define him forever. They fought about it. I heard them shouting about it after I was in bed, but he did it in the end. He did it for her. I'll never forget him running along behind me the first time I rode without stabilisers. He pretended to be holding on and, when I turned around, he was the other side of the playground.' Tom paused. 'He started riding again, too. We went for bike rides.'

'Excuse me,' I said. I pushed back my chair and elbowed my way through the bar, stumbling through groups of drinkers, searching for the toilets. How could he? I hadn't been allowed to ride my bike ever again. Slamming down the toilet seat, I sat on it, my head in my hands, my breathing hard and fast. I needed time to compose myself. Tom's revelation had told me one thing, underlined what I'd known all along; the one thing I didn't want to admit that, while Mum and I had continued living for twenty years in the shadow of Graham's death, Dad—the person under whose umbrella of care the accident had happened—had moved on.

'It's not Tom's fault,' I told myself. 'No matter how much it hurts, it's not his fault. It's not his fault, it's not his fault, it's not his fault.'

*

'I wondered if you were coming back,' said Tom when I returned to the table, a fragile smile on my face.

It's not his fault. I said it over and over in my head as I sat down. I'd only been gone a few minutes, but Tom had pretty much drained his glass. 'It's just... there are just so many shocks at the moment. I feel like I'm constantly being slapped on one cheek, then the other.'

'It's been a lot for you to learn in the last couple of weeks, hasn't it? On top of Dad, too.'

'Put it this way,' I said. 'When I left Dubai, I had no idea, no idea at all, about any of this. I thought I was coming to help Mum find Dad's Will, get in some sherry and get through the funeral. If I'd known about all this, maybe I'd have stayed put; invented an excuse; flown to India and hidden in an ashram.'

'Really? Aren't you glad you know now? That there are no more secrets? You've lost a dad, but you've gained a brother. That's got to be worth something?'

'It is. Of course it is.'

'I remember how I felt when I found out. The fact that he'd been such a great dad made me all the more angry with him when I found out what he'd done—about you and your mum, I mean. I'd grown up thinking he was perfect; he was my hero. I expected so much more from him. Suddenly Dad wasn't a superhero, he was a person who made mistakes—he was weak—and I felt so let down. So disappointed, Evie. I felt like he'd short-changed me. I'd believed in a person who didn't exist. It was like learning that Santa doesn't exist, or the tooth fairy, only a million times worse. I hated him.'

'I can't do that. How can I hate him? He's dead.'

'I know. It's different for you.'

Tom went to the bar. I remembered the pouch I'd brought for him containing Dad's watch and cufflinks. I'd taken out the photos; he didn't need those. It's not his fault, I thought. He may as well have something to remind him of his 'perfect' Dad. While Tom was still at the bar, I put the pouch on the table, in his place.

'What's this?' he asked, placing a fresh pint in front of me, another pint in front of him. He clearly thought we'd be here for some time.

'Open it.'

'Oh goodness,' he said, pulling out the cufflinks. 'I remember these.' He pulled out the watch, passed a hand through his hair. 'Oh God, and his watch. What are you going to do with them? '

'Would you like them?'

Tom looked at me, his eyes full of hope, as if he thought I was joking. 'Really? Are you sure?'

I nodded.

'I'd love them. Thank you. Thank you so much, Evie. You know, Dad set up a Trust for me because I couldn't be in the Will. But it was just financial. I had nothing of his. Nothing to remember him by. I guess he overlooked that bit. Thank you so much. I really appreciate it.'

'I wanted you to have them. It's not like I'd wear them.' I didn't tell him about Mum throwing out everything else. I was feeling much calmer again now. Seeing Tom's pleasure at having the watch and cufflinks made me feel a genuine bond with him for the first time. It made me realise how much Dad had meant to him, too; that there were two of us in life who could call the same man 'Dad'.

'It's weird, isn't it, that we both grew up in a web of

lies?' I asked, realising as I said it how true it was. We'd both been lied to.

'Yeah, I guess.'

'So how do you feel about it now? Now you've had so long to get over it? It's all still new to me. I can't imagine ever getting my head around this.'

'Well, as I said, I was angry with Dad to begin with. But then I started to get over it. I started to think of him as a good person caught in a bad situation. He just wanted to do the best by both of us. I think he wanted to be there for both his children. He just went about it the wrong way.'

'I'd like to believe that, too,' I said.

'We can believe what we want now he's gone. And we have a new sibling on the way.'

'How do you feel about that?'

Tom chewed his lip. 'Excited? Jealous? That kid will grow up without the lies.'

'But without a dad,' I pointed out.

'True.' There was a silence. Tom looked at his glass, then up at me. 'And how do you feel about my mum?' he asked. 'You know it's not entirely her fault either. She always wanted to know you. It wasn't her idea to keep us apart. I used to hear her arguing with Dad about it.'

'Really?'

'Yes. She hated the lies, too. She'd love to see you. She'll be able to tell you so much more; answer all your questions.'

'Hmm.'

'So would you do it? Meet her?' A pause. 'Please?'

I sighed. I have to admit, I was curious. I wanted to look at Zoe again, knowing what I now knew. I wanted to see what it was that Dad had seen in her.

'OK.'

CHAPTER 65

It wasn't late when I got home, but Mum was already in bed, her light still on. I crept upstairs and popped my head around the door. Fast asleep, still propped up on her pillows, the library book she'd been reading still lying open on the duvet. She looked so suburban, so normal in her white *broderie anglaise* nightie, rollers in her hair, a tube of hand cream next to her.

In sleep, her face was at peace, but the open packet of sleeping tablets on the bedside table told another story. She was a woman who, twenty years after the death of her son, still needed medication to get to sleep. Who knew what demons haunted her dreams? Our whole family had experienced Graham's death, lived with the aftermath, but it had left very different scars engraved on each of our souls. Mum had surprised me so much since Dad died that I was beginning to wonder if I knew her at all. I'd always seen her as weak, as someone who needed protecting, but now I began to wonder. It must have taken a great deal of strength to live with the knowledge that she'd had. Could I have done the same?

I closed the book, set it back on the table and clicked off
the light. I needed to talk to someone. The day had been
too momentous to get through alone. I called Luca. 'Can I
come over?'

*

Luca's apartment was the antithesis to Mum's silent house.
I could hear loud music before I even got to the door.
Classical. That surprised me.

'Hey, Evie,' he said, as he let me in. 'Good to see you.' He
slid his arms around me and kissed me slowly and deeply,
as if I were a rare delicacy he was savouring. His kitchen
table was covered in photographs and mountings—he'd
been mounting up his swan shoot. I noticed but didn't absorb
the fact that his pictures were stunning. I pulled away. Our
eyes met and I could see the question in his: why are you
here? What have you come for?

'You won't believe what happened today,' I said. 'I went
up to Warwick. I saw Tom again.'

'Wow. How did it go?'

'I had to listen to him telling me what a great father Dad
was.'

'And that's a problem because?'

'Well, you know how he practically ignored me after the
accident?' Luca nodded. 'Well, all the stuff he never did
with me, he did with Tom. Homework. Stories. Bike-riding.'
Luca raised one eyebrow. 'All that stuff.'

'Oh.'

'Anyway. What's done is done. I made my peace with

him. I'm glad I saw him again. We talked about our new "sibling". I just can't believe there's going to be three of us. He wants me to see his mum but, apart from that, I think all the worst is over now. There can't be any more secrets, can there!' I threw my hands in the air and walked to the patio doors. 'Can we go out? Onto your terrace? I really need some fresh air.'

'Sure... but hold on,' said Luca. 'Have you eaten? I don't know about you, but I could eat a horse. Why don't you make yourself at home while I run down and grab something for supper?'

I sank, suddenly feeling drained, onto his sofa, while he nipped down to Tesco Metro. He burst back into the apartment, plastic bags rustling and pulled out chicken breasts, a jar of *tikka masala* sauce and a bottle of wine.

'Gourmet, it ain't,' he said, opening the wine and handing me a glass, 'but it should fill a gap, and I think I've got some rice somewhere.' While he chopped an onion, got the chicken sizzling in the pan and put on the rice, I talked him through the conversation I'd had with Tom.

'I'm really proud of you for going,' he said. 'I think it's great if you two can pull something positive from all this mess.'

We ate outside. Luca got us each a fleece and moved his small kitchen table onto the terrace. We ate with the sounds of Woodside below us and the moon and stars above us. I loved that he'd cooked; I loved eating outside. After we'd eaten, Luca took my hand and led me to his bedroom.

'Leave it,' he said, nodding to the table, the dishes. Maybe it was the wine, maybe the emotion of the day but, ultimately, Luca was charming, I was tipsy and, well, I do believe I was finally over James.

CHAPTER 66

I woke the next morning and forgot, for a minute, where I was. The room was distinctly lacking in flowery wall-paper, for a start, and the bed sheets were charcoal grey. Early morning sunshine dripped lazily through the slats of a set of unfamiliar white shutters, and I realised that I was naked.

Slowly, I ran through events of the day before. The Dirty Duck. Tom. Luca. Oh yes, Luca. I could hear him clattering about in the kitchen. I squirmed in embarrassment. Sex with Luca had seemed like a good idea last night, even when he'd stopped to double-check — 'Are you sure this is what you want, Evie?' — and it had been great. But in the bright light of day I couldn't help wondering if I'd been a bit of a fool.

Before I had a chance to locate yesterday's knickers and drag a brush through my hair, Luca appeared with a mug in his hand and a local property magazine tucked under his arm. I smiled when I saw it: was he trying to tell me something?

'Here you go,' he said, placing both on the bedside table next to me. He was wearing boxer shorts and a t-shirt. I liked his bed hair. 'How are you feeling?'

Suddenly shy was how I was feeling, but I didn't want to admit it. 'Great,' I tried, making sure I was covered entirely by the duvet.

'Right, drink up,' he said brightly, 'then I'm taking you out for breakfast.'

He left the room, then popped his head back around the door, smiling cheekily. 'By the way, Evie? Um... do you think you could get used to this?'

*

Luca slipped his arm around me and pulled me close to him as we stepped out of his building into crisp, morning air that hit my brain like an excess of wasabi. The sky was so blue it could have been a summer's day, but it was so cold our breath came out in dragon puffs. Bundled up in coats and gloves, we walked to the shops near the station in silence. Luca strode out confidently and I wondered what he was thinking—most likely about what he was going to have for breakfast.

Myself, I was wondering how the pavement, the cars, the trees and the grass verges could continue to look the same when my life had changed so much. I hadn't done a good job of processing my thoughts, of filing them neatly.

In the space of a few weeks, I'd gone from being Evie-who-lives-in-Dubai—a fact that had previously defined me—to Evie-who-has-no-dad-a-brother-and-quite-possibly-a-slightly-mad-mother, not to mention Evie-who-appears-to-be-sleeping-with-her-ex. I didn't want to let myself believe that Luca saw it as anything more than a fling for

ANNABEL KANTARIA

old times' sake, but I couldn't suppress the little jig of hope that had started fluttering in my belly. I saw now that James had never been right for me. Luca made me feel so good about myself—we got on so well. Could we make it work? Should we even try? Could I move back to England? As we trudged up the hill, my emotions swirled. Was I jumping the gun to even think about a future with Luca?

'I just need to go to the ATM,' I told Luca when we reached the shops. 'Why don't you go ahead?'

He was waiting at a table in Caffè Nero when I got there—a lone young man amid a sea of latte-sipping, blue-rinsed old ladies. My lover. His film-star looks were lost neither on me nor on the grannies.

He'd ordered me a cappuccino and brought over a couple of newspapers. 'I didn't know what you wanted, but thought you could start with this,' he said. I sat down and took a sip, waiting for that first hit of caffeine.

'So,' said Luca.

I suppose it was testament to how well we knew each other that the one word could hold so much nuance. It encompassed everything that had happened last night, everything that had happened in our lives to date; the way our lives had entwined, separated and joined back together. It was a word that took in and embraced all that could be said about Luca and me, and a slight upward inflection made me realise that, for him, too, it also contained more than a fragment of hope.

'So,' I said in return, my one syllable packed with question marks, hesitations, hope and also with love.

He squeezed my hand and smiled.

'Let me buy you a butty,' I said, squeezing back.

*

After breakfast, I trudged up the road towards Mum's, my body weary, my face bare of make-up, my hair gathered messily in a clip. A second coffee and a couple of pain-killers had diminished the grip of my hangover, but I still had a hollow feeling from drinking too much and sleeping badly in an unfamiliar bed. My clothes smelt faintly of the curry and onions Luca had cooked, even though I'd stolen a squirt or two of his citrus aftershave.

It'd been many years since I'd done the 'walk of shame' and I was glad no one was around to care. Mum knew, obviously, where I'd been. I'd had to leave a note for her so she didn't worry and I hadn't had the mental capacity yesterday to lie. I was dreading her reaction to the news that I'd presumably got it on with Luca. She'd probably been choosing a hat and planning my wedding all morning. I was going to have to face her joyous reaction this morning and, on top of the remnants of my hangover, the thought made me feel sick.

My steps slowed as I neared the house. I rummaged in my bag for my keys as I turned into the driveway, my feet scrunching into the gravel. But I saw with a jolt that I wouldn't be needing them: Mum was standing on the doorstep, chatting with Richard. I stopped in my tracks. Mum looked at me. Richard looked at Mum. I looked from Mum to Richard and back again. There was something

about the way they looked. Guilt hung in the air above
them.

'Richard just brought me the paper,' said Mum, with a
smile, and it was then that I knew what I'd suspected all
along.

'How long?' I asked. 'Just how long has this been going
on? A week? A year? Five years? '

'Oh, Evie,' said Mum. Richard looked at the gravel.

'I asked you—I asked you both!—and you denied it.
How long?'

'Evie. It's not like that. It's not like that at all. Please
don't get the wrong idea.' She sighed. 'He's just... it's just
that your father was never here. Richard's been here for me.
You have to understand that. After yesterday.' Her words
came out in a rush.

Richard took a step towards me. 'Evie, I...'

'Save it,' I said, holding a hand up. 'It's just more secrets!
More lies!' I was shouting now, bags of pent-up anger coming out. I slapped my forehead theatrically. 'Why am I not
surprised? You could have just told me! You could have told
me! After all we've been through!' Tears threatened and I
shoved past the two of them into the porch. 'But it's just
more lies. Lies, lies, lies! When's it going to stop, Mum?
I'm an adult, for God's sake! Look at me! I'm twenty-eight
bloody years old! When are you going to stop lying to me?'
I slammed the door in their faces.

Chapter 67

A long, hot shower took the edge off my temper and, an hour later—without saying a word to Mum, who had somehow got back into the house—I took the bus to Bromley. While I didn't know the town that well, I knew where Café Rouge was, which is why I'd suggested it to Zoe as a place we could meet. There was a pleasant enough café in Woodside High Street, but it was too close to home. I got there ten minutes early and Zoe wasn't there. Like a dog making its bed for the night, I moved tables three times before settling on one facing the door, but tucked to the side, so we could talk privately without interruption from passing traffic. But then I felt sick. Apologising to the waitress, I stepped back out, walking quickly away from the café. I stopped outside a jewellery shop across the way and about thirty metres down, and, under the guise of looking in the shop window, I watched the entrance of the café.

Although I was nervous, I also wanted to know who she was, this woman who'd seduced my father, stolen his heart. What had he seen in her? Aside from her youth, what had Zoe had that Mum had not?

From my post at the jeweller's, I saw her arrive. She was wearing brown boots, dark-blue jeans and a brown pea coat with the same ice-blue scarf she'd worn to the funeral. She didn't look like an adulteress, a husband stealer. She looked nice, like someone with whom, in another life, I might have been friends.

I walked slowly over to the café, my hands fidgeting in my coat pockets. I flipped my hair and took a deep breath before pushing open the door.

'Oh hello again!' said the waitress. 'Back so soon?'

Zoe saw me at once and stood up. She'd sat at the same table I'd chosen, in the same seat facing the door. She smiled welcomingly at me. Her complexion was clear, glowing; her teeth white and even; her eyes bright; her smile open. Her shiny, dark hair hung loose, a strand falling over one eye. I walked towards her, aware of the sound my heels made on the wooden floorboards. I felt like I was walking the plank.

'Hello, Evie,' said Zoe, standing to greet me. She looked me up and down, a warm smile lighting up her face. 'At last. At last I get to meet you. And look at you, so beautiful. Photos don't do you credit. No wonder your father was so proud.' She put her arm around behind me to guide me to my chair and I caught the fragrance of her, of her skin, her hair—it was soft, powdery, clean, wholesome. An image of Dad holding her, loving her, flitted into my head.

Silently, I took off my coat, hung it over the back of the chair, and sat down.

'Thank you for coming,' Zoe said. 'I really appreciate it. I've wanted to meet you for so long.'

I tried to imagine what she'd looked like twenty years
ago. How old would she have been—twenty-two? Was
she skinny then? Pretty? All legs, eyes and cheekbones? It
was hard to imagine. Today, in the jeans and a sweater, she
looked neat, tidy, a little curvy.

'I'm very sorry about your father,' she said.

'Thank you.' It struck me that she'd loved Dad, too; that
she, too, had lost a loved one. 'Bit of a shock, wasn't it?'

'Well, yes…'

'You sound unsure?'

'Oh, it's just that… well, I'm probably wrong.' Zoe
shifted awkwardly in her seat and fiddled with the ring on
her wedding finger. 'But, well, I wondered if he'd had some
sort of premonition beforehand.'

I leaned forward. 'What do you mean?'

'Oh, don't mind me. It's nothing.'

'No—go on.'

Zoe sighed. 'Look, this probably sounds mad, but he
deposited some money in my account just before he died.
Quite a lot. It was unexpected and he didn't say what it
was for. He just put it there. And then he died. I can't stop
thinking about it. I don't know why he did it.' Zoe rubbed
her hand over her face.

'Maybe just a coincidence,' I said.

'But you know he paid maintenance for Tom?'

'Yes. A thousand a month in recent years. I worked that
one out myself.'

'Well, since we're talking figures, it was £22,000 and
I realised that there were twenty-two months until Tom

turned twenty-one. And, at twenty-one, his trust fund kicks in. Coincidence?' She stared at the table, her face clouded, then she looked up and smiled, the sunniness back. 'Oh ignore me,' she said. 'I'm not getting enough sleep at the moment. What would you like? Let me call the waitress.' She turned around and waved.

'It was heart failure,' I said, eyes fixed on the menu. 'He couldn't have known.'

'Yes. Exactly. I told you—I'm not sleeping well at the moment. Going mad!'

'Did you know he had a biopsy for cancer?'

Zoe's breath caught. 'What?'

'He hadn't told you? He'd had tests for prostate cancer. They were waiting to hear how advanced it was.' I shrugged, as if it were a secret to which I'd been privy. I enjoyed wrong-footing her.

Zoe's face had paled. 'He hadn't mentioned it. Are you sure?'

'Yes, absolutely. Mum told me. Apparently it wasn't related, though. He didn't die of cancer.'

A shadow passed across her face. I could see she was struggling not to show how upset she was. 'I had no idea.'

'Maybe he didn't tell you everything after all.'

'Rob wasn't a big talker when it came to health issues. Typical man.'

'He spoke to Mum about it.'

Zoe composed herself, then took a deep breath. 'Look, Evie, we're not here to score points. I can't tell you how

much it means to me that you and Tom have met. I've wanted so much for you to know each other.'

'Well, why didn't you tell us? Surely you could have
persuaded Dad? Worked on him over the years?'

'Rob—'she corrected herself '—your father wouldn't
hear of it.' She looked thoughtful. 'Not until last year. I think
he was just starting to change his mind. He was talking about
going to Dubai to see you. I think he planned to tell you
then. But, well... oh, it was complicated. I don't think he
ever felt truly happy with the way he handled the situation.
He was always torn. He felt a duty to your mum.' She said
it kindly, but the implication was there: he'd have preferred
to live with her and Tom.

'I don't understand why it was such a big secret,' I said.
'Like, in the beginning, maybe, when Mum was... you
know? But once she was better? I don't understand why he
didn't just tell her then. She'd have got over it.'

'Oh, Evie. I don't think your father thought she ever got
better.'

'What do you mean? She was fine. She had a job. Friends.'

Zoe didn't reply.

'It was nineteen years ago!'

'But you know how she was. Up and down? All right one
minute and not the next? She'd already tried to kill herself
once. Rob was worried she'd try to do it again.' There was
a silence. 'Or worse.'

'What do you mean? "Worse"? What's worse than trying
to kill yourself?'

Zoe just looked at me.

'What? I don't know what you're trying to say.' My voice rose.

'Him. He actually worried that she might try to harm him if she found out. He said she was volatile. He thought finding out something like this might send her over the edge. And the longer the secret went on for, the harder it became. He had to treat her with kid gloves.'

A laugh exploded out of me. I thought of how calmly Mum had handled it. 'Now that's just ridiculous! Seriously? Mum! Oh God. He had no idea. She tried to kill herself, like, nineteen years ago. And he still worried—*nineteen years later*—that she'd harm him? Oh, excuse me, but for heaven's sake!' My shoulders shook with laughter.

'I suppose, when you put it like that…' Zoe smiled. 'Look. I didn't know what state your mother was in. All I heard was what your father told me.'

'Like what? Give me an example.'

Zoe looked up while she racked her brains for an example. 'Well, there were those rumours about what happened to your grandfather.'

'What rumours?'

Zoe shifted on her seat. 'You know, when he died.'

'No, I don't know. Tell me. What are you trying to say?'

Zoe bit her lip. 'No. I'm wrong. It's nothing.'

'Well, clearly it's not nothing because you're claiming that Dad used whatever it is that you're now not telling me as an excuse not to leave Mum; that whatever it is you're implying happened between my mother and my grandfather was the reason why Dad thought his wife might murder him!' My voice rose in indignation as the words rained out of me. 'So what exactly is it you're trying to say?'

She shook her head. 'Nothing. Look, Evie, maybe there's someone in the family you can ask.'

I looked scathingly at her. 'I can assure you that there's nothing to find out. My father told you what suited him,' I said, 'and, for whatever reason, you lapped it up, whether or not it was true. I think we can both agree that he wasn't known for his confrontational style. He probably just wanted to maintain the status quo. It suited him because, whether or not you want to believe it, he loved Mum. Anyway, what neither of you knew is that Mum knew all along about the two of you shacked up in Maidstone.'

'What?' Zoe's face drained of colour. She held on to the edge of the table.

'She knows about you and Tom. Even the baby.' I looked at her stomach.

Zoe hugged her belly protectively. 'Seriously? No.' She looked around, as if Mum was hiding behind the bar. 'Does she know where I live?'

'What are you scared of? She won't *do* anything. She's known about you for years.' My tone was scathing. 'If she'd wanted to, she'd have confronted you years ago.'

'You don't know that, Evie. This—' she patted her belly '—this changes everything. Especially now Rob's dead. Oh, dear God.' Zoe was fanning herself with her hand again. Her face now looked flushed.

'You're being ridiculous.'

'Your mother's not normal, Evie. She's insane and she's got a history. Who knows what she might do?'

I knew how unpredictable Mum's moods could be but, seriously? Anger coursed through me. I stood up, shoving my chair back. 'Look, Zoe,' I said, my voice tight, controlled, 'I really want for us to get on. I really do. But you can't sit here and insult my mother and me like this and expect me just to take it. In the five minutes that I've been here you've told me my mother's barking mad and accused her of wanting to harm you, Dad—' I shook my head in disbelief '—and even an unborn baby. I'm sorry. There's absolutely no point in us continuing this conversation. I'll tell Tom I tried.' I shook my head at her and turned to go.

Zoe called after me, maybe she even got up, but I didn't stop. I didn't look back. The café door slammed behind me as I left.

*

I sat on the top deck of the bus home from Bromley. As I stared out at the identical houses of outer Woodside, at the cars parked in the driveways, and at the colour-coded wheelie bins lined up neatly by the front gates, I went over and over what Zoe had said. Maybe Dad had had reason to worry about Mum twenty years ago but, in the last decade—and in particular since she'd had her job—Mum had been pretty strong. And what had Zoe meant about my grandfather? He'd died before I was born and I hadn't heard anyone ever speak about his death.

There was only one person I could think of who might be

able to shed some light on all of this and, given what Zoe
had said, I now felt entirely justified in calling him. I needed
to get to the bottom of this. I rummaged in my bag for my
phone, scrolled through the address book and dialled. After
four rings, the line connected.

'Hello?' I said. 'Uncle David? It's Evie.'

CHAPTER 68

Tucked away around the back of Paddington Station, the coffee shop Uncle David had suggested we meet in didn't advertise its presence. I'd walked past its discreet, dark-painted door three times before I noticed it and now, as I stood nervously outside, I wondered why my uncle hadn't chosen somewhere a bit more mainstream for us to meet. It had been a long and frustrating slog for me to get there from Woodside but, with curiosity burning inside me, I'd have gone to Timbuktu if he'd have asked.

But, as soon as I pushed open the door, I understood why Uncle David had chosen the place: it was the antithesis of every coffee-shop chain I'd ever seen. Baroque in style, it was scattered with comfy, high-backed armchairs uphol-stered in jewel tones. The walls were wood-panelled and the overall effect was more gentlemen's club than coffee house. The aroma of coffee hung in the air; over the low burble of grown-up conversation I could hear blasts as milk was steamed for cappuccinos.

I looked around, unsure. I'd no idea what my uncle looked like and there were three men of about the right age sitting alone with their newspapers. One stood up and I knew then that it was him. There was a familiarity about his face—he had Mum's high cheekbones and his skin, under a bushy beard, was the same sort of pale, pinkish tone as Mum's and mine. His eyes, though, were what I noticed most: while they were the same piercing blue as Mum's, they looked in different directions and I realised with a jolt that one of them was glass. He was wearing a red-and-white checked shirt with blue jeans and a jacket. There was something jolly about his appearance that made me warm to him at once.

'Evie?' he asked, holding out a hand to shake. I offered mine and he clasped it in both of his. 'David Evans.' His voice was soft, languid and rich, almost musical in tone. He looked closely at me with his good eye. 'Nice to meet you. At last. I always hoped I'd get to see you one day. But Carole… well…' He shrugged. 'Does she know you're here?'

I shook my head and he acknowledged my deceit with a single nod. 'OK.'

We ordered our coffee, made the necessary small talk. Uncle David told me he was a musician. 'Well, of sorts,' he said. 'Some will say I sold out—went over to the dark side: these days I compose ditties for advertising companies. You know? Those irritating little jingles you hear on the radio? I'm too old to be a rock star or a struggling artist. I need to finance my retirement home in Thailand!' He laughed and I had no idea whether or not he was joking.

'I was sorry to hear about your dad,' he said, looking serious again. 'How's Carole taking it?'

'She seems… um… all right. Given the circumstances.'

'You don't sound too sure.'

'It's hard to say. She's up and down.' I thought about her screaming at me; hitting me when I tried to stop her throwing out Dad's things. 'Unpredictable, I suppose. I've talked to a counsellor and she thinks it might be some sort of grief dysfunction since my brother died. But I actually wonder if there's something else going on.' I paused, and then remembered the other reason why I was there. 'What I really wanted was to ask you—sorry, strange question—how your father died. No one's ever spoken about it and I was just wondering? If you don't mind?'

Uncle David stroked his beard thoughtfully. 'OK. We'll get to that. But, first, has Carole ever told you why we don't speak?' he asked. 'Why she "banished" me? I presume that's part of why you're here.'

I leaned forward, all ears. This was a secret I'd thought Mum would take with her to the grave. 'All I know is that you refused to go to her wedding.'

David laughed, a snort of a laugh. 'I didn't "refuse". I was, how shall we put it, "disinvited". But it goes further back than that. Carole always had quite a temper.' He tapped his glass eye with a finger. 'You see this eye? This comes courtesy of my sister.'

'Seriously? How?' I was horrified. My mother!

'There was a game we'd play in the garden when we were kids. It involved throwing stones at a target we'd made. Sort of like darts, I guess, only without darts and a dartboard. Mum hated us playing it, but we played anyway. The rule was, when one person went to pick up the stones or reset the target, the other wasn't allowed to throw.'

I could guess what was coming. Uncle David nodded. 'Yep. One day I went to reset the target and Carole threw one more stone. Got me smack in the eye. Good shot, my sister.'

'But it was an accident?'

'Well, that's what our parents wanted to believe, but I'm pretty sure it wasn't. Carole knew the rules; she knew I was there. But I was winning and, well...' He pursed his lips and shook his head. 'She always was very competitive. She couldn't bear anyone else to win.'

A shiver ran through me. Hadn't Mum said something about not wanting Zoe to 'win'? But misunderstandings, accidents like this happen all the time with kids. Maybe my uncle was reading too much into it. 'So that's why you stopped speaking?'

'No. Not at all. That was just background.' He took a sip of his coffee and I followed suit. 'No. The reason we don't speak is because of what happened with our father—your grandfather. This must be what you were getting at when you asked how he died. Did your mother ever tell you anything about it?'

I shook my head, desperate to hear more. Uncle David was a thoughtful speaker; he said his words slowly and with lots of pauses. I clasped my hands around my cup to repress my fidgets. Go on, I wanted to tell him. Hurry up!

'Our mother died when she was sixty. She and Dad had been married since they were seventeen. I think Mum had worked for a year or something before she got married, but she'd never actually had what you'd call a career. She'd dedicated her life to staying home and looking after Dad,

Carole and me. Nothing wrong with that, of course,' he said, fixing me with his good eye. 'It's just how it was in those days.'

I shrugged—I wasn't going to judge. I just wanted to hear the story. I picked a tiny pastry from the plate that had come with the coffee, and bit into it, nodding to get him to carry on.

'Dad hadn't learned to do anything around the house. He couldn't cook; didn't know what to use to do the cleaning. He probably didn't even know what the washing machine was for; he really was a domestic dinosaur.' I smiled at the thought, but Uncle David carried on. 'He hadn't a clue. After a few months, it became apparent that he was really struggling. He became thinner, started missing appointments. His clothes looked shabby; he stopped taking care of himself and retreated into himself. Carole and I talked about it and we agreed he'd have to move in with one of us while he readjusted to being single. I didn't ever imagine it would be a permanent move. I just thought one of us could "rehabilitate" him, so to speak; teach him how to cook and take care of himself. There was nothing physically or mentally wrong with him. It was just ineptitude.'

I nodded. The irony wasn't lost on me that Mum had also lost her life partner young. Thank heavens she knew how to take care of herself or I'd have been on a one-way ticket home from Dubai.

'Anyway, I was staying temporarily in Manchester for a work job, so it was decided that he would live with Carole rather than me. She'd teach him how to shop for ingredients and cook a few simple dishes; teach him how to do the washing and ironing and generally get him back on his feet.'

Uncle David stopped talking and stared into space.

'So what went wrong?' I said. Zoe's words were dancing in my head. I knew something bad was coming.

'Well, it was a good plan. I called every few days to check things were ticking along fine. Carole always sounded fine; she said things were going well and that Dad was frail and a bit reclusive, but he wasn't a burden. Then, one Saturday, I called as planned, and there was no reply. I tried again and again. I managed to get hold of the neighbour and asked her to go around. She had a key.' He paused. 'She found him lying face down in his own vomit.' I gasped. 'He'd hit his head as he'd fallen. We've no idea how long he'd been there. There was no sign of Carole.'

'How come? Where was she?'

'Well, it turned out she'd buggered off on holiday with her boyfriend. She claimed Dad had been fit and healthy and had given her his blessing to go, but it was obvious from the state of him that she hadn't been looking after him very well at all. He was frail, filthy and sick.'

'Oh my God. So then what happened?'

'Well. I blamed myself. I shouldn't have put so much responsibility on her. I quit the job in Manchester, and took Dad home with me to Oxford, where I concentrated on trying to nurse him back to health. He never really did recover, though.'

'So is that why you and Mum don't speak?' I nodded to myself, trying to piece it back together.

'No, no. That's not it at all. I told you. I blamed myself for that. It got worse when Dad died.'

My eyes widened. Both my grandparents had died before I was born, but I'd never really given a thought as to how or why. For me, my grandparents were imaginary, almost historical figures. I didn't know much about them at all.

'He didn't last long,' Uncle David continued. 'I think he died of a broken heart.' He looked sharply at me. 'No, don't laugh. He adored Mum and, ultimately, I don't think he had much will to carry on without her.'

'That's so sad.'

'That wasn't the end of it, though. In fact, it was after he died that it all started to go wrong. The autopsy showed a small amount of damage to his liver and kidneys that was consistent with having taken low doses of arsenic over a period of time.'

'What? Had he been trying to kill himself?' I imagined a heartbroken old man tipping arsenic into his coffee every day, waiting to die.

Uncle David shook his head. His voice was so quiet I strained to hear him. 'No. I didn't think it wasn't him.' He leaned forward and clasped his hands together. 'Forgive me for saying this, Evie. It was a difficult time. But I thought Carole had done it.'

'No!' I gasped, shaking my head vehemently. 'No! She would never have done that! You were wrong. You must have been wrong!'

But Uncle David lifted a hand to quieten me, and carried on. 'I thought she couldn't cope with having Dad there. Or maybe she'd thought she was being kind to him, giving him a quick way out or something. Trust me, I've thought about this constantly over the years and I'm not so sure now. But, at the time, I thought she'd given him a tiny bit every day and then gone away when she'd thought he was about to die.'

'Oh my God! You thought she tried to poison her own dad? Did she?' I thought of Zoe's accusation. 'Did anyone else ever find out?'

David looked bleakly at me. 'I'm afraid we'll never know if she did or not. There was an investigation. Carole and I were both questioned and let go. The police found a small bottle of arsenic hidden in the back of the wardrobe in Dad's room at Carole's so they couldn't prove that he hadn't actually taken it himself—grieving widower and all that. Ultimately, though, we were let go because the arsenic wasn't the cause of his death—the amount hadn't been enough to kill him, and it had obviously stopped when Dad had moved in with me. It was all very tenuous; the damage was slight. As I said, I think he died of a broken heart.'

I slumped back on my chair. 'Oh my God. I had no idea. No one ever mentioned this at home.'

'Well, why would they? It's not something Carole would ever have wanted dragged up. She probably tried to bury it as best she could.' Uncle David looked out of the window for a bit, even his normal eye looking glassy. Then he turned back to me. 'After it was all over, I confronted Carole.'

'And?' I couldn't believe all this had happened in my own family. Dad must have known—it must have been he who'd told Zoe, but I'd never heard a whisper about it.

'She went ballistic. Accused me of doing it myself. Tried to scratch my other eye out. Said she'd never forgive me for even thinking she would try to poison her own dad. Then she told me to get out. "I have no brother" were her words, if I remember correctly.' His voice was flat.

I took a deep breath and let it out slowly through my mouth. 'I'm in shock… So you not only lost both parents, but your sister as well.'

He closed his good eye for a moment, then opened it. 'Well. What can I do? Life goes on. My conscience is clear. I did all I could for Dad. I don't know about Carole, though. I wonder now if I was wrong about her. Maybe Dad *did* take the poison himself. I think about her. I thought about getting in touch, but…' His voice tailed off.

There was a silence. I was aware of the sounds of the coffee shop in the background. 'So you've never seen her since that day?' I asked.

Uncle David took a slug of tea. 'Not technically.'

'What on earth does that mean?'

'Well…' He smiled sadly, his voice cracking a little, his eye roaming towards the window again. He steepled his fingers under his chin. 'I did sort of go to her wedding. A friend we'd known growing up told me where and when, so I hid behind a hedge across the road from the church and I watched her arrive. I watched her get out of the car, arrange her dress and walk in. She was wearing ivory—not a big monstrosity of a dress, just a simple thing, and carrying pink roses. She looked beautiful. I waited to see her come out, married. That's the last time I saw her.' There was a long silence. 'Your dad looked like a nice chap. Was it a happy marriage, Evie? Did he make her happy?'

I put my head in my hands. 'Oh God. If you'd asked me this last week, I'd have said yes; yes they were very happy considering what they went through. You know about my brother, right?'

He nodded. 'I did hear. I sent flowers, a card with my number, but she never replied.'

'She was sick,' I said. I explained about Mum's suicide attempt and her incarceration. Uncle David sat there taking it all in.

'You've been through so much. I had no idea,' he said.

It was my turn to shrug. 'That's not the half of it. Since Dad died I've found out he had another family — a mistress and a son. He was leading a double life, staying with us all week and with them on the weekends.'

'Oh good God. You are joking, aren't you, Evie?'

'I wish. I wish I was joking. Nope. It's all true. I've met my half-brother. He told me.'

David let out a low laugh. 'You couldn't make it up. I'm guessing Carole doesn't know. I wouldn't have fancied your father's chances if she'd ever found out! As I said, she's very competitive.' He laughed again.

'She knew. She told me yesterday.'

Uncle David stopped laughing and leaned towards me. I could see tiny specks of cappuccino froth on his beard. 'How did you say your father died?'

'In his sleep. Heart failure.' I narrowed my eyes at him. 'Are you saying… ? No-no-no-no-no. Mum had known

about this for *years*. Like eighteen years or something.
Seriously. I think she'd actually got used to it. Maybe the
arrangement even suited her. She was very calm when she
told me about it yesterday. She got over it years ago. Don't
even go there!'

David sat back. 'Sorry, Evie. I wasn't implying that at
all. But, look, I'm glad you got in touch. If you need me,
you know where I am.'

'Need you?'

'In any way, Evie. I'm always here for you.' He patted
my hand awkwardly. 'In any way at all.'

*

I spent the majority of the journey home staring into space
in a daze, replaying my conversation with Uncle David in
my head. He thought my mother had killed her own father!
Every time I got to that bit of our talk, I shook my head.
'No!' I muttered. 'Just—no!'

I didn't know what had gone on between David and Mum
when they were growing up although, from the sounds of it,
it had clearly been a more combative relationship than I'd
had with Graham. Goodness, I'd heard of sibling rivalry,
but taking out your brother's eye? I could imagine, then,
that David must have had his own agenda; put his own spin
on what had happened between his dad and his sister. He
was a musician, for goodness' sake. I knew these creative
types: he probably wasn't unfamiliar with alcohol, maybe
even recreational drugs. Who knew what hallucinations he
might have had? I didn't doubt the facts of what he said,

just his analysis of what had happened. Maybe he felt guilty for not being there when his dad needed him, and blaming his sister was a way of exonerating himself.

Far from putting my mind at rest, the conversation with my uncle had made me feel uneasy. On the one hand, I was glad to have met him at last, and his assurances that he'd be there for me were good to hear, but, on the other hand, I still felt apprehensive about Mum. Did Zoe really have good reason to be scared of my mother? I shook my head again. Oh please.

I transited London on autopilot, still lost in thought and, before I knew it, I was on the local train back down to Woodside. As I stared out of the window, the back gardens of south London slipping past in a jumble of broken trampolines, uncut grass, rain-soaked patios, conservatories, garden sheds and washing lines, the germ of a thought, as yet unformed, knocked at the edge of my consciousness.

CHAPTER 69

I'd grown up seeing Benny's Removals trucks around town but, having lived in the same house all my life, it was a company that 'other people' used. Now, as my taxi pulled up outside my parents' house, the huge red-and-blue van parked outside looked out of place—it made the house look like someone else's house. It made me realise, too, that the days of calling this house 'home' were coming to a close. There was a certain poignancy to the moment.

There were eight packers ('That's the only way we'll do a job this size in two days, love.') and they were fast. They moved like a swarm of locusts around the house, wrapping everything in paper, placing each item in boxes with unexpected care before scribbling with thick marker pens on each box which room it was from. One even moved through the house with a camera, taking pictures of every room from every angle, 'to 'elp wiv the unpacking, love'. His accent was pure South London. 'Makes it easier.'

'That's a good idea,' I said. Mum and I didn't know what to do with ourselves. We perched in the living room, pretending to read magazines; Mum kept jumping up and offering to help.

'Look. I'll be honest,' said the man with the camera. 'It'll be much easier for us if you can go out for a bit, get out of our 'air. We'll be able to work quicker. Just make sure you've got yer valuables safe — jewellery, cash, passports — show us where the tea is and go for a late lunch and a bit of shopping, like?' He mimed a lady shopping, mincing along with bags in her hand and her nose in the air.

'You'll leave the beds till last, won't you?' I was anxious. 'We're sleeping here tonight.'

'Yep. Don't you worry about anyfing.' He grinned at us. 'I'll leave yer the beds and the microwave. Believe it or not, we've done this before. More than once.'

Upstairs, I looked into Graham's old room. Already it was missing the bed, bedside tables and lounge chair. All that remained was a slim dressing table and a chair. My chest tightened. This was where I came to speak to Graham; where I felt closest to him. Without this room to anchor my memories, would I forget the real Graham? Would he become just an ethereal idea; the floating concept of a boy who'd once existed?

'I think it's going to be all right,' I said to the room. 'She seems OK, doesn't she?'

I got down on my hands and knees and crawled under the dressing table to the point where the carpet met the skirting board in the far corner of the room. With my palm on the carpet, I felt around until I found a small lump. It was still there. I felt for the edge of the carpet and gently pulled it up, feeling with the other hand until it found what it was looking for.

I pulled out the plastic bag, reversed myself out from under the dressing table, pushing my hair back out of my eyes, and sat on the chair. I couldn't believe it was still there. Twenty-one years ago, when I was seven and Graham nine, we'd become fascinated with the idea of time capsules and had spent much of that entire summer first stripping the house and digging the garden in the hope that we'd find one someone had hidden, and then planning what we'd put into our own. This little sandwich bag was the result. Through the plastic, I could see a fraction of amateur joined-up writing in blunt pencil: '1992... Woodside, Kent, England... Robert, Carole, Graham, Evie... no spaceships... terrestrial car... Vauxhall Vectra... John Major...' The bump was from the 1p, 2p and 5p coins we'd put inside as an example of currency, along with a second-class postage stamp we'd stolen from our parents' desk drawer.

'What shall I do with it?' I asked the room, but I decided almost immediately to leave it. Crawling back under the dressing table, I pulled up the carpet again and slid the bag back underneath. I hoped the new people would have children who'd find the thought of a message from twenty years ago as exciting as we had.

*

We took the bus into Bromley and, after a quick mooch about the shops, Mum and I found ourselves facing each other over the scrubbed wooden table of one of my favourite cafés. We ordered smoked salmon wraps and a bottle of water but then, as the waiter turned to go, Mum suddenly asked for a bottle of Pinot Grigio and two glasses as well. 'Why not?' She shrugged as I pulled a *faux* shocked face at her. 'I'm not driving and we've nothing else to do.'

It was a good call—the wine went down well, making Mum a little giggly. Under the lunchtime influence, she became the mum I remembered from before Graham's death: a more carefree, happy Mum; a Mum who'd played on the floor with me, putting my Sindy dolls into ridiculous outfits and thinking up silly things for them to do. Not the tense, fragile Mum of later years.

'So tell me about Luca,' she said, leaning towards me over the table as if we were two girlfriends out for a gossip. 'Is he moving to Dubai, or can we expect to see you moving back here?'

'Would you like me to move back?' I studied my plate as I spoke. 'I mean… I could… ?'

'Move back for yourself, Evie,' said Mum. 'Move back for Luca. But don't move back for me. I'm fine. In case you haven't noticed.'

'Really? I worry.'

Mum rolled her eyes. 'You don't need to worry about me. But Luca? If I were you, I'd be doing everything I could to give that relationship a chance. You don't meet men like him every day.'

I took a sip of wine. She had a point. It was difficult to imagine how anti-relationships I had been just six weeks ago. Luca had been a game-changer. For the first time in six years, I'd started to question why I was in Dubai. I knew I'd been running away from Mum and from the sadness that had choked our family since Graham's death, but things had changed. Maybe it was time to come back.

'Look, Evie, everything else aside, Luca's a nice guy,' Mum said. 'He lights you up. No more, no less.'

I played with my napkin. Mum cocked her head expectantly.

'He's lovely,' I said finally. 'I'm wondering if it could work after all. Now we're older and all that.'

'I bet it could! You could always come back. I really don't know what keeps you over there in all that heat. And you of all people know how easy it is to move country. You've done it once before. Maybe it's time to come back. What is it the Buddhists say? "Nothing is permanent"? "Everything is possible"?'

'Hmm.' I tried to look non-committal as a smile wound its way round my insides. 'Anyway,' I said. 'I'm glad to see you looking so happy.'

'I *am* happy. Honestly, Evie? I'm glad to be moving out of that house.' Mum took another sip of wine and looked at her hands before continuing. 'It's a lovely house. And obviously it was your home, but there are too many bad memories tied up in it. It's time to move on. I feel so liberated to be moving to the new place. I can't wait. It feels like a new start.

'It *is* a new start.'

'But are you ready for it?' I asked. 'Are you sure it's not too soon?'

'I'm fine, darling. I'm stronger than you think. And Richard's been ever so helpful. It's very nice to have a chap like that around when you live on your own.' Mum looked carefully at me. It was the first time she'd alluded to Richard since I'd seen them on the doorstep that day.

I sighed. 'I know. I understand. Really, I do. Especially now I know what, um… happened with Dad.'

'He's a nice man,' Mum said. She smiled to herself. 'He's not an academic like your father but, if you got to know him, I think you'd like him.'

'I know, I know. I wasn't angry about him *per se*. I was angry that you didn't tell me. Even when I asked. It was another secret. It just seemed like there were so many secrets. Massive secrets! It was as if you didn't trust me with anything. That's what I was angry about.'

'I'm sorry, darling.' Mum patted my hand.

'You have to understand that it's just you and me now,' I said. 'We're all that's left. And I'm an adult. You don't have to shield me from this stuff any more.' As if you ever did, I thought. 'God! I mean, what could be worse than what we've been through in the last few weeks? A death, two affairs and a secret son! I swear, we could be on *The Jeremy Kyle Show*!'

'We don't have the tattoos,' Mum said deadpan. She took a sip of her wine. 'Anyway. You don't need to worry about me getting married. I'm never getting married again. Once was more than enough.' She laughed. Bitterly.

*

There are times in life when you're not sure if you're doing the right thing. As I rang the bell for the bus to stop a couple of stops too soon for Mum's road, I was full of doubt. If the wine hadn't dulled my sensitivity, I would never have done this. It took a second for Mum to realise what I was doing, and she looked sharply at me. Surrounded by strangers, we had a conversation in glances as I stood by the bus door. *Seriously?* she asked me with her eyes. *If you want to?* I asked her back. A pause, then Mum shrugged, stood up and joined me at the doors.

I took her arm as we got off and then I kept hold of it. It wasn't far to the crossing and our steps slowed as we got closer, both of us lost in our own thoughts. I was thinking, as I always did at this spot, how this view was the last thing Graham would have seen before he died. These trees, these buildings, this pavement. That pedestrian crossing button the last thing that he pressed. That spot of tarmac, which we were walking past now, was where he'd taken his last breath.

We reached the crossing and stood back from the road, our thoughts hanging heavy. The lilies I'd placed were long gone.

'I come here every year,' I told Mum.

'Me too. I come here often. Sometimes there are flowers, not from me. I always wonder who else it is that remembers him. But it's nice to know that someone else does.'

'I didn't realise you came.'

She shrugged. 'Darling, he was my son. My firstborn.'

'I didn't realise you were… able to?' I was referring to her breakdown, her suicide attempt.

'It was a difficult time for me. It was all too much. Your father… his "thing" with that woman… was no help. I loved your brother—both of you—very much. But he's happy now. I know he's happy now.'

'I like to think so, too. He'd like to see us both here today. I wonder if he's with Dad now.'

'Probably not,' said Mum. 'I like to think your brother went to heaven.' She paused. 'Anyway, let's hope we don't find out for a long time. Right, come on. Let's see how far those packers have got.'

*

Mum's front door was propped open. Removal men scrunched back and forth across the gravel with boxes, fitting them into the back of the van like they were playing an oversized game of Jenga. I walked up the driveway and peered into the van as I passed—it was now about ninety per cent full, many of the big pieces appeared to be in. I asked how it was going.

'Just fillin' up with boxes now, love. Give us 'alf an hour and we'll be ready to take this lot over before we come back for more.'

I followed him into the house. Without furniture, the rooms looked huge. Without the washing machine, fridge, freezer and dishwasher, the kitchen units looked like a giant's mouth with the teeth smashed out. Without Mum and Dad's things, the house had lost its soul. Even the acoustics were different; my footsteps echoed. The house was just a shell. I breathed in the old familiar smell—that was all that remained, and even that was underlain now with the scent of old dust disturbed.

Upstairs, the rooms were largely clear. I blew a kiss into Graham's room, then went into Mum's. She was standing at the window, watching the removal men on the drive below.

'How does it feel?'

'Exciting, scary. Like the start of a new chapter.' She paused. 'A chapter that should have started years ago.'

'I guess it's the end of an era.'

I couldn't summon the same enthusiasm: I loved my parents' house. I loved the high ceilings and huge sash windows, the way the sun fell into the living room, the big, square bedrooms. I sighed. Maybe Mum was right: the house was too full of memories, and she wasn't the only one who needed to let them go.

CHAPTER 70

The move gave Mum a new lease of life. Out of the confines of the old house, she blossomed; almost become a new person—perhaps the person she'd always been underneath, but a person I hadn't seen since before Graham had died. She was happy, outgoing, confident—she radiated from inside and it made her look younger, more beautiful. I hadn't realised how much the old house—and Dad's secret—had weighed her down. It really was a new start for her. A way overdue new start.

She amazed me with her energy. After the packers had put everything in roughly the right place, she'd attacked the unpacking with the enthusiasm of a child on a sugar high, waving away my offers of help.

'Go, have fun with Luca,' she'd said and I'd been only too happy to fit in as much time with him as I could before I had to leave.

Two days after the move, I marvelled at how settled Mum was. Apart from a stack of collapsed cardboard boxes waiting to be picked up by the packers, there was no evidence that she'd just moved in. Returning from Luca's that morning, I walked through the hall noticing that pictures were up on the walls, books were on the shelves and china was in the cabinets. There was even a vase of tulips by the phone. I followed the scent of freshly baked bread and found Mum standing at the hob, stirring something. It was as if she'd lived there all her life.

'You're just in time for lunch,' she said. 'Spicy pumpkin soup and fresh bread.'

'I'll leave you to it,' said Richard, entering the kitchen behind me. He looked dishevelled, his lashes fringed with dust. 'I'll leave the toolbox under the stairs.'

'Thank you so much, much obliged. See you later.' She blew him a kiss then turned to me. 'Richard put up the pictures and the curtain rails.'

He doffed an imaginary cap in her direction and left. 'I'll see myself out.'

'Now I'm all settled,' said Mum, opening the fridge, 'how about a little celebration drink? Look what I've got!' She pulled out a bottle of champagne and presented it like a game-show hostess. 'Ta da!'

Before I could reply, she popped it open, plucked two flutes from the dresser in the dining room and quickly located some cheesy biscuits. The new dining table hadn't been delivered so we sat in the kitchen, at a small folding table Mum had borrowed from Richard. We clinked glasses.

'Cheers!'

'Bottoms up!' That was Mum. She took a big swig.

'Here's to you,' I said. 'I can't believe how far you've come in six weeks. I was so worried when I first came over.

I thought you'd be a mess, but I'm so proud of the way you've handled everything.'

Mum laughed. 'There's life in the old goat yet.'

We sipped our drinks. 'Do you think you'd have told me about... all that stuff with Dad sooner if I lived here? Would it have been easier?' I asked.

'I don't know. It's hard to say. Maybe.' Mum took another glug, then looked pensively at her glass. 'It's not something I would have wanted to tell you over the phone. I suppose I could have told you when you were here one summer, but it never really crossed my mind. I was so used to suppressing it. I didn't really think about it very much; not until I found out "she" was pregnant. But you were doing so well in Dubai I didn't want to interrupt your life there and make you think about coming home. To be honest, I kind of hoped your father would tell you—it was his news to tell, not mine.'

She got up to check the soup, stirred it busily. 'Have you heard from him again? The son?'

'Oh y'know. We'll stay in touch.' I didn't want to say any more. I didn't want to hurt her feelings. 'Anyway, cheers! I feel we're on the brink of a new era, we Stevenses. Here's to no more secrets!'

'Cheers! No more secrets!' Mum lifted her half-empty glass, took another slug. 'Ooh, heavens, that's potent stuff on an empty stomach.' She looked down at the table, then up at me. She pursed her lips and rested her index finger on them thoughtfully. Her eyes narrowed and she looked at me almost challengingly.

'What?' I asked, defensive.

'Hmm,' she said, tapping her lips. 'Nothing.'

'What? We just agreed no more secrets. What's up?'

Mum looked down at the table, then back at me. 'Oh nothing. It's all worked out OK in the end, hasn't it?' She lifted her chin. A small smile played on her lips and suddenly I knew that there was something else she wasn't telling me.

'What, Mum? What do you mean "it's all worked out"? What's worked out?'

She gave a little laugh. 'Oh, Evie. It's probably better you don't know.' She took another slug of champagne and refilled her glass, nodding to herself as she did so. The half-formed thought I'd had coming back from seeing Uncle David suddenly took shape and I shook my head, trying to disperse it, but the clues were all there. Somehow, in Mum's new kitchen, they went from dancing randomly in my head to standing in a line, like schoolchildren at whistle-time: Mum's efficiency the day I'd arrived. Dad's money transfer to Zoe. The 'premonition' Zoe thought Dad had had. My mouth turned dry, the cheese biscuit I was eating stuck in lumps on my tongue.

'What are you not telling me?' I said, slowly shaking my head.

'I don't know what you mean.'

'You heard me. There's something you're not telling me about Dad's death. You knew he was going to die. You were ready for it. What was it? Did he commit suicide? Or did you have a hand in it? Did you kill him? I know all about you and Grandpa!'

Mum's hand flew to her chest. 'Oh, goodness, Evie. What a thing to say!'

I slammed my fist on the table, but my voice was quiet. 'I'm right, aren't I?' She shrunk from me, her hand over her mouth. 'Tell me! Tell me what happened!' My voice rose.

'Evie... I...'

'WHAT HAPPENED?'

Mum stared at the table and I waited, breathing hard. When she finally spoke, her hands were on her face, her fingers splayed over her cheeks. Her voice was fluttery. 'Look. You know I told you Dad had a biopsy done on his prostate?'

I nodded.

'I'm sorry, Evie. Sorry to say he did have cancer,' she said. 'The hospital called. The results came in.'

'And?'

'Well, your father was out at the time. I took the message. They gave me an appointment for him to see the consultant the following Monday.'

'And?'

'Well. I told Robert, of course. But we both knew what it meant. When you're asked to go in and discuss biopsy results with a consultant so quickly it can only mean one thing. It's not good news.'

I gestured at her to carry on. 'And so what happened? What did the consultant say?'

'Robert didn't go.'

'What do you mean he didn't go? That's ridiculous!'

'He refused point-blank to go. "I'm not going to sit there

and wait to be told by some quack how long I have to live,'
he said. He asked me to take a look at his file and see what
it said.'

'What? So you hacked into his file?'

Mum tutted. 'It's hardly hacking, Evie. I just pulled it
up and looked. I'm his next of kin, after all, and I had his
permission.'

'And?' My voice was a whisper. I couldn't imagine what
was coming, how this story was going to play out. I was
thinking: he died of heart failure. How can this be relevant?
'What was the result?'

'Cancer, Evie. Far worse than either of us could have
imagined. It had spread. Everywhere.'

'No!'

'He'd left it too late, Evie—by the time it was diagnosed,
he was riddled with it. It was in his lungs, his lymph nodes
and his liver.' Mum's voice was calm. It reminded me of
the nights she read me bedtime stories. 'The doctor had
written "palliative care only" on the file. Robert would
have had two, three months to live. And even that was
optimistic.'

I snapped my head up again, and slammed my fist into the
table, making the champagne glasses jump. 'I don't believe
you! He would have told me!'

Mum looked at me with flinty eyes. 'Would he really?
Your father never wrote to you; never got in contact with
you; never even told you you had a half-brother. Why do
you think he suddenly would then? To talk about his health?'

'But you would have told me!'

'I wanted to, Evie. Believe me. But he wouldn't let me. He didn't want anyone to know.'

I stared at Mum as if I'd never seen her before. 'But you should have told me anyway!'

'It wasn't fair to him, Evie. He was a dying man and he was adamant. Who was I to go against his wishes?'

'And what about Zoe? Did he tell her?' The thought that she'd known and hidden it from me made me nauseous. But Mum shook her head.

'Why? I don't get it. Why would he tell you and not her?'

Mum sighed and stared off into the middle distance, one hand on the table, the other circling the stem of her champagne glass. She smiled as she spoke. 'He loved me, Evie. That's the bit you keep forgetting. Your father may have thought he loved her, but I'm the one he stayed with. Can't you see that? At the end of the day, he loved me more than he loved her. It's obvious, isn't it? She may have won the odd battle, but I won the war.'

I flinched as she said it. 'And you should have told me! He was my dad! He'd have wanted me to know!' My chin trembled and I bit my lip to stop myself from crying.

'Evie.' Mum reached for my hand, but I pulled it away. 'He didn't want sympathy. He didn't want anyone to feel sorry for him—no one. Not his family, not his friends. He'd always said he wouldn't want to suffer and, credit to him, Evie, because it's not an easy decision to make but, yes, he decided he wanted to commit suicide rather than spend the last few months of his life in pain, and being a burden on me. It was a brave decision to make, Evie.'

'No!' I was shaking my head at her, beyond words. But even as I said it, I knew she was right. The clues were there: Dad had planned the whole thing. He'd even talked about Dignitas in public. Zoe's words came back to me: 'Maybe he had some sort of premonition beforehand,' she'd said. Even she'd guessed something was up. I leapt up. 'You *knew* Dad was going to commit suicide? And you didn't tell me? How could you? How could you *let* him?'

'I think I need more of this,' Mum said, pouring herself another glass of champagne. She took a mouthful, glugged it down, dabbed her mouth with a paper napkin. 'How could I have stopped him?' she asked. 'You know what he was like when his mind was made up about something. I tried to talk him out of it! But he was scared. He didn't want to suffer. And he didn't want us to watch him suffer.'

'Why didn't you tell me?' I shouted. 'I would have talked him out of it! I'd have come over, looked at treatments, argued until he backed down! We could have made him comfortable!'

'I'm sorry,' Mum was saying, wringing her hands now. 'I'm sorry. He knew you would try to talk him out of it. That's why he wouldn't let me tell you.'

'How did he do it? Obviously not at Dignitas.'

And then it hit me: Mum's comment after Dad's funeral when we'd talked about how Dad had died: 'It's for the best,' she'd said. 'He would have been a terrible patient.' I thought with a shudder about what Uncle David had told me about how much she'd hated looking after Grandpa. I thought about Zoe saying that Dad was scared Mum would harm him if she found out about their relationship; I thought about Zoe's new pregnancy; about Mum's cosy little relationship with Richard. I thought about the pink bedroom in the new-build house that Dad would have hated. And I remembered the champagne in her fridge the day I arrived from Dubai. A shiver ran through me.

'You were in on it, weren't you? Was it your idea?'

'No!' Mum got up and started pacing the kitchen, wringing her hands and looking at the floor. 'It's what he wanted, Evie. He was adamant that he didn't want to suffer.'

'Tell me what happened! Tell me now or I'm calling the police! I have to know!' I jumped up and ran towards Mum, ready to shake the truth out of her. I backed her up against the wall, glad of the extra inches I had over her.

'He suffocated!' she said, shrinking away from me.

I backed off. 'How? What did you do? Put a bag over his head?'

'Oh! Evie!' Mum looked horrified.

'Then how was it?' I screamed. 'Tell me!'

'He asked me to help him!'

'Help him do what?'

'Evie! Calm down! I'll tell you. Sit back down.' She shoved me back onto my chair.

'It was all his idea,' she said. 'He did some research and came up with a plan. He chose the date. It was the same date his father had died.'

I banged the table with my fist. 'He chose to die? And you helped him?' I paused. 'Does Richard know? Does he know what you did?'

Mum looked panicked. 'No! No, he doesn't! Please don't tell him. He can't know!'

'He can't know that he was an accessory when you helped your husband to die, you mean? It was Richard you called when you "found" him, wasn't it?'

Mum was shaking her head now, her voice was barely audible. 'You can't tell him. Please don't tell him.'

I ignored her plea. 'Come on then. Tell me. I'm waiting. How did you do it?'

Mum sat back down and twiddled with her champagne glass as she stared at the table. Then she took a deep breath and started to talk.

'Robert did a lot of research online. You have to understand, Evie, that this was his choice. I truly believe it was largely painless.'

'Largely?' I spat the word out.

My mother glowered at me. 'Hear me out. What I'm saying is that he chose how he wanted to do it. He'd read on the net about something called a "suicide bag". It's a method that many people choose as a way to commit suicide, but he wasn't sure he could do it alone, so he asked me to make sure it… it worked.'

My stomach convulsed. I clamped my hand over my mouth and shook my head as my mother spoke, as if the movement could erase the words I was hearing.

'Basically, it's a bag that's filled with a gas. Helium, I think he got. You—' Mum looked at me '—you fasten it over your head. You're unconscious very quickly, and then… you know. It's very hard for anyone to tell how you died. As long as you don't leave the evidence lying around. Robert wanted me to make sure the bag was properly on. "No half measures," he said. He bought all the bits on the net. There are places that sell this stuff, no questions asked. I don't know, really. I didn't ask. He just showed me what he wanted me to do. We did a dummy run without the gas. And he wanted me to hide the stuff afterwards; take it to the tip. That's all I had to do. He asked me to do it.'

Mum was staring at her champagne glass as she spoke. Her voice became quieter, then she gave herself a little shake, sat up straighter and continued.

'We had a lovely evening,' she said. 'Robert wanted to listen to Vivaldi. We had gin and tonics with pretzels and those wasabi nuts he liked?' I remembered the wasabi nuts. He'd always liked spicy things. 'I did smoked salmon *vol-au-vents* with a dab of cream cheese and some caviar for starters, and we had a glass of champagne with those.' The champagne Mum had offered me when I'd arrived.

'He wanted roast lamb for dinner. So I did it with roast potatoes, gravy, mint peas and carrots, and we managed to get through two bottles of Chianti Classico from the *Sunday Times* Wine Club. It was a good one! I'd not tried it before. I'd only got one bottle out of the wine cupboard, but he said he wanted more—he was hardly going to have a hangover, was he? How could I stop him? Even people on Death Row get what they want for their last meal. I only had a glass or two as I wanted to stay sober.

'I did a home-made baked Alaska for dessert. It was very fiddly. I offered to do apple pie, but he insisted.' She tutted. 'Trying to make life difficult for me to the very end! I practised the day before, just to make sure.' She sounded pleased with herself. 'I had a coffee and Dad had a couple of glasses of that posh whisky—you know, that single malt he keeps for Christmas? Then he gave me a kiss and we went upstairs. He connected the helium to the bag and got into bed. He breathed out and put the bag over his head and I tightened it round his neck. His eyes were open.' Mum stopped talking and traced her finger around her champagne glass. 'Anyway, it worked quickly. He breathed deeply. It was only a few breaths before he was unconscious. I sat in the room till I was sure he was gone. Twelve minutes, it took. He didn't struggle. I really doubt he felt a thing.'

The kitchen filled with noise. It was me screaming. 'No! No! No! You can't be telling me this! I can't believe you would do that!' I hurled my glass at the wall. It smashed with a satisfying explosion of sound. Champagne dripped down the tiles. I picked up Mum's. Threw that, too. Then the bowl of cheese biscuits.

I got to the sink in time to vomit up the champagne, half-chewed bits of cheesy biscuit. I couldn't get the image out of my head of Mum calmly saying goodnight to Dad as he went upstairs; of her slipping the bag over his head; of him looking at her as she fastened the elastic. What would he have been thinking as he watched her start to kill him? And how did she know he was dead? Did she keep checking his pulse? How long did she leave him before she called the ambulance? I remembered Mum calling me the next morning, faking her shock on the phone. I imagined her acting flustered on the phone to Richard. She'd known all along. No wonder she'd been so organised when I arrived from Dubai. No wonder she'd been so calm. She'd been prepared. It was beyond grotesque.

Strings of spit hung from my mouth and I looked around for something to wipe it on. Mum handed me the kitchen roll—I didn't want to talk to her, or to acknowledge her in any way. I grabbed the tissue, wiped my mouth, grabbed my handbag and ran for the front door. Mum followed me.

'Go away! I can't be near you right now! I can't! No wonder you never wore the ring I bought you!' I ripped my own ring off my finger and hurled it across the kitchen, where it ricocheted off a cabinet and spun under the cooker.

'Darling! It's what he wanted. Wait! He was worried you'd react like this. He wrote you a letter!' She shoved an envelope into my hand as I tore through the front door.

*

I ran down the street, my feet slamming against the pavement, as if a monster was hard behind me. I didn't look back; I ran in terror of the horrors I'd left behind. As I neared the end of the street, my lungs on fire, I saw the small path that led to the park and swerved down it. Hidden from view of the house, should my mother come after me, I doubled over against the wall and tried to catch my breath. My mouth still tasted of vomit; I could feel pieces stuck behind my gums and my throat burned with the acidity of the bile. I retched once more into the bushes and waited for my breathing to slow.

The playground was deserted and there was a bench near the swings. Straightening up, I walked slowly towards it, my breath still ragged. The trees, bare for winter, surrounded the playground like a garden of dismembered witches' hands, the branches like fingers beckoning; reaching towards the primary colours of the children's play equipment. I sat down and took out the envelope. It was sealed, my name in Dad's writing on the front. Slipping my finger under the seal, I opened it and pulled out the letter. A single sheet, handwritten.

*

My darling Evie

If you're reading this, your mother must have told you that I chose to take my own life. I didn't want her to tell you but, if she has, she must have had her reasons. I was riddled with cancer, Evie, it was everywhere, and I didn't want to wait for it to take me. You have your own life; I didn't want you and your mother spending weeks or months glued to my hospital bed while I wasted away in a haze of drugs and pain. Your mum and I agreed years ago that we'd rather just go quickly and quietly when the day came and—well—the day came.

When I found out the cancer was terminal, I had no option. I hope you can forgive me for not telling you. I knew you'd try to talk me out of it. I knew you'd want to research treatments that would just prolong the agony by a few months. I knew you'd argue and I didn't want to be argued with and, ultimately, I didn't want you to carry the guilt of allowing me to do it. Evie, you're a wonderful daughter. I'm so proud of you. I'm so proud of everything that you've done. I know I didn't always show it, especially after Graham, but I loved you more than anything. Please go through the rest of your life knowing my love is always with you.

Daddy

I looked up at the grey sky, at the silhouettes of the trees above me, and all the pain, the anguish, the frustration and the shock spilled out of me in a howl that had no language.

CHAPTER 71

'Luca! Luca! Open the door!' I bashed his bell three times, then banged on the wood with my knuckles. 'Please be home. Please, Luca! Open the door!' I slumped against the door, my forehead resting on it, my knocks getting smaller as I sank to the floor.

Then, the sound of footsteps on the other side, the lock clicking; Luca's socks in front of me.

'Hi, I was just—Evie! What's wrong? What's happened?' He pulled me to my feet, led me into his hallway and held me by the arms, looking into my face. 'What happened? Evie, are you hurt?'

But there were no words. 'Dad...' I tried. 'Mum... I...' I collapsed against Luca's chest, sobbing, while he stroked my hair.

*

Luca finally pulled away from me. He led me by the hand to his sofa and sat me down on it. He turned my face to his and traced his fingers over my cheeks. 'You're safe now. What can I get you? Some water?' I nodded, and he brought a glass. I took a few sips.

He rubbed his hand up and down my back. 'You're shaking.'

I realised I was freezing, my body racked with shivers. 'A bath,' I whispered. 'Can I have a bath?'

'Of course. Wait here.' Luca went off and I heard him moving about in the bathroom, the taps being turned on, water moving through the pipes. He came back and led me by the hand to the bathroom, where he helped me step out of my clothes and supported me as I climbed into the bath. His tub was big and I sank gratefully under the water, submerging my head completely. The nothingness of being underwater was soothing; right now, it was a world I preferred. I stayed under until my lungs felt they would burst. Then I took a breath and sunk back under. Is this what it felt like to suffocate? When I finally resurfaced, I saw Luca had put a cup of tea on the side of the bath.

For a long time, I lay motionless, unseeing, unfeeling, and let the water lap over me. Every now and then, I added more hot water. Luca knocked and came in with a pile of clean clothes. He smiled at me. 'For when you're ready,' he said, placing them on the chair and slinking out again. When I finally felt ready to get out, I dressed in his pyjama bottoms and t-shirt, wrapped myself in his robe and padded into his living room.

'That's better,' Luca said. 'You look a million miles more human now.'

'Thanks,' I breathed. Even that was too much of an effort.

He came over and took my hands in his. 'Can you tell me what happened?'

I shook my head.

'Are you hurt?'

I shook my head.

'Do you want to talk about it?'

I shook my head. Then, 'Can you get my phone? It's in my bag.' Luca did as I asked. 'Can you find Miss Dawson's number? Can you ask her to come?'

CHAPTER 72

I was lying on the sofa, still wrapped in the bathrobe, when there was a knock at the door. Luca went to open it. I heard him talking softly with a woman, then his hand was on my arm.

'Evie... Miss Dawson is here.'

I scrambled to stand up and shake her hand, the blood rushing to my head. 'You've come? Here?' Miss Dawson was a greyer version of the lady I remembered, but age suited her. She looked serious, wise. She rubbed her hands briskly together, the cold of outside still clinging to her.

'Luca said it was urgent.'

'I'm just nipping out,' said Luca, shrugging on his coat and edging towards the door. 'I'll leave you to it.' He waved towards the kitchen cupboards. 'Help yourselves to any-thing. Bye.' He closed the door quietly after him.

'Is that Luca, as in... ?' asked Miss Dawson. I nodded, and she smiled. 'That's nice. I always thought... anyway.'

She pulled a chair from Luca's kitchen table and brought it over to the sofa. I sank back down hugging my knees to me.

'So, Evie,' she said, 'what's this all about? What's

happened? Luca said you were in quite a state. Can you tell me what it's about? Is it to do with your mother?'

Slowly, struggling to find the words, I told Miss Dawson what Mum had told me. Miss Dawson didn't even flinch. She just sat, impassive, and listened. Every now and then she nodded. 'Ahh,' she said. 'I see.'

'Is that murder?' I asked when I'd got to the end. 'Did she murder him?'

'Can I see the letter?' Miss Dawson asked. 'Do you mind showing me?'

I rummaged in my bag and pulled it out and passed it to her. I watched as her eyes moved down the page, taking in my father's last message to me. She nodded to herself and handed it back to me.

'What your mother did is against the law. But it's in her favour that your father was terminally ill and that he asked her to do it. It's basically assisted suicide.'

'Will she go to jail?' I stared at my hands on my lap.

'Well. It's a topic of debate. Some people think assisted suicide should be legalised; there are people sympathetic to it. But, as far as I know—and I may be wrong; I can look it up for you—the Crown Prosecution Services says that family members who assist a loved one's suicide are "unlikely" to be prosecuted.'

'So she might get away with it?'

'Well, I'm guessing his death wasn't seen as suspicious or they would have done an autopsy?'

'Oh God. Mum said he'd had trouble with his heart a week or so before. She'd called the same doctor when she "found" him in the morning. He signed the medical certificate.'

'Well,' said Miss Dawson. 'So it's not suspicious in any way. I'm not going to tell the police anything else. Are you?'

I shook my head. 'I don't know what to do. At the moment, I hate her.'

'Evie, I know it's incredibly difficult. I know you feel like this decision was made without including you; I know you feel like you should have been a part of it.' I nodded. 'But it was a very personal decision your father made. It was his decision to make, not yours. And your mother did perhaps the most difficult thing, which was to help her husband do something with which she might not even have agreed. She's a strong woman.'

'You should have heard her telling me. She was so cold. So factual. There was no emotion at all.'

'I think she was probably protecting herself, not allowing herself to feel the emotions. It's probably the only way she got through having to do such a horrific thing. It must have been incredibly difficult.'

There was a silence. Miss Dawson was saying what I wanted to hear, but there was still something; something that made me feel uncomfortable.

I felt Miss Dawson's hand on my arm. 'Your mother's a brave woman. She helped her husband die with dignity. Really, Evie, what your mother did was the ultimate act of love.'

CHAPTER 73

The days passed in a haze. When Luca had gone to the house to collect my things, he'd told Mum I'd be staying with him for a few days. Apparently, she'd just nodded absently and waved him in without any questions. I was hardly expecting an argument. She must know how tenuous her situation was; that what she'd done was illegal. I passed a lot of time at Luca's sitting out on the terrace, wrapped in fleeces and a blanket, watching the sky and thinking.

Miss Dawson had painted the assisted suicide as an act of love, but she didn't know the background, the history of Zoe and Tom. In her eyes, my parents had stood by each other — Dad had confided in Mum and she'd repaid that confidence with what Miss Dawson had called the 'ultimate act of love' — the devoted wife risking potential incarceration to ease her husband's pain.

But was it really an act of love? Why would Mum help Dad, as she did, after everything that he'd done? I knew my mother, and I could see events from a different — darker — angle. Miss Dawson had framed the assisted suicide within the confines of a long-term, loving marriage, but that didn't sit well with me. Mum hadn't loved Dad as much as Miss

Dawson believed. She'd not only felt contempt for him, but she'd felt competitive with Zoe and, while Miss Dawson had imagined Dad's death had finally allowed Mum to grieve for Graham, I thought there was another type of release, too. Mum had lived a secret life, lying to everyone around her for twenty years. She'd hidden the fact that I had a half-brother from me while knowing how much I would have loved to have known. And, ultimately—unforgivably?—she'd helped my father to die without giving me a chance to say goodbye.

I couldn't help but wonder: when Dad had had his diagnosis, when they'd realised the cancer was terminal and he'd asked for her help to end his life, had there been a part of her that had rejoiced? A part of her that had thought she'd got her final, divine retribution? In her own words, she'd 'won the war'—things had worked out well for her. The thought made me physically sick.

I sat, almost catatonic, for several days, until I'd gained control of my thoughts; desensitised myself to what had happened. Only then did I realise what I had to do. Finally, I showered, dressed and booked a cab to Maidstone, to Zoe's.

The day still didn't know if it wanted to be sunny or cloudy; the sky was bright blue, but huge clouds blocked the sun every few minutes, casting the shadows of giants across the landscape. I was calm in the car. As I sat in the back watching the fields and hedges of Kent go by, I tried to focus on what I wanted to say to Zoe, and what I wanted to get out of the visit. My ticket back to Dubai was booked. I wanted to make peace with her before I left. I also wanted to see where it was that Dad had spent twenty years of weekends; where he'd gone when he'd left me and Mum every Friday.

As the cab pulled up, I took a deep breath. I was well prepared. I rang the doorbell and Zoe opened almost immediately.

'Thanks for letting me come over,' I said, holding out the packet of chocolate biscuits I'd brought as a peace offering.

'It's my pleasure,' she said. She touched my arm and I followed her into the house that had served as my father's second home. A faint scent of fresh coffee hung in the air. I couldn't stop thinking about Dad stepping over this threshold every Friday evening after leaving Mum and me. Did he knock, or had he had a key? Did she wait for him eagerly, coiffed and scented, in her best lingerie, or was she slobbing on the sofa when he arrived?

'Take a seat. I'll get some coffee,' said Zoe, waving a hand towards a door on the left, and I moved into the living room. It wasn't big, but it was nicely done up. Her style was shabby chic—cosy, comfortable, used, loved and a little cluttered: photo frames, vases, books and candle holders were scattered across whatever surfaces there were. I glanced quickly at each of the photos, not knowing how long Zoe would take to make the coffee and not wanting to be caught snooping. All of them were of her family: Tom, Zoe, two older people I imagined must be her parents. Then one of my father: my breath caught as I saw him smiling out at me.

I sat on the sofa then stood up again. I stood with my

back to the window and tried to absorb as many details of the room as I could. It was a small room—a small house compared to ours. The sofa was half hidden under a clutch of cushions; to the side, a basket overflowed with soft-looking blankets. A square coffee table sat on a thick oatmeal rug in the middle of the room; on it, a couple of coasters and a stack of coffee-table books. I tried to imagine Dad in this room every weekend; Dad watching television here; flicking through the books; playing with Tom; cuddling up to Zoe under one of the blankets. I picked up the top blanket and buried my nose in it, hoping for, but not finding, a trace of my father's scent.

By the time Zoe came back from the kitchen, I was sitting neatly on the sofa, flicking through a magazine I'd found on the coffee table while not taking in a thing. Zoe placed a wooden tray carefully on the table, then handed me a mug, the handle thoughtfully turned towards me as she took the hot cup in her own hand. The chocolate biscuits I'd brought sat on the tray. I thought I could see a slight rounding of her belly.

'So. Here we are,' she said, taking a seat across the room from me.

I nodded. 'Here we are.'

'I'm glad you and Tom managed to meet up again. He says you got on well?' Zoe's voice was gentle.

'Yes. He's great.'

'He is, isn't he? I'm so pleased you two finally had a good talk. I'd always hoped you would meet one day but your father was adamant until very recently that our two families shouldn't meet. As I said before, I think he was just starting to change his mind.'

'Well,' I said. 'We'll never know now.'

'Well,' she said. 'Let me show you something. Come.' She stood up and beckoned for me to follow her.

She led me out of the room and up a thinly carpeted staircase. I could smell the scent of fabric conditioner as we approached the landing. It was small with only three doors leading off it. She pushed one open and held it so I could go in ahead of her, but I stopped dead on the threshold. The room was nothing special: it wasn't big. There was just one sash window that faced the garden. Neither was it particularly pretty—it was a functional bedroom decorated in plain neutrals. A queen-sized bed was centred against one wall; there was a built-in wardrobe with white doors; a dresser; no *en suite* bathroom. I realised I was holding my breath. I expelled it with a big sigh.

'Go on,' said Zoe. 'Go in, I want to show you something.' She pointed to a bedside table, but I stared at the bed. This was the bed in which my father had woken up every Saturday and Sunday morning for the past twenty years. Those were the curtains he'd pulled. And then my eyes followed Zoe's hand and I saw what she was pointing at: on one of the bedside tables was a picture frame—in it, a photo of me, smiling at the camera on a trip we'd taken to Stonehenge when I was sixteen; it was one of my favourite photos.

'And here,' said Zoe, pointing to the dresser. On top of it, a cluster of frames—all of them pictures of Graham, Tom and me. Dad had cut some so we could all be in the same frame: his children. I caught my breath. Mum had taken down all pictures of Graham; stashed them away. Dad may have lived with us, but this was the only place he'd been able to truly be himself; to have pictures of all his children on display.

'That's what I wanted you to see.' Zoe was behind me, watching me look at her bedroom. 'He loved you very much. Let me show you something else.' She moved past me, opened one of the bedside drawers and pulled out a photo album. 'Pictures of you. He looked at them every week. He even took them on holiday when we went away.' She placed the album on the bed, turned back to the drawer, pulled out a folder. 'And this, too.'

'What is it?'

'Have a look.'

Zoe passed it across the bed and I opened it. I realised immediately what it was: a folder of things to do in Dubai. I stared at the folder, willing myself not to cry.

'He wanted to come and see you,' said Zoe. 'He wanted to tell you about Tom in person. He'd decided it was time to stop lying. He really wanted you and Tom to know each other. He thought you'd get on well. He was planning a trip to Dubai. He was planning what you could do together when he came.'

'Me too. I wanted it so badly. Was he going to come on his own?'

'Yes. I think he saw, with Tom, how close he could be to his child. He regretted that he wasn't that close to you.

ANNABEL KANTARIA

He missed you, Evie. He missed you and he wanted to put things right between you... Look through them... Take your time.'

Zoe left the room and I picked up the album. It included all the best photos of me from about the age of thirteen onwards: the years in which I'd thought Dad had ignored me. It was a loving record of my life. Then I leafed through the folder and imagined Dad planning his trip. It was very similar to the one I'd put together myself: he'd printed out information from the internet on deep-sea fishing, retro desert safaris, helicopter rides. He'd wanted to reconnect with me, too. It would have worked. It would.

*

In the bathroom, I splashed cold water onto my face.

'Thank you,' I said to Zoe, as I went back into the living room.

She smiled. 'Look, Evie, I know you must have lots of questions. Why don't you just ask me and I'll be as honest as I can?'

So we talked, my questions starting slowly but building to a torrent. Zoe portrayed Dad as deeply conflicted; torn between two women he wanted to protect in different ways; torn between his two children.

'I think having Tom made him realise how far he'd distanced himself from you after the accident. And it became even more important to him to hold on to you,' she said. 'If it hadn't been for you, I suspect he would have left Carole eventually. But he said she was—how to

say it—"unstable"?' Zoe said this carefully, checking my
reaction as she said it. I averted my eyes—an admission,
maybe—and she continued. 'He was petrified she'd stop
him from seeing you, and he didn't want to drag it through
the courts, not after what you'd all been through with your
brother's accident.'

I didn't say anything.

'It may have been an unconventional set-up,' she said,
'but your father tried to do what he thought was best for
everyone. He was a good man, caught in an impossible
situation.'

'How?' I asked. 'How did it come about in the first
place?'

'Please don't think I planned this. I never meant to
get involved with him,' she said. 'It takes two, Evie. It
wasn't just me. Your father was lonely. He felt very guilty
about the accident. Carole was—' she searched for a word
'—"unable" to support him. He needed someone and I was
there. For a while it stayed platonic, we'd talk for hours
after classes, but we were drawn to each other on every
level. I know it was wrong, but I don't regret it. And I don't
regret having Tom. I would never have wished you harm—I
would never have let Rob take you from your mother—but
what I wish is that Rob had handled it better; had found a
way to put an end to the lies. We both hated living with the
lies. But, as I said, he didn't want to lose you. You were his
top priority.' She paused. 'There were times when I hated
him for that, too.'

'So why did you put up with it? Why were you happy to

play second fiddle? You could have ended it; found some-one else.'

'Ohh,' Zoe sighed. 'I tried. Trust me, I tried. Rob never stopped me from seeing other men—in fact, he encouraged me to. I dated other guys, but I guess I was never emotionally available to them. Rob was the only one who did it for me. My heart was tied up with the father of my son. Is that so terrible?'

As she talked, I began to see that she wasn't the bad guy. That if I held the past against her, I was only going to harm my growing relationship with Tom. I had to let it go. My gut instinct when I'd first met Zoe outside the church had been right: she really did seem to be a nice person. And why wouldn't she be? She was, after all, the woman my father had loved.

*

Thank you,' I said at the door. 'Really, thank you.'

'Thank you for giving me the chance,' she said, giving me a little hug. 'Take care, Evie.' Then, 'Hang on!' She dashed up the stairs once more and came back down with Dad's photo album. She held it out to me. 'Would you like to keep it?'

'Would you mind?'

'Of course not. It should be yours. It's how your father remembered you.'

'Thank you.'

As the door closed behind me, I realised I'd found out what I wanted to know. I'd found out what it was that Dad had seen in Zoe: this was not some steamy, passionate affair, at least not these days. Zoe was not an overtly sexual being. The attraction possibly wasn't even intellectual. What Dad had seen in Zoe was far more ethereal. Dad had loved Zoe because she was everything that Mum was not: she was stable.

CHAPTER 74

I walked slowly towards Mum's new house, my feet dragging as I reached the driveway. I'd arranged for Luca to pick me up in a bit; my packed suitcase was already in his car. He'd offered to come with me, but this was something I wanted to do alone. My feet crunched over the gravel; I stepped onto the front step, took a deep breath and touched the bell, listening to the sound reverberate inside the house. I heard Mum scuffling about behind the door, then it opened and I looked up at her.

'Hello,' I said.

'Evie.' She held her arms out and I stepped forward. She held me tight, but from my side it was perfunctory. My body was stiff, my arm bent up behind her like a boomerang; my cheek turned away. She released me and I stepped into the house.

'Thank you for coming back,' she said. 'I thought you might leave without saying goodbye.'

'I just need to pick up some things.'

'It was what he wanted, Evie. I did what he wanted.' She followed me back into the house; called down the passage after me. 'One day you'll understand. It wasn't my decision to make.'

I turned in the doorway of my room, my voice exasperated. 'Look. I see why you did what you did. OK? But that's as much as you'll get from me. Don't push it. It doesn't mean I condone it. It doesn't mean I forgive you. You're lucky I'm not telling the police. Please let's never mention it again.'

'OK, Evie. OK. Thank you.'

I took what I needed from my room without emotion. I'd spent only a couple of nights here and the room didn't feel like mine. I looked around at the bland décor, the unfamiliar curtains and carpet. Nothing to miss. I closed the door behind me. There was no connection. For me, this house would always be tainted with the news Mum had delivered in the kitchen. I didn't know if I would ever come back.

'Do you still have the key to the old house?' I asked Mum.

'Yes. Why?'

'I'd like to have a last look.'

'Sure,' she said. She rummaged in the dresser and pulled out the old, familiar set of keys. 'Here you go. Can you just check everything's off as well? The lights and stuff? And make sure there's nothing left behind?'

The air was cold and crisp. I walked down the street breathing it deeply into my lungs, knowing it would be a long time until I breathed such fresh, cool air again. I was looking forward to going back to Dubai, to getting away from Woodside. Mum's confession had changed everything. The magazine was going from strength to strength; we were looking at launching franchises across Asia and I was set to be doing a lot of travelling for work in the months and years to come—all further East, away from England, away from the mess of my family.

Where that left Luca and me, I had no idea, but I hoped that time away would lessen the hurt I'd felt about my parents' multiple deceits. I was already some way to forgiving Dad. I bet he struggled every day to live with the decision he'd made about Zoe at what was, I suppose, a time of heightened emotion: Tom was born the same month that Mum tried to commit suicide; he must have been conceived three months after Graham's death. I think Dad genuinely believed he was trying to do the right thing for all of us. Under the impression—as we both were—that Mum was vulnerable, he'd tried to protect her, with more long-lasting consequences than he could have foreseen. I was glad, when I thought about it, when I reached through my own ego and hurt, that Dad had been happy with Zoe.

I hoped I'd be able to find a way to forgive him for not letting me say goodbye.

*

At the old house, I stood in Graham's room and looked around, trying to imprint every last detail on my mind. This was where I'd always come to connect with Graham, to talk to him, and my chest tightened to think this would be the last time. I lay down on the floor, on the carpet where Graham's bed had been, and looked up at the ceiling he would have seen when he'd lain in that same position. I closed my eyes and, for a second, I heard a whisper of the

noise and laughter that had filled our childhood; saw myself
bounding into his room, stocking in hand, on Christmas
mornings, yelling 'Wake up! Wake up! What did you get?'
I pictured his sleepy face changing from confusion to joy
as he realised Christmas morning had finally arrived, and
I smiled.

'Bye, big brother,' I whispered.

The only furniture now left in Graham's room was the
fitted wardrobe. Standing up again, I opened the doors and
half expected Graham's tennis racket, shoes, clothes and
boxes of Action Men to spring out as they always used to.
But, aside from the rack of floor-length dresses Mum had
kept in there for special occasions, the wardrobe had been
empty for years. I stretched up to sweep my hand along the
dusty top shelf and my fingertips touched on something
hard. I grappled to get it, but succeeded only in pushing it
even further towards the back of the cupboard.

I couldn't leave without seeing what it was. Maybe it was
something of Graham's — an old letter to Santa or the tooth
fairy, a piece of artwork, notes on a game we were playing,
a letter he'd left, like our time capsule, for future occupiers.
But there was nothing left in the house for me to stand
on, nothing for me to use to grasp it so I went downstairs,
hunting for something to use. The house was bare but I
found a small stick under the hedge outside — it would have
to do. Standing inside the bottom of the wardrobe to gain
a couple of extra inches, I stretched my arm awkwardly
around the top shelf and shoved the stick as deeply into the
shelf as I could, sweeping it around until I felt the object

hit the back wall. Pushing the stick down on it to get some purchase on whatever it was, I dragged it towards the edge of the shelf, where I grabbed it and slipped back onto the floor, breathing heavily with the effort. I'd overextended my shoulder and it hurt.

My reward was a brown paper bag, the sort shops used to give you before plastic became so common. The top was folded over twice. I opened it and pulled out a pink, girls' diary with a shiny silver lock on it, two tiny keys dangling. Also inside the bag was a birthday card, the envelope un-sealed. My name on the front. 'Happy birthday, Sister,' said the printed greeting. Inside, Graham's best ten-year-old joined-up writing: 'Dear Evie, Sometimes you're a pain but I'm glad you're my sister. I've made a copy of the key, ha ha. Gray'.

I swallowed, tears misting my eyes. Nineteen years ago, Graham had sworn he was saving his pocket money to buy me a lockable diary. I hadn't believed him. I stared at it, stroked its cover. I imagined him choosing it in the corner shop, picking it up and paying for it; carrying it home for me; hiding it here. I sank to the floor, hugging my pink, lockable diary to my chest.

*

Downstairs, the letterbox banged in a sound that was as familiar to me as my own voice. Post fell onto the mat. Closing Graham's door behind me, I checked the other rooms, closed all the doors and went down the stairs. I stopped in each room, trying to remember scenes from our family life, but I struggled. Without the prompts of the furniture and our possessions, it was just another house. I checked the heating and hot water were off, half closed the street-side curtains, picked the letter off the mat, shoved it in my bag and left, locking the front door behind me.

I walked slowly back to Mum's. Luca's car was parked outside; he was leaning against it, busy with his phone.

'I'll just give Mum back the keys then I'm ready,' I said.

Mum must have been watching for me. She opened the door and stepped out onto the gravel. I handed her the keys.

'It's all fine.'

We hugged stiffly.

'When will you be back?'

I shrugged. 'Not before the summer. I'm going to be busy at work… travelling…'

'Well. Safe journey,' she said. 'Look after yourself, darling.'

'Bye.' I turned and walked to Luca's car.

CHAPTER 75

'This is it.' I turned to Luca at the security door in the airport departure hall. 'You can't come any further.'

'Yep.' He pulled me to him and hugged me tight. I clung to him, breathing in his familiar smell and then I stepped back.

'Will you come back?' Luca asked.

I took his hands and looked into his eyes. If I'd learned one thing in the past six weeks, it was the importance of being honest with those you love.

'I was planning to come back,' I said. 'I was planning to wind things up in Dubai and move back. I wanted to see if… you know… you and me… ?' Luca was staring at me, his eyes devouring my face. 'But I just can't be near Mum right now. You understand that, don't you? For the first time in twenty years, she doesn't need me. And I don't want to be near her. I need to stay away for a bit.'

Luca was shaking his head. 'You'd been thinking of coming back? For me?'

'Yes.'

He grabbed me. 'Oh, Evie! I didn't even dare to hope. We'll make it work! I promise! We'll make it work long-distance if we have to. And when you're ready to come home, we'll get a place together, or maybe we'll move somewhere else. Away from Woodside. Whatever it takes!'

I laughed, tears spilling down my face.

'Hey, don't cry,' Luca said. 'It's good news!' He brushed my cheek with his fingers, kissed my eyes. 'I'll come and visit. I'll take some pictures of those skyscrapers of yours. See what all the fuss is about.'

'We've got flamingos.' I tried to smile. 'We don't have swans, but we have pink flamingos.'

'Even better. I'll come and photograph your pink flamingos. I'll look at flights as soon as I get home. I promise.' There was a pause; we stared at one another as if we'd never seen each other before. 'I love you, Evie Stevie,' he said.

I stood on tiptoes and kissed him softly. 'I love you too, Luca Rossi.'

*

On the plane, in darkness somewhere over the east of Europe, I remembered the letter. Much of the cabin was sleeping, but I was restless, my knitting needles flashing in the pool of the reading light. Stabbing the needles through the wool, I rummaged in my handbag and pulled out the envelope. The letter was addressed to Dad, on hospital stationery. I slit it open with my finger.

Department of Oncology
Woodside Hospital
Main Road
Woodside
BR4 9RT
Mr Robert Stevens
15 Mason's Court
Woodside
Kent BR5 4PH
November 19, 2013

Dear Mr Stevens,

The results of our investigative tests have established that you have early-stage and organ-confined prostate cancer. We could not detect any evidence that it has spread.

Given the low risk and your relatively young age, no treatment is advised at this stage. We will, however, keep you under active surveillance. This will require regular visits to the department for tests while we determine if the tumour is increasing in size.

The Urology department will be in touch at a later date to schedule the first of these appointments.

Yours faithfully,

Dr Harvey Clements
Head of Oncology

I read the letter several times, shaking my head until I understood; shaking my head until I worked out how events must have unfolded; what my mother must have done. My father had never spoken to the consultant. Mum had said she'd answered the phone. It was she who'd told Dad he had an urgent appointment with the consultant; it was she who'd checked his file and told him the devastating results.

I remembered the look of hatred that had flicked across her face when she'd mentioned Zoe's new pregnancy and I shivered, pulling the thin aeroplane blanket further up my lap. I imagined Mum reaching for Dad's hand as she told him about the fictitious phone call from the hospital. Perhaps she'd even been the one to offer to check his file. Perhaps she'd been thinking of Tom, or maybe of Zoe's new baby, while she'd sympathised with Dad; agreed that his only option was suicide; kindly agreed to help.

I took a large swig of my gin and tonic and swilled it around my mouth. I thought about the secrets that my mother had lived with; about how she must have felt, and about the look that she would have had in her eye as she'd suffocated my father. I thought about my uncle's glass eye and about the grandfather I'd never known.

In my hands, I held evidence that could see my mother jailed for murder. But what was she? A cold-blooded killer—or a woman pushed to her limits?

With clammy hands, I put the letter back in its envelope, folded it in half and zipped it carefully into the inner section of my handbag. Then I leaned back in my seat and stared out of the window at the darkness beyond.